T0040653

THE
PALACE JOB

The characters and events portrayed in this book are fictitious. Any similarity to real persons, living or dead, is coincidental and not intended by the author.

Text copyright © 2013 by Patrick Weekes
Originally published by Tyche Books, Ltd 2012

All rights reserved.
Printed in the United States of America.

No part of this book may be reproduced, or stored in a retrieval system, or transmitted in any form or by any means, electronic, mechanical, photo-copying, recording, or otherwise, without express written permission of the publisher.

Published by 47NORTH, Seattle
www.apub.com

ISBN-13: 9781477848203
ISBN-10: 1477848207
Library of Congress Control Number: 2013942314

Cover design & Illustration by: Lili Ibrahim

*For the Damsel, whose love, humor, and compassion
made me a better man:*

Thank you for helping me take pride in making people laugh

Table of Contents

Acknowledgments

This novel would not have been possible without the love, support, and occasional head-smacking I received from a great many people:

My mom, dad, and sister, for buying me every Hardy Boys book in existence, and then later every David Eddings book, thus ensuring that I grew up with a love for mystery and fantasy and a strong allergic reaction to sunlight.

Pat Murphy and Karen Joy Fowler, who tirelessly worked through my "undergraduate who just read Ulysses" phase in Science Fiction Writing at Stanford, and who didn't mention to the department that I took their class three separate times.

All the wonderful people at Strange Horizons, the science fiction webzine whose intelligent, multicultural criticism gave me the nerve to not make Loch a white guy.

My writing buddies from Clarion West, Second Draft, and the Penny Arcade Writer's Block, who critiqued not only this book but the additional 30,000 words that were quite necessarily cut from it—especially Jennifer Whitson and Miriam Hurst, who read multiple drafts and patiently pointed out when I was, as they say in better parts of the 'Net, Wearing No Pants.

And of course, the wonderful folks at both Tyche and Amazon, who took a chance on a heist caper in which a talking warhammer and a unicorn are important plot characters.

Most of the good parts of this work I owe to these great folks. The clunky bits are all mine.

THE
PALACE JOB

One

THE RULERS OF THE REPUBLIC LIVED ATOP THE GREAT FLYING city of Heaven's Spire, their magnificent palaces soaring above the world. From their great manses in the sky came the laws and decrees that kept the country in motion, and the commoners on the ground could look up every morning and see their rulers overhead.

The prisoners of the Republic lived *beneath* the great city of Heaven's Spire, scouring the *lapiscaela* whose magic kept the city aloft. For their terrible crimes, each man and woman served a life sentence, clinging to the pipes with only a mile of empty air beneath them. There was no chance of release, no hope of escape.

Today, however, Loch intended to change that.

"You sure this is the best way?" Kail asked. Like Loch, he clung upside-down to the pipes that anchored the *lapiscaela* in place, gripping a side-rail with one hand and his scouring broom with the other.

Loch nodded, giving him a lopsided grin, but said nothing. She was a tall, dark-skinned woman, muscular enough that she hadn't needed the protection of the women's gangs when she'd arrived last month. Her only concession to safety had been the silence she had maintained since arriving. An old superstition among the Republic's criminals held that old magic in the *lapiscaela* would steal the souls of prisoners who talked near them.

"Jeridan doesn't have what we need yet," Kail noted, "and we still haven't talked price."

Loch shrugged. They had to move while they were still newcomers, watched carefully and checked for signs of resistance. And, frankly, if she had to clean a damn magical rock with a damn magical broom one more time, she was going to go crazy and jump.

"Your confidence is inspiring, Captain. I'd follow you to the ends of the world if we weren't already in prison." Kail grinned sourly, his teeth bright white against his dark face, and swung himself upright. His leg-chain rattled against the pipes. "Whenever you're ready. No sense in putting in a full day's work."

Loch pulled herself up, her scouring broom tucked casually under one arm, so that they stood atop the pipe grid. Around them, other prisoners scurried, dull gray in their prison worksuits and lit from below by the great magical stones that kept the city in the sky.

A double grid of pipes secured the *lapiscaela*. During the day, when they caught light reflected from the great mirrors that hung along the rim of Heaven's Spire, the power of the enormous violet crystals held the city aloft, and the upper grid of pipes held them in place. At night, the stones sank down to rest in the lower grid, which held them safely while reserve-enchantments kept the city aloft until sunrise.

It was vital that the *lapiscaela* remain free of dust or grime to maximize the absorption of sunlight. When the ancient magic that polished the crystals had failed, the most dangerous prisoners in the Republic had been pulled into unwilling service in what had come to be called the Cleaners, scouring the *lapiscaela* with special brooms made to clear away the toughest dirt without risking a damaging scratch to the crystal surface. It was said that in the Cleaners, a prisoner's broom was worth more than his life.

Loch looked around, held her scouring broom out at arm's length, and let it go.

The broom clanged off the *lapiscaelum* they'd been assigned to clean, rang off the lower grid, and then fell into the distance.

Kail shook his head. "That should get their atten—"

"Broken chain!"

Loch and Kail turned toward the call, as did every prisoner on the grid. The rattle of leg-chains and the slow grunts of labor went deathly still.

"It's Soggs!" someone called. "South side. He's still got a grip!"

Loch took the grid-path at a run, one hand grabbing the cross-pipes for balance as she dashed along the narrow surface, the other yanking on her leg-chain as it rattled and jangled behind her. Kail was close behind. The other prisoners watched them run by, some shouting encouragement, most silent. "Which rock? Upper grid or lower?" Kail shouted.

"The Tooth! Lower grid!" Loch grimaced at the reply. The *lapiscaela* were irregularly shaped, like natural boulders. The Tooth was a jagged stalactite that hung down like a dragon's fang, its irregular shape so unusual that it necessitated a special frame to lock it into place. The Tooth had killed more men than any other stone on the grid. At the Cleaners, prisoners kept track of that sort of thing.

Loch and Kail had almost reached the Tooth when their pipes hit a junction.

"Guard!" Kail hollered. "We've got a man loose!"

Loch hit the corner as if she hadn't seen it, and her leg-chain snapped taut with a metallic twang that echoed across the grid.

Looking down, Loch could see Soggs—an older man, not a killer, probably in for something he had written or said or sung—clinging to a tiny spur on the great violet stone. His leg-chain snapped and jingled as he struggled to pull himself up.

"Guard!" Kail's voice bounced tinny echoes off the shadowed grid. "Switch me over!"

There was no way Loch could reach Soggs, not if she kept an arm on the pipes, probably not even if she leapt and trusted in her leg-chain to hold both their weights. She gripped the pipes until her knuckles turned white, keeping a scream of frustration in check through sheer willpower.

There were murderers and worse at the Cleaners. Soggs wasn't one of them.

"Guard!" Kail hollered up to the observation level. "Move your damn ass!"

In the maze of gray metal pipes lit from below by the vivid glow of the *lapiscaela*, the prisoners were completely alone.

"It's too far, Loch." Kail gripped the pipes.

Loch nodded, then extended a hand without looking at Kail.

With a sigh, he handed her his broom. "Soggs! She's coming!"

Soggs could see Loch through the grid of pipes between them. He looked into her dark eyes and nodded even as his sweat-slicked hands began to slip.

When she leapt, her whole body stretched to a single line that shattered into pain when her leg-chain stopped her fall. Soggs leapt as best he could for the broom she held extended for him.

He was perhaps a handbreadth short.

If he'd had a foothold to give him purchase, he might have reached her, even with Loch stuck on the wrong pipe and too far away.

Instead, one more prisoner escaped the Cleaners the only way he could.

He was too small to see after a few seconds, but everyone kept looking. The grid was silent but for the soft tinkle of chains tapping the pipes, and the regular, rusty squeak as Loch swung back and forth, her shackle digging into her ankle and the useless broom clutched in both hands.

Then Tawyer, one of the guards, slowly clambered down from one of the topside hatches, grunting as he hopped down. "You don't watch your tone, Kail, you'll spend the night dangling," he said easily. "Guards don't come down without a flying charm, no matter how you holler." He stepped lightly past where Kail stood silent and tight-fisted, then looked down at Loch. "So, your mute friend slipped, did she? Hey, Loch, you hold onto *that* broom or it's coming out of your hide!"

Tawyer chuckled. "Don't worry, boy. You two are good workers. We won't let *her* fall." He unlocked Kail's leg-chain, locked it back onto another pipe, and gestured for Kail to help Loch. "Byn-kodar's hell," he added with a laugh that echoed off the silent grid, "I had money on her to *catch* the bastard!"

Warden Orris huffed into the medical clinic where Prisoner Loch was being tended for cuts on her leg. Her hands and feet were shackled, as were those of Jeridan, a prisoner stocking supplies under a guard's watchful eye. Most prisoners hunched over a bit or shuffled when the shackles were put on, but Loch sat calmly, back straight, as a nurse applied the bandages.

This had to be handled carefully, Loch thought. Too soft, and he'd ignore it. Too hard, and he'd snap right here. She gave him a look devoid of anger or curiosity.

She knew Warden Orris didn't like her. It was probably her Urujar blood. Orris acted like he had Old Kingdom blood, and a dark-skinned woman who didn't act properly respectful would naturally put his back up. The fact that she was only half-Urujar would make him even angrier.

Orris waved the nurse and the guard out of the room, then stood before Loch, waiting expectantly. Jeridan put tools on the shelf, his shackles jangling.

"The guards tell me you lost a broom today," Orris finally said, pulling his jowly cheeks into a friendly smile. "Dropped your own and took someone else's to make up for it."

Loch said nothing.

"That's the story I heard, anyway. If you have a different story, I'd like to hear it." Orris gave her an encouraging smile.

She still said nothing.

"Loch, I want to help you here," Orris said, frowning. "I've tolerated this attitude… but that equipment you lost has to be paid for… one way or another." He tried a different smile this time. Across the room, Jeridan blanched and went back to stocking the shelves with jerky movements. His chains rattled more loudly.

A long and silent moment passed.

Orris wore a saber while at work, and he yanked the blade from its sheath now. It was a fine weapon, with a brass-plated guard, contoured mahogany grip, and a name worked into the blade in intricate calligraphy. He leveled it at Loch. "What happened to Soggs can happen to you! You will *give* me the respect I deserve!"

After another long moment, Loch gave him a low bow and shot him the tiniest suggestion of a smirk. He glared at her, so intent on catching the look that he completely missed the quick motion that sent several small tools into Jeridan's prison worksuit.

"Have it your way!" Orris shouted, and turned and left without a backward look.

When Orris was gone, Loch grinned. Perfect.

She tapped the metal frame of the bed gently, catching Jeridan's eye. She raised an eyebrow, and the other prisoner grinned, gave her a tiny nod, and went back to stocking the supplies as the guard and nurse came back in.

Back in his own office, Orris growled and tossed his grand-father's cavalry saber onto the chair. Stupid, getting flustered like that. He was in charge. He could take care of her if she wouldn't learn respect. But he couldn't kill her—the Voyancy was already going to investigate the death of Soggs.

Orris hung his grandfather's sword back up and asked his secretary to send for another prisoner.

Akus arrived a few minutes later, a burly man shuffling jerkily in the leg-shackles. He'd torn the sleeves off the gray worksuit, revealing ropy masses of muscle and knife scars along both arms. Orris should have disciplined him for damaging his worksuit, but the big man bowed low, then grinned and said, "Afternoon, Chief," and Orris decided to let it slide.

"I need a certain woman to have an accident." Orris smiled. "She needs to live, and I'll have to dangle you for a night afterward, but it'll pay."

Akus snorted. "Pay don't much matter. She's gotta live, you said?"

Orris nodded. "But anything short of killing her is fine." He leaned forward. *"Anything."*

Akus's mouth twisted into a broken-toothed grin.

The guards carried truncheons in the dining hall, as the dining hall was the only place aside from their own cells in which the prisoners were left unshackled. If the truncheons failed, the warden could activate a single crystal and send eldritch beams of energy sizzling across the metal floors, driving the prisoners to their knees in agony.

Riots ended quickly at the Cleaners.

Loch and Kail were waiting in line when Akus walked up and, without preamble, slammed his elbow into Loch's shoulder. "Hey!" he shouted. "Watch it! You messin' with me?"

"Watch yourself," Kail shot back. "She didn't—" Akus flung out an arm, and Kail staggered back. Kail grabbed for a sword that hadn't been at his waist since his old military days with Loch, then lifted a flimsy tin dining tray. He stopped when a guard's truncheon tapped gently on his shoulder.

"Settle down, son," Tawyer said affably. "You don't want more trouble." Using his truncheon, he gently steered Kail away from Akus and Loch.

"You messin' with me?" Akus blocked Loch's path as she tried to walk around him. "You say you're sorry real nice, maybe I'll forget about it." Seeing the crowd of prisoners slowly gathering around them, Akus grinned. "I like you breaking your vow of silence just for me."

Loch's eyes narrowed to thin slits, and she looked back at Kail. Kail gestured minutely at Tawyer, and Loch gave him a tiny nod, then turned around to walk the other way.

Akus's shove sent her crashing into a flimsy bench that shattered under the impact, leaving her face-down in a pile of splintered wood. "Don't you walk away from me!"

"Got what you asked for," Jeridan murmured as Kail stepped back into the crowd, which was starting to yell encouragement now. "But it's going to cost you."

"I'm a bit shy," Kail said, not making eye contact, "but if you're interested in a wager...."

"Always." Jeridan was in the Cleaners for winning a lot of money from very important people.

As Loch pushed herself to her knees, Akus kicked her hard in the side. "You're not gonna say my name, now. You're gonna *scream* it!"

"I'd take twenty at four to one," Kail said by way of opening.

Loch struggled back to her feet, and Akus strode over, shouting for the crowd, and pulled her to her feet by her thick black ponytail. She lashed out as she rose, her fists bloodying Akus's nose, and then broke his grip and slammed a fist into his broad gut.

Akus grunted and took Loch clear off her feet with a single backhand. She rolled and came up, shaking her head.

"You had your chance," Akus growled. "Pulling your hair's the *least* I'm gonna do."

"Two to one," Jeridan countered. "And at least a hundred, or why are we even talking?"

"Fifty at three to one. I'm no good for a hundred."

"Five to two?"

"I can do that," Kail said, and the two men shook on it.

Loch lunged in with high, fast jabs, but Akus had his hands up in a brawler's guard, and Kail heard him laughing as the smaller woman pounded his arms ineffectually. Then he ducked down, wrapped his arms around her knees, and yanked up. Loch slammed back onto the metal floor with a hiss of breath and rolled away desperately.

The crowd roared its approval.

"I'm impressed by your confidence," Jeridan said conversationally. "But really, against Akus?"

"Akus is the mighty oak," Kail said, "but Loch is the slender reed."

Pausing to acknowledge the cheers, Akus grinned, then looked to the dining hall doorway. Warden Orris was standing there, a mad leer on his face. He gave Akus a little nod.

As Loch pushed herself to her knees, leaning on the wall for support, Akus raised one boot to crush her spine.

The boot slammed into the wall a fraction of a second after Loch darted to the side, and Akus staggered. Loch's kick snapped into the back of his leg, and Akus crashed to his knees.

"And sometimes," Kail added, "the slender reed kicks the crap out of the mighty oak."

Loch slammed the heel of her palm into Akus's jaw with a crack that silenced the room, then hammered Akus's temple with an elbow. An uppercut snapped his head back up and sprayed blood across the room, and Loch grabbed a fistful of his hair and finished it by pulling him into a knee to the face.

Jeridan closed his mouth and looked at Kail.

Kail nodded thoughtfully. "So, about the one-twenty-five you owe me, and those items I wanted to buy...."

Akus wasn't moving. Loch pulled her blood-spattered gray worksuit back into place. She looked to the doorway, staring at Orris for a long moment. Then she sniffed, picked up her dining tray, and returned to the serving line.

Loch's silence since arriving at the Cleaners wasn't uncommon. The criminals who believed that the *lapiscaela* would catch the words and steal their souls often didn't talk for the first few weeks, until fear and loneliness and grim acceptance broke the barriers down.

In the small cell she shared with Kail, Loch kept her silence, saying not a single word.

Not aloud, anyway.

Are we clear? she signed to Kail. He had top bunk—Loch hated hearing him snore *beneath* her—and had swung his upper body down over the edge to look at her from above.

"Jeridan will get us the goods tomorrow," he said quietly. "You okay?"

Fine, she signed. *Hurry. Not much time.*

"You think the warden will move that soon?" Kail frowned. "Seems fast after sending the thug at you today."

Tomorrow. The sign-language she and Kail had learned as scouts didn't allow for nuance, but she put a fierce snap into each gesture. *He's killed before.*

"I'm sorry about Soggs." Kail sighed, then shrugged. "Did give you a chance to piss off the warden even more, though."

After a moment of silence, Kail's large eyes closed, two points of white blinking shut in the dim light. "I'm sorry. I didn't mean that."

Soggs was a civilian.

"I know, Loch. I'm sorry."

Fight the enemy, not their people. When Kail had joined her unit, that was the first thing she'd taught him. It was the first thing she'd learned herself when she'd joined, years before that. Every scout in the Republic's army learned that phrase, signed or spoke it before every mission. They were soldiers, not thieves, not murderers.

"I know." Kail sighed. "Tomorrow, then. Assuming the warden is as blood-crazy as he seems."

Tomorrow. Follow the plan. It will be okay.

"Where have I heard *that* before?" Kail shook his head and pulled himself back up onto the top bunk.

She'd caught the brief flash of his white teeth in the darkness, though, and the smile meant a lot that night.

When the prisoners lined up at the supply station desk that morning, Warden Orris was there alongside Tawyer. The change in routine had the prisoners nervously murmuring to each other. The warden greeted each prisoner as Tawyer switched the shackles for the leg-chain, handed them their broom, and called out their assignment.

"Morning, Rastik. How's Block C treating you? Lewerryn, you take it easy today, you hear? Haha!"

"Got it?" Kail murmured to Jeridan as they neared the desk. Loch was in front of them.

"Of course." Jeridan rocked gently and bumped into Kail, who staggered and pushed him back into place. A small, cloth-covered bundle disappeared into the sleeves of Kail's worksuit.

"Morning, Loch!" Orris said jovially. "Let's hope you run into less trouble today than yesterday! Haha!"

Loch stepped up to Tawyer and wordlessly held out her shackled arms.

"Not today, I think," Warden Orris said easily. "The lady lost a broom, nearly fell, got into a fight. She can keep the arm shackles on today. Hell, those Urujar are more comfortable in chains anyway, right?"

Tawyer chuckled weakly. "I have to sign off for each pair of shackles—"

"Just mark it down, Tawyer. Here, let me put my initials by it." Orris grabbed the pen. "There. Take her legs, though. Can't wear your leg shackles *and* the leg-chain."

"Right, sir." Tawyer didn't meet Loch's stare as she stepped onto the stand to have her leg shackles removed. "Here, I'll just—"

"No, no, Tawyer. Give her *this* leg-chain, here." Orris produced one with a smile. "Fasten it good and tight, too. I'd be real sad if anything should happen to her."

Tawyer fastened the leg-chain. "Where would you like—"

"The Tooth, I think." Warden Orris nodded thoughtfully. "She was so eager to get there yesterday, after all. Put them on the lower grid. In fact, why don't you go ahead and walk them there yourself?" He gave Loch a wide smile. "You take care now, girl."

Tawyer did Kail's shackles and leg-chain in silence, then snapped a single-use flying charm secure on his shoulder and followed them to the hatch nearest the Tooth. He carefully fastened each of their leg-chains to one of several vertical pipes labeled with different grid sections. They climbed down a short metal pipe along a rusted iron ladder, their leg-chains squeaking and rattling beside them.

At the bottom, Tawyer had to float a bit to get around them. "Go on," he muttered. "You know which way it is."

"He's gonna kill her," Kail said conversationally.

"That kind of talk gets a man a night dangling down under, Uru."

They started moving, Loch in the lead since her chain was connected to the pipe ahead of Kail's. They followed the pipe along the narrow walkway, the cold morning air still tasting of the metal of the grid.

"You think the warden can kill two prisoners in one week and not be investigated?" Kail asked. "When the heat comes down on the warden, who do you think he'll blame?"

"You just stay careful." Tawyer prodded Kail with his truncheon. "Can't blame the warden for getting angry. Byn-kodar's hell, all she had to do was show a little respect!"

"Oh, damn, Tawyer, you're right," Kail said as he and Loch turned a corner on the pipe, their leg-chains protesting the uneven fittings with shrill screeches. "I guess she has to die. What was I thinking?"

They reached the Tooth. From the upper grid, standing level with the top, it was a violet jewel. The sun hadn't risen above the rim of the city yet, and the Tooth shone with a clear brilliance as the sun's light caught it directly.

"Lower grid," Tawyer said sharply.

Loch and Kail moved to the junction where the upper grid linked to the special frame that locked the Tooth into place all four sides. A vertical pipe led down to the lower grid, which connected to the frame below as well.

"You think about what you did to make the warden so mad." Tawyer gestured for them to head down. "Maybe he'll change his mind."

"See," Kail said thoughtfully, "I don't *know* what I did to make him so mad. I *know* it wasn't sleepin' with his mama, because I was sleeping with *your* mama last night."

"Shut your fat mouth!"

"That's not what your mama said. Man, she couldn't get *enough* of my mouth. And your mama's a screamer, too—"

The truncheon came whistling down at Kail's head, and Kail dove back. The truncheon clanged off of the pipes instead, and then Loch's shackled arms crashed down on Tawyer's wrist.

As the truncheon clattered on the pipes, Loch's palms slammed into Tawyer's temples. Then she looped her shackles over the back of his neck, yanked down hard, and brought her knee up.

"So, today it is," Kail said as Tawyer hit the ground. He pulled a small bundle out of his sleeve, passed Loch what looked like a pair of thick cloth slippers, and produced another pair for himself.

Loch shot him a look and pulled on the cloth slippers.

"Yes, I always use it," Kail said, "every time. Because it always works."

Loch raised an eyebrow as she got to her feet.

"Swear to Gedesar, if I run into a guard who doesn't fall for it, I'll find a new one." Kail reached into his sleeve again, produced a thin metal wire, and bent down to work on the leg-chain. A moment later, it snapped free. "Here, let me see yours."

With a wry smile, she reached down and yanked hard, and the special leg-chain Warden Orris had saved for her snapped clean away.

"Or that," Kail allowed, and then, grinning, reached into the bundle to produce a pair of pipefitter's tools. "Shall we?"

Orris pounded the desk so hard that his hand throbbed. "Guards! *Guards, get in here!*"

As warden, he had access to several powerful artifacts. He'd taken a vicious pleasure in pulling out the flat disc of polished ivory, laying it flat on the table, breaking a vision charm over the artifact, and watching as the dust sprinkled down and the pale ivory surface resolved into a view of the grids. He shifted through the divining crystals set throughout the Cleaners until he found the perfect view of the Tooth, complete with Tawyer, Kail, and Loch herself.

Then he watched in helpless rage as she took down Tawyer with brutal efficiency, broke the chain he'd prepared for her, and got to her feet. She and Kail began to do something with metal tools on the pipes of the grid. *His* grid.

But he was still master of the grid, and he had a few surprises of his own. It had been a while since the Cleaners had seen *real* discipline.

Orris reached into a special drawer in his desk and drew out a narrow wand of polished crystal. At its tip was set a single gem, a muddy green-black whose whirling pattern constantly shifted.

A pair of guards came into the room, and one of them asked him what he needed. He ignored them.

Instead, he looked down into the polished ivory surface at Loch. "Time to dance, little princess." Then he touched his personal signet ring to the wand.

The screams that echoed up from the grid made the whole office vibrate, or perhaps it was the magic itself that shook the very underside of Heaven's Spire. Orris felt a lustful rush as he stared into the ivory, watched the writhing tendrils of scarlet fire snake across every metal surface on the grid. Every prisoner at work would curl up in helpless torment or fall screaming from the pipes until their metal leg-chains caught them. Then they would dangle, writhing in agony while the pain raced down their chains.

Loch and Kail jumped in surprise, then stopped and waited.

After half a minute, the scarlet flames flickered and died.

Loch grinned, turned to the divining crystal that she knew he was using to watch her, and waved.

The nurse sighed as the vibrations ran through the clinic. The containment magic was wonderful for neutralizing prisoners, but there were always injuries. He was going to have prisoners complaining of all sorts of aches and pains for the rest of the day, and the warden hated it when the nurse used supplies.

He looked down at his only overnight prisoner, a man who'd lost a fight in the dining hall and was shackled to the bed for treatment. "Count yourself lucky," the nurse said conversationally, leaning in to check the unconscious man's pulse. "Better to be in here than down there this—"

The man's shackled hand shot up, closed around the nurse's throat before he could pull back out of reach, and yanked him down toward the bed.

"Key," the prisoner growled.

The nurse tried to pull back, realized that that wasn't going to help his breathing, and sputtered frantically. "Can't escape!" he gasped. "They'll kill you as soon as you go up!"

The prisoner grinned horribly. "Not going up."

Orris watched helplessly as Loch and Kail started working on the pipes again.

"It can't be," he murmured again. "She played me. *She played me!*" He thrust the crystal wand at the ivory plate and focused his will, but the magic required time to gather its strength again. Orris hurled the wand and spun away as it shattered against the wall. "Get down there and... No!" With sheer force of will, he lowered his voice. "No. Tend to the prisoners." He pulled his grandfather's saber from the wall, unsheathed it, and tossed the scabbard aside.

"I'll deal with Loch myself."

His pronouncement was ruined when another guard burst into the room. "Sir! Sir!"

"You don't get *paid* to run around screaming, guard!" Orris barked, brandishing the saber. The intruding guard flinched back, sputtering. "I know damn well the security wards were activated!"

"That's not why I'm here, sir," the guard cut in, still eyeing Orris's saber nervously.

"Well, why the hell *are* you here?" Orris shouted, bustling forward and urging the guards out of his way with flourishes of his grandfather's saber.

"It's, well, it's about the prisoner who got beaten in the dining hall yesterday." The guard stepped back at Orris's stare. "He was at the clinic when the wards were activated, but it appears that in all the excitement...."

"Where is he now?" Orris asked, biting off each word.

"He, er..." The guard winced. "He subdued the orderly treating his injuries and told the man that he intended to settle a score with the woman."

Orris laughed. "Well, now, that's not bad news at *all*!" he declared grandly, heading for the drop-hatches with a jaunty step. "I just hope I get to see him do it!"

"Done." Kail stepped back from the upper grid. They'd worked fast since Orris had activated the wards and had gotten through most of the frame holding the Tooth in place. If not for the insulation slippers Kail had scrounged up, they'd likely have been dead already. "Want me to head down?"

Loch turned and nodded shortly, then jerked her head back to the eastern walkway where footsteps clanged in sharp contrast to the groans of shaken prisoners. Then came a roar of sheer hatred that could have been the war trumpet of Esajolar herself. "*LLLLLOCCCCH!*"

Akus came around the corner, a massive figure of battered flesh and rippling muscle. His nose was broken, and one eye was swollen nearly shut. He wore no worksuit, only boots and a clinic blanket wrapped around his waist several times like a kilt. His broad chest was covered with hair, knife scars, and purple-green bruises. She threw a punch, but he ignored it in his rage, slamming her against the pipes and driving the breath from her lungs.

"Get off her!" Kail shouted, leaping at the enormous man. His punch glanced harmlessly off Akus's shoulder, and with a grunt, Akus grabbed hold of Kail's worksuit with thick, knotted hands and lifted him off the ground.

"No leg-chain, little Urujar?" Akus growled. "That's gonna cost you." As Kail struggled helplessly, Akus walked to the edge of the upper grid. Then, with a smile, he flung Kail off the edge, laughed harshly, and turned back to Loch. "Hope your friend has a nice—"

Her elbow caught him in the gut. Her kick caught him in the groin. The open palms of her shackled hands smashed into his already-broken nose. And as he howled and lashed out blindly, her shoulder, with the full power of her lunging body behind it, caught him in the midsection, knocking him back a full three steps.

He'd only been two steps from the edge.

He screamed as he fell, and Loch spun away, not wanting to see it.

Instead, she saw Warden Orris himself, standing at the edge of the walkway with his saber raised in a mocking salute.

"That poor dumb brute was never in your league, Loch," the warden said conversationally, "but then, I guess your little friend Kail was never in *his* league."

Loch spread her arms as far apart as they could go, shackled as they were, and set herself in an unarmed fighting stance.

"What, nothing?" Orris shook his head. "You stupid girl, you *know* you're not leaving the Cleaners alive. You thought you could play me, do something to my grid, but I caught you. And *still* you cling to that stubborn pride?" His face reddened at her silence, and sweat began to bead on the thick jowls of his neck. "Or maybe you're too *stupid* to talk. Is that it? You too stupid to spit out any last words, *you Uru?*"

Loch walked forward, her padded feet nearly silent on the metal of the grid.

"Fine!" Orris shouted, raising his saber. "Die like the—"

Loch lunged in and kicked Orris in the shin. As he howled and brought the saber down, she raised her shackled arms, caught the saber on the shackles, crossed her wrists to trap the blade, and spun away, yanking the sword from his grasp. With practiced ease, she flipped the blade free of the chains and caught it with one hand.

Then she turned away from Orris and walked to the edge of the upper grid, her new sword held high to keep it clear of the shackles.

"I'll see you scream before you die, you..." Orris stammered to a halt. "Where are you going?"

Loch tapped the sword twice on the edge of the grid, looked down for a moment, and then strode to one of the corners. From the lower grid below, Kail's voice clearly called up, "Ready when you are, Captain!"

Orris dashed to the edge and stared down at the lower grid in dumbfounded shock. He'd clearly seen Kail thrown from the upper grid by Akus, who had then been knocked off by Loch.

Kail and Akus were working side by side. Akus was naked except for his boots, and the large blanket Akus had worn wrapped around his waist was now wrapped around the Tooth, covering the vast majority of its lower surface like a massive stocking.

Blocking it from the light of the sun.

Orris was not a stupid man. The Tooth was so irregular and so large that it required a special frame to connect it to the grid. His gaping stare took in the missing screws and broken pins on that frame, both on the upper grid and the lower grid.

There was only one major support pipe still connected to the Tooth's harness, and it was creaking ominously, metal whining in protest as Loch approached it.

"You *can't!*" Orris blurted, then felt himself reddening as Loch turned and raised an eyebrow. "You'll be... That's... You're a madwoman!"

Loch smiled, and it was that more than anything that made Orris backpedal frantically. She raised the sword in her shackled arms, her whole body bending like a fully stretched bow, and then she brought the blade down on the last junction holding the entire Tooth and its frame in place.

There was a sharp metallic crack, followed an interminable moment later by a low creak that built rapidly in pitch and volume as the entire structure of the grid around the Tooth began to sink. Small pipes twisted, bent, and snapped under the weight of the great stone, and as Orris scrambled back, the entire section of scaffolding sheared away in a screaming crescendo of tearing metal.

The last thing Orris saw as the Tooth and the three prisoners fell away to freedom was Loch's smiling face. One shackled arm clung to the twisted wreckage of the grid around the stone, and the other held his grandfather's sword. Orris watched that face until he could no longer see it, and then, when his shaking legs would bear his weight again, he pulled himself back to his feet.

Behind him, the prisoners began cheering.

Kail had insisted that he had timed it exactly, but Loch was very near the end of her trust when, below her on the remains of the lower grid, Kail shouted, *"Three! Two! One! Now!"*

As the ground raced toward them, green and brown and blue resolving into fields and rivers, farms and townships, Kail and Akus yanked hard on the sheet and pulled it free from the Tooth. The wind caught it, and in seconds, the blanket was far above them, floating gently on its lazy path to the ground.

As the Tooth caught the morning sunlight, its dull purple surface blossomed into violet and its ancient magic slowed their plummeting descent. The wind that threatened to tear Loch free from the grid fell from a scream to a throaty whisper, and the ground that had been hurtling toward them at breakneck speed slowed to the comparative crawl of a galloping horse.

Which, Loch noted as she hit the damp turf of a dazzling green meadow and rolled, taking the impact in her legs and shoulders and hips and back, was still faster than you wanted to be going when you hit the ground.

Loch found herself lying face-down in the damp grass. The sword stood embedded in the earth a few paces away, vibrating from the impact. She took in a deep breath, heard the ominous creak of metal, and rolled away instinctively. Sparks of light trailed dizzily across her eyes, but she still got a good look.

Its glow now rising to its normal dazzling violet brilliance, the Tooth rose from the shattered wreckage of the grid. It moved slowly at first, rocking and swaying like a charm dangling on a chain. Then, picking up speed, it leapt into the heavens, straight back toward the glowing purple disk that hung high above them like a sullen sun, the only glimpse of Heaven's Spire most citizens ever saw. It would, Loch guessed, be going *quite* fast by the time it returned to the Cleaners.

"Damn!" Akus groaned as he pushed himself back to his feet. "I don't know who hits harder, Loch, you or the damn ground." He looked up at Heaven's Spire high above and laughed. "Still, worth a few beatings. Anybody seen my blanket?"

"I'm looking, believe me," Kail said shakily, leaning on the wreckage of the grid. "I don't need my first glimpse of freedom ruined by your sorry naked body."

"Hah!" Akus clapped Kail on the shoulder. "Almost wish I could see Orris's face when the Tooth gets back. Hope it hits him square in the ass."

"Given the size of his ass, you've got good odds," Kail said, and Akus laughed again.

"Damn straight! Hey, you ever got a job that needs some muscle, you let me know."

"Will do," said Kail. "Thanks again for coming to us when Orris made his offer. I had no idea how in Byn-kodar's hell we were going to smuggle a tarp out to the grid."

"Worked out for all of us." Akus looked to Loch, who was still staring upward. "Ma'am, I'm going to put some distance between me and this wreckage before the airships come looking. Pleasure working with you."

Loch smiled and raised a fist in a warrior's salute. He returned it, ducked his head, and walked off toward the woods to the east, naked and whistling off-key.

"So, Captain," Kail said, still swaying where he stood, "what now?"

Loch reached down and ran her hand along the damp grass, then licked the dew from her palm. She swallowed, tasting the sweet water as it loosened her throat. High overhead, she imagined she could see a sudden blossom of light across the underside of Heaven's Spire.

"Now," she said, "we pay back the son of a bitch who put us there."

Two

Justicar Pyvic strode into his office, looked at the board for a moment in silence, and then went to see Melich. He knocked on the office door, then walked in without waiting for an answer. "I heard the most interesting joke this morning, sir."

"Pyvic...." Melich wasn't much older than Pyvic, but he had a bad leg that had kept him out of the army during the war, so he'd had more time to rise through the ranks of the justicars. He was balding, carried a truly absurd cane so that the limp didn't show, and had a face prematurely lined from worry and laughter both.

"What's the difference between a justicar and a porter?"

"I was going to send word—"

"When a case gets taken from a *porter*, somebody *tips* him." Pyvic was tall, which had been a disadvantage in the war, and fast, which was an advantage almost anywhere. His dark eyes narrowed as he leaned over Melich's desk. "Where are my cases, *sir?*"

"They're not yours. You're on special assignment." Melich didn't lose eye contact.

"What's the assignment?"

"Political."

"Use Derenky. He loves that crap. Why did you give my death-curse case to Tomlin?"

"It has to be you." Melich blinked this time. "And Tomlin has family history with the wizards. It might give him an in."

"Everyone in Tomlin's family is a wizard, sir. Do you know why he isn't?"

"Because he had a deep desire to protect the helpless?" Melich deadpanned.

"Because he's an idiot. He's good with pushpins and a map, and that's about it. And I ruled out the wizards. It's either a fairy creature or a rogue priest. You should give it to Jyrre."

"You know," Melich mused, "I thought that when they gave me this little star on my uniform, it meant I got to make those decisions."

"Why me, sir?"

"*Because* Derenky loves politics." Melich grimaced. "Someone escaped from the Cleaners."

Pyvic blinked. "You're calling me in on a suicide?"

"No, they *actually* escaped," Melich said irately, "and now the Skilled are saying that the Learned warden appointee was incompetent, and the Learned are saying that the Skilled have been slashing the budget to make it impossible to keep order. They're demanding an independent investigation from the justicars."

"You need someone impartial," Pyvic guessed.

"I need someone who can get it done fast and right." Melich handed him a folder.

"What was he in for?"

"It was a trio, but the leader was a woman. And the information is in the file. Why are you asking me?"

Pyvic smiled tightly. "Because the death-curse killed an eight-year-old girl on her way home from a solstice dance. I wanted to know what was more important than that."

"Dismissed, Pyvic."

He walked out, folder crinkling in his clenched fist, sparing a moment for a brief nod when he heard, back behind him, Melich ordering Jyrre to take over the death-curse case.

Loch held up her purse, but the old white woman behind the counter of the small general store didn't even look at it.

"I've got money," Loch said for the third time. She'd covered her worksuit with mud to disguise it as much as possible. "I'm telling you, I was robbed on the road, but I was able to keep—"

"Get out!" The old woman was holding her broom like a sword. "You're not fooling me! This is a shop for honest folk!"

Loch shook the purse. "Would you like me to leave this on the counter while I browse? You can even check that it's real money. I just need some new traveling clothes and—"

"If you don't leave," the old woman hissed, "I'll call the guard and tell them you've been stealing. One look at you, and they'll believe it."

"One look at me?" Loch stepped in close to the counter, and the woman flinched back. "What exactly do I *look* like?"

The old woman just glared, lips pressed together in a tight grimace, and Loch sighed. She tossed the purse up into the air, caught it with the other hand, and walked out of the store.

Kail met her outside. He was wearing one pack and carrying another, along with Loch's new sword. "Nice old lady. Didn't call you a dirty Uru out *loud*, anyway."

Loch sighed. "So, what did she have in the back room?"

"Traveling clothes, boots, and enough food to get us to Twobridge." Kail grinned and handed her the pack and the warden's sword.

"Good." Loch gave Kail the purse. "That's more money we can put toward a wagon ride, then."

Kail hefted the purse, and then it disappeared into a pocket. "Would you really have given that old bat our money if she hadn't thrown you out?"

"Fight the enemy, Kail. Not their people."

Loch and Kail got off a wagon and walked into Twobridge a few days later.

A puppeteer was giving the news as they entered the town square. It covered their entrance nicely.

"Now, how about this prison break?" the dragon asked the two other puppets. "Is this something that citizens should be concerned about?"

"I think it raises a lot of questions," said the griffon, flying around the stage and raising its lion's paws while flapping its great eagle wings. The crowd laughed. "I mean, the Learned Party prides itself on being the party of security for the Republic, and here their appointed officer lets three dangerous criminals escape!"

"So," Kail murmured, "do we have a more direct plan?"

"A job." Loch nudged Kail, and they made their way into the outer edges of the crowd, close enough to blend in but far enough out that they weren't getting in people's way.

"Well, I'd figured. Who?"

"These partisan attacks are exactly the reason the people don't trust the Skilled Party!" cried the manticore, battering the griffon with a stick and swishing its scorpion's tail. "The Skilled have stabbed Corrective Services in the back for years, and now they try to blame people for something nobody could have predicted!"

"I wouldn't say that the Skilled Party stabbed Corrective Services—" the griffon said weakly, trying to escape the manticore's assault.

"Acting like they could have done better. It just shows you how much the Skilled Party hates the good honest working folk of the Republic!" The manticore was now chasing the griffon around the stage, flapping its great bat wings while the dragon harrumphed loudly and tried to calm things down. The crowd roared with laughter.

Loch pursed her lips. "We can't use any of the other scouts. Uribin's got the restaurant, and Voshik's a lieutenant. I don't want to drag them into this."

"There's always Jyelle," Kail said with a small grin, and then winced as Loch elbowed him.

"For something like this," Loch said, "we need professionals. People who can handle magic. Gedesar knows there's enough of it up there."

"I know a few people," Kail said hopefully. "A wizard. Old, but good with safes."

"That's not a fair accusation!" cried the griffon. "All of Heaven's Spire has security problems—"

"You're endangering our security just by saying that!" shouted the manticore, pouncing on the griffon. "I can't understand how you can sit there and put the lives of our men and women at risk from Imperial spies!"

"I've got an old friend with some tricks," Loch mused. "Usually sticks to the woods, though."

"Heated arguments from both sides," declared the dragon, marking the announcement with a little puff of alchemical flame. "We'll keep you updated with the latest news! Remember, everyone, *it's your republic!*"

"*Stay informed!*" the crowd shouted back, and then erupted into applause.

"Well, how do you propose to find a team that can hit the Spire?" Kail muttered under the applause.

Loch pointed with her chin. Kail looked, then nodded.

After the performance, the crowd broke up, and the puppeteer, a balding old Urujar man with a limp, began to break down the stage. Loch and Kail ambled over.

"Afternoon, *Yeshki,*" Loch said with a little nod. "That was a lovely performance."

"*Aitha.*" The old puppeteer gave her a wrinkled smile, then nodded to Kail. "*Ithki.* I'm glad you enjoyed it. Tell me, if you don't mind... which do you favor? The griffon or the manticore?"

Loch looked at the griffon, an eagle's head and wings on a lion's body, and the manticore, a lion with bat wings and a scorpion's tail.

"Funny thing, *Yeshki.* You get right down to it, they're both mostly big cats."

The old puppeteer chuckled. "I doubt the men on the Spire would appreciate your answer."

"You seemed to be playing up the manticore," Kail said, looking at the puppets.

The puppeteer shrugged. "We get the news from the Spire, but they let us play it how we like." He looked around. "Town like this, they go for the Learned. Play it that way, the crowd's happy, and you end up with more coins in the cup."

"As a puppeteer, I bet you get around pretty good," Loch said idly. "We're looking for a few talented individuals for a job."

The puppeteer shrank back. "I don't know who told you what, but I'm an honest man. I don't know anything about that."

"*Ynkuveth,*" Kail said reassuringly, raising his hands in a placating gesture. "We're not with anybody."

"What kind of people are you looking for?" the puppeteer asked cautiously. "Might be I've met a few people in my travels. Nothing definite, mind you, but—"

"A lock-man, a second-storey operator, and somebody who can jigger with the crystals the Ancients used," Loch said crisply, "plus anybody who can handle magic and isn't insane, evil, or overly religious."

"Hey, I told you, I've got a magic guy!" Kail said irately.

"Gedesar's fingers!" the puppeteer said in a choked whisper. "What kind of job are you planning?"

"A very profitable one," said Loch, and gave the old Urujar man a winning smile and some money.

Justicar Pyvic had been a soldier once, back in the war against the Empire. He'd been good at that. After the war, he'd been an excellent justicar, tracking down criminals too clever or strong for the local laws. He'd liked the job, gotten comfortable with the rhythm.

And now this.

Archvoyant Silestin was eating breakfast with Warden Orris when Pyvic was shown in. Pyvic hadn't seen the Archvoyant up-close since the war, when he'd been *Colonel* Silestin. He was still trim, and he filled out the shoulders of the dress-white uniform he wore instead of an Archvoyant's robes. Silestin's hair and beard had gone from black to salt-and-pepper, but he still had a robust energy as he piled eggs onto his toast.

"Bureaucrats!" Silestin declared. "Whining as though dogs wouldn't crap if they held the leash!"

Archvoyant Silestin, first among equals in the Voyancy. Leader of the Learned Party, with an impressive military background and a platform of making the Republic great again by protecting it from all enemies. The churches loved him because he tithed generously and supported legislation to lift restrictions on their economic activities. The Urujar loved him because he'd adopted an Urujar girl whose parents had died in the war and helped put the first Urujar Voyant into office. The merchants loved him because he made them more money.

Orris nodded with enthusiasm. "Damn right, sir!"

"So here's what we're going to do," Silestin said, leaning in. He hadn't looked at Pyvic yet. "You're going to take point, lead a team down on the ground and get those prisoners back in hand. You do that, and any doubts about how you run the Cleaners go away."

"I'll take care of it, sir!"

"Now," Silestin went on, "the damned Skilled insisted on picking the justicar who'd accompany you—and they were bent on making it hot for us, so we had to let them have their way on this one. So he's some Skilled brown-noser who's going to nanny about. You, what's your name?"

"No," Pyvic said pleasantly.

Orris looked confused. Silestin, quicker on the uptake, looked somewhere between speculative and angry. "No, what?" the Archvoyant asked quietly.

"No, I am not a Skilled brown-noser," Pyvic said crisply. His army days were over, and there was no way he was calling this man "sir." "And no, I will not be accompanying Warden Orris on his mission. Warden Orris will be accompanying *me* on mine."

"Right," said Silestin, "whatever. The point, Justicar Pyvic—"

"The point, Archvoyant Silestin, is that you remembered my name quite conveniently after appearing not to know it earlier. The point is that you *need* me on this mission to avoid the appearance of trying to cover up your mistakes." Pyvic smiled. "The point is that if I walk away claiming that you're more interested in playing politics than capturing prisoners, it's going to be a bad day for you."

Orris grew red. Silestin pursed his lips behind his beard. "You're an observant man, Pyvic."

"My record reflects that," Pyvic said evenly. "That's *likely* why I was chosen."

"Warden Orris will coordinate with you." Silestin smiled.

"I appreciate the gesture," Pyvic said.

Tern watched as Icy headed into the town jail to blackmail Sheriff Gaist for the death of Guildmaster Halistan.

Icy was an Imperial, short and slender, and his golden robes billowed around him as he went up the stairs and inside. Tern watched him go, muttered a quick prayer to Gedesar, and then headed over to the town square.

Guildmaster Halistan had, according to Icy, been killed with clean slashes that suggested a duelist's precision. Before his appointment to sheriff, Gaist had been a blademaster with more than fifty wins in both first-blood and death matches.

According to the Textile Guild, Halistan's signet ring would have recorded the last few moments of his life. It should offer enough proof for the Textile Guild to go to the justicars and bring down Gaist.

At which point, Tern and Icy would get paid.

Tern wandered the market for a quarter of an hour. She blended in, a mousy woman with spectacles and a brown crafter's dress with a lot of pockets.

Finally, she picked out her target, a stall selling expensive scented candles. A scowling middle-aged man looked at her suspiciously as she examined his wares.

"Is this ginger?" she asked, sniffing one of them. "It smells more like vanilla."

"It's a mixture of several different spices," the candle-seller said, trying not to sneer.

"Great. Icy will love this. I'll take it." She tucked the candle into one of her dress's many pockets.

The candle-seller jumped. "Ah, that will be twenty-five—"

"Oh, I don't need to pay." Tern fished out a piece of paper with a gold seal on it. "Diplomatic Writ of Accommodation. You'll be fully compensated by the Empire. Thanks!" She walked off without looking back as the candle-seller sputtered behind her.

She hit a stall with expensive bath salts next, and was getting ready to flash the Diplomatic Writ of Accommodation to a woman selling watches when the guards closed in from either side.

A few minutes later, she was hauled into the town jail, protesting loudly.

"I thought the Republic was the bastion of freedom for all men, but *apparently* that doesn't apply to women," she yelled as she took in the room, "and if you're from another country, well, that precious *freedom* doesn't apply to—"

"Just give us a minute," one of the guards cut her off, and knocked on Sheriff Gaist's door. "Sir?"

"What?" Gaist shouted back. His voice had the rusty roughness that came from a lot of long nights at the tavern.

"Woman here who says she's with an Imperial," the guard said to the door.

"I demand to see the sheriff!" Tern added. "If you people are going to cause a diplomatic incident, I'd *prefer* that you do it to my face!"

"Fine!" Gaist shouted. It sounded like he was moving something, and Tern caught the click-clank of something metal snapping shut. "Come in."

"It's about time," Tern muttered as the guards pulled her into Gaist's office. "Maybe *now* we can clear up this idiotic misunderstanding, so I can get back to my—"

"You're not an Imperial," Gaist cut in. He'd lost the lean build of his dueling days, but he still wore the sword.

"How could you tell, Sheriff?" Tern shot back. "But I *am* the attaché of an important official from the Empire, and as such, I am entitled to the full protections of—"

"She was stealing in the merchant square," one of the guards told Gaist. "Claimed she didn't have to pay anything because of some legal thing."

There was no sign of Icy in the room. In fact, there was little sign of anything much at all in the room, save a battered desk, a knife-scarred dartboard, and a truly impressive safe. The safe was, if Tern wasn't mistaken, of dwarven manufacture, straight from the smiths of Ajeveth. It was nearly indestructible, constructed from an *yvkefer* alloy that made it impossible to open with magic.

"The *legal thing* you're referring to is a Diplomatic Writ of Accommodation!" Tern said when it became clear that the guards weren't going to explain. "Now, my master, an official from the Empire, was coming to see you here, I believe. If you'll simply *talk* with him, you ignorant yokels, he will *prove* that I am entitled to requisition items for personal use—"

"There's no official here, miss," Gaist said flatly, cutting her off.

Tern sputtered for a moment. "But he said he needed to speak to the sheriff about something—"

"He's not here," Gaist insisted.

Tern looked at Gaist's hand, which clutched at his sword scabbard tightly enough to whiten his knuckles. She looked at Gaist's boots, which were flecked with blood. She looked at the small trail of blood, barely noticeable unless one was looking for it, that suggested something had been dragged to the safe. While bleeding.

She tried a smile. "Sheriff, I'm certain that we can put this little..." She swallowed. "...misunderstanding... behind us. I'd be happy to—"

"Oh, we ignorant yokels like to see these things through," Gaist said, smiling grimly. "We'll keep an eye out for your Imperial official, but in the meantime, you'll enjoy our accommodations."

"But I've got diplomatic immunity as an attaché of—this is a complete abrogation of—you don't understand how important this man—"

She kept yelling while the guards shoved her into the cell whose iron bars formed one wall of Gaist's office and locked her inside. "When my master arrives, you're going to find yourself apologizing to people on *both* sides of the border," she said, her cheeks red with anger, "and I have to tell you, I for one am not going to be quiet about my treatment—"

"Lady," Gaist said in a voice that stopped her cold, "you'd best hope that your little yellow friend shows up at all. Otherwise, things could be very unpleasant for you." With a gesture to his guards, he turned and left his office, shutting the door behind him.

Tern waited a few minutes, just to make sure he was gone.

"*Lady,*" she muttered in a fair imitation of Gaist's wine-soaked voice, "*you'd best hope that your little yellow friend shows up at all.*" She paced back and forth in the jail cell, tugging at her plain brown braid. "Why do they always say *lady* like that?" With her fingers, she eased a lock of hair out of the braid and began to pull on it. "Is that supposed to be some clever dichotomy, or are they completely unaware of the irony of… hah! Got it!" She yanked the lock of hair free, revealing a long length of thin wire with a few tiny hooks near the end.

"*Things could get very unpleasant for you.*" Tern snaked the thin wire through the bars and into the lock on the other side. "How about being jailed in a backward village with a jackass sheriff?" she muttered as she made careful motions with the wire. "Little unpleasant for me right there—ahhh." The cell door gave a tiny click and opened to Tern's push.

"*Enjoy our accommodations.*" Tern strode to the back wall of the sheriff's office. She unbuckled her boots, massive steel-toed clunkers that looked like they belonged on someone much taller and wearing many studded leather accessories. Then she wrenched the heel of one boot sharply. A hidden compartment snapped open, revealing a small pouch filled with gritty gray powder. "Like *that* hasn't been done to death...." A moment later, the other boot revealed a similar compartment containing a small cup of viscous sludge. "Thought duelists were supposed to have snappy comebacks...." She upended the cup near the wall, waiting until the dark material settled fully, and then gingerly sprinkled the pouch of powder onto the sludge.

"Nice safe though." Tern slid her boots back on and tromped back across the office. "Heard they're nigh unbreakable. Great place to store your incriminating evidence." She stopped before the safe and pulled a small listening tube from one of her brown dress's many pockets and a pressure wrench from another. "In fact, the dwarves claim that the only way you could crack one of their safes was..." Her dry voice dropped about three octaves and adopted a dwarven brogue. "...*to have somebody inside it.*"

She knocked twice on the safe door and, in the silence that followed, nervously took off her spectacles and cleaned them on the hem of her dress. A moment later, two knocks answered her, and she let out a long breath.

Once the pressure wrench was latched onto the combination faceplate, it was just a matter of turning it slowly enough for Icy to be able to knock each time he caught the telltale click of changing tumblers from inside the safe. Once his knock alerted her, Tern could listen through the tube to figure out whether the click meant "keep turning this way" or "start turning that way"—only the tumblers themselves were soundproofed. It *was* a sophisticated safe, though, and it took Tern and Icy a good ten or fifteen minutes to get it open.

Finally, Tern felt the handle release, and she opened the door. "You okay?"

"The sheriff dislocated several joints to fit me into the safe," Icy reported slowly, crunching as he slowly uncurled and slid out onto the floor, "but I am essentially unharmed." He held out Guildmaster Halistan's ring in one bloodstained hand. "And the ring was indeed stored here, where the *yvkefer* alloy prevented the Textile Guild from finding it with tracking spells."

"From which we profit. You had enough air?" Tern rifled the safe, pocketing a fair amount of money that Icy had left behind.

"I was preparing to lower my heart-rate," Icy noted, "but you were quite efficient; my standard meditative state sufficed."

"And him stabbing you?" Tern drew a sealed packet from yet another pocket and affixed it to the side of the safe. She affixed the seal to the inside of the door, then swung the safe door until only a crack remained open.

"His reflexes were slowed enough from alcohol for me to redirect his attack, as we anticipated. The blood packet on my hand worked adequately to suggest a mortal injury." Icy rolled out his neck and producing more crunching sounds. "However, I unintentionally swallowed the pellet under my tongue while conversing with the sheriff."

"You *what?*" Tern reached up to her hair and untwined the cord holding her braid in place. She strode to the wall, her boots clomping on the wooden floor, and stuck one end of the cord carefully into the dark sludge, into which the sprinkled powder had now dissolved. "How did you do the blood-on-the-mouth thing, then? You need blood-on-the-mouth to sell the kill."

"I ruptured a small vein under my tongue." Icy arched his back, catlike, before rising to his feet. "It served much the same effect."

"Probably easier to just not swallow the blood pellet, Icy." Tern put a hand to a pocket, then frowned and tried another one.

"I become flustered when acting dishonestly. I have already reordered my energies to heal my mouth, and the blood pellet seems innocuous, though I suspect I shall pass... Is there some problem?"

Tern tried another pocket. "Dammit! Hey, remember when I used my special striker to light the candles at the inn last night? Do you by any chance remember seeing me put that back in my pocket?"

"You have misplaced your striker?" Icy rolled out his shoulders some more and popped a few more joints. Tern suspected that he was just showing off now.

"That's the general idea, yes."

"I do not believe our plan is severely compromised," Icy said with a small bow. "If I may?"

"Oh, get over there." Tern positioned herself behind the safe as Icy sauntered over to the cord sticking from the sludge, held the tip between his middle finger and thumb, concentrated for a moment, and then snapped his fingers with the cord between them. The tip of the cord burst into flame and promptly began hissing as the fuse burned down, and Icy trotted over and got next to her.

The explosion a few moments later was small, more of a rapid burn than an actual explosion *per se*. It did, however, open a tidy hole in the wall, and when the acrid purple smoke had cleared enough for safe breathing, Icy and Tern were on their way.

"Almost wish I could be there to see the look on his face when he opens the safe," Tern said as they reached the market square.

"What did you do?" Icy asked. "I assumed you had simply removed evidence that could incriminate us."

"Oh, no. When he opens it, a bunch of papers with *I killed Guildmaster Halistan* written on them are going to burst out and fly all over the room like an Imperial party favor. He's going to know *exactly* why we took him down."

Icy glanced back at the town jail behind them. "The hole we left in the wall probably communicated the same message."

"Don't ruin the moment for me, Icy." Tern sighed as the shouts began. "Oh, forget it. Looks like we're running."

When the stiff-necked justicar and the warden had gone, Archvoyant Silestin turned to the shadows near the door. "The white prisoner dies before he tells any embarrassing stories. The two Urujar come back. Make sure this wasn't a double-cross by the guild leader who turned them in." He turned back to his plate, then raised an eyebrow as another thought came to him. "And deal with Pyvic if you deem it necessary," he added, pointing with his fork.

The shadows rippled and slid into a perfectly black humanoid shape, the colors streaming off like water down an oiled raincoat.

Silestin's First Blade bowed once, turned, and then was gone.

Loch and Kail found their first potential recruits on the road outside town.

"Look about right?" Loch asked as they neared the other pair.

"An Imperial guy in robes and a woman in spectacles? Not a usual combination." Kail nodded as the other pair stopped, watching them. "I'm guessing they're ours."

"The woman with the spectacles has really good hearing," said the woman, raising a crossbow with a lot of gears and fiddly bits attached to it.

"Almost positive," Kail added to Loch, and then said to the woman, "I'm looking for a safecracker named Tern and a man named, ah, Cold?"

"Icy," said the Imperial man. "You have found us."

"This isn't one of those silence-the-thief deals, is it?" Tern asked. "Because I've been double-crossed before, but if the *Textile* Guild is screwing me—"

"Relax." Loch held up a hand and made the shape of the local guild for this province. "I'm Loch. This is Kail. We've got a job for a tinker and someone comfortable in uncomfortable spaces. Word on the street says you've taken down a lot of rich bastards."

"Well, the poor bastards don't have much money, or any challenging safes." Tern squinted behind her spectacles. "What's the job?"

"Long story," said Loch. "High-risk, high-reward."

"We must finish our business before entertaining new prospects," Icy said politely. "Where would we meet you if we were interested?"

"Ever been to Ros-Uitosuf?" Kail asked.

"A few days north of Ros-Sesuf?" Tern said.

"There's a restaurant named Uribin's," Loch said. "They serve the best damn catfish you've ever had."

"Crusted with sweet potatoes," Kail added, "in a cream sauce. We'll see you there two weeks from today."

"Two weeks?" Tern asked. "Heading to a few more cities to recruit?"

"Actually," Loch said with a smile, "we're heading into the woods."

Three

"**J**ERIDAN!" CAME THE GUARD'S CALL, AND EVERYONE IN THE Cleaners' dining hall paused.

People had kept quiet since the escape. Orris was gone, but Tawyer was throwing his weight around, making sure that prisoners weren't going to escape on his watch. People who mouthed off spent a night dangling by a leg-chain.

And some bastards Jeridan had won money from were whispering that he had helped Loch, Kail, and Akus escape. It was true, but they were still bastards for saying so.

"Jeridan! Tawyer wants to see you." The guard smiled.

Jeridan got to his feet slowly. "He say why?"

"Nothing *bad*, Jeridan!" The guard laughed and clapped him on the shoulder. "Warden Tawyer just wants to talk to you!"

Jeridan filed away the plans he'd secreted in his bunk, the things people could prove he'd done. He'd been planning his story ever since the escape. He was ready.

Nobody in the Cleaners ever saw him again.

"I don't love it," Kail said as they hopped off the wagon and walked the last quarter mile into Woodsedge.

"I'm hurt, Kail."

"There was a fairy on the thieves' guild register back in the last town," Kail said. "Reasonable rates, references available—"

"You have to be careful with magical creatures, Kail." Loch looked at Woodsedge as they approached, the wagon slowly pulling ahead of them. It was a new settlement, freshly carved out of the forest, with none of the smoke and smell of an established town.

"That's why they have references, Captain."

"Kail, how'd you end up in my unit?"

"It was either join the scouts or go to jail after the rest of my team threw me to the sheriff, and yes, I see your point, honor among thieves, fine." Kail squinted at a hunting party heading back into town. They were empty handed, clutching weapons and looking back over their shoulders. "And these fine people have found something bad in the woods."

"Ogres." Loch pointed off to scratch marks on the larger trees. "See the territory markers?"

"I did study *some* of the scouting manual." Kail looked up at the spring clouds. "And they'd just be coming out of hibernation. These people are digging themselves right into a bloodbath."

"Looks like." Loch looked at the hunting party again. They had reached the village already and were yelling excitedly. One of them, a rangy young man who couldn't have been more than eighteen, hung back from the crowd. "And this is where she'll be."

"This fairy you know and trust, even though she isn't on the register."

"Magical creatures have their own motives," Loch said and smiled. "I know hers. She's here."

"And how do we find her?" Kail asked, scanning the crowd of villagers gathering around the hunting party.

Loch gestured. While the rest of the crowd yelled angrily and drew their weapons, the rangy young man was making his way slowly back into the woods.

"We watch him."

The humans had come, and with them had come axes and fire.

Ululenia stood in the clearing and waited. Around her, light danced, catching the pure white of her snowy flanks. Butterflies circled her shining horn, and then fluttered away when she sent them off with a blessing of peace and the promise of sweet nectar in the bushes nearby.

Axes and fire killed, as swiftly as the hunter's arrow, as surely as the mountain lion's fangs. As surely as an ogre's spiked war staff.

Ululenia waited. Though the spring was still new, flowers shot from the earth and blossomed around her hooves.

But fire was part of the forest. No man brought the thunderstorms whose lightning ignited the forest. And when it finished burning, new growth rose from the ashes of the old.

Ululenia waited, and finally Merigan came.

He saw her, saw her snowy flanks that denied the shadows, her horn that shone like a rainbow before a waterfall, and he dropped his hunting bow and stared.

You alone can stop the bloodshed, Merigan, she spoke in his mind. *You alone must lead your people.*

He dropped to his knees. "W-why me?"

Because when you hunt in my woods, your thoughts are of food for your family and not death for your target, Ululenia said, and her horn blazed. *Because when you saw the signs left by the ogres, your thoughts were not of the glory and terror of spilled blood, but asking why the ogres would do this. Because you alone are the spark that will burn clean and let the new growth come.*

Merigan flushed and dropped his eyes. "What would you have me do?"

Ululenia told him.

Loch and Kail filed into the village hall. It was filled with a lot of scared people, and the yelling had already started. Villagers scuffed the sawdust on the floor and brandished clubs and knives while a tall, dark-bearded man standing behind a table banged a wooden mallet and called for order.

"Jerl Blackspear," Kail murmured beneath the noise of the crowd. "Village speaker. Wants to be mayor, once they're big enough to merit one. Trades on having fought in the war."

"To order!" Jerl yelled, and the crowd finally settled down. "Everyone be quiet! We all know why we're here, so settle down, and let's talk about ogres."

At the word, the crowd went still. Jerl smiled.

"That's right!" Jerl called to the now-silent crowd. "That's what we've got. Ogres. And I know you're scared. Scared they'll come kill your children, scared they'll crush you under those huge clubs like that bear we found smashed like an egg in the woods." He let it sink in. "But I know all about ogres. I killed a good dozen when they raided Hendkirk's barony. You let me plan this, you listen good and careful, and we'll do the same here."

"Captain, this is going to be bloody," Kail said quietly. "You sure we can't find someplace safer to go recruiting?"

"You're saying the beasts will attack?" asked an old woodsman.

"It's all under control." Loch smiled slightly.

Kail grimaced. "What can your friend do against a mob of angry villagers? Or an ogre clan?"

"As I recall... arrogant apple." Loch raised a finger as Kail shot her a look.

"Hell, yes, I'm saying they'll attack!" Jerl barked. "They're arrogant, and they'll bite into our children's heads like you'd bite into an apple!"

Kail pursed his lips. "Okay. I'm curious."

"Arrogant apple, babbling brook," Loch said without looking at him.

"And you want us to put our lives in your hands?" a matronly woman with flour-dusted hands called out.

"Who else is it going to be?" Jerl snarled. "You'd just babble like a brook while they... while they kill us all! These beasts are arrogant, and... but I've fought them before!"

"So your fairy friend..." Kail began.

"Didn't say she was a fairy," Loch said. "Arrogant apple, babbling brook, creeping cat."

"If you think you can just creep like a cat into their lairs by the babbling brook, you're just a dawdling duck!" Jerl stammered to a halt, blinking rapidly.

"Dawdling duck?" Kail asked.

Loch nodded. "She's got the rhythm, now."

"So your magical-creature friend who may or may not be a fairy," Kail said, "can play with people's thoughts?"

Loch grinned. "Picked that up all on your own, did you?"

Over the confused mutters of the crowd, the rangy young hunter that Loch had watched walk back into the forest raised his hand. "I would like to try to stop the ogres myself. I think I can do it."

"And she always uses the same pattern?" Kail asked.

"Says the man who always leads with the mother insults," Loch said without looking at him.

Jerl shook his head, grimacing. "Merigan! You think you can... you apple-cheeked, babbling cat dawdling while... No!" he snapped over the growing calls from the crowd. "No! I can lead us! You can't kill an ogre with excellent eggs!"

Loch looked over at Kail. "Excellent eggs was the next one."

Kail snorted. "Got that, thanks. After that?"

"Fondling fern, gullible something... Honestly, they usually fall over around this point."

"I respect your experience, Speaker Blackspear," Merigan said firmly, "but I would like to try nevertheless." He turned to the crowd. "Send me out alone, and if I fail, then let Woodsedge do as it must!"

Jerl had dropped his hammer and now clutched the table with both hands. "I can fondle more ogres than... babbling... not arrogant, I just..." Over the laughter and calls from the crowd, he shouted, "Creeping like ferns!"

"Will you let me try?" Merigan called. "Give me one chance. I will stop the ogres or die in the attempt."

"You're out of order! It's not your turn to arrogant apple, babbling brook, creeping cat," Jerl shouted, and then added, "dawdling duckling, excellent eggshells, fondling fern, gullible goat!"

And with that, the speaker for Woodsedge fell over.

"Okay, she may be better than the fairy on the register," Kail admitted. "Where is she, anyway?"

As the calls rose from the room for Merigan to take his chance against the ogres, Loch pointed at the rafters.

There, unnoticed by most, a shining white dove perched and looked out over the crowd.

Bathed in sunbeams that crept through the twisting branches to find her, Ululenia fluttered into the camp of the *Besnisti*. The great creatures were arguing as she came, and she wore the form of the snowy white dove, so none took notice of her.

"The small ones have defiled our sacred place!" one of the elders growled, baring her tusks at the threat to the clan. "They have stolen the snowmelt-bear we offered to the forest spirits! They will offer it to their own spirits now and make war upon us!"

Another elder stood and extended a massive hand. After a moment, the one who had spoken passed over the Staff of Words, and the new speaker said, "We are newly wakened from the winter-sleep, and our people are hungry. If we bathe our clubs in anger-blood, we will not have time to hunt."

The *Besnisti* watching the discussion nodded, and Ululenia watched them from a low branch at the edge of the clearing. They were a simple people, violent but careful to follow the tenets of the land.

The first speaker angrily took back the Staff of Words. "Does the deer who sees the wolf drawing near keep gnawing at leaves? *The small ones hunt us!*" She looked to her people. "They do not follow the ways of the forest! They have brought fire! They have broken the great trees to make room for their huts! I am eldest among us, and I have seen the *Besnisti* driven away before. If we do not defend ourselves, they will kill us all!"

Ululenia looked at the mind of the elder and knew sorrow, for she was not wrong in her fears. The ogres had lost much of their woodlands to the humans in Ululenia's lifetime. When the ogres ignored the humans, the humans attacked and slaughtered the ogres. When the ogres attacked first, the humans died but returned later with warriors in great numbers.

And then, as Ululenia felt the elder's despair, one of the *Besnisti* in the crowd spoke.

"Why?"

It was one of the young adults, newly grown during his winter-long sleep. The others shuffled and coughed uncomfortably, since he was not an elder, and did not hold the Staff of Words.

But Ululenia saw hope.

"Why did they take the snowmelt-bear?" the young male asked. "They live in huts instead of under the trees and stars. What if they don't know why we leave the bear for the forest spirits? What if they only see a broken bear and thought we wanted to break them, too?"

The elder with the Staff of Words growled. "You are young, and know not your words," she said. "While you ask questions, the small ones sharpen their spears to—"

She broke off as the Staff of Words quivered in her hands.

A moment later, she stumbled back with a cry as it jerked itself from her grasp. It landed in the soft earth, and as the *Besnisti* gasped, roots shot from the base of the staff and dug into the ground. The stone spikes on the staff's striking head sprang off with little popping sounds as branches stretched out, already dotted with new green leaves.

Ululenia landed in the clearing and took her true form. Her horn blazed in every color of nature's glory as she stood in front of the new sapling and looked out upon the *Besnisti*.

As one, they dropped to their knees before her.

Whickering softly, Ululenia pawed the soft earth, and into their minds said, *I ask that you heed the wisdom that comes from youth.* Then she turned to the young male who had asked the right question. *This is what you must do....*

"A unicorn."

"That's the common word for her, yes."

Loch and Kail stood with the villagers at the perimeter of Woodsedge, watching the forest.

"She was a bird."

"Shapeshifter."

Merigan, the young man who had asked for a chance to deal with the ogres himself, stood at the front of the group. He had told everyone that morning that he'd had a dream, and the ogres would come today. Loch saw that the young man was unarmored—a village woodcutter would never have been able to afford any protection worth wearing—but carried an old infantry blade that must have belonged to his father.

"And, what, she usually just wants to look like a horse with a big point on its head?"

"Evidently, Kail."

"I'm not sure I'd want a team member who thought that walking around as a horse was the best plan."

"She's a magical creature. That might be her natural..." Loch started, then paused at cries from the crowd. She followed the pointing fingers and saw the ogres at the edge of the forest, a hundred yards distant. "Here we go."

Kail cracked his knuckles. "Sure about this, Captain? You know they're scared of fire. We could—"

"She's got this."

"*She* being the magical creature that wants to look like a pointy-headed horse."

"The same, yes." Loch pointed at Merigan with her chin. "He had a dream last night. This is going to be okay."

She ignored Kail's muttered response as one of the ogres stepped out from the trees and came toward the village. He was nine feet tall, garbed in heavy furs, and he held a great staff set with bone teeth at either end. His skin was dark and leathery, and a pair of horns curled out from his head.

"Only one set of horns, and they don't even form a complete circle." Kail cocked his head. "He's practically a *kid*."

Loch nodded. "Just like Merigan." The young man was walking forward as well, his sword held before him.

The ogre gestured at Merigan with his great staff and roared a challenge in his own tongue.

Merigan raised his sword. "For Woodsedge, I challenge you!"

The two figures met midway between the trees and the village. The ogre lifted its great war staff with a roar, and Merigan lunged in and swung his sword. The blow struck the ogre on the chest, glancing off his thick furs.

And with a barely perceptible pause, the ogre fell down, dropped his staff, and raised his hands in surrender.

"You are *kidding* me," Kail said under the villagers' cheers. "There wasn't even any *blood*."

"Spirit of the thing, Kail." Loch smiled as Merigan raised his sword, then looked sharply off into the forest.

"I'm just saying, as someone who occasionally rigs fights, I'm offended by the lack of professionalism."

Instead of bringing his blade down for the killing blow, Merigan stepped back, still looking into the forest. Then he turned to the villagers and called out, "They have been defeated! And now that they know our strength, they will never threaten us again. Instead..." Merigan held out a hand. After a moment's pause, the ogre took it, and pulled himself back to his feet. "...we will have peace."

Loch and Kail were guests for the somewhat confused but still celebratory feast held in the village square. When it ended later that afternoon, they headed into the woods.

"Okay, so I think I get it," Kail said as they found an animal trail and lost sight of Woodsedge. "The villagers aren't afraid anymore, because they think the ogres have been beaten."

Loch noted several broken branches and followed the trail. "They'll probably get a fair amount of trade from the ogres as a result. Furs, rare herbs..."

"Right. Meanwhile, the ogres all know that the fight was rigged—poorly."

"Get over it, Kail."

"So they're just happy the humans aren't going to burn down the whole forest."

Loch paused, sniffed the air, and then pushed through the thick bushes ahead. "They also get access to fine metals through trade, along with a much better chance to hold onto their land, since the humans see them as trading partners and not savages."

"Granted. So what does your magical friend get out of this?" Kail asked.

"Two things." Loch spotted a clearing up ahead and pushed forward with a grin. "First, the woods she lives in and nurtures are free from conflict, and second... Did you notice that Merigan ducked out of the celebratory feast?"

"Yeah, I figured that—*whoah*, hey, afternoon, there!"

Merigan of Woodsedge lay on a bed of soft grass near a sparkling pond in the middle of a clearing. He was flushed, drowsy eyed, and about half dressed. "I'm sorry!" he said, pulling his pants up. "I was..."

Loch smiled at Merigan. "I'm sorry to disturb you, Mayor Merigan. The lady who was with you..."

"I, um, er..." said the young mayor of Woodsedge.

"Virgins, huh?" Kail asked. "So that's not just a myth?"

"Be at peace," Loch said as Merigan finished dressing. "We're friends. I know that she spoke in your mind, and in your dreams."

Merigan coughed. "She said that she had to leave, that our time together was precious, but she was as the last melting snow of winter, flowing away in the river of —"

"Did she head off in any particular direction?" Kail asked. Merigan pointed.

"Damn it, she should still be back there with him," Loch muttered as they hiked deeper into the woods. "She *never* leaves that quickly."

"Well," Kail said behind her, "if it was Merigan's first time, it might not have taken that long."

"Thank you, Kail."

"That's the thing about guys that age. They can pretty much—"

"*Thank you*, Kail." Loch found another small animal trail. "She couldn't have gotten far."

"Broken branches over there," Kail added. "Big ones. Must be getting close to ogre territory. I hope they're still feeling peaceful."

Then they came into a clearing, and both Loch and Kail were silent.

Our time together was precious, said the pale ogre female with the glowing horn to the young ogre male who'd thrown the fight, *but I am as the last melting snow of winter, flowing away in the river of spring.* Loch heard the words clearly in her head, which was disconcerting.

She'd take any distraction she could get at the moment, though, given that neither of the ogres was wearing a stitch of clothing.

The young male ogre grunted something in response. Loch and Kail backed away.

"So... also a virgin," Kail said after a moment, leaning against a tree.

"I'm trying really hard not to think about it."

"Weird how her voice just pops right into your head, though."

"Definitely." Loch found a good place to sit. "From what I've read, the horn isn't really a solid bit of bone. It's magical energy. Did you see how it shimmered?"

"Sorry, Captain, I couldn't see anything but naked ogre."

Loch sighed and went back to trying to get the image out of her head.

A few minutes later, the unicorn trotted into the small clearing where they waited. The air shimmered around it, and a moment later, it was a small, slender woman with ash-blond hair and the same rainbow-shimmering horn set in her pale forehead.

She saw Loch and gasped. "Little One!" Her horn shone in delight, and she pulled Loch into a warm hug.

"It's Loch, for the moment," Loch muttered, hugging Ululenia back.

"Little One?" Kail asked.

"She did some work for my father," Loch said. "Helped make the river flow cleanly again."

"*Little One?*"

"We've got a job, Ululenia," Loch cut in. "We could use a shapeshifter, and I thought of you."

"Whatever you did to Jerl's mind could be helpful, too," Kail added.

"Does this job benefit the untamed realms of nature?" Ululenia asked.

"It's going to pay *really* well," Kail said after a moment. "Well enough to buy a lot of nature for yourself."

Ululenia frowned. "Is there any chance that young muscular virgins will be involved?"

Loch's lips quirked into a grin. "I can probably arrange that."

"Wonderful," Ululenia said with a warm smile, her rainbow horn flaring in the middle of her pale brow. "When do we start?"

In the town of Ros-Aelafuir, a pair of scruffy men in nondescript clothing looked at the town jail, which had a large hole in one wall. The town's former sheriff was being held in the basement until the jail was repaired.

"And nobody cleared it with the local contacts?"

"Nope."

Riffe exhaled slowly. He hated small towns. "Did you get a description?"

"Yep." After a short silence, Ketch, the local contact, coughed and said, "Mousy girl and an Imperial fellow. They didn't register."

A mousy girl and an Imperial. While that might be traceable, it didn't put Riffe in a good mood. "Can you give me anything else to take back to the boss?"

There was a thoughtful pause. Or, Riffe suspected, simply a pause.

"Mousy girl and the Imperial met up with a pair of Urujar outside town," Ketch finally added. "And the Urujar *did* register."

"Perhaps," Riffe suggested slowly, "you could get me their names."

"I could look," Ketch said grudgingly.

"I'd really appreciate it," Riffe said with infinite patience. Ketch stalked off, leaving Riffe to look at the hole in the wall.

Jyelle had passed the word for regional directors to watch for a pair of Urujar right after the news of the Cleaners breakout had come around. She'd been furious. Evidently they'd crossed Jyelle a few years ago. Riffe tried not to think about such things. He prided himself on fast hands, keen eyes, and a complete disregard for matters worth killing people over.

Riffe's keen eyes noticed something in the shadows near the wall. Dust from the wall's shattered frame skittered and sprayed whenever the wind blew, but in the dull afternoon light, it looked like the dust was billowing *around* something. Something that wasn't really there. Maybe magic.

Jyelle didn't pay him enough for this. Riffe stepped back, but the wind gusted again, and this time the dust billowed around something closer, a shape moving *toward* him.

He turned to run.

The blade went cleanly across his throat.

Four

FATHER BERTRUS WAS SURPRISED WHEN THE CLERGYMAN'S WEEKLY game of *suf-gesuf* picked up a new addition, but not disappointed. Sister Desidora was a pretty woman whose short-cropped auburn hair framed a cheerful face tanned from travel. Her olive-green robes were unadorned, but that was only prudent in these troubled times.

Of greater note was the warhammer that rode on her hip, catching the light with a glittering sparkle. Where an ordinary warhammer looked much like a long-handled carpenter's hammer, this great weapon had a thick silver hilt inlaid with rivulets of tiny rubies, and a massive double-hammer head of solid platinum, banded with strips of rune-carved gold just behind the head. Desidora claimed it as a religious artifact of her order, a weapon of the ancients that she was carrying to a border shrine.

So taken was Father Bertrus by the pretty woman that he neglected to ask which deity she worshipped, and by the time he realized it, he was too embarrassed to ask. The other priests had already shown up by then: big bluff Cordagar who headed the sparring shrine of Io-fergajar, stout old Hesna who over-saw the birth-houses of Jairyur, and even rangy old Sholrin who tended the local forge of Pesyr. They accepted the new addition with courtesy (and gentle flirting on Sholrin's part) and asked for news.

"I'll prop Ghylspwr up here, if no one minds," Desidora said as the others drifted toward the *suf-gesuf* table. Then, with a smile, she added, "I assume that a temple of Ael-meseth is safe enough that I need not request a storeroom?"

Bertrus chuckled. "We do imbibe a bit, Sister, but rarely are we rendered insensate. And should anyone trouble us here, I should note that these humble chambers lie directly over the temple vault. A number of strapping acolytes will ensure our protection."

The chambers were, in fact, opulently decorated, as the Republic had been kind to Ael-meseth in general and Father Bertrus in particular. The table was inlaid with elaborate copper swirls that formed fanciful patterns of dragons and griffons cavorting, and every cup in the room was made of gold.

Desidora laughed, and Bertrus dealt the first hand. Cordagar raised without even looking at his hidden cards, as was his tra-dition, while Hesna traded in one hidden card and two of her showing cards. Sholrin examined his hidden cards carefully and eventually kept what he had. It was the new priestess's turn, and she frowned at her cards for a long moment.

"I'm so sorry," she said, embarrassed. "I haven't played in... Perhaps I should fold and observe the first hand—"

"Kutesosh gajair'is!" shouted the warhammer.

"Oh, hush!" she called back. "I'm trying to relax!"

"The artifact speaks?" Sholrin looked at the silver warhammer with newfound respect.

"That's up for some debate," Desidora said wryly. "It may have held the mind of an ancient sage in centuries past, but now it merely spouts gibberish." She shook her head.

The others agreed that the gifts of the ancients and the gods were sometimes confusing, and Desidora did eventually decide to stay in. It turned out to be lucky that she did, as she neatly swept the hand.

Bertrus was quietly troubled. Sentient magic was rare and often dangerous. When the ancient lands had been tamed by the Old Kingdom colonies that would later form the Republic, many artifacts had been destroyed; it was said that the founders had nearly destroyed Heaven's Spire itself rather than take it as the home of the Voyancy.

They played several hands without incident. Desidora was better at *suf-gesuf* than she had implied, and Bertrus wondered if perhaps she was a wandering priestess of Gedesar. They'd been visited by one of the thief-priests once. Cordagar had nearly killed the little swindler.

"What news have I missed in my travels?" Desidora asked. "I heard there was some trouble on the Spire—something to do with escaped prisoners?"

"That was last week," Sholrin muttered while flipping the cards out to each of them. They all paused to check their hidden cards. "The news up there these days is about the Glimmering Folk."

"Really? How exciting! I'll raise twenty, I think," she said dismissively, then smiled in interest. "Have the Glimmering Folk returned, then?"

"Kun-kabynalti osu fuir'is!" shouted Ghylspwr from his corner of Bertrus's opulent chamber.

"Quiet, you!" Desidora shook her head. "Oh, is the three of swords a shared card or one of Sholrin's open cards? I thought it was shared. In that case, I shall fold this hand."

"They have not returned in great numbers," Hesna said, while Sholrin caught Bertrus's eye with a knowing smirk. "One of their lords, Bi'ul, has come from the shining realms to meet with the Voyancy, though."

They finished the hand, and Cordagar took it neatly. They played another round in silence, with Sholrin and Bertrus watching and Hesna slowly catching on. "It seems that I have been out of touch with the reports," Desidora admitted. "My order has little dealing with the Voyancy, while it seems that you four are *quite* in the Voyancy's favor."

"Men who serve the spirits must also serve the material world." Bertrus smiled. "And the Republic is a great nation, Sister. In the Empire to the east, only those of the proper caste may rule, while here, any man—or woman," he added with a tolerant smile, "may rise as far as his ability takes him, regardless of his birth."

"How surprising, then, that all twelve of the Voyants come from noble houses," Desidora murmured, looking at her cards. "I will stand."

"Kutesosh gajair'is!"

"Actually, this should be my last hand," Desidora said quickly. "I might as well make it memorable. I will raise forty."

Sholrin grinned widely. "It is not the fault of the Voyants that they are best suited to lead. Indeed, their training in the noble houses likely gave them excellent preparation for politics. Or would you have unlettered laborers deciding the course of the Republic?"

"I simply do not see how the Eastern Empire's caste system is so different," said Desidora, "if both result in rich men ruling poor men. This Lord Bi'ul of the Glimmering Folk—is he meeting the people on the ground, or is he up on the Spire, with the wealthy heirs of the old kingdom?"

Hesna's face was stern. "He meets Archvoyant Silestin on the Spire, as is only proper. It would not do for such a great creature to walk the world of men, where he could meet laborers... or thieves."

"Tell me, *Sister*," Sholrin added, "in all our talk, I have forgotten... which god has favored you with his divine presence?"

"You have not forgotten," Desidora said primly. "I have not said."

"I would think such an *impassioned* young woman, with such a powerful artifact as that ancient hammer, would be proud to name the god she serves," Bertrus said, gathering the divine energies of Ael-meseth about him. "Unless of course, she serves no god, and came upon the hammer by accident or evil... and is now using it to steal."

"If it *is* an artifact of true power," Sholrin said with a dismissive sniff. "Likely brass and tin, painted over, with a wizard's spell that lasts but a few hours." Bertrus could not sense the magic Sholrin wielded, as the rangy man served Pesyr, but he had no doubt from the dark heat of the man's stare that his power had been brought into play.

"Did you really think your parlor tricks could fool us, girl?" Hesna asked acidly. "A magic hammer that conveniently speaks when it is your turn to bet on the hand? You might have taken a few coins in a tavern, but here you deal with the chosen of the gods. Now declare your god, or fight if you are foolish."

"Try me," Desidora said, her heart-shaped face unchanged. "A single woman should pose no threat... unless your own corruption has offended the gods."

Bertrus lunged to strike, and the power of his god would have obliterated her the moment his hand struck her cheek had his blow landed. In fact, however, he was locked in place, the very air turned to stone around him. Across the table, Sholrin grunted and then began to pant, his eyes wide as he struggled. Hesna's small squeaks bespoke a similar struggle.

"Which god has favored me?" Desidora asked the now-silent assembly as she rose to her feet. "Which god could lock you in place with the very magic you sought to wield against me?" And before Bertrus's terrified eyes, her hair shimmered and turned black, and her tan skin faded to alabaster. Her dress, in an instant, was a glistening black, and the golden cup in her grasp, decorated with nymphs and satyrs, crackled and twisted into tarnished silver, into which ivory skulls were set. "Which god could snare four priests of such power, do you think?" she asked, and laughed.

"Three," growled Cordagar as he rose to his feet. "Not four priests, three. Your dark magic twisted their own spells against them, but those who serve Io-fergajar wield no magic save the gifts of forge and sweat, of bone and blood. Your tricks give you away, even if your foul visage did not. You have fallen to the dark temptations of Byn-kodar the Life-Stealer, but you do not hold me in your sway." His broadsword slid from its sheath. "Now die, death-witch!"

He kicked the table aside and lunged at the pale death priestess, his blade cleaving down like an unstoppable avalanche of steel.

There was a sound like the striking of a bell, and Cordagar stumbled back, his great sword shaking in his hand.

Ghylspwr the warhammer had appeared in Desidora's hands and, held aloft by the pale, slender woman with the dark hair and the midnight eyes, had driven back Cordagar's great blow. Bertrus had seen oxen felled by Cordagar's empty fist.

Cordagar roared and spun into a mighty backhand blow that could have cloven a stone column in twain. Desidora lifted the warhammer, and the mighty broadsword rang again and then clattered to the floor. *"Kutesosh gajair'is!"* cried the warhammer in a warrior's voice as Cordagar gripped his own wrist in pain and rage.

Bertrus was looking at the death-witch, and so he could see clearly when it happened. She stood over Cordagar, the warhammer raised, and she was cold as ice, but then the color crept back into her skin and hair, slowly, grudgingly. Discarded on the floor, the ivory skulls on her golden goblet slowly twisted back into golden nymphs.

"Alive, please," the auburn-haired woman murmured.

"Kun-kabynalti osu fuir'is," the warhammer said grudgingly, and swung down and then up in a massive arc that actually pulled the slight woman off the ground. The head of the hammer caught the light in a silvery glow as it crashed down upon Cordagar's head.

Bertrus had seen men die in battle, and he knew how it looked. He averted his eyes to avoid the sight. When he finally looked, however, Cordagar was unconscious but alive. This was odd, considering that he had been driven waist-deep through the floorboards.

"Nicely done," Desidora said, returning the warhammer to her belt.

"Besyn larveth'is," it said in evident satisfaction, and then jerked in Bertrus's direction and added, *"Kutesosh gajair'is?"*

"I'm not sure," she said thoughtfully. "Father Bertrus, do *you* think I should kill you?" For a moment, the color bled from her skin, but she shook her head briskly, and the color slowly returned.

"You'll never survive," he vowed, forcing the words through frozen lips. "I triggered the wards. My acolytes will be here in minutes."

"I'm pleased to hear that." Desidora turned to the doorway. "I see you've also activated a long-standing ward to prevent me from fleeing. How brave of you. If only I could somehow manipulate the very magic of that ward, just as I manipulated all your magical auras?" She pursed her lips, head tilted, and stared at the door for a long moment. Bertrus watched the color bleed from her face again, and she tossed her black hair back with a cold laugh. "Oh. I can. How fortunate for me. With just a few alterations to the aura, your burly acolytes are locked *out.*"

She turned to the unconscious form of Cordagar. "I do apologize," she said, "but you've made me two-thirds of a very nice doorway." She turned to Bertrus and smiled again, her pale lips curved like a sickle moon. "You *did* say that these opulent chambers lay directly over the temple vault? I *suppose* that means that I'll be able to pilfer everything in there and then take my leave while all the acolytes batter the now-locked door."

Then, ignoring Bertrus's inarticulate ranting, she raised a dainty foot, shoved Cordagar down through the hole, and climbed down after him.

"I heard there was a woman named Desidora hitting the temples," said the Urujar warrior-woman as she stepped out into the street. There was a man with her, and judging by his aura, he was very loyal to his friend and very interested in having sex with Desidora. Behind them, alarm bells rang and warriors shouted.

"How'd you find me?" Desidora asked. Her aura was almost normal. Her hair and skin were their usual tone, and her dress was just a bit dark.

"*Kutesosh gajair'is?*" Ghylspwr asked.

"A friend told us you were hitting temples that had gotten money from the Voyancy," the man noted. "Father Bertrus had a reputation. We've been waiting."

"Not just yet," Desidora told the warhammer, smiling wryly.

"We've got a job," the Urujar woman said. "Likely involving magic. If you can break through the temple wards, you could be just what I need."

Desidora let the aura slide back in, felt her skin cool and her hair tighten into glossy black, the ice creep into her voice. "I could break through the temple's wards because I'm a death priestess."

"*Besyn larveth'is!*"

She glanced down at Ghylspwr in irritation. "There is little point hiding it."

"You're a death priestess?" the man asked. His urge to have sex with her had diminished greatly, though not entirely. "Like, sacrificing babies and devouring souls to gain the power of daemons and all that?"

Desidora thought for a moment. There were ideas, suggestions, not hers. She forced them away, forced the colors of life back into her skin and hair. "I don't really know. I hope not."

"Loch, we don't need this," said the man. "My wizard can get us through any safe."

"Then we'll be twice as lucky to have him as well."

"Are you the two Jyelle is up in arms about?" Desidora asked.

"Jyelle?" the woman asked quickly.

"Master of the thieves' guild for most of the province," Desidora said.

"Dammit!" The man turned to the woman. "And here we've been playing nice, registering in every damn town we pass through!"

"Maybe she'll let it lie," the woman suggested.

"Based on what I've heard," Desidora said, "probably not."

"She ratted us out before, Loch," the man said. "If she's guildmaster, that's a complication."

"It'll be dealt with," Loch said. "Like I said, I'm looking for someone who can break wards. You interested?"

"I'm not for hire," said Desidora, but then checked herself and asked, "Where is the job?"

The woman jerked her head up to the night sky. "Heaven's Spire."

Desidora nodded. The gods provided. "I'm in."

It was nearly midnight when Akus emerged, drunk and reeling and squinting in the torchlight, from the tavern Pyvic had tracked him to.

"Prisoner Akus," Pyvic said calmly, "you're surrounded."

"Thought you could escape, now, didja?" Orris cut in. "Well, you thought wrong, Akus!"

Akus looked from Orris to Pyvic in confusion, then grinned at Orris. "Hey, Orris. Sorry I left. Just had to give it a try, you know?"

"Had to give—*had to give it a try?*" Orris stomped forward, and Pyvic followed, sword ready in case Orris's antics turned him into a hostage. "You make a fool of me, and that's all you can say? You're gonna be dangling every night for the next month, Akus! You and—"

"Enough." Pyvic silenced Orris with a glare, then turned to the town guards he'd pulled in to help. "You four, put Akus in chains. We'll want him for questioning. You three." He pointed. "You're with me."

"As you say, Justicar." They were good men, a luxury in small towns like this.

Inside, the tavern was loud and filthy. Loch and Kail had been in the Cleaners for unlawful entry into Heaven's Spire—which usually meant smuggling yourself in a crate. They'd been caught when an informant, Jyelle, had tipped off Customs agents. Loch and Kail could be two-bit thieves hoping to get lucky in the magical capitol city of the Republic, or they could have had a bigger plan. If it were the former, then this was their kind of tavern, too.

It wasn't, from what Pyvic could see. He made the rounds, staring down a few drunks who got angry when they saw uniforms and asking the bartender a few polite questions. He even let the bartender get his digs in, so that he could hold his head up after Pyvic left. A good justicar knew when to take a little lip. The bartender would remember that Pyvic hadn't made it hard for him if Pyvic ever came back.

After poking through the back rooms, Pyvic thanked the occupants of the tavern for their time and stepped outside into the cool darkness.

Warden Orris had a big sweaty smile. "Well, Justicar, it doesn't look like you found anything, but I found us a lead!"

"What's that, Warden?"

"Akus split from Loch and Kail as soon as they landed, but *before* they broke out, he heard them talking about their plan!" Orris wiped his palms. "They're putting a team together for something."

"How does that help us find them?" Pyvic asked, and then, to be civil, added, "Not that I'm complaining. Anything we learn can help us. If Akus can give us the names of contacts, we might be able to put a little pressure on them."

Orris made a dismissive gesture. "We don't need to do that. Akus told me everything. They're putting a team together, and they're not leaving the province. That should do us just fine."

Pyvic nodded again to be civil. "I'll question Akus as well; he might be more forthcoming with the threat of an unfamiliar face…"

Orris coughed. "Well, the fact is, Akus didn't want to tell me anything. I had to let him go in exchange for telling me that."

Pyvic stopped nodding. "Where is the prisoner now?"

"Well, I *promised*," Orris said with a helpless shrug. "And he did help us out. Loch and Kail, *they're* the ones we want!"

Pyvic tried to control his temper. "You *let* our prisoner *go?*"

Orris laughed. "Don't worry so much, Pyvic. I put two of the men on him. If he tries to warn them, he'll lead us right to 'em instead."

Pyvic felt a slow heat building in his gut, spreading across his chest, building in his throat until it finally came out with a hiss. "Idiot! You don't let a prisoner go when he tells you something you can't verify! You don't put two men on someone who's already escaped once!" Pyvic leaned in until he was inches from Orris's sweaty face. "I don't know whose ass you kissed to get this job, Warden, but this is *my* command. If you even *think* of questioning a prisoner without me present, much *less* offering him anything, I will have you charged with conspiracy to abet the escape of a prisoner, and you'll spend the rest of your days in the Cleaners scrubbing stones instead of pushing papers. *Am I clear?*"

The warden sputtered, stumbling back. "You can't talk to me like that!"

"I'm guessing you've never served in the Republic's army, Warden." Pyvic had Orris backed up to the wall. "You disobeyed orders, you compromised my command, and you just let one of the mission objectives walk away. As the one who has to deal with that mess, I *can* talk to you that way. Now haul your sorry carcass after Akus with half the men."

Pyvic turned his back on Orris and walked away, the rage within him vented but still there, smoldering. He could feel the warden's anger, could tell that Orris wanted nothing more than to lay into Pyvic.

"You don't understand, Captain," Orris said through gritted teeth. "It's not about Akus. It's about Loch. *Nothing matters except getting her back.*"

"Get moving, Warden. That's an order." Pyvic turned and smiled. "And it's the last one I'm going to give you."

Orris swallowed, then turned and yelled at the guards to get after Akus.

"The rest of you, with me. Double-time to the town gates."

Without turning to see if they'd follow, Pyvic ran into the night to see what he could salvage.

Five

HESSLER DIDN'T KNOW WHETHER YOU HAD TO BE ACTUALLY *thrown* in order for it to be considered "being thrown out." He wasn't, in fact, but the security attendants did hustle him down the front steps.

"—conduct unbecoming a University Arcanologist, above and beyond the monetary cost of the infraction," the Chair of Illusion was blustering, "makes it clear that this is no isolated matter that—"

"As if you even care, Porisporant," Hessler cut in, adjusting his robes. "If you were smart enough to get away with it, you'd have done so in a moment, and then you'd be a wealthy man instead of a second-rate shadow-weaver chasing University tenure!"

Hessler was a tall, squint-eyed man permanently in need of a shave. He tended to hunch inside his robes, and he gestured a lot with his hands in ways that made others irritated. His most memorable feature was his mouth, mainly for what came out of it.

"Your disrespectful attitude and pilfering could have been tolerated," Porisporant went on, red-faced and pointing now, "had your remarks been restricted to matters of the arcane. But by your public attitude, you have misrepresented the University's regard for the Voyancy and the Republic!"

Hessler manipulated the air with twitching fingers. "But, but, but the entire premise of the Republic involves free speech, which should imply that—"

"The Republic *must* be clear on the University's respect and admiration for the policies of the Voyancy," Porisporant said, "especially in these trying times."

"Am I being suspended for pilfering," Hessler asked, "or for what I said?"

"For your crimes against the University—" Porisporant intoned as though someone important were listening.

"I only did that to pay for my moth—"

"—taken in light of your pernicious and unpatriotic attitude—" Porisporant went on.

Hessler shook his head with a sneer. "So I'd get different treatment if I—"

"—you are hereby *expelled*," Porisporant finished with a malicious leer. "Guards, this man is not to re-enter campus, and his goods are hereby claimed to help pay off the debt he incurred through his thievery."

"Oh, you can't be..." Hessler began, and when Porisporant turned away, raised his voice. "You can't be serious! You can't expel me! The *founders of this university* were warlocks who trafficked with daemons! A few magic trinkets can't be cause for—I'll go to Professor Cestran! He'll overturn this, you frog-eyed Republic lickspittle! You'll see! I'll be back in two weeks!"

Porisporant closed the door behind him. The guards stayed outside, watching.

When it became clear that the conversation was over, Hessler stalked off. Cestran was on vacation, as Hessler had last heard, in the port city of Ros-Sesuf, where the elderly wizard made his home. It was several days away on horseback. Hessler hadn't had much on him when Porisporant had arrived with the guards, and he had nothing stashed away.

But Hessler was, as even Porisporant had to admit after discovering the black-market trinkets, a creative individual.

"The sign says you're looking for guards," he said to a fat, bearded caravan master a few hours later. "You're headed to Ros-Sesuf."

"How d'you know that?" The caravan master glared suspiciously at the gangly man in the shimmering purple robes. "You some kind of wizard?"

"As a matter of fact, I am," Hessler said in irritation, "but it's obvious you're going to Ros-Sesuf without any magic at all." He pointed at the wagon. "The smell from your wagons clearly shows that you were carrying greenroot, which you'd have gotten from inland and sold here. But you're now carrying dye and silks, judging by the guild stamps on the crates. You couldn't sell those inland, and that means you must be heading to Ros-Sesuf, to sell the expensive items in a port city." He snorted. "Why, you'd be a fool *not* to notice."

The caravan master grimaced. "But you're a wizard."

"Of course I am!" Hessler declared, waving his arms. "Look at the robe!"

"Official and licensed and all?" the caravan master asked with a squint. "Went to the university in town here, did you?"

"I did indeed go to that university," Hessler proclaimed, "and may Jairytnef, mistress of magic, strike me dead if I lie." This was not a technical falsehood, which was good, as Hessler preferred to remain truthful when daring the gods to slay him if he were lying.

"Fine," the caravan master grunted. "Pays food and five per day, ten if we see trouble. You ride with the new boy."

The new boy turned out to be a fresh-faced young lad named Rybindaris, who tried not to gawk as they rode out of town. He had seen sixteen summers, if that, and he was running away from something.

"Have you been a guard for long, Magister Hessler?"

"Don't call me that, lad. And no. No, I'm new. Just like you."

"What should I call you then?" The kid had sandy blond hair and sky-blue eyes. Given the dusky, dark-eyed stock of the average peasants around here, Hessler guessed the kid to be some noble's son from the wrong side of the sheets.

"Just Hessler. That's fine."

"Okay, Mister Hessler."

"Or that."

"Mister Hessler?"

"Yes, Ryban... what do people call you when they don't want to toss out the full four syllables?"

"What, Mister Hessler?"

"For short, lad. What do they call you for short?"

"They, er... they call me Dairy, Mister Hessler. Since I was found as a baby in the barn where the cows sleep."

"That's adorable, lad."

"Mister Hessler?"

"Yes, Dairy?"

"Are you a good wizard?"

Hessler was not given to long conversations unless he had someone interesting to argue with. "Do you mean good as in ethical or good as in capable, Dairy?"

"Er... is there a difference, Mister Hessler?" As Hessler turned, mouth open to deliver a truly blistering retort, he looked directly into Dairy's sky-blue eyes. "I mean, wouldn't a wizard who wanted to do good be better at using magic than a wizard who wanted to do evil?"

Hessler couldn't quite bring himself to say it. "Sure, lad," he said quietly, shifting in the saddle to stretch his already-sore legs. "Yes, I'm a good wizard."

The kid was looking forward again, and being as casual as a sixteen-year-old can. "Do you know a spell to drive away blood-gargoyles?"

"Bloo... is that what you farmers call the *pyrkafir?*" At Dairy's blank look, Hessler waved in annoyance. "Scales, wings, man-sized with little flames coming out of their mouths?" Dairy nodded mutely. "Why in Jairytnef's name would a lad like you be worried about *pyrkafir?*"

"Er... no reason, Mister Hessler," Dairy said quickly, flushing pink and gripping his horse's reins nervously. "It's just something I heard once."

Hessler sighed. The *pyrkafir* were damnably tough to conjure and command, but they were wonderful assassins. Seeing something like that stalking through the darkness could easily send a kid running from the farm where he'd grown up. Hessler wondered who on the kid's farm had been worth killing.

"I doubt we'll run into any blood-gargoyles on this trip, lad," he finally said. "And if we do, you just stay near me. I'm sure I can deal with them."

Not entirely true. Not even remotely true, in fact. But unlikely to come up, Hessler figured.

They didn't encounter any blood-gargoyles on the trip. They didn't encounter *anything* on the trip. The only threats came from the other guards, after Hessler won at the nightly gambling a bit too often and wasn't properly contrite. He'd been accused of cheating with his magic. (He had, in fact, been doing so, but he was pretty sure that the others were cheating with their own natural skill.) By the end of the trip, the only one still speaking to him was Dairy, who wouldn't leave him alone. It was a joy when they finally reached the port city of Ros-Sesuf.

Until it came time to claim his pay.

"There's only five in here," he said indignantly to the caravan master, holding the far-too-light pouch. He wondered if the man had made a mistake. He didn't seem terribly educated.

"I docked you fifteen for causing trouble with the others," the caravan master said, spitting to the side. "Damned wizards are bad enough luck as it is, without you cheating the men with your magic."

"Cheat the—did you dock *them* for cheating? And who has proof that I cheated?" Hessler pointed an accusing finger. "And how am I bad luck? You seemed eager for my help when you feared danger on the road!"

"And we didn't run into any danger," the caravan master replied, "so I didn't get to *see* any of that skill. All I saw was you angering the men. So get out of here and be grateful I'm paying you anything!"

"I hope your damn dye spoils in the salt air!" Hessler snapped. "I hope moths get into your silks and ruin the whole damn shipment!" He stalked away, clenching the too-small coin pouch in his knotted fingers. It didn't matter. He'd gotten to Ros-Sesuf, and Professor Cestran would take care of everything. He'd be back at the university in no time.

"When, exactly, did he die?" Hessler asked approximately two hours later.

"More than a week, young wizard," the steward said with sad weariness. "He wished to retire here to Ros-Sesuf to spend his last days. He went peacefully, though, in his sleep. A great man. He shall be missed."

"But... he didn't *look* sick!" Hessler said insistently. "He looked fine! He told us that he was just leaving to see his home once more. He didn't say—"

"I doubt," the steward said firmly, "that he wished to alarm his students. And as for his appearance, the master always looked as he wished." With a faint smile, he added, "I am certain you understand."

"Yes, of course," Hessler said irritably, "but you have to understand, I needed him to... I... he was supposed to...." He trailed off.

"Good day, young wizard," the steward said with faint asperity. "I shall let the mistress know that you offered your condolences." He shut the door.

"Yes. Thank you," Hessler said to the door. "I'll just... find someone else, then."

Several hours later, having exhausted the five coins on bad drink and bad food, he did indeed find someone else in a darkened street outside a cheap sailor's tavern. Namely, the guards from the caravan.

"There he is!" one of them shouted. "There's the bastard now! Get him!"

Hessler could have conjured figments to terrify them into fleeing or summoned an illusion to cover his retreat, but he was drunk enough to have trouble concentrating, and he only got as far as raising his hands and declaring, "You have no id—" before a small pouch filled with pebbles crunched down on his arm, and then his back, and then his head.

He awoke in the dockside jail with shackles at his wrists and ankles and a racking collar chained to his throat. The shackles had an *yvkefer* alloy in them to prevent his escape. They had to be expensive. He didn't see how cheating at cards really made it worthwhile.

"I'm sorry, Mister Hessler," came a voice from the cell beside him. Hessler turned.

"Dairy, what are you doing here?"

"The caravan master became very angry after you left," the kid said to the floor. "He was complaining about the cargo."

"What about the cargo?" Hessler looked at the shackles. As far as non-illusion classes, he'd taken a course in wards against daemons and an introductory conjuring seminar, but that was about it. Most of the students didn't fulfill the non-specialist requirements until their fourth or fifth year.

"He said you'd cursed it, and then he went to the city's magical hall and had them cast a spell, and then he said that you'd never graduated from the university."

Hessler winced. He hadn't thought that the verification lists would have been updated so quickly. "What happened to the cargo?"

"The dye went bad and moths got into the silks."

Hessler winced again. Those were both common problems with shipping in these areas. His father had been a merchant, and he'd told Hessler about such things. Dye from arid climates could spoil if not properly sealed against humid salt air, and anyone who didn't pack the silks in wormweed to keep the moths away had nobody but themselves to blame.

Unless, of course, a wizard who didn't actually have a license to practice magic had been heard to utter what could be construed as a curse. Then you *definitely* had somebody else to blame.

Had Hessler actually had the power to do that sort of thing, he would have laughed.

"What are *you* doing in here, Dairy?" he finally asked instead.

"The guards went to find you," the kid said, still talking to the floor. "They said they were going to hurt you. I followed, and they didn't stop hitting you once you were down. So I tried to help. I knocked two of them down, and they say I broke another guard's arm."

"What, with a club?"

"Er... with my fist, Mister Hessler." Dairy sighed. "I'm really sorry I didn't stop them before the town constables arrived."

"Me too, lad." After a moment, Hessler generously added, "Thank you for trying. I didn't curse that cargo, and I appreciate your help."

"They said you cheated at cards, too," Dairy added from his cell.

"Well, people say many things." Hessler's shackles weren't coming off. "Did they say what the punishment for using magic without a license is? If they find me guilty of cursing the cargo?"

"They don't have the magic they need to bind you," Dairy said quietly, his shackles clinking. "They said that without that, there was only one way to keep the town safe from you. They didn't say what it was."

Hessler took a guess. "And you? They can't charge you, can they?"

"They, er, said that I hurt those men more than I could have. Since I joined the guards when you did, they're saying I'm a daemon conjured by you."

"Oh. Crap."

"I'm really sorry, Mister Hessler."

"You and me both, lad."

Time passed. The night got deeper and darker. They'd come for him in the morning. People taking care of wizards liked to do so by daylight, preferably with priests around to bless the event.

This shouldn't have happened. Ros-Sesuf was a *port* city, a *cultured* city! There should have been someone to talk to, someone who could explain this misunderstanding.

Professor Cestran would have been ideal. Failing that, the university would have vouched for him, had that day on the steps gone a bit differently....

Hessler tried to summon his magic. It came, fitfully, but there nonetheless. He was warded against cloaking or altering himself, but the *yvkefer* bonds only blocked magic affecting the self and powerful magic directed outward. Illusion was often said to be the weakest of the magical branches, as it used the least magical energy.

"Dairy," Hessler said quietly, "I want you to do something."

"What's that, Mister Hessler?"

"I'm going to make you invisible. In the morning, when they come for me, I'll say that you were a daemon, and the bonds kept me from binding you any longer. They'll come in and unlock the shackles to check, and then you can escape. Do you understand?"

"Wouldn't that be lying, though, Mister Hessler?"

Hessler lowered his head. "It's not really a lie if it's said to counter a lie that someone else told," he improvised. "Like that caravan master. He lied about you, so I have to lie about you to counter it."

There was a thoughtful silence. "I don't think I understand, Mister Hessler."

"You're a good lad, Dairy."

"But what about you? Maybe... maybe when they unlock my shackles, I can—"

"Just run," Hessler said impatiently. "Run as fast as you can and get out of town. I'll..." He stared into a dark abyss of truth, then deliberately looked away and said in a tone Professor Cestran would have admired, "I'll be fine. I have a trick to escape, but I can't take you with me, so I'm going to let you escape that way. It's only fair."

"Oh. Okay, Mister Hessler."

"Right, then. Here we go." Hessler summoned his energies again, constrained as they were by the shackles, and sent out a small spell to render Dairy invisible.

Nothing happened. Maybe the collar, maybe Hessler being tired and aching from the beating the vengeful guards had given him.

"Damn," Hessler said very quietly.

"Is there a problem, Mister Hessler?"

"I... I think I should wait until morning. I want to preserve my strength. We'll do it later."

"Okay, Mister Hessler," the kid said, smiling. "I'll try to get some sleep, then. So I'm rested when it comes time to escape."

"Good. Good plan."

"Thank you, Mister Hessler," the kid added. "I was really scared, but I'm not scared anymore."

"That's… good, lad. That's good to hear."

The wizard Kail had been touting for the past several days turned out to have died peacefully in his sleep.

"You said he was the *best*," Loch complained as she trudged through the night streets of Ros-Sesuf with Kail beside her. The others—the tinker and her acrobatic Imperial friend, the unicorn, and the death priestess with her enthusiastic warhammer—were set to meet them in Ros-Uitosuf in a few days.

"Being the best doesn't mean you don't die," Kail pointed out. "And we knew he was old."

"If he's that old, why did he still have his name out for jobs?" Loch was not precisely in the mood to be reasonable. They'd ridden hard to get to Ros-Sesuf, and they had nothing to show for it.

"Got me," Kail said. "Nothing to do for it now, though."

"You don't think the death priestess could—"

"No, Loch, I really don't. I really profoundly don't."

"Let's hit the taverns."

In the dockside taverns, drink was cheap, and people didn't watch what they said too closely. Still, nobody talked. In fact, they clammed up as soon as she and Kail came into the room. Loch figured that Jyelle had been passing the word.

"Do we really *need* a wizard?" Kail murmured a few hours later as they left. "We've got the tinker. We've got the death priestess. Hell, I bet the unicorn could do in a pinch."

"You don't take a hill without cavalry," Loch said. "You don't guard a pass without archers. And you sure as *hell* don't take Heaven's Spire without a wizard."

"See, you say that like it's an aphorism, but I've never heard that before."

"There's a lot you've never heard before, Kail."

They kept listening. Around midnight, an angry guard told them his story about a wizard who'd cursed some caravan's cargo. The wizard was slated for a quick death in the morning. He was shackled in the dockside jail.

Loch and Kail wandered over. The jailhouse door had only a single lock, and Kail had them inside in moments. The lone guard was asleep at his desk. Loch thoughtfully woke him up by prodding his throat with her sword, and it was agreed that the guard would spend the night peacefully and quietly bound and gagged in the broom closet.

There were only two occupied cells. A sandy-haired kid was asleep in one of them. A squinting dark-haired guy was crouched in the other, wearing all kinds of shackles. "You the wizard?" Kail asked.

The wizard looked up and glowered. "No, I'm just wearing these robes because they're so comfortable."

"We've got a job," Kail said. "We need a wizard."

"What kind of job?" the wizard asked.

"The kind where we unlock that cell and all those shackles," Loch put in.

"I think I'd be interested in that kind of job," said the wizard.

"Glad to hear it. Kail, help the man." Kail dropped to one knee, leaned in, and got to work on the cell door, humming to himself, and Loch added, "What's your specialty?"

The wizard squinted. "What would you *like* my specialty to be?"

"The truth," Loch said as Kail snickered and twisted open the cell door. "Look, we've got a schedule, and that Cestran guy is dead, so you're our wizard. I just want to know what I'm dealing with."

"Cestran was...." The wizard looked dumbfounded. Kail snapped open the lock to his foot-shackles.

"Oh, he was good," Kail said. "You ever needed a helpful little daemon or a gout of fire, Cestran was your man. There wasn't a safe in the country that man couldn't burn through... well, except for the dwarven-made ones. But that's because of the stuff they put in the sides."

"*Yvkefer*," the wizard said to no one in particular. "He was supposed to get me back into the university. He was a thief? I do illusions."

"Illusions?" Kail got another shackle undone. "But you can still, like, throw gouts of fire when you have to, right?"

"Illusionary ones, yes," said the wizard irritably.

"Oh. Well, we'll figure out something for you to do."

"Listen," said the wizard, "the kid has to come too." He gestured at the boy in the next cell.

Loch looked at the boy, who showed no particular talent save the ability to sleep through a jailbreak. "No."

"That's the deal. He comes, or I... so help me, I'll stay in this cell!"

The noise woke up the kid. "Mister Hessler, are you all right?" he asked, blinking and getting up. "Are these people hurting you?" His arms were bare, and in the flickering candlelight, Loch saw something on his arm.

"Evening, kid." She looked closer. "What is that, a tattoo?"

"It's, er, my birthmark," said the kid, flushing angrily. "And I don't care what you say. You wouldn't be the first to make fun of it!"

"Kid, I'm Urujar. Making fun of your birthmark would be the pot calling the kettle… forget it. Kail, spring the kid, too. He's with us."

"Really?"

"Really. I'll be outside." She sheathed her sword and left the jailhouse.

The men she'd heard were waiting in the street. Just two of them, wearing loose nondescript clothes and holding quarterstaffs whose metal-shod ends had nails driven through them. "Jyelle have message for you," one of them said, his nasal accent marking him as a sailor from the old country. They began to spin the staffs.

"Jyelle should remember that a good scout doesn't send messages she could deliver herself," Loch noted.

"Jyelle say you are fool to come back to her province," said the other one. "You should have run away when you had the chance."

"Her province? Jyelle was a two-bit thief when I saw her in Ros-Oanki," Loch said. "Are you happy taking orders from a girl who rats out guild members?"

That gave one of them the pause—nobody liked a rat. The other one kept spinning his staff. "She tell us what happen," he sneered. "You leave her in the war. Leave her for dead in the Empire. She just put you in jail."

The door creaked open behind Loch. She didn't turn. Instead, she stepped forward, hands raised.

"Kail, please don't make any sudden movements," she said. "Jyelle says that we left her for dead behind enemy lines during the war. Do you remember doing that?"

Kail grunted thoughtfully. "There was that brief disagreement when she tried to kill an Imperial family for their food."

"Oh, that." Loch shrugged. "Fight the enemy, not their people."

"I'm guessing Jyelle never took that one to heart, Captain."

The sailor nearest Loch finished his spin with a mocking salutation, his staff jabbing the air just shy of her throat. "Maybe we bring you to her... later, no? It is some time since I have an Urujar woman!"

"Peut-être je vous connais," Kail said suddenly and flawlessly in the language of the old country. *"Je ne veux pas de problème. Je suis passé beaucoup de temps dans la mer."*

The sailors regarded Kail skeptically. *"Dans quelle mer, Urujar?"*

Kail grinned. *"Dans ta mère!"*

The sailors' looks turned murderous, and in that moment, as the one with the staff held at Loch's throat turned toward Kail, Loch moved.

Her hands snapped up, closed around the staff just behind the nail-studded head, and slammed it back into the sailor's face. As he dropped to his knees with a wet moan, she pulled his staff away and speared it like a harpoon down onto the foot of the other sailor.

As he shouted, she cracked the staff up between his legs, spun it as he dropped into the crouch every man in the world recognized, and came down hard on the back of his head. He didn't move.

"You said something about his mother again, didn't you?" Loch asked over her shoulder.

"Don't mess with success, Captain."

"Remind me not to threaten her," the wizard noted, "ever."

"Gosh!" said the kid.

Loch turned to the sailor she'd hit first. He had his hands over his mouth.

"You tell Jyelle that her old captain intends to do business in the area," she said. "She can be in my way, or she can be out of my way. Tell her that where she decides to stand isn't going to change my plan. Think you can pass that on?" The sailor nodded mutely. "Good." The staff landed beside him with a clatter. "Oh, and tell her that she was always a lousy scout."

She headed for the city gates without looking back.

Six

Ros-Uitosuf sat near a small, fast river that had once been a large, slow river, a tumbled collection of grand old houses and humble modern homes. It was hot and humid. The kahva-houses and restaurants paid Urujar children and pretty women to swing fans in the doorways.

The sign outside one restaurant read simply "Uribin's," and showed a plate covered with catfish and potatoes. Loch and Kail went inside, tossing a coin to the Urujar girl fanning cool air their way.

"*Ynk'ura ciel'urti!*" said Uribin, leaping to his feet as they came in. He was still big and bald, and he'd been eating a lot of his own food over the past few years. He wore an apron with a lobster on it, and his bare arms were still muscular.

"*Darveth'isti!*" Loch said, offering a handshake and getting an enormous hug instead. "What's an old friend have to do to get some decent catfish?"

"Ros-Uitosuf is the best in the province, Cap'n," Uribin said with a big toothy grin. "And Uribin's is the best in Ros-Uitosuf."

"Got a private room?" Loch looked out at the gently lit main room, where people—most Urujar, but more white than she'd expected—drank good wine and ate hot, spicy food. "Business."

"Done, Cap'n." Uribin gestured to a young woman whose lighter complexion mirrored Loch's. "Denia, show the lady to the back room. Set as many places as she needs." Loch left with Denia, leaving Kail and Uribin alone for a moment. "Trouble?"

"Possibly," Kail said with a wry smile.

"You and the cap'n are family," Uribin said quietly.

"Understood." Kail nodded.

"Family doesn't cause trouble unless they have to."

"Also understood." Kail looked around the room. "You have any problems with Jyelle?"

Uribin snorted. "Some men came once, asking for protection money. I insulted their mothers and then hit them when they got angry. No problems since then."

Kail nodded solemnly. "That usually works for me."

"You're certain, Ketch?" Pyvic asked, relaxing his hold slightly. "I want you to think carefully."

"Definitely, Justicar," said the man with Pyvic's sword pressing against his throat. "Two Urujar, a man and a woman. They met up with a safecracker and her Imperial friend here in town, then left."

"Which way did they leave?" Pyvic's sword didn't move.

"Separately, Justicar. The safecracker and her friend went west, and the Urujar went north. Only thing to the north is Woodsedge!"

Pyvic lowered his sword. Ketch collapsed, holding his throat and staring at Pyvic with big eyes. "Next time I come into town saying I just want to talk, don't go for your knife." As the thief glowered, Pyvic added, "I've heard rumors of a boss in the area, a woman. Tell her that I want the Urujar. I've got no other worries unless someone puts herself in my way. Clear?"

"Clear." The thief nodded. "Thank you, Justicar."

Pyvic turned to Orris. "Get the men ready, Warden. We ride for Woodsedge."

They all sat in the large back room with only three walls—the fourth was a balcony overlooking the river, and the entire restaurant was on stilts on a steep sloping hill. A single lamp lit the room in soft flickering orange, and most of the plates were laden with catfish crusted with sweet potatoes and pecans—save for one plate, which had stir-fried vegetables on it instead.

"The waiters won't be back for an hour," Loch said, breaking the silence. "You all know me. You may not know each other." She took a bite of catfish, closed her eyes and paused for a long moment. "Damn. Missed that." Then she started pointing with the fork.

"Magister Hessler. He does illusions, and he's an expert in magical artifacts."

Hessler squinted. "I wouldn't say I'm an expert, technically, since—" He broke off as everyone looked at him. "Sure, fine, I'm an expert."

The fork pointed again. "Ululenia. Unicorn and shape-shifter, and she can mess with minds."

"I can also purify water, encourage plants to grow, and speak with forest animals," Ululenia added, her horn a rainbow shimmer flickering on her pale brow, "although I don't imagine that will come up."

"You're a *unicorn?*" Dairy exclaimed.

"And serendipitously seated next to a virgin," Ululenia murmured with a sweetly curving smile. Dairy flushed beet-red.

"See? I promised." Loch pointed again. "Icy Fist. Contortionist, acrobat. He's our man on the walls."

"Do you radiate cold magic when you punch people?" Kail asked.

"I do not engage in physical combat," Icy replied, taking a bite from his vegetable plate, "and I possess no elemental magical ability."

"Then why Icy Fist?"

"It is short for 'Indomitable Courteous Fist,' which is my full name."

"That's significantly less cool, Icy."

"Tern. Lock-man and tinker."

"Lock-*person.*"

"Lock-*person* and tinker." Loch rolled her eyes. "She recently took out a dwarf-made safe in Ros-Aelafuir, and blew out a jailhouse wall to boot."

"That was you?" Desidora asked. "That was really impressive!" Tern smiled and lifted a wineglass in thanks.

"Sister Desidora," Loch went on. "Death priestess." Tern dropped her wineglass. "She'll be working with Hessler on magical defenses, and she's got an ancient warhammer that will help if it comes to a fight. Which is *not* the plan."

"*Besyn larveth'is,*" Ghylspwr declared.

Hessler leaned forward, looking from Ghylspwr to Desidora. "Could I maybe see your talking warhammer for just a minute or two?"

"Kutesosh gajair'is!"

"Maybe not right at the moment," Desidora said.

"And this is Dairy," Loch finished, watching as the boy went beet-red again. "He's here to... well, he's here." She looked around the table. "That's it. Eight of us."

"Nine," Desidora corrected, holding up Ghylspwr.

"Nine?" Hessler asked incredulously. "It's a *warhammer.*"

"If your little brother counts," Desidora said, dark eyes narrowing, "Ghylspwr counts."

"Besyn larveth'is!"

"I'm not his brother," Dairy mumbled. "I'm an orphan."

"As each petal, gently curving in satin embrace, is valued by the rose, so should we count the sweet virgin among our number." Ululenia paused. "He should definitely count. Definitely."

"Nine it is," Loch said, rapping the table with her fork. "The nine of us are going to get this job done."

"And that job is?" Tern asked.

"We're going to sneak up to Heaven's Spire, break into an Archvoyant's palace, and steal back something he stole from my family, something expensive enough for us all to retire on." In the stunned silence, Loch took another bite of the catfish. "Gods, this is good."

"Yes, sir, I've seen them," Merigan said to Pyvic as they walked the freshly-laid streets of Woodsedge. "They passed through a few weeks ago." He looked back behind them.

"Does your assistant need help? We could get him some soothing herbs."

"Your *assistant?*" Orris shouted from behind them. "I'm the warden for Heaven's Spire! I'm in charge of—"

"He's in charge of assisting me, at the moment," Pyvic said mildly. "And he's not accustomed to hard riding. Can you tell me where they went?"

"Yes, sir," Merigan said promptly. "They asked where the largest and wealthiest temple in the nearby area was, and then left for the regional temple of Ael-meseth on the westward trail."

"My thanks, Mayor Merigan," Pyvic said. "I appreciate your help." The young man ducked his head, and Pyvic looked curiously at the massive humanoid figures at the edge of town. "And you really made peace with the ogres?"

Merigan smiled. "Yes, sir. Just have to show them you're not going to back down. I think they'd rather talk than fight, too, when it comes down to it."

"Glad to hear it." Pyvic chuckled. "Good day, Mayor." He gestured for Orris to follow.

"Pompous little... He thought I was your assistant!" Orris shouted once they were a safe distance away. "That little boy should have been taught a lesson!"

"More flies with honey, Warden," Pyvic said, not turning. "It seems the young mayor learned that. Perhaps you should, too."

When the shouting died down, Loch finished off her catfish, pushed her plate away, and said, "Questions?"

"Are you *insane?*" Hessler's eyes actually opened all the way, he was so excited.

"Not as of yet," Loch said calmly. "Tern?"

"Why Heaven's Spire?" The tinker cleaned her spectacles with a soft rag produced from one of her dress's many pockets. "The Voyants might be the most powerful men in the Republic, but they're not the richest, at least not in terms of things we can carry out. And I *know* they've got the best security."

"Captain's got a plan," Kail said. "She's always got a plan."

"Do they always work, Little One?" Ululenia asked. It *looked* like she was asking innocently.

Loch decided not to field that one.

"I can't help you," Father Bertrus said shortly, adjusting the neckline of his vestments. "We've seen no one like that here. Other, more pressing matters have demanded our attention."

"What *has* demanded your attention, Father?" Pyvic asked shortly. "We know that the prisoners came this way after asking about wealthy temples in the area."

Father Bertrus stiffened. "Perhaps they were with her," he murmured, and then a grim smile lit his face. "It is good news for me if the woes of my temple involve you, though it may not be good news for *you*, Justicar."

"I'm listening, Father." Pyvic kept his tone polite and formal.

"Our temple was attacked by a death priestess." Bertrus lowered his voice to a grim whisper. "The temptress attempted to entice us with her unholy wiles, and when we were not swayed, she used dark sorcery to steal several priceless relics from our vault."

"Do you know which way she went when leaving town, Father?"

Bertrus gave him a sour look. "South, much good it will do you. The road hits a major crossroads a day or two out of town. She could be anywhere by now. Now, if you will excuse me." He stalked back into his temple without waiting for Pyvic to reply.

"Looks like we're out of luck now," Orris said with a snicker. "Bet you're wishing you'd paid a bit more attention to what *I* got us from Akus."

"I know where they'll be," Pyvic said. "Come. We're headed south."

"But you heard the man!" Orris grabbed Pyvic's shoulder. "We don't know where she's going! She could be anywhere!" He flinched as Pyvic took the hand off his shoulder, then sneered. "Get as mad as you like. You wanted to be in charge, and now you'll have to go explain why you didn't get the job done."

"Think for a minute." Pyvic glowered. "We don't need to know where Loch and Kail went if we know where they're going." Orris stared at him blankly, and Pyvic sighed and started ticking off points. "Wherever Loch went, something strange has happened—either a crime, like robbing the temple or cracking the dwarven safe, or this sudden peace with the ogres in Woodsedge."

"But Loch didn't do any of that." From Orris's mouth, it sounded more like a whine than an argument.

"Exactly, Warden. So what does that tell us?"

Orris thought for a minute, and then it hit him. "She's recruiting."

"That she is. She's going around with Kail to make contact, and she's asking them all to meet her somewhere. We don't need to know where *she's* going. We just need to know where the death priestess was headed, because that's where Loch will be."

Orris frowned. "I don't see it, Pyvic. That's pretty justicar thinking, there, but we still don't know where the death priestess was going."

Pyvic reached into a pouch and withdrew a small but serviceable folding map of the province. "Here we are," he said, pointing, "and here's the road south from town. Here's where it intersects the East-West merchant way. The death priestess can go in four directions. But going north brings her right back into town here, so she wouldn't do that." He crossed off that direction with a slash of his finger. "East takes her to back to Ros-Aelafuir, which is unlikely, since they've already attracted attention in the area."

"That leaves Ros-Sesuf to the south and Ros-Uitosuf to the west." Orris grunted. "Even odds."

"Not really. They'll be in Ros-Uitosuf." Pyvic gave Orris a frosty smile. "Do I have to remind you, Warden, what your prisoner was in for?" When Orris gave him a blank stare, Pyvic grimaced. "She was in for attempting to infiltrate Heaven's Spire. Once her group is gathered, they'll eventually head for the port city of Ros-Oanki to try to steal an airship. And the only major town on the way to Ros-Oanki is Ros-Uitosuf."

"Fine. Whatever you say, Justicar." Orris turned and spat as he walked away. "We'll see soon enough if you're just blowing smoke."

"What is the target?" Desidora asked, pulling her auburn hair out of her face. Of all of them, she looked the least perturbed. "Also, can we get any more of that bread to soak up the sauce?"

"Archvoyant Silestin," Loch said, and the room went quiet, "fancies himself quite the collector. He's come into possession of an ancient elven manuscript that once belonged to my family. If we get that, the elves will pay enough that we'll never need to work again. It's high risk, but I believe the reward is worth it. If you want out, let me know now."

Everyone looked at each other, guilty or appraising or frustrated. Kail passed Desidora a loaf of bread.

"Right." Loch gestured with the fork. "The elven manuscript is an original copy of *The Love Song of Eillenfiniel*, signed by the three poets and with an intact enchantment of the fairy song that inspired them, recorded as they were composing." Desidora's jaw dropped. Tern nodded, lips pursed. Everyone else looked politely ignorant. "It's worth at least seven million to the elves."

"How did your family get such an heirloom?" Hessler asked.

"My father was a baron," Loch said shortly. "Minor nobility, with this as our most prized possession. My parents died during the war, and Silestin took guardianship of the land until my sister comes of age."

Hessler squinted. "Aren't *you* of age?"

"The captain was off fighting during the war," Kail said. "It's hard to keep track of who lives and who dies in the big battles." He grinned sourly. "The captain's efforts to reclaim her family's title have been...."

"Problematic," Loch finished, smiling thinly, "and irrelevant. But I know the book exists, and I know Silestin has it in his vault."

"Which we can't get into," Tern said, "since it's impossible to crack one of those vaults even if I had time to study one. And since we *don't* have that—"

"We will," Loch said, "once we get up to Heaven's Spire. I've got a friend who will help."

"So you don't *know* how to beat it right now?" Hessler asked acidly.

"No, Magister, I don't. Much as you didn't know how you were getting out of that jail cell."

"That's not fair!" Dairy leapt to his feet. "Mister Hessler was going to escape! And he was going to help me escape, too! You're... you're nothing but *thieves*!" Red-faced, he ran from the room, slamming the door shut behind him.

"Well... you don't set up a heist with *non*-thieves," Tern commented. "That doesn't work as well."

"Did you really have a plan to escape?" Desidora asked Hessler.

"Oh, *hell*, no. I had nothing."

"So that's the plan," Loch cut in. "We steal an airship, get up to Heaven's Spire, and meet my contact, who can get us into Silestin's palace. I don't know what we'll need, which is why I've got a wide range of skills at the table. When we've got a solid plan, we lift the book and contact the elves."

"The dew is as constant as the spring mornings," Ululenia said, "and the zephyr is as unchanging as the afternoon sun. But the elves are fickle, flighty, infrequently found. What means have you, fair maiden, to bend their gaze to the world of men?"

"The elves were always interested in buying the book from my father." Loch shrugged. "They told him how to contact them if he ever changed his mind. I'm assuming it's still valid, and that they're still interested. My contact can get us down to earth whenever we're ready. Even split, we all retire. Or purchase a large tract of forest. Or... whatever it is that unicorns do."

"Frolic, primarily." Ululenia frowned. "When will my virgin return to me?"

"Oh, lay off the lad," Hessler said with a sour look.

"In sooth, I had planned—"

"Even split?" Tern asked. "The kid and the warhammer each get as much as I do?"

"I'm sure Ghylspwr and Dairy will both prove their worth to the team," Loch said calmly. "Even split. The math is easier."

Hessler sniffed. "That assumes that this plan, and I use the word 'plan' *extremely* loosely, actually works."

"Those safes don't crack themselves, Loch. That's all I'm saying."

"Unlike your plans, Magister," Kail said brightly, "Loch's plans come together without complications."

The door crashed open.

Pyvic shouldered open the door to Uribin's with his sword drawn. Diners jumped to their feet as he strode in, scanning the room.

"*Ynk'ura ciel'urti,*" said a big bald black man in an apron.

"Pleased to be here." Pyvic nodded. "I am Justicar Pyvic, following two escaped prisoners. I wish no harm on your establishment, but I must conduct a search."

Behind him, the town guards looked at their friends nervously.

"You with him?" Uribin pointed into the main room. Pyvic looked. Pyvic glared.

Orris stumbled to his feet, tossing aside the shell of a half-devoured shellfish and wiping buttery fingers on a napkin. "Didn't think you were coming in until nine."

"I got concerned about the number of people entering and leaving. *Why are you not outside guarding the back?*" Pyvic felt the slow rage burning in him again.

"The other guards are doing it, Justicar." Orris gave a self-satisfied smirk. "Reckoned I'd see if she were here. Can't have you stealing the credit."

"You were supposed to be outside so that she wouldn't see you—or did you think that a fat, old, white man in a military uniform would blend in here?" Pyvic gestured sharply at the main dining room.

Orris shot Pyvic a defiant glare. "She ain't in here—"

"We heard otherwise." Pyvic looked at the hallway that led to the kitchens. "Uribin, you've got a back room? One for private parties? I'll need to search it." Without waiting for permission, he strode down the hallway.

"We've got a room, sure, but we don't use it," Uribin protested, wringing his big hands as he stopped before a large door. "It's not good to go in—"

"Save it," Pyvic snapped, moving Uribin aside with his sword. Then he stepped in and put a shoulder to the door. It crashed open.

"See?" Uribin said mildly after a long moment of silence. "We don't use it because of the big hole in the floor. Can't serve food in here. Somebody'd fall through and break a leg."

"And the plates with the half-eaten food on them, still warm?" Pyvic asked acidly.

Uribin gave him a broad grin. "The dishwasher goes too slow on busy nights. Sometimes we put the dirty dishes out here for a bit."

"Of course." Pyvic strode to the balcony and looked down to see the rest of the town guards, dim silhouettes just visible against the purple-gray of the water. "See anything down there?"

"Arrogant apple, babbling brook, creeping cat?" one of them called back, and then fell over with a splash.

"Damn it!" Pyvic stalked out of the restaurant with his men, ignoring Uribin's grinning farewell. "Orris, walk with me. The rest of you, tend to the men, then start searching. They can't be far." The other men darted off, leaving Pyvic and Orris alone in the street outside Uribin's.

"Reckon that Urujar cook's playin' you," Orris noted sagely.

"Of course he is." Pyvic rammed his sword back into its sheath.

"We could question him. If you don't think you can do it, I—"

"I told you to stay outside, *Warden*. You didn't. I didn't want you to be seen. You were. I wanted to catch the prisoners. They have escaped."

"You were going to claim all the credit," Orris whined.

"Orris, they escaped on your watch. I'm trying to fix *your* mistake. Stop getting in my way. In fact, get out of my way entirely." Pyvic let out a long breath. "I'm stationing you back in Ros-Oanki. You can watch the ships heading up to the Spire."

Orris made a strangled noise. Pyvic stood silent. Finally, the warden spat at Pyvic's feet. "You think you can do any better, Justicar? You think you can make me your scapegoat?

I'll be back up on the Spire, talking with folks who'll be watching you *real* close." He stomped away, gesticulating wildly as he shouted to himself.

Pyvic shook his head. He'd pay for what he'd said to Orris, but not tonight.

In the darkness downstream, eight people and one warhammer made quiet progress through the bushes.

"Okay," Tern said quietly, "even split, including the kid and the warhammer."

"That's the fastest I've ever seen *anyone* break through a floor." Kail's voice shone with admiration.

"Besyn larveth'is," Ghylspwr said modestly.

"How did you know they were coming?" Loch asked Dairy quietly. The boy had given them less than a minute of warning when he'd burst into the room.

"The big angry man was ordering food." Dairy was looking around wildly, but he kept pace with the group. "He was glaring at the black... er, the Urujar..."

"Black people is fine," Kail cut in. Loch glared him to silence.

"Then Mister Uribin asked him if there were a problem, and the big angry man yelled that he wanted some food, that he had friends arriving soon, and although he smiled when he said it, it wasn't a nice smile. And with his uniform, I just thought...."

"You thought right." Hessler patted his shoulder. "Good job, Dairy."

"How do these events change our plan?" Icy asked, his breath still even as they ran.

"Not at all." Loch grinned. "Except that I don't think we'll stay the night in Ros-Uitosuf."

Kail grimaced. "Straight on to Ros-Oanki, Captain?"

"No rest for the wicked, Kail."

Akus tore around the corner, quieted his rasping breath, and looked for something he could use if it came to a fight.

He should've learned his lesson. After that near scrape with the justicar and Orris, he should have stopped telling the stories. Instead, he'd kept getting free drinks in each town he passed through, telling the story of how he'd broken out of the Cleaners.

The two guild enforcers stopped at the entrance to the alley. Akus went still. They had torches, which he didn't like much, and swords, which Akus didn't like at *all*.

Guild guys had jumped him in the last town. One of them had let slip that Jyelle had a beef with the two Urujar and anyone who'd helped them. Apparently she'd ratted the Urujar out to send them to the Cleaners in the first place.

"Give it a look," one of the guys muttered, and started in with his torch raised high. Akus cursed Gedesar silently and offered Io-fergajar a quick whispered prayer.

Akus had gathered rumors over the next few nights. Word had it that Loch had left Jyelle to die over in the Empire during the war. Word also had it that Jyelle had been trying to kill peasants when Loch did it. Akus didn't care about that. If she and some guild leader wanted to gut each other over an old feud, Akus wanted no part of it.

"Hang on," said the guy in the lead. "I think—" And then Akus jumped out from around the corner and hit him with the rotten plank he'd scooped out of the mud. It caught the guy on the arm and knocked his torch back toward his face, and he flinched. Akus lunged in, broke the guy's nose, grabbed the torch, threw it at the other guy, and shoved him hard into the wall. Then he started running.

People always underestimated Akus. That was why he was still alive. They saw the big guy with the scars and they thought, he's too dumb to run away. He's got too much pride.

Akus ran two blocks, then turned and made for the shadows. He'd hide until morning, head out of town with a merchant train. He was going to live a happy man someplace where they'd never heard of Loch or Jyelle, even if he did have to buy his own drinks.

The shadows twisted beside him, and then a blade sliced cleanly through his hamstring.

He yelled, lunged, connected with nothing. He dropped to one knee, trying to keep quiet.

The second blade stabbed into his ankle.

"This ain't got nothin' to do with me," Akus panted when he'd managed to bite off the scream. "Nothin' to do with me."

"If it did," said a voice from the shadow, "you might be worth something."

The guild enforcers stepped into the alley, and Akus, with one bad leg and one bad ankle, raised his callused fists.

They still had their swords.

Seven

THEY'D PURCHASED PASSAGE WITH A CARAVAN HEADING TO ROS-Oanki. Most of them rode in the wagons, while Ululenia accompanied the caravan as a magnificent snowy white mare whose mane shone in the morning light and whose horn was almost visible to the casual observer. She wouldn't let anyone but Dairy ride her.

There was a pause one day when they reached a small crossroads and found something placed on a sign near the junction.

While the wagoners calmed horses made nervous by the smell of blood, Loch neared the sign. Kail was already there. He didn't look at Loch.

There was a note pinned to the tattered remains of Akus's shirt. It fluttered in the wind, but Loch made it out quickly enough.

Captain,
Hope your time away has been relaxing. Looking forward to showing you what I've learned since our time together.
Jyelle

Kail made a small gesture of blessing. "Couldn't have known."

"Doesn't matter." Loch didn't look over.

"His fault for spreading the story. He had to know—"

"Doesn't matter."

Kail sighed. "No, not really. I'm sorry, Captain."

Loch bit her lip, nodded shortly. "Doesn't matter. But thanks." She turned to the wagoners. "I'll get him buried. It won't be long." They nodded their thanks, still calming the horses and trying to keep the women and children from seeing anything.

When Loch looked back to the wagons, Tern was there. Her rosy cheeks had gone pale.

"Wow, Loch." She squinted, reading the note. "You've got lovely enemies."

"It's a gift," Kail said shortly. "Come on. Help me find a shovel."

"And while *some* of my fellow Voyants want to spend more on programs for the lazy," Silestin called down from the podium, "I'm going to fight them tooth and nail! I'm going to help the hardworking citizens of the Republic keep *their* money in *their* pockets!"

The crowd, a mixed group of white and Urujar laborers who'd been brought up to the Spire to hear Silestin speak, clapped loudly.

"You're good people, dedicated, churchgoing people!" Silestin declared. "You don't need Skilled handouts! You need your people on the Spire to keep you safe, so that you can make this Republic the best country in the world!" As the crowd applauded again, Silestin gestured. A young Urujar woman, beautiful even with a band of smoky crystal obscuring her eyes, came out onto Silestin's stage, her movements steady but careful.

"You hear the Skilled talk about helping others," Silestin continued, his voice pitched lower now. "They want to legislate charity. Kind of makes you wonder what kind of person thinks charity has to be forced, doesn't it?" The young woman smiled at the crowd, and then Silestin led her to the podium. "I didn't see the Skilled Party helping young Naria when Imperials took her eyes and her family during the war. Did the Skilled help you? They must have been helping *some-body*," he said with a chuckle, looking around the crowd, "to hear how they talk about their programs and taxes, but mostly, I think they're helping themselves."

Silestin caught sight of Warden Orris standing at the edge of the crowd and cut smoothly to the end of his speech. "The Skilled would like you to believe that the Republic isn't on the right path. They think we need to bow down to the Empire, and I'm sure the Empire would like that." Silestin's adopted daughter Naria shook her head angrily. "But that's not the kind of man I am," Silestin went on. "I think the Republic needs to move forward, not back! Ambassador Bi'ul, come on up here."

From the front row, a tall, lean figure stood. His ivory skin flickered with a multicolored aura, like a rainbow beside a waterfall, and his loose black robe rippled like oil as he moved. "This is Ambassador Bi'ul of the Glimmering Folk," Silestin said to the suddenly hushed crowd. "He's here meeting with the Voyancy, the first of the Glimmering Folk in a thousand years to do *any* nation that honor! That's the kind of strength the Republic has, people! That's how we're keeping you safe!"

Silestin, the ambassador, and Naria waved to the cheering crowd for a while. Then Silestin and Naria shook some hands. When enough of a crowd had gathered around Naria, Silestin slipped off to Warden Orris, who was smiling broadly.

"Great speech, sir!" Orris declared.

"Just telling it like I see it," Silestin said, smiling at the workers nearby. In a lower voice, he added, "I thought you were taking care of the problem on the ground."

"This is the former warden?" asked Ambassador Bi'ul suddenly. He had approached silently, carving out a circle as the workers moved aside for him. His voice was light and twangy, as if it were not a real voice but a clever reconstruction. "The one who lost the prisoners?"

"Indeed." Silestin clapped Orris on the shoulder. "He was rounding them back up. How's that going, Orris?"

Orris shook his head. "Well, to be honest, sir, Pyvic is causing all kinds of trouble. Getting in my way, keeping me from doing my job."

"Wait. You don't have them?" Silestin looked from Orris to Bi'ul in evident confusion. The crowd was moving around Naria now, leaving Silestin, Orris, and Bi'ul alone.

"If he doesn't have his prisoners," Bi'ul said, his head cocked curiously, "why has he returned?"

Orris fidgeted. "Well, Silestin, you have to know how it was."

Silestin frowned. "I really wanted you down there as part of the effort."

"I, I, that is, I delegated it, Archvoyant."

"Sure, delegated, that's good." Silestin cupped his jaw. "Hard to explain to the politicians, though."

"They will assume that the warden was incompetent again," Bi'ul agreed.

"No!" Orris was starting to sweat again. "I'll go back down, sir, if that's—"

"Can't go back down now, Orris." Silestin cut him off with an impatient slash of the arm. "Can't look indecisive. You're up, and you'll stay up." He glanced at the crowd. "We'll have to play it different, that's all. You'll be there when the ship docks." He turned back to Orris and smiled, and his voice warmed. "Now, if you'll excuse me, I've got to greet the rest of these people."

With that, Silestin moved back to the common people, shaking hands and leaving Orris behind.

They hit Ros-Oanki a few days later. It was a slow afternoon, and the locals looked up curiously at the sight of two Urujar, an Imperial, a wizard, three women and a kid coming through the gates.

"We've got eyes," Kail murmured as they entered the market square nearest the gates, heels clicking on the freshly laid flagstones. Ros-Oanki had profited from its status as a port town for the Spire, raking in enough tax money to have bronze fountains and large marble arches with patriotic mosaics done on the sides. "Right, two pair."

"Over or under?" Loch turned to a stall where a vendor was selling clothes and, in a louder voice, said, "Let's make nice, everyone. Meet up where and when we agreed." The others went their separate ways, with Dairy being wrenched in two directions simultaneously by Hessler and Ululenia until the wizard finally proved victorious.

"Under," Kail said as Loch picked through several hats. "Oooh, I like the red one with the floppy brim. Very neo-Uru."

"I do try to keep up with the times." Loch paid for the floppy red hat, then moved to a stall selling weapons. "Still with us?"

"Oh yeah. Moving in now, by the produce wagon."

"The white wagon with the Imperial vendor, or the unpainted one with the apples?" A pair of knives caught her eye, and she smiled at the merchant. "Are these balanced for throwing?"

"Ten, fifteen paces." The merchant shrugged. "Cost too much to throw them away, though. Twenty apiece."

"The one with the apples," Kail said. "You want me to go mention their mothers?"

"Thirty-five for the pair, and they'd better be good from fifteen," Loch said to the merchant, and then to Kail, "Let's not play your only card just yet."

The merchant grunted. "No credit. You miss at fifteen, it's on you, not them."

Loch put several coins on the merchant's table. "Just a moment." She picked up the knives, hefted them carefully, then spun and threw.

The marketplace erupted into screams, mothers grabbed their children, and merchants began slamming their cases shut. Loch crossed the square toward the produce wagon, where two scruffy-looking men were tugging frantically at their shirtsleeves, which had been neatly pinned to the wagon. She drew her sword, adjusted the brim of her floppy red hat, and hollered, "Everyone take a look! You tell everyone you know that Loch is in town, and Byn-kodar himself is with her!" Then she leveled her sword at the two men. "I'm taking down Jyelle. You run and let her know, or you have no use to me."

The two men finally tore their ragged sleeves free and bolted without another look, and Loch sheathed her blade, stalked to the wagon, and pulled out her knives. She nodded to the apple merchant, an old woman in a faded blue dress, then tossed a coin. "Ma'am. For the damage to your wagon." The old woman sniffed in disdain, but she also neatly caught the coin.

Kail joined her as she strode from the square. "Picked up the sheaths, Captain. I assumed you'd want them."

"No, Kail, I planned to hold a knife in each hand for the next few weeks."

"With you, Captain, I never know."

Pyvic reached Ros-Oanki in the early afternoon and asked around the market, hoping for some sign of Loch.

He was in luck.

"Enormous woman!" declared a hat vendor. "She blotted out the sun, muscles like melons!"

"Tiny, barely more than a girl," said a weapons merchant. "Fast like an adder and twice as poisonous!"

"I honestly didn't get a good look at her," said an old crone selling vegetables. "Just the red hat and the sword."

Pyvic blinked. "The sword?"

The old woman nodded. "Single-edge, brass hand guard, contoured mahogany grip, and some name etched into the blade."

Pyvic came away from it without much more than he'd started with. An Urujar woman with Warden Orris's prized saber... and a big red hat.

He filed it away and started investigating the taverns and kahva-houses.

It seemed that Loch was a feather, not a rock. If you wanted to catch a rock somebody had thrown, you grabbed fast and hard to make sure you got hold of it. But with a feather, you watched carefully, spread your hands, and waited.

The first few taverns yielded only garbled accounts of the incident in the market. The kahva-houses yielded even less, until he walked into a warmly lit place with green leaves hanging from the doorway and cinnamon wafting through the air. Before he could even start the speech about people helping the Republic by answering questions, something was whipping through the air toward him with a glint of metal.

He sidestepped and caught it by reflex. A coin.

"For your kahva, Justicar," came a strong alto voice with laughter just beneath its velvet surface. "You *are* in a kahva-house, after all."

Pyvic looked at her as the chuckles fluttered across the room. She was an Urujar, skin the color of burnished leather or fine whiskey. Her silky black hair hung carelessly over her shoulders, and her loose shirt and breeches could have been the outfit of a trader, a crafter, or an off-duty guard. There were tiny laugh-lines crinkled around her deep eyes, but as she stared up at him, he couldn't quite say that she was mocking him. There was something too intense in the look, and Pyvic found himself flushing.

Then, because he was damned if he was going to let some woman in a kahva-house show him up, he went to the counter and ordered a drink. The vendor handed him a cheap waxed-paper cup filled with steaming dark liquid, and he made his way to the table where the woman sat alone, her rough hands cradling a chipped ceramic mug.

It was too easy. Prisoner Loch wouldn't have advertised herself to him like this. But then, nobody else would have done so, either.

He let a few coins clink on the table as he sat down across from her. "Here's your change."

She raised an eyebrow, and those deep dark eyes cut right through him with a glance. "I usually tip the server. It's polite."

"Did you learn your manners at home, or in prison?"

"Assuming all Urujar are convicts?" she asked, raising an eyebrow. "What charming behavior."

"What do you do, then?"

She pursed her lips, tiny dimples appearing on her cheeks as she stifled a smile. "I'm a bookseller."

"You don't have any books on you."

The smile grew. "You don't have a dozen thugs with truncheons, but you're a justicar nonetheless."

"Not all justicars work that way," Pyvic said with a hard smile. "And how did you know I was one?"

She sipped her kahva. It was the same color as her skin, and the sight of her closing her eyes and touching the drink to her lips shot little sparks through Pyvic's gut. "You're in military uniform. If you were in active service, you'd be in a tavern with your men. Also, you've got an officer's insignia but a standard-issue sword at your waist." She half-closed her eyes. "And only a justicar walks into a kahva-house, lets a single woman buy him a drink, and then asks if she's been in prison."

"Why did a single woman buy me a drink?" Pyvic asked a little hoarsely. The woman was making him sweat, and he doubted hot kahva would help matters.

She shrugged. "Has to be hard, walking and asking questions all day. I'm sure they don't pay you enough."

"The travel's not so bad. I imagine you travel a lot yourself as a bookbinder."

"Book*seller*, Justicar," the woman corrected. "And the travel isn't so bad. You go where you have to in order to get what you want."

Pyvic leaned forward, pushing his kahva aside. "I'm looking for an Urujar woman who fits your description. What if I arrested you right here, just to be safe?"

"I'd never buy a justicar a drink again," the woman deadpanned, "and that would be truly tragic. Brooding men in uniform, shoulders broad from swordplay, legs firm from riding... I'd hate to lose that."

Pyvic coughed. "What can you tell me about the escaped prisoners?"

"They're in town, but then, everyone's heard that." The woman sipped her kahva again, then grinned crookedly, the dimples flashing. "Word has it that she's got a problem with some big thief in the area. If I were you, I'd have your ears out for fighting in the streets. Better chance of finding her there than in a nice kahva-house like this."

"I'll bear that in mind," Pyvic murmured. "Have you seen her? Can you tell me what she looks like?"

The woman took one last sip of her kahva, then set the mug aside and stood. "Oh, you know how it is, Justicar," she said, brushing her hair back over her shoulders. "Those Urujar women all look alike." Then she turned and walked out of the kahva-house, her hips swaying as though exciting music were playing just out of earshot.

"I wouldn't say that *at all*," Pyvic said, and sat back to sip his kahva for a while.

"Hook's baited," Loch said to Kail a few blocks from the kahva-house at the fountain where they'd agreed to meet. "He'll be there." The fountain was bronze, a tall figure holding a walking staff in one hand and a merchant's scales in the other. Gedesar the Wanderer, god of merchants, travelers, and fortune-seekers. And thieves, too, although somehow that hadn't made it into the display. Loch tugged her hair back into its normal ponytail.

"You're sure? Here's your stupid hat." Kail passed her the sword-belt as well. "Last time we got to the Spire, we got out of the crates to see a bunch of guards grinning at us. If we do all this and see the same guards giving us the same grin... well, I'm going to be disappointed, Captain."

"You know, I really *like* this hat," Loch confessed, slapping it back on. "Any word on your end?"

"I asked a few questions around the market. It appears Warden Orris is no longer working groundside." Kail grinned. "One less thing to worry about, anyway."

"I talked to a fence while parting with the last of the trinkets from my vault job," said Desidora as she came out of an alley, Ghylspwr at her side. Her hair was darker than its normal auburn, and her green robe was more of an olive color. "Jyelle spread the word. She wants a meeting. Ninth bell at a fountain in Tratter Square." She smiled, her skin pale even in the bright afternoon light. "The air is thick with their fear."

Loch thought a moment, lips pursed. "Trap?"

"*Kutesosh gajair'is,*" Ghylspwr said grimly.

"Of course," Desidora said coldly, then seemed to catch herself. She shut her eyes, and some of the color came back into her cheeks.

"Tratter Square?" Loch glanced at Kail.

"Haven't seen it, Captain. Didn't want to tip anything."

"There were watchers," said Icy as he joined them, "but none were watching the spire of Esa-jolar's nearby temple, which affords an excellent view."

"A pure white dove circling gently through cerulean skies went similarly unobserved," Ululenia agreed, stepping past them to touch her hands to the water of the fountain.

"Well, hell, I was just invisible," Hessler grunted as he and Dairy joined them, and then glared at the fountain. "What are you... are those *lily-pads?*"

"Excellent," said Loch. "How does it look?"

"It is located in the poor quarter," Icy said, frowning slightly. "The ground appears muddy and uneven, and the exits are more alleys than roads. The fountain itself is dry and its statue gone. One may still access the pipe system through which the water once flowed, however."

"Ululenia?"

"'Tis a sad place," she said softly, her ash-white hair falling into her face as she stared down into the fountain. "I sense unshed tears in earth long paved with stone and brick and tears and blood."

"That's... slightly less helpful, but thank you for trying. Hessler?"

"Great place for a trap," he said sourly. "It's the kind of forgotten maze where she can hide dozens of her gang."

"Noted. So... the invitation's on the table." Loch grinned. "We can spring the trap or back out."

"*Kutesosh gajair'is!*"

"Ghylspwr favors springing the trap," Desidora translated, smiling faintly. "As do I." Her hair was back to red now.

Kail squinted. "But isn't that the same thing he said when—"

"There are a lot of subtle tonal differences, Kail. You really have to listen for it."

"I don't like it," Hessler said, "but then, I'm not the one who'll be walking into it."

"Good team spirit, Magister. Icy?"

"Fortune favors the bold, though statistics favor the cautious."

"I have not journeyed so far to retreat to safer pastures now," Ululenia said firmly.

"I don't know, Loch," Kail said. "We've got surprises available, but she *really* hates you. What she did to Akus...."

"Sorry I'm late," Tern called out breathlessly as she dashed out from an alley.

"Pursuit?" Loch asked sharply.

"No," the mousy woman said cheerily. "Just lost track of time. The locals seem pretty riled up about an Urujar woman in a red hat. Any thoughts?"

"Just one." Loch smiled. "We spring the trap."

The fountain in Tratter Square had been torn down years ago.

When the Voyants of Heaven's Spire had chosen Ros-Oanki as one of the few lucky cities it would visit in the course of its migration across the Republic, the city had been a minor trading hub with a small but thriving artistic community and an exotic multicultural presence. Becoming the capitol city of the province had brought in hordes of commerce.

It had also brought in a sizeable military presence, a ton of government contracts, and a seething mass of farmers, crafters, merchants, and servants to keep everyone fed, clothed, trendy, and sexually sated.

Tratter Square was a victim of the city's expansion. Once part of a residential neighborhood where the smells of exotic

Imperial-spiced meals would fill the air along with sounds of folksongs from the old country, shouted banter in Urujar, and the distinct but universal cries of young couples in love, the square had long ago had its apartments gutted and converted into warehouses. The square itself served as the back lot for four separate warehouse clusters, and the roads leading to the square were clogged with leftover crates, packing materials, damaged merchandise, and junk.

The ground of the square, untouched for years, was now a very small marsh as a result of the spring rains. Where the fountain had once been, there was now only a grimy, leaf-strewn crater with a wide rusted pipe jutting from the ground in the middle.

It was dark and moonless that night, and the lights of the city left the sky a sooty orange-gray but did little to illuminate Tratter Square itself.

As the ninth bell tolled through the city, Loch carefully eased through the wall of crates and entered the square, blinking and squinting in the darkness. Her hat was cocked jauntily on her head, and her sword was still at her waist.

Jyelle stood on the small raised rim of the old fountain. In the darkness, Loch had no idea whether the years had been kind to her, but it was undoubtedly the woman Loch had trained, trusted, and then left in the woods back during the war. She was mixed race, like Loch, but lighter—able to pass for white if she tried, with hair that had the tight Urujar curls but the old-country color and skin the color of old paper. She wore simple, loose clothes, and held only a quarterstaff.

"Hello, Captain." Jyelle saluted with an elaborate twirl of the quarterstaff. "Get my note?" Her voice was dry, light, mocking.

"How long did you rehearse that?" Loch asked, still moving forward. She drew her sword. "Have you had that one in mind for a while, or did you come up with it while trying to talk the cold sweats away earlier tonight?"

"You think I'm scared of you?" Jyelle laughed. "I've killed better warriors than you two at a time, *Captain*. I've walked away from bloodbaths that made our little scouting skirmishes look like children playing with sticks."

"Which is why you're now holding one." Loch wondered if she should hop up onto the fountain's edge or stab from below. "Did you train those sailors who came after me? I didn't even draw my sword against them." She decided to stay below. "All I want is to come through, Jyelle. What do *you* want?"

Jyelle laughed. "I spent a long time thinking that I wanted to kill you, Loch." She began spinning her quarterstaff. "But then I realized that that wasn't it. I wanted to *beat* you. That's why I'm holding this little stick. I'm going to break your arms, and your knees, and—"

"That's more detail than I wanted," Loch said, and ran Jyelle through.

Her sword passed clean through the staff, and then clean through the woman's body, with no resistance whatsoever.

The image of Jyelle smiled down at Loch. "Surprise." Then it exploded with a blazing flash of light that ripped into Loch's face like the blinding radiance of the desert sun.

Loch stumbled backward, clutching at her eyes, as the *real* Jyelle stood up from where she had lain inside the fountain.

"It's expensive as hell to have your own pet illusionist," she said conversationally as Loch shook her head frantically, "but in my line of work, it's worth it." Like her illusory double, she had a quarterstaff. "Really kills the night vision if it sneaks up like that, doesn't it?" She lashed out and knocked the blade from Loch's hand. Loch groped for it, and Jyelle swept her legs out with another strike, sending Loch to the ground.

"You can't... my team..." Loch rolled away as Jyelle brought the staff down where she had lain, then rolled back, clutching desperately at the staff. She got hold of it and used her leverage to wrench it from Jyelle's grasp.

Stumbling to her feet, Loch swung wildly, and Jyelle coolly stepped aside, kicked Loch in the ankle, and drove a fist into her gut.

"You probably can't hear it right now," Jyelle said, "but your team is being ambushed as we speak." Loch stumbled back, still blinking, and Jyelle paused to retrieve Loch's sword. "You should feel honored, Captain. I'm spending a lot of money tonight. But nothing is too good for old friends like you."

She stabbed at Loch's knee, and Loch barely sidestepped it. Jyelle's follow-up slash just missed Loch's face and sent her red hat flying. "After all," Jyelle went on, "how else could I pay back the woman who made me what I am?"

"I didn't make you a murderer and a coward, Jyelle." Loch put her staff through a defensive spin. "*Fight the enemy, not their people.* It's the first thing we learn."

"Trying to catch me by the sound of my voice, Captain? Maybe keep me talking while your eyes recover?" Jyelle chuckled. "I've learned a few lessons of my own." She stepped in and slashed, and Loch stumbled back, tripping over the edge of the fountain and falling heavily inside.

"Loch, honey, I don't know if you can see me yet, but I'm putting on your hat." Jyelle cocked it at just the right angle as Loch pulled herself upright, using the rough edges of the rusted metal pipe in the center of the fountain for support. "You told everyone to look at you, and I want everyone to see *me* tomorrow, wearing that very same hat, carrying the very same sword, so that *everyone* knows *exactly* what happened."

From behind her, at the edge of the square, came the sound of crashing crates and ripping wood.

Loch hopped up onto the metal pipe that had once fed water into the fountain, one foot on either rusted edge. "Jyelle, honey," she said quietly, "that was more or less the plan."

And she stared right at Jyelle, her vision clean and unwavering, and smiled.

"Prisoner Loch!" came a shout from behind Jyelle.

As Jyelle gasped, Loch jumped lightly into the air, brought her feet and arms together, and dropped down into the pipe, vanishing into the darkness.

"Blinding flashes of light are covered in the first week of the illusion curriculum," came Hessler's voice, just loud enough for Loch and Jyelle to hear it. "Now, creating shields of darkness to protect someone's eyes, *that* you don't get until the advanced classes." Down in the darkness of the pipes, Loch shook her head as Jyelle swung her blade wildly. "Don't embarrass yourself. This is an illusion. I'm actually smirking at you from the roof."

"Prisoner Loch! Surrender yourself now!"

Jyelle could probably have explained herself to the guards, Loch mused. Despite the hat, despite the sword, if she'd had time to talk, she could have explained everything.

Which was why it was probably for the best that Hessler chose that moment to project an excellent impersonation of

Jyelle's voice shouting, "I'm not going back, you Republic bastards! You'll never take me alive!"

It took a lot of work from the guards Pyvic had pressed into service for the night's raid, but Prisoner Loch was, in fact, taken alive in the end.

She kept yelling even after she lost her sword, but one of the town guards, an Urujar fellow, showed some initiative and gagged her. Even after that, Pyvic had to knock her out cold to get the shackles on. She was going to be sore and unhappy when she woke up on Heaven's Spire.

"Report," he ordered as he came out of the alley to meet the rest of the town guards.

"We tried the trick with the flour and found a couple of invisible people, but they ran before we could bring them down," said the Urujar guard. "We did catch the Imperial and one of the women. Haven't said anything, though. Shall we question them?"

"No." Pyvic gestured at the three local guards who held the two prisoners in their shackles. "You're still attached to me. We'll bring them all back up to the Spire and make them someone else's problem."

"Captain doesn't wish to give up custody, Justicar," said one of the other guards, a lean fellow with a warhammer. "Doesn't want it said he let them out of his sight if they get away."

"You can personally hand them over to the Archvoyant," Pyvic promised. "I don't care whose name the puppets shout in the news, as long as they're in custody. Come on. Think of it as a holiday." He grinned. "How many of you have ever gotten to see Heaven's Spire close up?"

It was late, and Pyvic was tired and giddy from finally catching one of the escapees, which was likely why the voice of the guard with the warhammer seemed slightly wrong—a bit high, almost musical, for the aura of professional combat power it definitely exuded. That was probably also why he kept catching flickers at the edge of his vision, tiny flashes of movement that revealed themselves to be shadows dancing in the torchlight when he turned to look.

It probably even accounted for the dove Pyvic would have sworn was following them as they marched through the city. Or the sense that the prisoners (the two conscious ones, anyway), despite their downtrodden stares and helpless eyes, somehow seemed just a bit too smug, considering the circumstances.

He would kick himself about that later.

Eight

THE AIRSHIP THAT CARRIED THEM UP TO THE SPIRE WAS A SMALL passenger model, not one of the massive cargo lifters onto which Loch and Kail had smuggled themselves last time. Instead of huddling in a crate, Loch stood serenely on the deck, watching the pre-dawn world recede below. Invisible, of course, and under strict orders to move slowly if she had to move at all.

The ship's crew was…wrong. Loch couldn't place it, but they all moved with downcast eyes and didn't speak as they went about their tasks. She suspected that they were Silestin's personal men, along to ensure a smooth ride.

Loch hadn't seen many airships, except for the battleships during the war, and her experience then had mostly involved looking at the flag, diving for cover, and hoping that the ship had exhausted its magical flamecannons and could only drop grapeshot on them as it flew overhead. The passenger carrier had no guns that Loch could see.

It wasn't shaped like a real ship. Overhead, an enormous elliptical balloon contained a trapped wind-daemon. The deck was a big wooden oval with railings all around and a single control station with levers and multicolored crystals. There were a few chairs, but most people simply clung to handrails. There was complicated-looking rigging knotted all over the place.

Off to either side of the main ship's body, six great sailwings were tucked in close at the moment, ready to be extended to make a tight turn. Below the deck, instead of crew quarters and cargo holds, there was only a great ridge of wood hanging down to stabilize the deck.

Tern and Icy were seated, as their shackles made it hard for them to hold the handrails. They were being diligently guarded by Dairy, Kail, and Desidora, the last of whom wasn't even wearing a guard's uniform. No one had given the aura-manipulating death priestess a second glance, despite her alabaster skin and her pitch-black robes.

Ululenia was a dove perched on the rigging. Hessler could be anywhere, but he was definitely near enough to keep watch on Loch. He'd gone on at length about how difficult it was to keep someone else invisible when they were moving around.

She'd gotten all of them together, and all nine of them were on their way up to the Spire. And the woman who'd blown her cover last time was shackled and gagged in the seat next to Tern and Icy.

"I had no idea how dangerous these things were," Hessler's voice hissed in her ear.

Loch smiled and stared out over the edge some more. With his little whisper trick, the illusionist could make his voice appear right inside Loch's ear.

"Do you have any idea how much energy this ship has devoted to warding the wind-daemon inside that balloon?

And how much more is devoted to making sure the balloon doesn't tear open on a passing tree branch?"

Loch sighed quietly.

"Ancients be damned, this thing is a *deathtrap*. I don't understand how they can—careful, careful, when you fidget like that, it's hard to keep the invisibility field on you. If you could hold still, that would be perfect."

He kept talking. Loch stopped listening. Overhead, the tiny sliver of sky not filled by the balloon began to be filled with the underside of Heaven's Spire. The violet *lapiscaela* had already begun to glow as the sunrise hit them high overhead.

Just a few minutes more, Loch thought, and they'd be there. Everything was going perfectly.

"Not long now!" Archvoyant Silestin declared to the crowd at the airdock as the passenger ship approached. "You can run, and you can hide, but eventually the law catches up with you!"

The open-air dock was connected to an enormous hangar where the ships were stowed, their wind-daemons banished when not in use. It was a cold, bright morning. Silestin wore his military uniform. The crowd included several other Voyants, a few news writers, and a number of general hangers-on.

Beside him, Warden Orris made as though to say something, but Silestin quieted him with a casual gesture.

"What do you plan to say to them, Archvoyant?" one of the writers asked.

Silestin chuckled. "I thought I'd just tell them, 'Nice try.'" The crowd laughed.

"Odd," said Ambassador Bi'ul, staring down at the ship.

"What's that, Ambassador?" Silestin asked, glancing at the crowd of onlookers and giving an amused shrug.

The ambassador kept looking at the approaching ship. "As I examined the supple threads that knit your world into the fabric in which your souls exist, I sensed an... unusual... pattern. Something very old, but unfamiliar to me, though—"

"Loch's got a death priestess," Orris chimed in. "I bet that's it."

"I'm sure," Silestin said firmly, "that it's nothing our boys on the ship can't handle."

Just a little longer, Pyvic thought, and it would be over. Everything was going perfectly, except for the nagging feeling in his gut whenever he looked at the crew.

He'd taken the trip up to the Spire dozens of times, and something with the crew wasn't right. He'd worked a case once involving a crazed alchemist. When he'd finally caught the bastard, Pyvic had had the feeling that the man wasn't really there—that when he stared at the man, there was something he wasn't seeing, something pulling the strings. The alchemist had died rather than surrender, and Pyvic had never worked up the energy to regret it.

The airship crew, to a man, reminded him of that alchemist.

He watched the Spire draw closer. They were almost directly under the great disc of glowing violet that formed the underbelly of the city. Pyvic didn't know why the helmsmen always took them up that way—he'd heard the ship had to come up inside the magical field that protected the city from storms, but a magical field with a great big hole in the bottom didn't make much sense.

And then one of the guards, the young one who hadn't talked much, cleared his throat nervously and asked, "Are we going to hit the glowing things on the city?"

Pyvic would've sworn he saw one of the other guards drop his head and sigh, would have sworn that he *heard* another sigh coming from off to his left, though there was no one over there.

"Of course not," one of the crewmen said in a low rusty voice with a coiled snarl lurking at the edges.

The other crewmen stopped what they were doing and turned to the guards in unison. "A trooper from Ros-Oanki would know that," another one added.

The first crewman poked the young guard hard in the chest. "Who are you?"

Pyvic looked at the other two guards, blinking as he saw them by daylight. The Urujar's armor didn't fit right, and the... the third one was somehow hard to focus on, but it was almost like he wasn't even wearing armor... and that warhammer certainly wasn't standard issue.

"Hell, how could you *not* know who I am?" the Urujar guard demanded indignantly. "Your mother was shouting my name *all night long!*" Then he cold-cocked the man with a right cross to the jaw. "Loch! Plan B!"

The nineteen crewmen had their swords out before the twentieth had hit the deck, and they drew with the same motion and snarled with the same voice. The helmsman was trying very hard to ignore everyone, the guards themselves were leaping into motion, and the prisoners....

The Imperial slid out of his shackles and leaped into the rigging as blades crashed down onto the chair where he'd been sitting. Pyvic shouted, "Wait, we need them alive!" while draw-ing his blade, and then the mousy woman in the brown dress with all the pockets lifted her shackled arms, smiled at Pyvic, and touched one of the metal studs on the shackle chains.

A dart hissed against Pyvic's neck, and he had time to swear before the world went dark.

"Something is happening," Bi'ul said, his dry voice cutting through the murmurs of the crowd.

"I don't see how you could tell," Orris huffed. "All we can see is the balloon."

"Do you make a habit out of proclaiming things in ignorance?" Bi'ul asked. He sounded genuinely curious. "Is misplaced confidence sufficient to advance an otherwise unskilled mortal into a position of comfort, or is it simply a behavioral flaw on your part?"

"I'm sure everything is fine," Orris declared. "You may not know Archvoyant Silestin like I do, but he runs a pretty tight ship!"

"Be quiet, Orris," Silestin said, glancing at the crowd. The other Voyants were giving him speculative looks. "Let's all move back a bit. Don't want to crowd the ship when it lands."

As the smooth ride went all to hell, Loch darted out of the safety of her invisibility field, grabbed a crewman from behind as he cocked his arm back to hurl a knife at Dairy, looped her other arm between her legs, and unceremoniously heaved him over the railing.

Tern had unsnapped her false shackles and had darted behind Desidora, who was holding four men at bay with great sweeps of Ghylspwr. Dairy whipped out a truncheon, but Kail had thankfully gotten between the boy and any real harm, and was parrying like a madman.

Most airship crews had little combat training, but everyone except the helmsman was slashing and stabbing with skill. Every man had his teeth pulled back in the same vicious snarl, and every man's eyes were dead and cold. It was as if they were wearing masks.

As Loch grabbed her sword from Pyvic's unconscious body, one of the men darted in too close, and Ghylspwr smashed the blade down, arced around in a complete circle that sent Desidora leaping into the air with its sheer momentum, and then crashed down on the thug's head with a cry of *"Kutesosh gajair'is!"* The thug went down—*straight* down, through the deck into the open air below, tearing a good-sized hole in the planks in the process.

"Over the side, not through the damn hull!" Loch shouted. A half-dozen of the crew caught sight of her and moved her way, and she knocked aside one slash, kicked one of them in the shins, leaped aside, and brought her saber down on a line attached to the sailwings. With a horrific creak and tear of metal, the wing snapped out. A coil of rope whipped out taut in one swift motion, clotheslining two of the men and sending them overboard. On the other end of the ship, the helmsman screamed.

A flash of movement caught Loch's eye as the ship heaved to the side and everyone stumbled. Off the starboard bow, four crewmen flew majestically over the railing like ocean spray. Glancing back, Loch saw Desidora with Ghylspwr held in a truly impressive follow-through pose. In the rigging overhead, Icy leaped from rope to rope while crewmen hurled knives at him. One missed him by a handbreadth and continued on its upward path to strike the balloon, only to bounce off harmlessly.

Another crewman lunged in, face still fixed with that same inhuman snarl, and Loch parried the stab, moved in, and hammered the man's arm against the rail, sending the sword flying away. As he stumbled, Loch grabbed his collar, moved in for a throw...

"Loch."

And looking at his face again, past the rictus snarl and the dead eyes, Loch saw Jeridan, the gambler who'd fixed Kail up with supplies in the Cleaners.

"Help me." It was barely a whisper. His face was still snarling, but something warred behind his eyes. Jeridan had never been a fighter. He'd barely known one end of a sword from the other.

Loch hesitated, and Jeridan broke her grip and grabbed for her sword. She punched him in the face and swept his legs out from under him, sending him crashing to the deck. "What the hell happened?"

Jeridan, the man with a glass jaw and a tendency to cry when hit, pushed himself back to his feet. "Loch, help me. I can't... I can't..." He was looking at her sword. "Please."

He lunged, as much at the blade as her, and she spun aside and hilt-punched him behind the ear. "No. Tell me what happened, and we'll—"

Behind Kail, Dairy drew back his truncheon and hurled it. It arced past Kail, threaded a maze of rigging without touching a single rope, and slammed into the helmsman's forehead. He reeled drunkenly and then collapsed across the control panel, pushing countless levers and crystals as he slid to the ground.

The ship gave a terrible wrenching, creaking, cracking, tearing noise that started in the deck and worked its way through Loch's body like the bellow of an ox suddenly realizing that it outweighed the angry farmer by at least half a ton.

The balloon flickered with blue light, and several of the sailwings leapt into motion. Two wings sprang out, one began to extend and retract repeatedly, and one wrenched backward and tore itself from the ship in a crashing explosion of splinters, to sweep across the deck in an enormous arc of wood and canvas.

Loch regained her senses to find herself prone on the deck, her saber quite some ways away and her entire left side sore. There were a few crewmen still on deck, and Hessler was suddenly visible, lying unconscious in a heap by the railing.

Everyone was on the ground, or at least on their knees. Loch tried to get up, failed, and thought she'd taken a shot to the head before realizing that the ship was swinging with wild movements while still moving forward and skyward.

Jeridan clung to the rigging, hanging over empty space. "Free." And with the effort of a man lifting a mountain, he let go.

"No! Damn it!" Loch fought her way to her knees, but he was already gone, a speck far below.

"Sorry!" Dairy called from across the deck. "I didn't mean—"

Loch got to her feet. "You're doing fine. *Don't throw anything else!*" A flash of movement from the corner of her eye was followed by a stunning pain that sent her into the railing. She dived sideways as a boot splintered the wood of the railing where she'd lain.

"Mmrff rrmrrmm," Jyelle growled, and then tore the gag from her mouth and tossed it to the deck, next to the unlocked shackles and the key she'd gotten from Pyvic's unconscious body. "This time, *Captain,* I'll see you dead."

The crowd roared as the passenger ship reared up over the dock like an ancient dragon come to life. The balloon missed the dock itself by no more than a few feet, sailwings lashing the air, and one whipping rope sent a section of planking whizzing past Silestin's head.

On the torn and splintered remains of the deck, men and women were locked in combat. Silestin caught a glimpse of two Urujar women fighting near the railing, and then the ship whooshed over his head and reeled drunkenly over the city with sawdust falling behind it. In the bright morning air of Heaven's Spire, shouts erupted in the streets.

For a moment, the crowd was silent. Silestin gave them a quick look.

Then he turned to Orris and, in a shocked and angry voice, demanded, "Warden, just what the hell was that?"

Kail was still parrying. Desidora was driving most of the remaining crew back on their heels with great sweeping strikes. Dairy was making his way to Hessler, either incredibly lucky or incredibly skilled at avoiding the lashing ropes and flying debris over at that end of the ship. Tern's plate, at the moment, was mostly empty.

"Um, Loch?" Tern called. "If we pass over the city, that's going to negatively impact the plan!"

"Little busy!" called Loch, who was engaged in an enthusiastic knife-fight with Jyelle. "Ever flown a ship?"

"I'm sure it's like driving a wagon!" Tern reached into a pocket and withdrew a vial of purple powder. She tore the stopper free with her teeth and flung the contents past Kail into a crewman's snarling face, and the man yelled and clutched at his eyes until Kail kicked him over the edge.

Tern had never driven a wagon, either, but since Loch was involved in a knife fight, Tern was ready to get outside her comfort zone.

Carefully pulling herself along the railing with a few nasty surprises at the ready in case the few remaining crewmen came her way, Tern made her way over to the helm. She pushed the unconscious navigator aside and studied the helm.

The six levers obviously corresponded to the sailwings, and she was reasonably certain that the large crystal surrounded by a bunch of smaller crystals (many of them blinking red, which was almost never good) had something to do with the big balloon.

"What do you want me to make it do?" Tern looked over. Loch and Jyelle were doing some kind of intricate dance of death, their blades moving faster than Tern's eyes could follow as the two women circled the rubble-strewn deck. Tern wished she'd learned something about knife-fighting, but she was really good at cracking safes, and safes didn't usually stab you in the stomach when you botched the tumblers.

"Land!" Loch shouted, and then stumbled on one of the holes Ghylspwr had made in the deck and barely ducked under a slash that would have taken out an eye. The two women collapsed into a tangle of arms and legs and knives, and Tern, who really didn't want to even *think* about the logistics of adding wrestling into the knife-fight equation, went back to consulting the helm.

Landing, landing, landing. Well, if her limited grasp of Ancient was any good, that panel marked *"Oankilar"* probably had something to do with descending, but there were several buttons in that area, and there was probably some all-important procedure to follow with—

"Die!" Tern looked up to see one of the crewmen glaring at her, arm raised to throw a knife. Before she could do anything, he hurled it at her, and then a flash of gold obscured her vision, and all at once Icy was there, crouched in a coiled warrior's pose after leaping from the rigging, one arm flung to the heavens.

"Icy!" Tern cried. "No!"

"There is no need for apprehension," Icy said calmly. "I knocked the blade aside harmlessly." The crewman snarled and went off to find greener pastures.

"No!" Tern grabbed Icy's shoulder and pointed up. "What I was *going* to say was, 'Icy, no, you knocked the knife straight up, and it appears to have torn a hole in the balloon overhead, and now the wind-daemon is trying to claw its way out!'"

Icy looked up at the balloon, where a smoky, mustard-yellow tentacle with a dozen barbed claws was wriggling out of a tiny tear. "Ah. Did Loch not instruct you to land the airship?"

"I'll get right on it."

As the ship's balloon distended, Bi'ul sniffed the air, then smiled. "Wind-daemon. Lovely bouquet."

"Archvoyant, you can't blame me for this!" Orris insisted. "I left before they *found* her! I wasn't even *there!*"

"All I know," Silestin said ominously, "is that this was your chance to put everything right, Orris, and now one of the Republic's ships is coming apart at the seams. I don't know what to say. I'm beginning to think the Skilled were wrong to put you and Justicar Pyvic on that task force. "

"It gains substance as it interacts with the elements of this little world," said Bi'ul, and made a face. "Pity. They taste so much better when fresh."

The news writers started scribbling.

They were losing altitude now, either because of what Tern had done or because the damn wind-daemon was trying to claw its way to freedom. As Loch circled, breathing hard and hoping Jyelle was feeling the small cuts on her arms and side as much as Loch was feeling the ones on her leg and shoulder, she saw a church steeple rise into view ahead.

"Down!" Loch shouted, rolling away from Jyelle's slash just as the shuddering impact knocked everyone off their feet.

The entire starboard railing tore away in a series of ear-splitting cracks. The helmsman, lucky unconscious bastard that he was, landed gently on a rooftop. One of the crew, not quite so lucky, had a much longer fall and a much harder landing. Loch, flung to the port railing hard enough to bruise a rib, got a quick look ahead and saw the rim approaching. "Everyone get ready to jump ship!"

"Leaving so soon?" Jyelle called from behind her, and Loch scrambled to her feet, barely knocking aside a wicked slash and diving away, her own knife coming back in a wide sweep to keep Jyelle at bay. "You wanted to get on this ship! Why don't you stay awhile?"

Jyelle lunged in again, her off-hand hidden, which could mean only one thing. Loch parried the first stab and desperately jumped away from the slash from the second knife Jyelle had picked up.

Now the advantage was wholly Jyelle's, and Loch gave ground. The airship hit another building and lost most of its aft section. Loch dropped her knife and clung to a flailing rope as the deck slid out from under her, and she felt open air yawning sickeningly beneath her dangling legs.

"Reached the end of your rope, Loch?" Jyelle stood on the edge of the shattered planking, her knives raised to slash at the rope Loch clung to, eyes wild and smile vicious. "I figure cutting this rope is a bit like you leaving me—"

"Jyelle!" Loch ignored the jagged pain of the knife cuts and the dull ache of battered muscle as she hauled herself up hand over hand.

"What is it, Loch? Do you want to plead for your miserable life?" Jyelle grabbed the rope, and raised the other knife to start sawing. "Do you want to beg me for mercy?"

"Well, I *was* going to warn you about the wind-daemon," Loch muttered as mustard-yellow claws closed around Jyelle, "if you'd let me get a word in edgewise." She grabbed the shattered decking, ignoring the jabs of splinters, and pulled herself up. Overhead, Jyelle disappeared into the writhing mass of coiled tentacles billowing out of the now-large hole in the balloon.

A quick backward glance revealed that the fall might not kill anyone from this height. A quick forward glance revealed a lot of open sky ahead. *"Everybody out, now!"*

An ash-white eagle the size of a draft horse flapped ponderously away, Dairy clutched in one claw and Hessler in the other. Icy leapt from the ship, Tern hugging his back—he landed with limbs splayed on the side of a brick building, slid down a bit, and then snagged a ledge. Loch saw Desidora and Kail leap from the side as well, nodded in swift satisfaction, and then saw the prone form of Pyvic lying alone on the deck.

It took precious seconds, but the man was only trying to do his job, Loch thought as she slung him over her shoulder, staggered to the railing, and flung herself and Pyvic overboard.

She tried to roll as best she could, and this section of Heaven's Spire appeared to be a gentle garden area, because she hit a hedge, fortunately, and then a tree, unfortunately.

The morning sky whirled dizzily overhead, but she was alive. Judging by the nearby groans, so was Kail. Loch blinked the dizziness away and saw Desidora standing in the middle of a large impact crater, apparently unharmed—she didn't know exactly how, but she guessed it had something to do with the hammer. The white eagle crash-landed awkwardly on a lawn, dumping Dairy and Hessler, and then turned in a flash of light into a beautiful white mare with a glowing horn and some grass stains.

All nine, alive and evidently unharmed. Loch glanced over at Pyvic, saw that he was still breathing.

She got to her feet and looked at the rim, all of twenty feet away. Beyond it, the wind-daemon writhed in the balloon like three cats in a potato sack, dragging the shattered remains of the ship in its wake. A trio of Republic warships was already in the air, chasing the runaway daemon.

"Any landing you can walk away from," Loch said. "Come on."

In the alley near Tratter Square, an ambitious pickpocket looked through the wreckage of crates.

Jyelle had disappeared—some said captured, some said killed. Some said she'd beaten that other Urujar woman she'd had the guild hunting, and some said the other Urujar had beaten her.

The only thing anyone knew for sure was that whatever had happened had happened in Tratter Square.

And to the ambitious pickpocket, that meant power. He sifted through the rotten cloth of a crate, then moved on, his fingers gliding easily over everything.

Knowledge was power. If he found Jyelle dead, he'd be the first to bring the news to one of the new contenders. He examined scuff marks in the dried mud, frowned, and looked at the wall.

Magic was power. If the fight had been frantic, Jyelle or the other Urujar might have dropped something he could sell... or even use himself. He tensed as a tiny sound whispered through the alley. He'd lived his whole life trusting his senses without doubt or hesitation. A small pile of crates had just shifted slightly.

Gratitude was power. If Jyelle had been hurt, even gotten cracked over the head and lost in the darkness, and he found her, she'd owe him a favor. He crept to the pile of crates. Underneath, he could see something—not a person, but darkness deeper than seemed natural in the morning light.

"Jyelle?" he asked quietly. "That you?"

There was a small, soft groan, and the crates shifted again. He pulled some of the wreckage aside. "I knew you'd have something up your sleeve, ma'am," he said, staring at the inky blackness underneath.

The knife went straight through his right eye.

Heaven's Spire wasn't a real city at all, Tern decided. The sound was all wrong.

They'd gotten out of the park quickly, Ululenia staggering (and back in human form, but so dazed that her horn was showing) and Hessler slung over Icy's shoulder. They'd been far away by the time the local guard had reached the scene.

Heaven's Spire had a market district, a residential district, and taverns and inns and palaces (twelve of them, one for each Voyant, arranged around the city). If you saw a picture of it, you might not even realize that it was floating in the heavens. But the ground was paved with a shiny gray material. It was *shaped* like flagstones, but the texture was different—more slick, like crystal or hematite. With every step, Tern's steel-toed boots made a dull *click-thump* instead of the normal *clop-clop* of boots on cobblestones or the even more normal *clop-shlup* of boots on cobblestones that hadn't been replaced in years and had a lot of mud squelching out from between them.

There were merchants hawking their wares, but no street sweepers pushing their brooms and banging pots for tips. There were people shopping in the streets, but no beggars calling for charity. Tern heard the clink of money changing hands and the creak of small wagons, but couldn't smell the stink of the slaughterhouse or the tannery.

It was a city that started at "gentry" and went up from there.

Tern decided that she hated the place.

"The air," Desidora said. "It's not... real. It is refined by magic somehow." She didn't have the weird death priestess aura on—her hair was still red, and her dress was still green.

"Kutesosh gajair'is?"

"I'm not certain, but it is very old."

"We're clear ahead," Kail reported, limping back from the corner of the alley they had paused in. "This the right way?"

"Will they not find us in this hedged garden?" Ululenia asked, still shaky.

"It's not much further." Loch pushed off from the alley wall and motioned for them to go.

"We're going to be easy to track," Kail noted, "if things keep blooming wherever the unicorn walks."

Ululenia glanced back into the alley, where a barrel she had leaned against had put forth small branches and buds. "Sorry." She gestured, and the buds bloomed into green leaves that rapidly turned golden, then red, and then fell off.

"Great," said Kail. "We're fine, then, unless Dairy here asks someone a question or throws his truncheon again and turns off all the magic in the city." He slung Hessler over one shoulder and followed Loch out of the alley.

"I'm really sorry, Mister Kail!" Dairy yelped, darting after him.

"You know," Tern said to Icy as they started moving again, "I think I figured out what happened to turn off the shield on the balloon."

"You possess a curious mind," Icy responded, "capable of cutting to the heart of puzzling matters. It is an admirable trait."

"See, the balloon was protected by a magical shield to stop things like, well, you deflecting a knife up and tearing it. In order for that shield to be taken offline, someone would have to override safety procedures. Then they would have to disengage the shield matrix maintenance protocols from the daemon-summoning system, which is a bitch and a half, since the whole point is to have the shield up *whenever* the daemon is summoned. *Then* they would have had to reroute the shield matrix energy to an alternate subsystem!'"

"I understand," said Icy, "that what you are saying is a matter of critical import to you."

"I am saying," said Tern, "that the odds of that happening by accident are…very small."

"The helmsman was unconscious," Icy said. "If the probability of such an event occurring is greater than zero, it must simply be the result of chance."

"I don't know." Tern frowned and looked at Dairy. "It just seems wrong."

They came through the wagon-street, darted through another alley, and came out near the rim again. Loch motioned, and they darted across the broad circumference street and down a side road between a palace and an old museum.

After a block or so, they stopped at a side-gate leading into the palace's courtyard. "Loch?" Tern asked. "You need me to—"

"We're good," Kail said. Loch leaned in close to the gate and said something Tern couldn't make out. The gate opened. "Okay, everyone inside."

They were moving quickly, so there wasn't much time to gawk, but they made their way through a good-sized garden, across a broad and well-maintained lawn, and finally to one of the side-doors of the palace. Loch moved in and said something again, and the door opened to her touch.

Tern was becoming curious about the word Loch was using. That kind of thing could be handy.

Again, Kail gestured for them to get moving, and everyone was quickly inside. Inside turned out to be a gorgeous room with marble floors and gold scrollwork and expensive paintings. Tern looked at an Imperial vase and guessed it to be from the Liu dynasty, which would be nearly enough for Tern to retire on. She glanced at Icy, who caught her stare and nodded.

"We're here," Loch finally said, looking around the room. Tern had expected her voice to hold a triumphant edge, but instead she sounded resigned.

"This is our contact?" Tern asked.

"Gosh!" said Dairy.

"Besyn larveth'is?"

"Looks like," Desidora murmured.

"Put Hessler on one of the couches," Loch said. "I'll bring back the owner."

A side door blew in off its hinges, and Tern spun to see gem-studded security golems the size of ogres, holding enormous crystal swords. "Unnecessary," came a voice from behind the golems. "Unluckily for you, the security isn't *quite* as poor as it appears."

The crystal swords shimmered with scarlet light, and the golems stepped forward.

Nine

"**T**ODAY'S DISCUSSION: SECURITY," INTONED THE DRAGON IN the puppet show the next morning. "With today's debacle, the Republic has lost an airship complete with wind-daemon, and three dangerous prisoners have escaped justice."

"If I could just start," the manticore butted in, knocking the dragon aside as the crowd laughed, "I think *debacle* is a very loaded term. We've got people assigned to their jobs, and they're doing their jobs, and it's very presumptuous to judge how they're doing."

"Well, any time you lose a ship," suggested the griffon, "you have to wonder whether things are being done prop—"

"Silence!" steamed the dragon, driving the griffon back with alchemical flames, and the crowd applauded. "We're here for a civilized discussion!"

"But I think that this event, when taken within the context of the earlier escape, points to an overall lack of performance by the Learned," shouted the griffon from the edge of the stage, hiding from the flames.

"Wait, now, you can't play politics with national security!" The manticore jumped onto the griffon, its stinger flashing, and the griffon howled and tried to buck it off. "And I'll have you know that the leader of the task force, a justicar with a shady past and a reputation for playing loose with the rules, was appointed by the *Skilled*. They're the ones who should be answering for this."

"But that isn't true!" cried the griffon. "Justicar Pyvic has an excellent reputation and—"

"Let's not get off topic!" the dragon proclaimed, belching a puff of fire that stopped both of the other puppets in their tracks. It raised a claw toward the manticore, and the griffon took the opportunity to run to the other side of the stage. The crowd laughed derisively. "What do you have to say about Warden Orris's resignation yesterday?"

"Totally unrelated," the manticore said promptly, "and if you listen to what he has to say, you'll know that." The manticore yanked on a leash, and a goat puppet was reluctantly dragged onto the stage. The crowd hooted.

"...proud of what we've accomplished," said the goat in the whiny whistling voice that signified a cheap recording crystal, "but now is... and now I intend to spend more time with my family. I know that others will continue this important work." The goat broke off as the manticore's jaws clamped down on it and tore off its head. The manticore then snatched up the body and shook it violently, throwing small candies out into the crowd.

"There you have it!" declared the manticore with a burp.

"But the timing," protested the griffon, only to be knocked down by the manticore's giant bat-wings.

"I honestly don't know why we're even having this discussion!" boomed the manticore. "This is the Skilled

Party's fault for putting this Pyvic fellow in charge, and if you want to play the partisan blame game, Warden Orris has already resigned. Why can't you people let a good man retire in peace?"

"Strong words!" boomed the dragon. "We'll keep you informed of any updates on this fast-breaking story!" It threw more candy out to the crowd while intoning the ritual words. "Remember, everyone, *it's your republic!*"

"Stay informed!"

"You're clever," said the man behind the golems, "and have gone to a lot of trouble. I appreciate that. Just a few years back, that pass phrase would have gotten you inside undetected. Sadly for you, the inner wards on my household were upgraded recently. Now, I could order my large metal friends to spray your liquefied organs across this very nice sitting room... or you could tell me where you learned the word."

"From my father," said Loch, stepping to the front of the group and staring past the golems to the man behind them. "He told me on my thirteenth birthday, in case I ever needed to speak with his friend, Lord Cevirt."

"Kill," said the man, and the golems clanked forward, swords raised.

"What?" shouted Tern.

"I'm just a university student!" cried Hessler weakly from the couch.

"It's the truth," said Loch, voice level as the golems advanced.

"I very much doubt that," said the man, "since I *am* Voyant Cevirt, and I only told one man that phrase. And his daughter is a beautiful blind girl who does not much resemble you."

The golem nearest Loch lifted its sword overhead. Loch could see herself reflected in the shining crystal of the blade. She didn't move, but instead asked, "And his other daughter?"

"Hold."

The golems froze in place.

From around them stepped a small man, Urujar in complexion with closely cropped hair. He was wearing the traditional robes of the Voyancy, which snapped around him as he came past the golems to Loch.

"My friend's *other* daughter," said Voyant Cevirt, "is dead."

Loch smiled crookedly. "I very much doubt that."

It was the smile that convinced him. He stepped back, his eyes wide, then moved in with a darting birdlike movement. "Isa?" he asked softly, looking at her as though searching. "*Aitha,* is that you?"

"Uncle," said Loch, "I need your help."

"Anything!" he cried, and lunged forward to pull her into a hug. "Isa, you're alive! You don't know how I've.... Have you talked with Naria yet? We can set you up with—"

Loch pushed him back gently. "Uncle, I need a way into Archvoyant Silestin's palace," she said flatly, "and access to your private vault and security room."

Cevirt blinked.

"Mister Hessler?" said Dairy. "Isn't the contact supposed to know he's the contact?"

"I don't know, kid. I'm still picking up the fine points of all this."

"Patrol," Cevirt called back over his shoulder, "standard formation. Recognize guests." The golems clanked off, swords sliding back into sheaths, and Cevirt looked past Loch. "I need to speak with Isa in private for a moment. There's a small bar in the next room. Please make yourselves comfortable."

He walked off without another word. After a moment, Loch followed.

She followed him to a much smaller room, where he closed the door after her, pressed a glowing red crystal on his desk, which hummed and turned green. He gestured at a chair, and she sat.

"I forced an inquiry," he said, sitting. His arms rested on the desk, and his fingers were steepled, the index fingers tapping idly.

"So I gathered," said Loch.

"They determined that you deserted." The fingers tapped faster. "I refused to believe it."

"That was awfully nice of you."

"I refused to believe," he continued, "that Isafesira de Lochenville, who had snuck off to join the army against her father's wishes, would desert in the middle of a war."

"So you pulled a few strings."

"I protected your family name!" His palms slammed down on the table. "Your father and mother were dead! Your sister was blind and orphaned and didn't need her older sister's reputation as a deserter hanging around her neck! I assumed you had died," he grated, eyes flashing with anger, "and so, yes, *I pulled a few strings.*"

"And now," said Loch, "here I sit."

"You okay?" came the voice as the darkness faded to a gray, and then to vague shapes, and finally to Captain Melich's ugly and concerned face.

"No?" Pyvic tried. He sat up slowly, wincing as knives of pain stabbed through him. "No." He recognized the shabby drawing of a human body, complete with old graffiti, on the far wall by a shelf. "How'd I get to the justicars' infirmary?"

"By stretcher," Melich deadpanned, sitting down on the edge of the bed and poking at Pyvic's shoulder. Pyvic winced at the sudden pain, and Melich made a face and tightened a bandage. "We found you out cold in the grass near the border. Apparently when the wind-daemon tore the ship to shreds, bits and pieces landed everywhere. You got lucky." Melich squinted. "Real lucky."

"Wind-daemon?" Pyvic tried standing, caught his balance on the edge of the bed, and settled on leaning. "I thought there were magical protocols to stop them from getting loose."

"Not enough, apparently. It had to be abjured by a cadre of local priests."

"Oh, so it worked out fine, then." Pyvic let go of the bed and rolled out his shoulders. It hurt like a bitch, but at least the room had stopped spinning.

"Pretty much had to back a wagon up to the treasury and fill it up, though."

"I get the impression there's a report I should be reading."

"There's a report you should be *writing*, Pyvic." Melich lowered his voice. "What went wrong up there? The prisoners are gone. The only other survivor is a helmsman who was knocked out cold early on."

"Same thing happened to me," Pyvic said, and sighed. "My guess? We got played. Prisoner Loch wasn't Prisoner Loch. They used me to get up to Heaven's Spire, which is where they wanted to be the whole time."

Melich winced. "Might want to clean that up in the report."

"It's the truth." Pyvic shrugged, then winced. His shoulder was going to be sore for a while. "If Orris hadn't deserted, I'd have had an observer on the ground to confirm that it was Loch."

"So the entire hunt was a wash?" Melich asked.

"Well, I met a woman," Pyvic noted. "Where's my sword?"

Melich reached under the infirmary bed and handed Pyvic's sword over. "The woman isn't Loch, is it?"

"I wasn't sure at the time, but I wanted to feel her out. Anyway, she didn't look like..." Pyvic trailed off, sighed, and brought the sheathed sword up to gently knock himself on the head.

"She didn't look like the woman you arrested, thinking she was Loch, who was most likely set up just like you as part of the plan to get up to the Spire?" Melich finished innocently.

"I guess they *did* give you the captain's bars for a reason," Pyvic muttered. "By the way, how's the death-curse case going?"

"Jyrre closed it." Melich smiled wryly.

"Keep the politicians off me as long as you can," Pyvic said, hooking the sword scabbard onto his belt. "I've got to talk to the helmsman."

"You're going out like that?" Melich asked, and Pyvic hooked his fingers into his belt and looked at him flatly. "I'll do what I can."

"Thanks." Pyvic headed for the door, slowly but steadily. "And tell Jyrre good job."

The small bar turned out to have every drink Kail, Tern, and Icy combined had ever heard of.

"Nice place." Kail was behind the bar, pouring drinks. "Being a Voyant pays big. Hessler, ice?"

"For my head, yes," said the wizard from where he still lay on the couch. "For my drink, never."

"Should've figured you as neat. What can I get you, Dairy?"

Dairy looked up from Hessler. "The woman who found me as an orphan used to give me hot milk sweetened with a little honey, Mister Kail."

Kail pursed his lips. "I'll see what we've got."

"No alcohol for the boy," said Desidora.

"*Kun-kabynalti osu fuir'is,*" muttered Ghylspwr.

"Because he's *sixteen,*" Desidora insisted. "Kail, *you will not* give him alcohol. Do I make myself clear?" Her hair darkened perceptibly.

"You just *had* to play the death priestess card." Kail grunted. "Fine. Virgin for the kid."

"Virgin," said Ululenia, smiling dreamily, her horn shining brightly on her pale forehead. "Mmm." Dairy blushed.

"So," said Tern, sipping from a cocktail glass filled with something pink and fruity, "what's the deal with Loch and the Voyant?"

"Got me." Kail topped off an ale for himself, then sat back on a barstool. "I just pour the drinks."

"Dammit, Isa, give me something!" Cevirt stood and began to pace furiously. "Tell me your heartbreaking tale of being captured by Imperials and forced to serve in slavery until you heroically escaped!"

Loch nodded thoughtfully. "Wow, Uncle. That's pretty good. Guess the Voyancy keeps you sharp."

He turned and glared. "Always, *Aitha*. Give me something."

"Why?" Loch stood and faced him squarely. "So you can assuage your conscience?"

"Yes, dammit! I lied for you!"

"You lied to keep your record clean," Loch said evenly, "so there'd be no little blots on your acquaintances' record when you rode Silestin's coat-tails up to this nice palace."

The slap caught her hard on the cheek, snapped her head back.

"Do you have *any* idea, little girl, what it's like to be an Urujar Voyant?" Cevirt asked coldly. "To try to convince this proud old brotherhood that the color of my skin doesn't make me a fool? Do you know what I have to swallow to get myself invited to the meetings where the real decisions get made?"

"I gather," said Loch, "that it means falsifying records." Her cheek stung like hell. "The pay looks good, though."

"How *dare* you judge me? While you've been doing Gedesar-knows-what all these years, I've been getting schools built in poor provinces. I've gotten good sheriffs put in our towns, not the washed-up lordlings with enough power to beg a favor! I've got roads coming into Urujar towns that will bring them trade. Our people live better lives today because of what I do up here."

Loch stepped back, circling around the desk and looking at the rich room. "So I'm not supposed to believe that you sold your soul for a little comfort?"

He stared at her, eyes wide, and when he spoke, his voice was soft. "How could you ever believe that about me?"

Loch sat down in *his* chair, rested her arms on the desk, and steepled her fingers. "*Give me something*, Uncle."

He sagged as the breath went out of him. "I apologize."

"I got caught behind enemy lines," she said. "It took me a while to get back." He nodded, and she continued. "You were just trying to help Naria by covering it up."

"I was trying to protect your family name." Cevirt sighed raggedly. "I never thought...."

"You were sure you were right," Loch said, "that it hadn't happened the way the report guessed. You even checked with someone else before doing it, to make sure it wouldn't be taken amiss."

"Silestin suggested it himself, actually," said Cevirt. "He thought it unnecessary to add insult to injury, and—"

"And then he became Naria's ward, using Lochenville's resources to reach the Voyancy while keeping up the appearance of a progressive public figure," Loch finished.

Cevirt stepped back as though she'd slapped him, then sat down in the other chair. "Loch, he isn't like that."

"It's my inheritance." Loch's voice was even, not angry.

"Loch, do you know how powerful the Archvoyant is?"

"It's *mine*." Loch leaned forward. "I don't care if Naria gets the rest when she comes of age. I don't care if Silestin uses her and you as proof that the Republic is fair and equal while spending my money and taxing my people. I don't want all of it. I just want one thing."

Cevirt leapt to his feet again, came around the desk. "Gods, Loch, do you know what could *happen?*"

"Would it be worse than being declared a deserter?" Loch asked. "Worse than finding out that your family is dead, that your sister is being used as political currency?"

"Yes," Cevirt said, looking her square in the face. His eyes were full of things that probably kept him awake at night. "Yes, Isafesira, it would be." He sighed, looked away. "So be damn careful." Then he pulled her into a rough embrace.

"Thank you." Her eyes stung, and she squeezed them shut as she returned the hug. The first time he had hugged her had been when she was six years old, showing him how she could swing her wooden sword when he had come to Lochenville to visit her father. "Thank you, Uncle."

"You're foolish and headstrong, *Aitha,* and you never know when to walk away," he said hoarsely. "But if you mean to try now, you won't do it alone."

Then he stepped away, chuckling and clearing his throat. "So why don't you introduce me to this gang of thieves and murderers you've gotten mixed up with?"

Ten

TERN LISTENED.

After a moment, she sighed and stepped back from the *yvkefer*-plated vault door. Voyant Cevirt spun the dial through the proper combinations, and the vault door clicked open.

Icy poked his head out. "I was unable to detect the tumblers. Perhaps if I were in a meditative state—"

"Hang on, dammit." Tern shouldered Cevirt out of the way and looked at the door. "Wait. Crap. These aren't even tumblers. These are... I don't know *what* these are. Who in Byn-kodar's hell makes a vault without tumblers?"

"Nobody," said Desidora the death priestess cheerfully from the other corner of the room, "that I know of." She and Hessler were working on auras or something.

"Well, you *are* the one with working knowledge of Byn-kodar's hell," Tern muttered, glaring at the crystal lattice set behind the combination dial. "Let me see... Cevirt, mind if I pop the dial off? I can probably do that while the vault is open."

"Um..."

"Good, good."

Cevirt stepped back and watched the little lockpicker go to work. The only other person in the room was Kail, who appeared to have no responsibilities beyond getting drinks. "They're disassembling my vault," Cevirt murmured, smiling through gritted teeth.

"The captain really appreciates this," Kail said, handing him a beer. It had a lime in it. Cevirt had never told anyone about his favorite drink, and he looked over at Kail curiously. The younger man sipped his own beer absently while watching Hessler and Desidora.

"What about altering the aural-recognition ward through a low-level daemonic conjuration across the lattice?" Hessler asked. Sparkling lights arced between his splayed fingers, and he was squinting at the sparkles intently.

"Good idea!" said Desidora, rocking her weight from her heels to her toes and tossing her auburn locks. "The daemon would only have to remain stable for an instant to disintegrate the warding pattern!"

"...*disintegrate the warding pattern*," Tern muttered in a slightly too-chipper version of Desidora's voice, climbing back into the vault and tapping the inside of the vault door with what looked to Cevirt like a golden tuning fork. "*I am a death priestess,*" Tern's voice echoed out of the vault, "*but I'm bouncy and I have pretty hair....*"

Kail coughed into his beer.

"And if we have another ward ready to overlay the existing pattern...." Hessler said, still staring at his sparkles.

"We can replace it before the entire field collapses and sounds the alarm!" Desidora finished, giving Hessler an impulsive hug.

"*She did* not *just hug him,*" Tern muttered from inside the vault.

"I am certain that that is not the case." Icy poked his head out, glanced at Desidora and Hessler, and added, "And even if she did—"

"Shut up, Icy."

"Good team your captain picked out." Cevirt squeezed his lime into the beer, then took a sip.

"Best of the best," said Kail, smiling vaguely at Desidora as she disengaged from a flushed and stammering Hessler.

"It sort of sounded like they were going to summon a daemon inside my vault, Kail."

"Well, we're not wizards, Voyant. Who are we to say that it isn't some completely harmless magical term—"

"Kail?"

"Yes, Voyant?"

"Please stop snowing me."

"Yes, Voyant."

"I'm a much better liar than you are, and I hate to see it done badly."

"The captain really appreciates this, Voyant."

"That's immensely reassuring, Kail."

"Care for another beer? I can probably dig up another slice of lime."

"I'm sure you can," Cevirt said acidly. "They're *my* limes."

"We should prime the area with a harmonic diffusion mist," Hessler said.

"To slow the ward-incursion response." Desidora nodded. "I wonder if Tern has any powdered *yvkefer?* That would provide us with a larger window of opportunity to safely interrupt the ward."

A small pouch sailed over the vault's half-open door without comment and landed at Desidora's feet.

"She's such a dear," Desidora murmured as she picked up the bag. Cevirt took a couple of casual steps to see into the vault, and was able to confirm that Tern was making a terrible but hilarious face while tapping some sort of crystal against the walls.

"You've got an exceptional grasp of aural pattern manipulation," Hessler said earnestly, making the sparkles do some sort of dance between his fingers.

"It comes with the training." Desidora winked and gave Hessler a mischievous smile. "Before I turned to Byn-kodar, I was a love priestess of Tasheveth."

"That is *so* hot," Kail murmured.

Inside the vault, Cevirt caught the sound of Tern breaking her crystal against the wall, followed by a muttered curse.

Desidora tossed a pinch of silvery powder into the air over the vault door, and she and Hessler began a rapid chant. Cevirt took an involuntary step backward as the healthy tan bled from Desidora's skin, leaving flawless white behind. Her hair darkened to glossy black, as did her dress, and the pattern on the pouch she'd been holding, which Cevirt remembered as being horses in a meadow, took on a skull-and-spider motif.

A moment later, the crystalline lights in the ceiling shot sparks, flared with blinding intensity, and then went out. In the darkness, Cevirt saw only purple afterimages but heard a sudden loud crash.

After a few moments of blinking, he realized that there *was* still some light in the chamber. It came from Desidora and Hessler, who appeared to be frozen in a glowing blue nimbus of energy.

After another moment, Cevirt realized that the vault door had slammed shut.

"The captain *really* appreciates this, Voyant," said Kail, draining the last of his tankard.

"I think, Kail," said Cevirt, digging around in his pocket for the warding crystal that would let him free his god-daughter's friends, "that I *will* have another beer."

The summons had come from Archvoyant Silestin, but Justicar Pyvic had seen only his secretary so far. The two men stood in one of the airship hangars, Pyvic with his hands in his trouser pockets, the secretary shivering in the cold afternoon air.

"Did he say *when* he'd be here?" Pyvic asked after a moment. He had leads, and leads didn't generally get warmer while he sat around waiting.

"The Archvoyant is exceedingly busy in these difficult times," the secretary said crisply.

"Listen..." Pyvic paused. "I didn't get your name."

"No," said the secretary with a pleased, fussy little smile, "you didn't."

Pyvic waited. The secretary remained silent.

Pyvic shrugged and started to walk away.

"Wait!" cried the secretary behind him. "What are you doing? You can't just walk away from Archvoyant Silestin!"

Pyvic stopped, turned, and gave the secretary a hard smile. "If Archvoyant Silestin wants to show up late to yank my leash, he has that power. But if his secretary gives me lip, I've got better things to do than sit and wait."

"I would hate," the secretary said with a sniff, "to think that a justicar would be so short-tempered as to stalk off when his personal needs weren't made the highest priority."

"I would hate," Pyvic said evenly, "to include a mention of Silestin's secretary failing to provide information pertinent to my investigation in my formal report to the Voyancy."

The secretary bristled, then controlled himself with an effort and said, "Archvoyant Silestin is currently at an important meeting with the Eastern—"

"Eastern Mining Council, a large group of landed gentry with some nobles kept on a tight leash to give the illusion of tradition. We're waiting here because after Silestin gives away a long-term mining contract in exchange for political support in the coming election, he's on his way down earthside to give a speech at an Urujar school about the virtues of education and make the first throw in a local league game of *aelaciel.*" The secretary's eyes went wide as Pyvic continued. "After he makes nice with the locals, he's putting in the warding keystone at a nearby wizard's university and hearing what they have to offer to swing his vote on the conjuration referendum currently working its way through the Sub-Committee on Ethics and Magic." Pyvic smiled. "I'm aware of the Archvoyant's affairs. I didn't ask *where* he was. I asked *when* he'd bother to show up for the meeting *he* initiated."

"Well, Pyvic, it's hard to keep these things on a schedule," came a lazy drawl from behind him. Pyvic managed to avoid wincing as he turned around.

"Archvoyant Silestin," he said with a crisp nod. "Reporting as ordered."

"You play *suf-gesuf,* Justicar?" Silestin smiled. "You've got the face for it… if not the mouth."

"I've got an airship navigator who can tell me who fell off where, provided I can walk him through the town," Pyvic said. "I've got a diviner of Ael-meseth who thinks he can tell me which way the death priestess went, but I need to meet personally with priests of Jairytnef and Tasheveth to obtain clearance to request the rite. I've got people on the street to befriend, harass, or bribe. Right now, I'm doing none of those things."

"Sounds busy," Silestin observed. "Got to put in an effort, make them see that it wasn't your fault when everything went into Byn-kodar's teeth a few mornings back."

"If you'd wanted me off the case," Pyvic said politely, "I'd be sweeping floors by now."

Silestin laughed. "Again, Justicar, the face but not the mouth!" He stepped in. "Tricky to say, though, why you came out with a few bumps and bruises while all those other men died. Could make a man wonder."

"Not my problem," Pyvic said, and because he was being prodded, and because there were few things he hated more than being prodded, he added, "I'm not in politics. All that matters is whether the job gets done."

Silestin raised an eyebrow. "Be careful, Justicar. You lost my men."

"Orris lost your men, Archvoyant."

"I'm putting additional forces on this," Silestin said smoothly, ignoring Pyvic's last remark. "Unofficially, of course. This is still your case."

"Unofficially in this case meaning that you're not obtaining formal clearances?" Pyvic asked, and then saw anger flash in Silestin's eyes.

"Pushing, Pyvic. You want to report it, you'll wish you'd stayed on the ship with that wind-daemon tearing loose." Silestin turned away. "They won't be in your way. Keep me informed of your progress. I'll let you know if they find anything."

Pyvic remained silent as Silestin stalked off to his personal airship. The Archvoyant turned at the end with a wolfish look that had even Pyvic nervous until he realized that it wasn't aimed at him.

"And Elkinsair," Silestin added, carefully enunciating the name, "don't anger my justicar needlessly."

Then the Archvoyant hiked up the gangplank and shook hands with the captain, and Pyvic stalked out of the hangar to get back to work.

In the one brief glance he spared Elkinsair, the little secretary looked furious.

Loch and the others gathered in the enormous waiting room. Kail was behind the bar again. Ululenia was in horse form—the waiting room was big enough, and she claimed that it was relaxing—munching on carrots that Dairy fed to her while Hessler scowled from a couch. Icy was seated cross-legged on the carpet, and Desidora had an entire sofa to herself, with Ghylspwr resting on one of the pillows. Cevirt sat on one of his barstools, still looking somewhat bemused as he took them all in.

Loch stood behind the couch, arms folded, a glass of red wine on a pedestal nearby, and scowled at Tern, who was standing at the center of everyone's attention, save possibly Ululenia, who was whickering and nudging Dairy.

"So," said Tern finally after finishing her fruity drink, "not much from what passes for the guild up here about the general security. Nobody's been able to bribe his guards."

"There's *always* a guard you can bribe," Kail said.

"I know, right?" Tern tried to sip her drink, looked down, and blinked at the empty glass. "But that's what everyone said. Totally unbribable. And beyond normal guards, Silestin has his Blades—trained assassins and bodyguards."

"I've heard rumors of those who cause trouble for Silestin dying under mysterious circumstances." Cevirt shook his head. "I assumed it was the usual hyperbole."

"So we avoid the Blades." Loch nodded. "What about the vault?"

"I have mixed news."

"Like good and bad?" Kail asked, pouring himself a drink.

"Like bad, *very* bad, *hell no,* and maybe," Tern clarified.

"Desidora and I were ensnared in an extremely uncomfortable warding field," Hessler groused.

"See?" Tern smiled. "Not *all* bad."

"Excellent team spirit, *Aitha*," Cevirt said, sipping his drink.

Loch gestured to Tern. "Go ahead."

"There are three layers of security around these palace vaults," Tern began, then stopped to sip her already-empty drink, which made the straw rattle noisily, until Kail got up to make her another one. "First, a ward on the door that checks for an aura specifically bestowed upon current Voyancy members. I'll let the death priestess field this one."

Desidora raised a fluted glass in Tern's direction. "Impossible to duplicate well enough to fool the ward."

Loch pursed her lips. "That's it?"

Desidora nodded. "It's simply too complex, even for a skilled aura manipulator."

Loch's eyes narrowed. "I got you *up* here, Priestess. The assumption was that you'd be useful."

Desidora paled slightly, which could have been taken as a sign of fear, except that her fluted glass also grew a couple of skull-faced gargoyles. "Try anyone else you like, Loch. No one can imitate that aura."

Loch glanced at Kail, who shrugged. "Okay. Tern, next?"

Tern blinked. "Honestly, I sort of thought that one was a show stopper."

Kail snorted. Dairy looked confused.

If the lake is frozen over, Ululenia broadcast to the room, *drink from the river that feeds it.*

"Exactly. I think." Loch pointed at Hessler. "What runs the thing that checks the aura?"

"The *thing?*" Hessler looked outraged. "To call a complex crystal lattice still functioning since the days of the Ancients a *thing* is—"

"The *Lapitemperum* in the middle of the city," Tern chimed in, coming to Hessler's rescue. "It's the big building where pretty much everything that relates to the Ancient systems is monitored. Even if they don't control it directly, they'll have the schematics that tell us where the... *thing*...that controls the auras is controlled from."

"I'll go in and take a look around," Kail suggested.

"They've *got* guards," Hessler said with the tiniest trace of a sneer.

"Which would make it *difficult,*" Kail said, swiping Hessler's drink with a quick movement and pouring him another one, "which, correct me if I'm wrong, Magister, is better than *impossible.*"

"Tern," Loch said, pointing back at the apple-cheeked woman who was sipping her fruity drink and watching the argument, "next?"

"Once we're inside the chamber," Tern said, "we need Archvoyant Silestin's *personal* aural signature to open the door."

Loch looked at Desidora. Desidora shook her head, and Loch lost it slightly. "Oh, *come on!*"

The personal aura of an individual is sacrosanct, Ululenia broadcast. *Even those with the gifts of the gods cannot duplicate such a thing.*

"Crap," Loch muttered. "Why the hell do we even *have* a death priestess, anyway?" Desidora's gown went flat black, as did the upholstery on her couch. The legs of the couch grew little clawed feet, and tiny silver spikes popped out in lines near the seams.

"Well, if you need a few zombies or something...." Tern ventured.

"Kutesosh gajair'is!"

"Just try it, big guy." Tern glared at the warhammer. "I've sold better artifacts than you for scrap metal."

"Ghyl, that's not necessary." Desidora laid an alabaster hand on the hammer.

"Kun-kabynalti osu fuir'is," Ghylspwr muttered.

"Can we crack the personal aura deal from the *Lapitemperum?"* Loch asked.

Hessler shook his head. "It's on the vault itself."

"Actually," Desidora said, "speaking of zombies...." Her skin was slowly regrowing its healthy color.

"I told you!" Tern shouted.

"Oh, for the love of...." Loch pinched the bridge of her nose. "What have you got for me, Priestess?"

"Voyant Cevirt," Desidora said, smiling, "you told me that Archvoyant Silestin is not the first of his family to bear the title?"

Cevirt nodded. "His great-grandfather, I believe, was also Archvoyant."

"Which just goes to show you what a sham the supposed democratic election process is," Hessler said to Dairy, "since all the Voyants and Archvoyants come from the noble families—"

"And all Archvoyants are buried in the mausoleum on the Archvoyant's palace grounds?" Desidora asked.

Cevirt nodded again, then paused. "You're not suggesting—"

"With the aura of the grandfather," Desidora said, smiling winsomely, "I can duplicate the aura of Silestin." She went just a touch pale and added, "Would *that* be suitably useful, Loch?"

Loch glanced at Ululenia. "Any chance of you getting the Archvoyant to open it himself for us?"

I would need to test his defenses, Ululenia broadcast, whickering and nosing Dairy.

"Do it. Desidora, visit the mausoleum and check the defenses. You're our backup plan." Desidora smiled, and Loch turned back to Tern. "Next?"

"Last order of business," Tern said, "is the lock itself, which uses a combination that changes every few seconds. It seems to use a code that relies on two very large prime numbers to...." She trailed off as Loch made a get-on-with-it gesture. "Okay, short version: I've got no way to crack it—"

"Kind of a pessimistic team you've built, here, Captain," Cevirt observed.

"—*unless* we can steal a matching encryption crystal," Tern finished. "Get me that crystal, and I think I can figure out the combination from that."

Loch nodded slowly. "Cevirt?"

He frowned. "It will be on him," he said after a moment's thought, "or with his secretary, at best."

"Good." She turned to Kail. "Set up a watch on him. Find me a weakness. He's a Voyant, so he'll have a lot of public speaking events. Up here, security will be lighter. Maybe a short con." She took a sip of her wine, finally, which was damn good wine after all that. "So what does that tell us?"

"That I should have stayed in my damn cell," Hessler muttered.

"I believe," said Icy, "that this information necessitates a change in plan. We were prepared for a short investigation of the palace security followed by a break-in utilizing our skills as necessary. Instead, we must now target Archvoyant Silestin specifically."

"Exactly," said Loch. "This just ceased to be a grab-and-run. It's an *operation* now."

"When does it become too dangerous?" Hessler grimaced. "Not that I'm not grateful, but there have to be better jobs out there, if you examine the profit-to-risk ratio."

Loch bared her teeth in a hard grin. "Magister, if you see me running past you, that'll be your cue to get out."

The captain knew to halt the ship's descent when he saw the telltale gleam of black crystal coming up toward them from below. He waited, of course. Archvoyant Silestin encouraged displays of initiative in very limited ways.

But when the Archvoyant gave the order, the captain had merely to nod his head, and the navigator followed the captain's pre-arranged orders and brought the airship to a halt, hovering in the sky hundreds of feet below the Spire.

Their steady presence allowed it to approach.

It was all black, and the captain thought it was made of crystal, though it did not glitter in the late afternoon sun. It seemed to suck in the light, and the air around it rippled. It was shaped like a broad "V," or like a pair of outstretched bird's wings.

It sliced cleanly through the air and came to a halt before the captain's ship.

"One moment," said Silestin, as he always did. "And if you don't mind, I'd appreciate a bit of privacy," which he always added.

Once, a crewman had snuck close to listen. He'd been found dead in his bed a few days later, his chest covered with stab wounds that formed the words "too curious" in his lacerated flesh. The captain did not have to order his men away after that.

He watched as the Archvoyant stepped to the black crystal ship. A hole opened in its side, and in the deeper darkness the captain could see something. A ripple of black on black, nothing more. He looked away.

He looked up again when the Archvoyant stomped noisily back his way. "Excuses," the Archvoyant said with a sniff. "Like assholes, Captain. Everybody has one."

"And they all stink, Archvoyant," the captain ventured. The black crystal ship was gone, but the air near the ship still rippled.

The Archvoyant rewarded him with a smile. "Indeed, Captain. Now let's get this boat moving, shall we?"

Eleven

A FEW DAYS LATER, ARCHVOYANT SILESTIN WALKED DOWN Voyancy Street. He wore a military uniform that glittered with medals. Dairy looked until his eyes hurt.

"Gedesar's fingers, kid, you don't need to stare that hard." Mister Kail elbowed Dairy. They were sitting at a table outside a kahva-house, which Mister Kail had said was a good vantage point on account of its good view of the street and its excellent kahva.

"I thought we had to look hard so Ululenia could get the picture from our minds," Dairy said, risking a quick glance back up. There were two men with the Archvoyant, but he couldn't see them through the crowded street.

"Sure, but not so hard that the mark sees us, right?" Mister Kail looked over at Dairy, then sighed. "Mark, kid. It means the target, the guy you're trying to rob. Or, well, murder, but we're not murderers. We're thieves." He said that proudly.

"Mister Kail, do you ever read the Book of the Four-and-Twenty?" Dairy took a sip of his milk and honey.

"Um... sure, kid." Mister Kail shifted in his seat.

"Doesn't the Book say that stealing is wrong?" Dairy asked plaintively. This had been troubling him for some time.

"Well, yeah, but you have to figure that this isn't exactly stealing, is it?" Mister Kail looked over at him, nodding hopefully. "I mean, Silestin is a bad guy. He stole the book from Loch. But because he's got so much power, we can never arrest him. What we can do, though, is hurt him for all the bad things he's done. It's sort of like we're doing justice very quietly on our own."

Dairy thought for a moment. "The world shouldn't be like that, Mister Kail."

"Damn right it shouldn't, kid."

The men walking with the Archvoyant came into view. They both wore robes. One of them, a small man, tittered along nervously behind the Archvoyant, but the other wore a shimmering black robe and had skin that flickered in the light. Dairy felt the world go still around him, as though everything else had paused.

"Mister Kail," he said softly, "who is that man?"

"Damn," Mister Kail murmured. "Silestin's got one of the Glimmering Folk with him. I heard about that in the puppet show. There are some nasty old Urujar folktales...." He looked over at Dairy with some concern. "You okay, kid? It's... well, it's *really* okay to be scared of him."

"I'm not scared, Mister Kail." The Glimmering Man looked around as though searching for something, and Dairy quickly looked down again.

"Well, I am." Mister Kail took a big drink of his kahva. When Dairy glanced back up, the Glimmering Man was walking away.

"He makes me feel sort of tingly," Dairy said, frowning as he tried to explain it. "Like something deep inside me is trying to say something important."

"Huh." Mister Kail pursed his lips. "Uh, do you feel that kind of tingly feeling when you look at your unicorn friend, Ululenia? Or maybe Desidora?" Mister Kail sipped his kahva and smiled. "She's got those big dark eyes and that dangerous death priestess thing going on, huh?"

Dairy frowned. "I don't think so, Mister Kail. I've never felt it until I looked at that man."

"Maybe you should ask Hessler about this," Mister Kail said, coughing. "I'm sure it's, you know, perfectly natural, but... yeah, you should really talk with him about it."

"Do we go back and report to Loch now, Mister Kail?" Dairy asked as the Archvoyant and the two men with him turned and walked up a bunch of steps into the Hall of the Voyancy, a big white building with guards out front.

Mister Kail looked at his kahva. "Let's finish our drinks, make sure the Archvoyant doesn't come back out. Have to be thorough and all that."

"Thanks for helping me learn how to be a good thief, Mister Kail." Dairy sipped his milk.

"My pleasure, kid."

Pyvic found Orris in the Cleaners, sitting at one of the guard stations. "Good morning, Orris."

Orris looked up at him blankly, then went red-faced. "You. Hope you're happy, you son of a bitch."

"Orris, Archvoyant Silestin has ordered me to speak with you about Prisoners Loch and Kail. He'd like me to get a description to help with conducting my investigation."

"So it's your investigation now, is it?" Orris sniffed, and Pyvic simply stood there for a long moment, counting in his head as his old superior had taught him, until the former warden ducked his head again. "Fine. Whatever gets you out of my face. You've done enough already."

Pyvic took Orris to a private room and took notes for the better part of an hour until he had a decent idea of the appearance of both prisoners. Kail was easy—by the end of the interview, Pyvic was certain that the Urujar guard who'd thrown the first punch when the young guard had given away their ruse was Prisoner Kail.

Loch was harder. Orris said she was bony, then said she had arms like a man's, which didn't sound bony at all. In one of Orris's tirades, she was an ungainly stomping monster who'd kick you if you called her a woman. In another, she became a sly seductress who had probably convinced Akus to help her with what Orris called "her animalistic wanton ways." Orris was screaming obscenities about her by this point.

By the end of it, all Pyvic really had to go on were the eyes. No matter his other inconsistencies, Orris always yelled that they seemed to look right through him, hard and sharp and alert, always measuring.

Pyvic had seen eyes like that on an Urujar woman recently. He wished he hadn't.

Icy Fist watched as Archvoyant Silestin strode through the main gate of his palace and shook hands with visitors who had come to take a look at the palace gardens. By proud tradition, the gardens were open to the public except during emergencies or parties, and so the cultivated hedges and sparkling fountains were surrounded by businessmen trying to impress their associates, young nobles visiting on vacation, and those few common folks who could afford the travel fees and security inspections necessary for a trip to the Spire.

Just past the hedges and garden paths and behind a wrought-iron gate whose presence indicated that it was *not* part of the public tour lay the impressive bulk of the Archvoyant's mausoleum. Its marble columns were pale in the afternoon light, even the parts sculpted with a fake ivy pattern.

Most of the wrought-iron gate was bounded by hedges, and Icy leaned against one of them comfortably, watching for approaching guards while Desidora, who had snuck into the off-limits area, examined the mausoleum's magical aura for defenses. He had a small white lizard perched on his shoulder.

You are most nimble, Ululenia said in his mind. *I would not have believed a man of flesh and blood, untouched by the magic of nature, could climb that wall in order to get over the gate and open it for Desidora.*

"I was fortunate that the ancient stone had acceptable handholds," Icy said modestly. He'd had to time it properly, given that tourists and visitors could have seen him as well.

Also, the part where you leaped off the building, grabbed that hanging pipe, and swung around before vaulting out into the air and catching hold of the obelisk statue, said Ululenia as they waited. *That was really impressive.*

A pair of palace guards were coming his way, so Icy made his way back toward the gift stalls. Ululenia would let him know if Desidora needed help getting back out again.

"It is a useful skill, but hardly of merit," Icy said, blending with the crowd as a pair of palace guards strode by. "I am but a beginner on the great path of knowledge."

Did you know, Indomitable Courteous Fist, that when I read your mind, I can tell when you are using false modesty?

Icy looked through a selection of rich silk robes emblazoned with the colors of the Republic. "That is greatly unfor-
tunate," Icy murmured, "as false humility is necessary for an
Imperial living among the Republic barbarians."

*Or a creature of magic. As the arctic fox takes up its snowy
pelt to blend into the icy white of winter, so we outsiders must
make ourselves small and innocent to soothe the fear of these
angry mortals.* Icy moved on to a stall that sold suede and
leather gloves for dueling. *What little pride we may retain
is—oh, my virgin needs a good pair of gloves.*

"Dairy?" Icy blinked. "I do not believe he is *your....*"
After a brief pause, he gave that up. "You believe that his
lack of handwear presents a problem?"

The gray suede ones. The tiny reptilian form under Icy's
collar dug in her claws. *Can you not see him wearing them?
Them, and nothing el—*

"I shall purchase them immediately," Icy promised, "provided that you refrain from further discussion of this topic."

Had Dairy, with whatever unintentional magnetism he possessed, not so ensnared Ululenia that she insisted upon the
purchase of the gloves, Icy would not have taken the few extra
moments to purchase them. He would have walked around the
corner and out of sight without incident, never the wiser.

And so it was, in a way, due to Dairy that Icy walked back
toward Desidora and the mausoleum when he did, and col-
lided with a beautiful young Urujar woman whose eyes were
covered with a band of smoked crystal, walking quickly
but unevenly, wearing expensive silks and an expression of
delighted terror.

"Please, please, you must hide me!" she declared, her
voice smooth and cultured. Her hands moved in front of Icy,

fluttering nervously, and Icy realized that the woman was blind. "The guards! They will be furious—"

"Do not trouble yourself," Icy said quickly. "Please, take my hand, and I will lead you to safety."

He darted back through the gift stalls and pulled her into one of the hedge mazes, taller than a man stood, all of them with rare flowers and rich golden statues in their centers to reward those who could navigate them. She followed, and in mere moments they were safely out of view.

"My thanks," said the beautiful young woman. "I... I know it is foolish, but—"

"They were pursuing you?"

"They are my guardians," she said, smiling and lowering her head. "The guardians of my guardian. You see, I'm a ward of Archvoyant Silestin."

"You are Naria de Lochenville?" Icy asked in surprise, belatedly remembering Loch's sister.

"I am." She shook her head, then wiped angrily at her eyes behind the crystal band. "Of course you would know my name. The Archvoyant names me his daughter and parades me around to show what a great man he is."

"I am Indomitable Courteous Fist." Icy took her hand again. "It is a pleasure to meet you."

"I thank you, my Indomitable defender." Her lips curved into a sweet smile. "I so rarely find my way to freedom from it all. Is there... is there any chance that you could take me through the city my father protects me from?"

"I..." In the silence of his mind, Icy thought very hard about how he had just purchased expensive gloves on someone's behalf, and how someone might consider repaying a favor in such a fashion.

I shall help Desidora, Ululenia said, her laughter a silvery flash in his mind. *Embrace your freedom, fellow outsider.*

"...believe I can spare a few hours to escort a beautiful woman around the city," Icy finished.

As they left the hedge maze and headed for the main gates, Icy flicked an arm casually behind Naria's back, and a white dove flew out of his sleeve.

Pyvic found himself on the Spire at sunset with nowhere to go. His quarters at the justicar precinct held little appeal after several days flat on his back, so he collected his meal allowance and went out.

The entertainment district of the Spire was coming alive with nightfall. Businesses that could afford magical lighting arrayed signs in a glow of gentle lavender or sultry crimson. Businesses that couldn't afford the magic lit lamps with colored glass panels to achieve the same effect. Pyvic passed a lane of restaurants whose glittering lights and expensively attired clientele proclaimed them far beyond his meal allowance.

A lamplit sign marked a dark-painted kahva-house at the corner of the restaurant lane. It said that it served meals as well, and, thinking of his last kahva-house experience, Pyvic smiled and strode inside, squinting at the candlelight that cast a dim golden glow across the room.

Most of the people inside were Urujar, and Pyvic was one of a handful of white customers. The kitchen had evidently just opened, and waiters were pushing scarred wooden tables together for larger dinner parties and politely requesting that the folks lingering over their kahva either order dinner or leave.

The woman from the kahva-house in Ros-Oanki was there at a small table, reading a thin leather-bound book. Her hair was bound back in a simple ponytail that suited her better than the loose-flowing cascade she'd worn before, and her skin shone like polished bronze in the candlelight as she frowned thoughtfully over a passage.

Pyvic considered the timing.

The coin landed on the book, and she looked up sharply, slamming the pages shut to catch it. She *did* have piercing brown eyes. When she saw him, her frown turned up into a crooked smile.

"They're kicking out anyone who isn't buying dinner," Pyvic said. "You looked like you wanted to stay."

She opened the book slightly. The coin slid free. "This isn't much for dinner on the Spire, Justicar."

"Pyvic." He shrugged, then grinned. "It's a down payment. You get the rest when you let me share your table."

She weighed the coin in her palm, giving him a look that slid right through him. Then she kicked the other chair out from the table. "If this is the start of a negotiated purchase of affection, you're in for a disappointing evening... Pyvic." Her lips were pursed in a barely contained smile.

He sat, pulled up the chair, and tried to figure out what to do with his hands. "I recall a woman in a kahva-house saying that she liked intense brooding men in uniform."

She smirked. "You've got a good memory."

"I still don't recall your name, though." Pyvic gave her a casual grin. "Or what you did for a living. What was it, again?"

"Bookseller," she said. "You keep asking like the answer is going to change. And you never heard my name." She paused, and Pyvic saw her take a slight breath, the kind that most people wouldn't ascribe any deep meaning to, and then she said, "Isafesira."

"That's a lovely name." She put the book in her knapsack, but not before he'd caught the title. *The Uncovering of Bounty in Inhospitable Climates.* Wei Lin, famous Imperial strategist. Odd reading material for a bookseller... or are you planning to sell that?" An actual bookseller wouldn't be caught dead creasing and staining the pages of something she planned to sell in a kahva-house.

"Hardly." She grinned. "A gift from a friend with whom I'm staying."

"That's a rare book, especially in the Republic. Your friend has deep pockets... and an odd notion of books a lady might enjoy."

"Voyant Cevirt was my commanding officer back during the war." She clipped her knapsack shut. "He thought I'd appreciate a rare book on tactics."

"Not just tactics." Pyvic raised an eyebrow. The book had been required reading material for officers commanding scouts, although they hadn't gotten first editions. "Tactics of infiltration—getting in and out like thieves in the night."

"That's such a very justicar-ish way of thinking about it." She sipped her kahva. An Urujar waiter brought them menus, and she smiled politely and said something in their old language. Pyvic took his menu with a nod.

When the waiter was gone, Pyvic said, "A justicar has to think like a justicar. All the time."

"All the time?" She arched an eyebrow. "I suppose that means you're looking at Archvoyant Silestin as well, then."

He gave her a polite, confused smile. "Should I be?"

"According to the puppeteers, you were put onto this case for political reasons. A justicar with your record might be wondering what makes this case so important... what the Archvoyant had to hide."

He chuckled. "And what do you think that might be?"

"I'm just a bookseller, Pyvic," she said, and smiled. "How would I know?"

"You seem awfully well informed for a bookseller," Pyvic said, putting no particular heat into the words. "I met you in Ros-Oanki, while the escaped prisoner I'm looking for was in Ros-Oanki. She came up to the Spire, and now you're up on the Spire at the exact same time. Maybe I just have a suspicious mind."

She snorted. "Damn right you have a suspicious mind. Any justicar worth a damn has to have one." She leaned forward. "Of *course* you saw me there and then up here. Why the hell do you think I was down in Ros-Oanki? I needed to book passage up here so that I could sell Voyant Cevirt a book." She sniffed. "And apparently get interrogated by a nice-looking justicar who's talking himself out of buying me dinner."

He sat back, stung. Her eyes were the same shining bronze as her skin when she was angry. "You don't talk like a bookseller."

"And if you actually thought I was this prisoner, you'd be watching me from across the street or taking me into custody. You wouldn't be badgering me over kahva." Her eyes narrowed. "Unless Silestin has you bullied into submission."

"And I should be investigating him on, what? The word of a *bookseller?*"

"On the suspicions of a justicar," she said evenly, "unless those only work on women in kahva-houses."

Pyvic blinked, looked away. "I'm sorry, Isafesira. I suppose I deserved that."

"Damn right you did." She sipped her kahva again.

"So…" He looked at the menu, then at the… not beautiful. No makeup, no painted nails, no low-cut silk dress, no dangling black tresses. But striking. A much better word for the woman across the table. She could strike you with her eyes, her words, probably her fists if it came to it. She had the build of a woman used to pulling her own weight. She'd served in the army. "Shall I leave you, then, or shall we order?"

"Before you were a justicar, you served in the army," she said. "What were you?"

He blinked again—she kept throwing him off track. "I captained a scouting patrol."

Her eyes softened, crinkled with laugh lines around the edges. She smiled.

They ordered.

Archvoyant Silestin walked through the night-time crowd that filled the Boulevard of Enchantment.

Light-globes lit the city street gaily, and from salons and taverns came rich music, laughter, and heady debate. Stalking beside him was a massively built man in peculiar golden armor, complete with a mask that obscured his face, and a flowing green cloak. The strange man carried an ancient barbed spear, and the crowds of drunk, laughing aristocrats parted before his palpable menace while Silestin himself laughed and shook hands.

"Do you trust the death priestess?" Tern asked, stomping through the crowd defiantly. People looking at her sturdy brown dress seemed inclined to think her a servant and jostle her aside, and a few had learned about the steel-toed boots firsthand.

"I don't understand the parameters of the question." Hessler wore the white robes of a scholar. "Trust is a more complex philosophical issue than the average layperson can understand."

"Thanks." Tern kicked someone who got in her way.

"For example," Hessler mused, "I'm walking here with you, and your face is known by that justicar and the helmsman, so there's a chance that we could be seen. I am essentially trusting your ability as a career criminal to avoid detection."

"Stop, Magister, I'm blushing."

Archvoyant Silestin and his associate stopped at a four-storey building whose vivid murals and expensive illusions marked it as a temple of Tasheveth, the only goddess who would be caught in the pleasure district. Tern and Hessler caught a glimpse of rich red carpets and gilded bronze columns in the entry room, and then the great door slammed shut behind them.

"On the other hand, as a career criminal, you—and any of the others—would likely leave me behind if need be." Hessler nodded in triumphant calculation. "Thus, my level of trust for any of you is *logically* a case-by-case examination of the current threat level measured against your perceived need for my abilities."

"Weren't you shackled in a cell when Loch found you?" Tern stomped on a nobleman's foot as she and Hessler started back the way they had come.

"Only because I was framed!"

"So, like I asked earlier, non-criminal, do you trust the death priestess?"

"Why is she any different from the rest of you?" Hessler asked bluntly.

They paused beside a fountain of a frolicking water nymph. "Well, I don't raise zombies from *hell* on behalf of a daemon-god who consumes souls," said Tern. "I mean, how do we know what she's saying about that hammer is true? How do we know that it isn't some poor guy whose mortal essence was enslaved?"

Hessler considered this option. "I don't really see Desidora as the type of woman who would *want* a magical talking warhammer."

"She sacrifices victims in obscene rites to fuel her horrific, world-shattering enchantments!"

"Which we haven't seen," Hessler noted, "and only know through secondhand anecdotal evidence from unreliable storytellers. Really, Tern, it's almost like you have some built-in prejudice against Desidora."

"She's a *death priestess!*" Tern said in a voice that made onlookers pause and stare at them. "Can't you feel the weight of her evil stare?"

"She used to be a love priestess, and her eyes are actually quite attractive," Hessler said, followed by, "Ow! That was—"

"Look, he's back," Tern said quietly as the Archvoyant came outside with a wrapped package tucked under one arm. "Now that's a *lot* sooner than I expected to see him come." She heard the cough behind her and added, "*Outside,*" archly. "Come on. Let's see where he's headed."

She stalked off into the crowd, and Hessler followed, limping slightly and muttering to himself.

"This," Pyvic said while nibbling on Loch's neck and helping her out of her blouse, "is a massive mistake."

"Mmmm-hmmm," Loch agreed, working her hands under his shirt and raking her fingers across the taut muscles of Pyvic's back. She'd already flung his jacket over the door handle and tossed her own coat over the small chair that, aside from the bed, was the only furniture in the room they'd rented.

"I should be hunting," Pyvic murmured into Loch's hair as his strong fingers slipped beneath her undershirt and traced hot patterns across her skin.

"Mmm-mmm." Loch tugged his shirt free from his pants—but not off. She liked the look of it, rumpled and unbuttoned but still hanging over his broad shoulders. "For your thief?"

"For the truth, Isafesira," he said, and her heart pounded hard against her chest for a moment. Why had she told him her real name? Stupid, stupid, stupid. "I should be..." His wonderful warm hands came up to rest on her shoulders. "... hunting for the truth."

She felt the moment pass and took one selfish second to feel the warmth of him against her before she let him push her away.

"Well, then," she said, and drew a finger along his arm as he stepped back, "good hunting."

His breath was shaky as he grabbed his jacket and stalked out.

So was hers, damn him.

Twelve

KAIL APPROACHED THE *LAPITEMPERUM* EARLY THE FOLLOWING morning, wearing the lavender robes of a lapitect and carrying a thick ream of paper. He was sweating and grouchy and dimly aware that Cevirt's free bar might not always be his friend.

The guards outside the big brick building were grumpy as well. People always thought that grumpy guards were harder to talk through, but, well, people were stupid.

He jerked his chin at the one on the right as he stomped up the steps. "Hey."

The guards gave him a sour look. "Badge?"

Kail grimaced, shifted the ream of papers to his other hand, fumbled in the robe pocket, and then dropped the ream of papers between the two guards, scattering them everywhere. "Son of a bitch!" Kail dropped to his knees and began grabbing papers. "Dammit! Dammit! Da... hey, come on, man, could you help me out here?" A gust of wind, sent helpfully by a small white dove across the street, swept the remaining stack of papers down the steps. "Oh, that's *just* what I need! Jackass guard needs to see my *badge.* "

"Right, right, don't get your knickers in a twist," one of the sour-faced guards growled and bent down to help gather the papers. In an audible undertone, he added, "Bunch of pansy fiddlers...."

"And... hell, what was I thinking?" Kail sighed and shook his head. "I don't even work at this station. I don't even *have* a badge that would work for you."

The security, as explained by Tern, was top-notch, using some of the oldest and most powerful magic the Ancients had had. It included a verifier ward that would fire a warning glamour on anyone who knowingly told a falsehood.

As such, Kail was being *completely honest* when he said that he didn't work at that station and didn't have a badge.

"You don't have a badge?" the first guard said with a sour look. "We're not supposed to let you in without a badge."

"Well, fine," Kail said shortly. "Would *you* like to present a dissertation on ablating the magnification-decay ratio in null-source thaumaturgic enchantments, then?"

That was a question, so it wasn't *exactly* a lie.

Also, that had been the entirety of Kail's knowledge of ancient magical artifact terminology as patiently repeated to him by Hessler.

"Gods." The other guard shook his head. "S'too early for this crap. Here. We'll drop it for you. Just get inside and remember your damn badge next time."

"Thanks, man. I really appreciate it." Also entirely true. Kail ducked his head while the guard reached inside, put his palm to a blue crystal panel just beyond the door, and shut his eyes in concentration. The panel flashed green, and the other guard jerked his chin toward the doorway. Kail muttered his thanks again and hurried inside.

Kail stepped into an airy entryway lit by beautiful magic chandeliers and pristine windows. A matronly woman sat at the lobby desk, and busy lapitects, all in lavender robes like Kail's, marched to and fro with folders and crystals and wands and notepads.

"Hey!" one of the guards called sharply behind him. Kail considered running, opted not to, but did make a fist inside the pocket of his robe as he turned around.

The guard held out one crumpled sheet of paper. It was muddy and had a dirty boot print on it. "Missed this one," the guard said with a smirk.

Kail snatched it, made a good show of wiping it off before tucking it back in with the rest of the papers. "Thanks again," he said with a brisk nod, and hurried into the complex itself.

Kail walked purposefully until he saw a set of stairs, and then he headed up to the second floor and walked some more, giving brief, distracted nods to anyone who made eye contact with him.

When he saw a white-haired old guy with a rumpled robe and some papers of his own step out of an office on the window-side of the hallway, Kail angled toward the man. The man shut his office door, locked it carefully, turned to start walking, and ran directly into Kail. There was a brief explosive tangle of flying paper and lavender robes.

"Second time this morning, dammit!" Kail said, which was, again, not a lie, as he helped the other man up and also removed the man's badge and keys from his pocket. "Here, this paper is yours, I think, and so's this one. Man, that was my fault."

"You should watch where you're going," the old man said severely, and stalked off. Kail spent a good long while adjusting his papers and the hem of his robes, and when the old man was around the corner, Kail unlocked the man's door and stepped inside.

After many hours of brainstorming and planning and expletives, Tern and Hessler had concluded that there was no way that Kail was going to be able to find the *lapisavantum*, which was apparently something he was supposed to find, and pull the energy matrix records for Archvoyant Silestin's palace, which Tern had finally dumbed down enough for Kail to understand by saying that it was like a sketch of a lock showing you where the tumblers were.

And even if Kail could find it, there was no way he was going to access it. That just wasn't his thing. It was Tern's thing, but Tern couldn't very well smuggle herself in, and it was Hessler's thing, too, but the illusion magic he'd use to get inside would apparently set off all kinds of alarm bells.

And so Kail had a different partner. He glanced briefly at the old man's office, which looked a great deal like the office of any old man with a lot of intellectual power. Then he moved aside a pile of books that was half-blocking the window, threw back the curtains, coughed at the dust he'd kicked up, and eased the window open.

The street below—a small side street, pretty much empty this time of morning—shone bright and clean in the pale sunlight, and the building across the street was a tall brick office. Icy Fist stood on the roof, also wearing borrowed lapitect robes. He had a pole, perhaps ten feet long, in one hand, and he waved with his free hand when he saw Kail.

Kail attached the security badge to a handy paperweight with a bit of twine, hefted the package to get the weight of it, took two hopping steps to the window, and hurled it out and across the street. Icy leaped, caught it in his free hand, and then turned and ran out of view.

Icy had seemed confident when describing this aspect of the plan. Kail didn't know if that was just an Imperial fearlessness or what, but the physics the little Imperial described when explaining why a pole would let him jump across the street were more of the Tern-and-Hessler variety than the Kail variety. Because Icy was on his team, now, Kail said a quick prayer to Gedesar.

A moment later, Icy Fist flew from the edge of the tax building like he'd been hurled by a catapult, flying across the street with his pole trailing behind him.

But he wasn't going to make it. Kail leaned out the window with his arms ready to grab hold, maybe catch Icy by the arm....

A moment later, Kail regained his senses. Primarily his sense of touch, which was telling him about the desk lodged in his back and the Imperial who had just slammed into him harder than anything had ever hit Kail, ever, including the ground when they'd leaped from the airship last week or from the Spire a couple of weeks before that.

"I calculated the distance carefully," Icy said.

"Mrf." Kail was going to have some wonderful bruises.

"I appreciate the sentiment, however." Icy rolled off him, and Kail, now unpinned from the desk, crumpled slowly to the floor.

When he opened his eyes a moment later, wincing, he saw that Icy still had the damn pole in one hand. One end was sticking out the window, and he pulled it the rest of the way through, angling it sideways so that it went from one corner of the small office to the other.

"Are you prepared to continue?" Icy asked, bouncing lightly on the balls of his feet. "Our timeline is flexible."

"What, me?" Kail pushed himself to his feet, ignoring the screaming pain in his back. Judging by the indentations in the carpet, he and Icy had knocked the desk a good couple feet, and it wasn't a small desk. "I'm fine." A flare of purple radiance lit in the air over Kail's head.

"That would appear to be the ambient ward that detects falsehoods," Icy said politely.

"Stupid ward's probably just misfiring." Kail snorted. Another flare of purple radiance lit in the air. "Let's hit it."

He didn't think of himself as a proud man, but he was damned if he was going to limp as he opened the door and ushered Icy out into the hallway.

"Which way?" Kail murmured, and Icy turned confidently to the right and started down the hallway. Kail fell in behind him.

They walked down some hallways and up another flight of stairs. Icy walked without hesitation or pause, and Kail, who got lost after about three turns, just walked alongside him staring at nothing.

"Hold on just one moment!" Kail blinked and looked at the portly lapitect who stood in their path. "I don't recognize you two! What are you doing here?"

And then Kail was back in charge.

"Oh, come on, man," he said indignantly as Icy began to stutter out a response. "What do you *think* we're doing here?"

The portly man turned to Kail and raised a finger. "Security is a vital part of maintaining the *Lapitemperum*, and it is not only the right but the *responsibility* of all staff to verify—"

"Sure," Kail cut in, "so if you saw a couple of *white* technicians coming in to perform a, a, a..."

"Time-curve analysis of energy dispersion for the Spire's levitation field," Icy finished.

"Right. If you saw white technicians coming in to do that, you'd ask them the same thing? And you've recognized everyone else you've passed in the halls today?"

"I..." The portly lapitect flushed. "It's simply a matter of—"

"Oh, afraid to answer the question?" Kail crossed his arms indignantly. "Maybe afraid you'd get a little flare of purple over your head?"

The lapitect glared. "That's the most... I don't have to stand here and listen to this!" He brushed past them and stomped away.

"I am impressed," Icy said after a moment, "by your ability to dissemble within such limited parameters."

"It's not so hard," Kail said. "Most people, you ask questions at them, they just want to get rid of you as quick as they can. You learn to work that, you can get a lot of doors opened."

Icy started down the hallway again. "It is as though your body is entirely motivated by *kaj* energy. " Seeing Kail's blank look, he added, "We of the Empire believe that the body is made of two energies: the *jar*, or receptive, quiet, female energy, and the *kaj*, or aggressive, loud, male energy."

"So I'm, like, more male then most men?" Kail asked with a hint of pride.

Icy pursed his lips. "That is certainly one way of interpreting my statement," he said, and glanced briefly overhead before continuing. "And you seem almost to transmit this disharmony to others by your speech and attitudes, such that your very presence disrupts the balance of their spirit."

"You're saying I get them mad and confused?" Kail asked.

"I... yes." Icy stopped at a door marked "Primary *Lapisavantum* Chamber—Authorized Personnel Only."

"I can work with that. We here?"

"We are."

Kail studied the door. "Just like Tern said. Mechanical lock, no crystals or anything." He pulled Iofecyl from her special case (which he'd sewn into his sleeve last night) and got to work on the lock. "Come on, baby, let's make this fast...."

"Tern theorized that the ambient magic of the *lapisavantum* would preclude... are you anthropomorphizing your lockpick?"

Kail squinted, trying to feel the tumblers. "You know, she really works better when it's quiet."

"Tern often says the same thing." Icy shrugged, went back to keeping a lookout. "Although she does not, to my knowledge, anthropomorphize her lockpicks."

A few moments later, Kail felt the tumblers click as he raked his one true love gently across the grooved surface. He gave a quiet "Hah!", pulled the door open, and darted inside with Icy close behind.

It could have been a broom closet, except that one entire wall was made of glowing blue crystal, and the blue crystal had hundreds of sparkly lights in it, some blinking in different colors. "All you, Icy. Do your thing."

Icy nodded and stepped up to the rock. He touched one glowing thing, then another. Some of the lights changed colors. He touched another glowing thing and moved his finger across the crystal's surface, and the lights started flashing crazily.

"Hey, are they supposed to do that?" Kail asked.

"Tern did not mention that particular pattern," Icy said absently, "but then, I was instructed only to follow a specific course of action."

"Right, but if they're not supposed to do that—"

"I memorized the specific pattern of actions Tern described," Icy said, "and interrupting me in mid-application is unlikely to prove beneficial."

"Oh, fine." Kail leaned against one of the side walls, which was blank except for a lot of narrow slots that might have held levers or extra crystals or something. "I'll just sit here and shut up, then."

"Thank you." Icy pressed a final glowing thing, and there was a *plink* noise, and a crystal popped out of one of the little slots in the wall. "I believe that this should be what Tern wished us to retrieve."

Kail grabbed the crystal, opened the door, and ushered Icy out. "So, are you two...?"

"We are simply friends and partners," Icy said. "Much like you and Loch." He coughed. "Actually, I may be seeing someone as of yesterday."

"And just what are you two doing in the *lapisavantum* chamber?" came a sharp voice from around the corner and out of Kail's view, stuck as he was behind Icy.

There was a brief and hopeful silence.

"What do you think we are doing in the *lapisavantum* chamber?" Icy asked carefully.

Kail made a mental note to spend some time discussing the importance of *delivery*.

"Right, the two of you just stay where you are!" the sharp voice declared. "I don't know who you are, but you're not going anywhere until—"

"Hey, come on!" Kail pushed into the hallway and saw an ascetic-looking man whose lapitect robes had some little stars on the collar. "We're trying to work, here! Do I go down to where your mother works and push the sailors out of her bed?"

The thin man stiffened in outrage, and Kail cold-cocked him, caught him as he fell, tossed his body into the room with the big blue crystal, and shut the door firmly. A few lapitects down at the end of the hall were moving their way with concerned looks.

"Your actions were indicative of just the form of disharmonizing influence I described earlier," said Icy, starting back the way they had come at a fast walk.

"And *your* actions were indicative of you not being able to lie worth a damn," Kail said, keeping pace while listening behind him. Someone called out in his direction, but they were calling it out like a question. "Okay, new plan. Do you think we can both do that pole-vault thing you did?"

Icy looked at Kail speculatively. "Do you have any formal acrobatic training?"

"Not formal, no, not really, I guess you could say." They got to the corner, which had been Kail's big goal for that twenty-second period. Behind them, someone started shouting, and Icy and Kail started jogging by mutual agreement. "Hey!" Kail shouted at some lapitects coming their way. "There's some problem, someone unconscious back there! Get help!" A few of them ran past Kail and Icy. A few ran in the other direction, presumably to get help. Nobody tried to apprehend him. This fulfilled another one of Kail's goals.

"My plan to reach the streets was to leap from the window, strike the pole upon the ground vertically, and slide down as the pole began to tilt, trusting that my balance and tumbling ability would cushion the resulting fall."

Kail pursed his lips and jogged faster. "Yeah, I don't see that working for me."

They had just gotten back to the office when the alarms started chiming. As Kail slammed the door shut, Icy picked up the pole and gave Kail a questioning look. "Go, dammit, I'll be fine." Purple light flared over his head. "Oh, and take this." He passed Icy the crystal.

Icy pocketed the crystal, hefted his pole, and leaped out the window. Kail followed and saw the man do a kind of controlled falling slide down the pole to the ground, roll smoothly to his feet, and jog down the street and around a corner, disappearing into safety.

The fall looked to be about twenty-five or thirty feet. Not a killer—the ship had been worse, but then, the ship had had a lawn underneath it.

The chiming took on a new intensity, and red lights began dancing on the ceiling. Kail decided to risk it, got a running start, and dove out the window. He got about a foot and a half before crashing into an invisible wall and bouncing back into the office, now bruised in a *new* damn place.

Tern had mentioned something about barrier wards if things went wrong. Kail had sort of been counting on things not going wrong.

Running wouldn't help, not if they had wards up. Kail took a seat in the office and stared at the flashing red lights on the ceiling.

About fifteen minutes later, the guards showed up. He heard the booted feet on the stairs, heard them banging doors open and shouting to each other. Kail wondered if Warden Orris would be happy to see him.

He ducked down behind the desk. The door banged open. Two guards stepped in.

"All clear," said one of them—Kail couldn't see him, as he was still hiding behind the desk, but he sounded young. "Wait, it looks like this desk has been moved. And the window is open…." He came around the corner, saw Kail, and stared speechlessly for a moment.

"Please don't." The other guard cracked the first guard neatly on the temple with the butt of her truncheon. "It's too early for one of your lines about people's mothers. You're just lucky Ululenia could hex one of the guards to sleep for us."

"You look tense, Loch," Kail said, catching the unconscious young guard. "Weren't you going to get a massage or sauna package or something last night? How come you still look tense?"

Loch glared from beneath her helmet. "Get dressed, Kail. We've got two minutes until Ululenia and Hessler make a big distraction outside and all the guards run out to chase them. "

"Good, good." Kail slapped on the young guard's helmet and got to work on the jacket. "But really. You got a scented-water immersion or an herbal treatment at one of the baths or something, right?"

"Yes, Kail. Not that it's any of your business, but I had a very relaxing herbal treatment last night."

A purple light flared over her head. Kail figured it out and started laughing.

"Get dressed," Loch muttered, and went to guard the door. "When that outside alarm shuts down, we're leaving, even if you're bare-ass naked."

"You bringing up bare-assed nakedness for any reason in particular?" Kail asked innocently.

"Shut up, Kail."

"Happy to oblige, Captain."

Thirteen

TERN WAS WAITING OUTSIDE THE TEMPLE OF TASHEVETH, BY THE fountain where she and Hessler had watched Archvoyant Silestin. The frolicking water nymph spouting the water was pissing Tern off. She began hunting through her pockets.

When Desidora finally came out, hair red, skin tan, and robes a nice flirty green, she gave the water nymph a concerned look. "What happened to its head?"

"Minor alchemical accident," Tern said flatly. "So, did they buy the act?"

Desidora blinked. "If by *the act,* you mean my faithful assumption of my former duties as a priestess of Tasheveth—"

"Right, before you sold your soul to Byn-kodar."

"Kutesosh gajair'is!"

The green robes darkened slightly. "Tern, this may be an eldritch glimmering beyond the comprehension of man causing my sight to betray me, but I'm sensing some veiled hostility."

Tern narrowed her eyes. "Look, you can get the guys all lovestruck with the smoldering eyes and the 'former love priestess' angle, but I've seen warlocks with great daemon-augmented smiles, so I'm not buying it. You worship a *death god*. That's *evil*."

"You crack safes," Desidora pointed out.

"You say that like it's a comeback!" Tern stamped her steel-toed boot, cracking the pavement slightly and causing the remains of the frolicking water nymph's head to fall off. "Safes! Not people! If you can't see past that, we have nothing to talk about."

Tern watched Desidora's hair and face change color and had a brief realization that perhaps she could have told the death priestess off with witnesses other than a mentally deficient warhammer present. "Not all stories of the priesthood of Byn-kodar are true," Desidora said carefully.

"Really?" Tern asked acidly. "So you were bluffing when you told Loch you could rig up something with zombies?"

Desidora winced. "Not precisely. But the priesthood is not necessarily one of killing—"

"Which is why you have a talking magical warhammer."

"*Besyn larveth'is!*"

"Hey, Ghyl."

"Ghylspwr is not merely a weapon," Desidora said softly, "and not merely a tool. He is ancient, and he is wise, and he has seen things neither you nor I could understand or accept. He came to me on the night I became what I am today. He is not an object of violence, Tern, but of Prophecy."

She said it with capital letters and everything.

"I don't believe in prophecies," Tern said.

"If you can't see past that," Desidora shot back wryly, "we have nothing to talk about." But her short-cropped hair was back to glossy auburn, and her robes were green again.

"Well," Tern said, coughing and shifting her weight, "how did it go in there?"

"Archvoyant Silestin visited a priestess who specializes in creating items of love-magic and trickery," Desidora said crisply. "And in return for some promised latitude in the taxation of buildings operating in the pleasure district, the Archvoyant received a very expensive magical vestment known as the robes of *Nef'kemet.*"

"Which are?" Tern raised an eyebrow.

"Commonly known as chameleon robes."

"Wait. He promised tax incentives and all kinds of corrupt bureaucratic crap just to get robes that change color?"

Desidora smiled. "And I know how he's going to use them. And I believe I know how we're going to get that crystal off of him."

The temple of Ael-meseth on the Spire was the most glorious of all the temples. Its inner sanctum was bedecked with marble columns flecked with gold, vast murals of kings and warriors of antiquity, fonts of holy wine, and bronze gongs to summon the faithful. The temple's outer courtyard could comfortably hold several hundred people, and today it was packed full.

Many of those standing and watching the upper balcony wore the robes of other gods—Pesyr the Smith, Esa-jolar the General, and even Jairytnef the Sorceress. The priests sat on plush couches in an area roped off from the businessmen and politicians who came to listen and the news writers who came to take notes to pass down to the puppeteers.

Tern paid for their tickets. She and Desidora stepped into the crowd, and the crowd made way for them mindlessly, moving aside without ever looking their way. Desidora smiled, slightly pale, and Tern kept her eyes to the front and her feet moving.

When they reached the doors to the inner sanctum, guards stopped them. Tern opened her mouth to launch into the spiel, but Desidora checked her with a small motion and instead said, "Tell the Prime that a visitor says, '*Ynku hesyur dar'ur Ael-meseth.*'"

The guards looked at her in confusion, but one of them left. Tern put on her best expression of bored contempt. A minute later the guard returned, pale and shaken, and showed them into the inner sanctum.

Tern had been in temples before, although usually the presence of a guard meant that something had gone horribly wrong (or that Icy was going to be breaking in through the wall). They came to a lavish room where a tall and imposing man in expensive robes sat at what was only nominally a chair instead of a throne. The guards left.

"You choose a difficult time to speak the words that can bind even the Prime of Ael-meseth," the man said. His voice was calm, tranquil even. "Might I interest you in refreshments while I attend the trifling matters outside?"

Tern opened her mouth to launch into the spiel, but Desidora checked her again and said, "I bear the hammer Ghylspwr, who was king of the Ancients and whose return to this world bespeaks the coming of prophecy." Her voice was cold. She drew out Ghylspwr from her robes, and he shone and shouted, "*Besyn-larveth'is!*" impressively.

On his throne, the Prime of Ael-meseth paled and shrank back. "I thought that was just.... Of course, I am yours to command. Few indeed know the—"

"Yes," said Desidora, cutting off the high priest of the god of rulers with a short motion. "I need an impression crystal. Any simple one will suffice."

"As you say," the Prime said quickly, coming down from his throne and rummaging through the pockets of his robes. He held up a wand that glowed a shining violet. "This crystal controls the wards for this humble temple, but if it suits your needs—"

"Two birds with one stone," said Desidora, and brought Ghylspwr down on his head.

"*Kun-kabynalti osu fuir'is*," Ghylspwr offered as the Prime crumpled gently to the ground.

"Well, that was nice of you, yes. Killing him isn't necessary."

Tern got the crystal that the Prime had held and tossed it to Desidora, then dragged the Prime into a private chamber to the side of the throne. "You think maybe he's going to report this when he wakes up?"

"The Prime of Ael-meseth?" Desidora asked wryly. "Admitting that two women and a talking warhammer defeated him in his inner sanctum? I doubt it. Not unless we make it public." She held up the crystal and focused her gaze intently, and a low hum that Tern hadn't even realized she'd been hearing suddenly snapped off. "Which is not, I believe, the plan."

"Wards?" Tern asked, looking around.

"Not anymore." Desidora smiled as the violet glow flickered and died. Her skin was growing steadily more pale. She drew a medallion out from under her robes, and Tern saw that it was engraved with a twisting shape she couldn't place. Then Desidora touched the medallion and shut her eyes, and the shape slid into the crown and scepter of Ael-meseth.

A pair of acolytes stepped into the room. "Who are you?" they demanded, their violet robes shining and their gold-braided tassels snapping as they strode forward. "Where is the Prime? The Archvoyant is here for the address!"

Tern opened her mouth to launch into the spiel, then paused. Desidora nudged her slightly, and Tern realized that she was indeed here for a reason.

"What in Byn-kodar's name took you so long?" she snapped, stomping forward. "The Prime wanted him brought here *immediately*. Do you have any idea how important this is? I don't have to tell you how far Mother Haeldatha traveled to give the damn blessing—"

"My secretary speaks, of course, of the Rite of Conferral," Desidora added serenely, adjusting her medallion.

"Whatever, Mother. What you and the gods call it is up to you. Making it happen on *time* is up to me." Tern fixed the acolytes with the chilly smile that every functionary knew. "Now if you two will hurry the hell up, we can actually try to get this thing done."

The acolytes blinked. They had no idea what was going on, but the small, apple-cheeked woman in the brown dress didn't seem to know or care about that. And if there were any trouble, the wards would have triggered an alarm.

Public events are hell for any organization. The weary and frazzled acolytes nodded in mute relief at having somebody around who seemed to know what she was doing.

Archvoyant Silestin strode into the temple about a quarter of an hour before his speech. The temple guards ushered him in and led him to the Chamber of Conferral, which was where the Prime would do the ceremony and give him the robes.

"We good to go, Elkinsair?" he murmured without looking at his little secretary.

"Of course, sir."

"Capital." Ordinarily, he wouldn't have asked. Elkinsair was nothing if not dependable. But today was important.

The Chamber of Conferral was small and dark and shaped like an octagon, lit only by crystals that reflected off triangular mirrors set on each wall. Each of the eight triangular mirrors had a deity's symbol set at each point of the triangle, so that all twenty-four of the recognized gods shone their collective light upon the room. As the ruler of the gods, Ael-meseth had a slightly larger logo.

The Prime wasn't there. Instead, an imposing young red-headed priestess was there, along with what Silestin guessed was her assistant, a peasant girl in brown.

"You come seeking the blessing of the four-and-twenty, Archvoyant," the priestess said formally.

"I do," said Silestin. He'd rehearsed. "Now, the Prime was supposed to—"

"None may gain the blessing of the four-and-twenty unless they speak their words from the heart, for all to see their true intent," the priestess went on. "Will you bare your soul to all you wish your words to reach?"

"I will. Listen, where is the Prime?"

She raised an eyebrow, and Silestin found himself in the rare position of discomfiture. "The supreme representative of the gods does not explain himself to a ruler of men," she said. "If you do not wish to undergo the Conferral—"

"Fine, fine." Silestin cut her off, took charge of the conversation again with a brief note of satisfaction at her affronted look. "Let's get moving."

"Yes," the assistant chimed in. "We're behind schedule, and it's very important that we get this going as quickly as possible." The priestess glared down at her, and she flushed bright red and went silent.

"All are naked in the eyes of the four-and-twenty," said the priestess. "Remove your vestments and kneel to receive the Conferral."

Silestin unbuttoned his jacket and pulled it off. When he made to hand it to Elkinsair, however, the priestess stopped him with an imperious gesture. "None may interfere in your death and rebirth, Archvoyant. Your guest remains at our sufferance, and because the temple wishes to offer no disrespect, but your mortal vestments *must* remain untouched until you return. To do otherwise violates the Conferral and revokes the offer of the four-and-twenty to affirm the intentions of your soul." She smiled archly at the last bit.

Silestin stripped down. The priestess didn't even look at him, but the assistant blushed and looked at her shoes. He folded his uniform neatly and knelt, naked, before the priestess.

"The man who entered this room lies in his shed trappings on the floor," the priestess intoned, holding out the shimmering robe Silestin would be wearing. "It is his immortal soul that now moves to address the people, so that all may know the truth of his words."

She handed Silestin the robes. He put them on quickly, grimacing as they immediately shifted from shimmering gray to an angry swirling mix of red and black.

"Control yourself, Archvoyant." The priestess sniffed. "You wished this, according to the Prime. Do not envy the authority of the gods."

Silestin rose to his feet, shifted the robes around him. "The Prime told me I could have a few words with my secretary before I head out."

The priestess raised an eyebrow. "Then you misunderstood him, Archvoyant."

"Priestess!" the assistant gasped. "This is the Arch—"

The priestess rode right over her. "None may interact with you or your mortal garments until your speech is concluded. To do otherwise violates—"

"Right, right. It's just that the Prime said...." Silestin glanced at Elkinsair, who gave him a barely perceptible nod without directly looking his way. "Fine. Whatever. Let's get going."

"My assistant will show you to the podium. I shall remain here as a conduit for the blessing of the four-and-twenty." She glanced at Elkinsair disdainfully. "Your secretary may remain if he wishes... and if he is silent."

"Whatever." With a confidence marred only slightly by the frustrated lines of red and yellow that shot across the robes, Silestin followed the assistant out toward the podium where he would give the most important speech of his career.

Desidora gave the secretary a minute and a half, tops.

The *Nef'kemet* robes were in a tiny folded bundle under his own robes, visible only for the aura that few people, even among the priesthood, would be able to see. The switch was obviously supposed to have taken place during that brief private moment, which the Prime had apparently been ready to allow despite centuries of established protocol. Desidora was lying about some of the rules of the Ceremony of Conferral, but not all of it.

She wondered briefly if the Prime had been bribed or was just playing politics, keeping her face serene and her aura authoritative but calm as she knelt in the middle of the room.

The secretary shifted his weight, took a few steps, then stopped and put his hands behind his back. Desidora could feel the stress pouring off him in waves. It had to be a big speech—the Archvoyant wouldn't bow to the temples unless he needed a *large* audience, as well as the hook of having his heart quite literally worn on his sleeve for all to see his sincerity.

Or at least, the illusion of sincerity. The secretary shifted his weight again, and Desidora favored him with a glare for interrupting her peaceful meditations.

The secretary glared back at her and strode to the door. "I'll be back," he muttered, spitting the words her way as he left.

Desidora let the door swing shut behind him, gave him another few seconds just for safety, and then dove into Silestin's uniform and rifled the pockets. In an inner pocket in the jacket, she found the encryption crystal, a small wand that glowed in complex swirling patterns of color.

She refolded Silestin's jacket, got back into meditation position, and raised her arms to either side. Her right hand held Silestin's crystal, scintillating and wild. Her left hand held the Prime's warding crystal, now a blank slate as the result of an aural cleansing.

She shut her eyes, opened herself to the power of death, and felt the air chill around her. She knew her skin had gone chalk-white, her hair pitch-black. Part of her hated it. A new part of her, a frightening part, didn't care.

As the power of Byn-kodar flowed through her, the blank crystal slowly began to glow.

"Bit high-strung, isn't she?" the Archvoyant observed as Tern led him toward the podium.

"I, er, I couldn't really say, sir," Tern said, getting as flustered as she could.

The Archvoyant laughed. "If you can't even say that, she must really be bad!"

Tern gave him a tiny smile. "I'm sorry she was so difficult, sir."

He edged a little closer as they walked. "Nothing I don't deal with every day," the Archvoyant said ruefully. "The Voyancy, the priests, the nobles... hell, even the banking companies make sure I know my place!"

"Yes, sir."

"I bet she makes sure you know yours, too." The Archvoyant stopped, and Tern took a few nervous steps, then hesitantly turned to look back at him. "Tell me, miss... I'm sorry, she never even told me your name."

"Laridae, sir." Icy hated it when she used that name.

"Listen, Laridae, did you wake up one morning and say to yourself, 'You know, I really want to be the whipping-girl for some stuck-up priestess?'" His voice was gentle, full of concern. If the Republic still had kings, he'd be a prince.

"I needed to take care of my parents," Tern stammered, "and the temple said they'd teach me to be a good scribe, provided I was willing to work for them for ten years."

"Oh, one of those deals." The Archvoyant nodded thoughtfully. "Well, Laridae, sometimes people need to move in a different direction. You seem like a talented young woman, and I think I know a few Voyants who might need a good scribe." He leaned in a bit closer. "Especially one who can be flexible."

"I…" Tern looked around, paused for one second to make sure that it looked like a tough choice, and then said, "That sounds wonderful, sir, but—"

"The thing is," the Archvoyant said, putting a companionable arm around her shoulder, "this is a very important speech, and I want everything to go right. And, well, to be honest…" And here he smiled, and *damn,* he was good. It was a great smile. "…I'm not that good at speeches. I get flustered. I forget what I wanted to say." He looked around the hallway, saw a doorway with a tiny meeting room inside. "And my secretary had my notes." He steered Tern gently toward the hallway. "Now, I would never ask you to violate the laws of the temple, but I *do* need those notes for this speech. So I'm asking you to walk a few steps down that hallway and not turn around. Can you do that for me, Laridae?" He was nodding as he asked, and Tern nodded along with him, wide-eyed. "Good." The companionable arm dropped away, and the Archvoyant stepped into the small side room. "I'll just be a moment," he said with a golden smile.

Tern obediently walked out and turned her back. A moment later, she rolled her eyes and pretended not to hear the secretary creeping down the narrow hallway behind her into the meeting room.

You couldn't con an innocent man. But fortunately, in the case of Archvoyant Silestin, that was not a problem.

The crystals were nearly identical now, the shimmering glow dancing off of all the mirrors. Desidora kept the energy flowing, smoothing the flow of power on the left-hand crystal. It was getting closer. At the *Lapitemperum,* there were ancient artifacts that could do what Desidora was doing in a matter of hours. She figured she had a minute or two, if that.

Tern poked her head into the room, gave her a questioning look. Desidora gave her a quick headshake, and Tern rolled her eyes, mouthed something vile, and took off back down the hallway.

"I am concerned, Archvoyant," said Elkinsair, helping Silestin into the chameleon robe.

"Noted."

"The absence of the Prime—"

"Will be investigated." Silestin grimaced. "Thoroughly." He shrugged the new robe on, smiling as the colors swirled into patterns of sincerity, gravity, and hope. Perfect.

"The aura of the priestess troubles me as well," Elkinsair added. Silestin raised an eyebrow. "It conforms perfectly to that of a priestess of Ael-meseth. Almost *too* perfectly."

"Could be because of the Ceremony." Silestin rifled through a small set of notecards. He didn't need them—any speech worth giving was worth giving from memory—but props were important in any lie. "Have to get the most formal of the priests to do it."

"Possible," Elkinsair admitted, "but I would like to investigate further."

"Do it." Silestin turned on his smile. "I'll expect a report tomorrow morning."

"And the assistant?" Elkinsair asked.

They got to the door, and Elkinsair pushed, then frowned. He pushed harder, then glared helplessly at Silestin.

A moment later, the door opened a crack, and Laridae poked her head in, eyes wide. "I had to keep the door closed," she whispered. "There were *guards!*"

Silestin smiled at Elkinsair. "I think that other matter we were discussing is under control. Good thinking, Laridae." He held up his notecards and saw her guilty smile. "Now, where do I give this speech?"

One last flow, one tiny detail that, for a crystal attuned to the patterns of energy, meant the difference between the encryption crystal that would open the vault and a very expensive glowing paperweight. Desidora pushed, grimacing as it flowed through her. It was hateful and cold and very, very angry. The symbols of the gods were changing around all the mirrors. She knew which symbols she'd see there now, if she bothered to look. Part of her welcomed it, gloried in it.

An aura approaching in the hallway. She could sense them better when she let it in, but at such a cost. She looked to the flow. She needed one more moment.

She forced it, slammed the energy into place, then cut it off ruthlessly inside her. It hurt, forcing the change back so quickly. She could feel it pulling through her very soul as it slid back to the place it lived when she didn't call it. She sagged, momentarily breathless. The footsteps were almost to the doorway.

The crystal was there.

So was Elkinsair.

"Friends, fellow Voyants, members of the nobility and the various temples all throughout our beloved land, wizards of our proud universities, and most honored and distinguished of all, citizens of the Republic.... I come before you today not as a leader, not as a politician, not as a member of the Learned Party... but as a man who loves his country. *And I praise all the gods to see that I am not alone.*"

The robe shone with the power of his humble belief, his awe-inspiring sincerity.

The crowd greeted Archvoyant Silestin with thunderous applause.

Elkinsair blinked as he came back into the Chamber of Conferral. The crystals were flickering faintly, and everything seemed dimmer. The haughty priestess looked pale in the dim light. He shot her a questioning look, to which she responded by stiffening her posture and pointedly ignoring him.

Elkinsair sniffed, looked at the symbols of the gods on the wall for a moment to make sure that they weren't actually moving, and settled in to wait.

Tern led the Archvoyant back to the Chamber of Conferral about an hour later and found Silestin's secretary and Desidora both still there.

"As you return to the world, the gods return the privacy of your mortal soul," Desidora intoned, rising smoothly to her feet. "Recover your vestments."

She turned her back on the Archvoyant, and Tern did the same, thus allowing him to swap the actual robe back in.

Tern raised an eyebrow. Desidora winced and withdrew *two* glowing crystals from the folds of her robe. Tern's eyes widened, and Desidora gave her a helpless shrug.

Risking a quick glance back, Tern saw that the Archvoyant and his secretary were still occupied. She held a hand out, and Desidora, after seeing Tern's insistent nod, slipped the crystal to her.

"Which pocket?" Tern breathed. Desidora touched a finger to her heart, and Tern nodded.

"You can turn around now, ladies," the Archvoyant said cheerfully, and Tern jumped, then turned. Silestin was back in his dashing military uniform.

"You are free to return to the world of men," Desidora proclaimed, "but remember that your soul has been bared for all to see."

"Noted," the Archvoyant murmured, and turned to go.

"Archvoyant?" Tern asked, stepping forward boldly and blushing just a little. "I just wanted to tell you that your speech was *wonderful*. I think it will be a, a, a life-changing thing, and one day I'll be able to tell my children that I saw it. Thank you *so much!*" And with her eyes, she put out just a little desperation, a little wide-eyed reminder that he'd made her an offer.

"Good people like you," the Archvoyant said, smiling fondly, "are the reason that what I said today is so important. I think that good things are coming for everybody," he said, and he nodded and gave her a knowing smile. "You take care of yourself, young lady," he added, and gave her that same companionable pat on the shoulder.

Then he and the secretary left, and as soon as they were gone, both Tern and Desidora sagged against the wall.

"Slipped it into his jacket pocket during the shoulder-pat?" Desidora asked.

"Yep. You got the encryption crystal mapped?"

"Indeed." Desidora let out a long breath. "I do *not* have smoldering eyes. Or intentions regarding your illusionist wizard."

"Who says he's *my* illusionist wizard?"

"I'm a former love priestess, Tern. I can read auras."

"They do smolder a bit. Is there *any* chance you could tone it down?"

"I'll work on it."

"Thanks. Desidora?"

"Yes?"

"Left jacket pocket or right jacket pocket?"

The death priestess pursed her lips. "Right."

"Oh. We should probably be going, then."

Fourteen

"**W**HAT IN THE HELL KIND OF TEMPLE ARE YOU RUNNING, Kuoric?"

Yesterday's speech had gotten rave reviews, and even without the Prime there to turn his back and let Silestin make his special preparations, things had gone well.

None of which apparently mattered.

The Prime of Ael-meseth, highest representative of the ruler of the gods, shrank back. "You have little cause to complain—"

The Archvoyant cut him off with a gesture. "We had a *deal*. You didn't carry through on it. Even more, someone tampered with my belongings. Now either you're *incompetent* enough to let this happen, or you were *in on it*." Silestin narrowed his eyes. "For your sake, Kuoric, you'd better hope that it was incompetence."

"I will not be threatened!" The Prime rose and glowered down at Silestin. "You presume much, Archvoyant."

"Do you know what happened yesterday, you little twit?" Silestin snarled. "The *Lapitemperum* was broken into by someone who copied information about the security wards for my palace. And while I left my personal items, including an encryption crystal, in the care of your *priestess*, they were touched, possibly altered! I *presume* that you're either an idiot or part of a plan to stab me in the back, and I'd like to know which."

The Prime stiffened. "You mistake yourself, *Silestin.* Guards?" Several acolytes stepped into the room. "Show the Archvoyant out. Then summon the senior priests."

"Fifteen minutes," Silestin murmured, and shook his head. Then he looked up at the Prime. "Goodbye, Kuoric."

Then he turned and left with his fussy little secretary in tow.

They were back in Cevirt's lounge. Loch was swirling another glass of red wine, watching the trails it left around the glass. "So... talk to me," she said, and drank. It was good wine, and she was drinking it now just in case she heard anything that was going to disappoint her later.

"The party is in five days," Cevirt began. "It's a Victory Ball, to celebrate the treaty with the Empire. There will be hundreds of people in the palace."

"And among such foliage, our natural colors shall serve to conceal?" asked Ululenia, who was in human form tonight, her horn shining brightly. Dairy sat on an ottoman next to her, flushing as she wove flowers into his hair.

"If you mean are you invited," Cevirt said, turning to Loch with a raised eyebrow, "the answer is yes. As Voyant, I can procure enough invitations to get you inside."

"Good enough." Loch raised her glass in a silent toast, then took a sip. It was *still* damn good wine. She was afraid she was getting used to the good stuff again. "Tern?"

"We got the encryption crystal," Tern said, holding it up behind the fruity pink stuff in her glass so that the scintillating colors played through it. "I'll tinker to see if I can pull anything about Silestin's personal code out of it, but at the very least, this makes it *possible* for me to crack the vault." She glanced over at Desidora, looked like she was about to say something snide, and then actually stopped herself.

"Good. Desidora, the *Lapitemperum* crystal. Was it worth me going in to save Kail?"

"I wouldn't go that far," the death priestess said, tossing her auburn hair with a little smile at Kail, who flushed and spilled his beer, "but I believe that with it, Magister Hessler and I can find the source of the Voyancy Aura ward and shut it down."

"Good. If you can find out where it's likely to be in Silestin's palace, we can come up with a plan to get into it. Since," Loch added dryly, looking at Hessler, "there's some small chance that there'll be guards. Ululenia, how about Silestin himself?"

"His mind is as a stone in a grassy field, silent and unmoving," said Ululenia, frowning. One of the flowers in Dairy's hair sprouted a few new buds.

"So... no, then." Loch turned to Desidora. "How about the mausoleum?"

"Difficult but possible." The priestess paled slightly and looked at Tern. "I'll need help breaking the security."

Tern gulped her drink. "Sure. Happy to help. I just don't wanna see the zombie, okay? That's where I draw the line."

"Good. Now... exit strategy?"

"If nothing goes wrong, you can simply leave with me," Cevirt offered.

"Something always goes wrong," Loch said dryly.

Cevirt nodded. "In that case... if you're already getting into the vault, you could use the escape rune. There's one in the vault room of every palace. Activate it, and it magically transports everyone in the room to the airship hangar."

"Perfect. Show Desidora and Hessler how to activate it." Loch turned to everyone else. "The party is in five days." She grinned. "We know what we need to do. Hit the research, ask quietly for whatever additional information we need. The clock is running."

"Study the old books," the Prime ordered. "If she wields Ghylspwr, then she is chosen by prophecy, and if she could mask her own magic to falsify our aura...." He shuddered, and the senior priests of Ael-meseth fell back in fear. "She may be of Byn-kodar."

"How could a servant of the death-daemon be chosen by the gods?" one of the priests asked.

"That is none of your concern!" the Prime snapped. "Investigate the Archvoyant as well. What has he done to attract the attention of prophecy? We must know, so that we may act as the gods decree."

"He has been seen with one of the Glimmering Folk," one of the priests, an Urujar, suggested. "There are old Urujar folk tales—"

"This is not the time for silly superstitions!" Massaging his temples, the Prime paused for a moment. "But we must try all avenues. Yes, investigate the stories of the Glimmering Folk. And find out everything known about the warhammer." He shook his head. "She is the instrument of the gods themselves, and she wants something relating to the Archvoyant. Find out what it is. This is your holy charge."

They left. They were wise men and women, efficient and strong in their command of the resources of the temple. They would carry out the Prime's will, so that he might carry out Ael-meseth's will in turn. It might come about that the Prime had been wrong, and if that were the case, he would make amends, then exile himself to a monastery for his retirement. He was a proud man, more than a little accustomed to the politics of the Spire, but if that was necessary, he would do it.

"Whatever we must do, my lord," he whispered, clutching his amulet in an old gesture of faith. "If the Archvoyant is your foe, then—"

"Fifteen minutes," came a quiet voice beside him, and the blade slashed across his throat.

Orris walked to the Twilight Park. The park always faced the sunset, and as it was set right at the edge of the city, there was always a gorgeous and unobstructed view.

It was also the park where Loch and her gang had landed, where Orris's life had been ruined by her conniving ways. The gardeners had cleaned up the torn grass, but there were burn marks on some of the nearby buildings that still attested to her passage.

Orris's wife had left him when he'd lost his position. Orris leaned on a railing overlooking the great drop and stared down at the world below, trying to find his place in it.

"You cannot jump," came a voice from behind him, and Orris turned, startled, to see the rainbow-flickering form of Ambassador Bi'ul standing behind him. "I can sense the protective wards beneath the ground." He gestured. "If you jumped, you would bounce back inside."

"I wasn't planning to jump," Orris retorted.

"The justicar makes progress on tracking down the woman," Bi'ul said. "I believe he will locate her soon."

"So you've come to rub it in, have you?" Orris said bitterly, turning back to glare at the Glimmering Man.

Bi'ul blinked. "I would have to care about your opinion to, as you say, *rub it in.*" He chuckled at the thought. "No, Orris, I am here to offer you my assistance."

The air before him rippled, and he reached into that ripple and pulled out the most magnificent suit of armor Orris had ever seen.

It was an old-fashioned set of plate armor, with chain at the throat and the joints for flexibility. It was black, shimmering and glossy, as though it were covered in oil. Curved spikes jutted out from the joints. The helmet had a horrific daemon-faceplate, and red lenses set into the eyeholes glowed with a smoky radiance.

Orris knew that it would fit him. He'd be able to break a man's neck with one hand. He'd laugh while blades glanced harmlessly off him. His voice cracked as he asked, "Why me?"

"You appear desperate enough to accept it," Bi'ul said, unperturbed. "And I wish for the matter of the escaped prisoners to be resolved. It distracts Archvoyant Silestin from his dealings with me." The Glimmering Man paused. "And I am… troubled by the strange presence I felt on the airship. I wish to resolve this matter."

"That's the why," Orris said cautiously. "But what's the catch?"

"There is a cost," Bi'ul said with a shrug. "There is always a cost. In this case, the cost is the soul of a single mortal."

Orris licked his lips. "Does it have to be mine?"

Bi'ul smiled. "I would accept Loch's in exchange."

"You'll have it," said Orris, and reached out to don the Glimmering Man's gift.

Naria walked through the market square with two guards flanking her and another helping her find her way.

Then a commotion on the far side of the market caught the attention of the guards, and they left her at a stall on her own for a moment, feeling the soft silks whose beautiful colors she could not see, and a moment later, Icy's voice came to her from above. "Can I offer my assistance, fair Naria?"

She jumped and turned her face to either side, and when he said her name again, she realized that he was above her, and she raised her arms. His strong hands caught her wrists, and then she was rising into the air, sliding over the awning, and falling into Icy's arms.

"My indomitable courteous savior returns," she murmured, settling into the awning. Below her, the guards came around the corner and gave startled exclamations at the disappearance of their charge.

When they were gone, Icy said, "I did not wish to intrude, but if you wished to wander the market with greater freedom, I felt obliged to help."

"It is no intrusion," Naria said, smiling shyly. "The Archvoyant wishes to protect me, but his protection is often more than I can bear."

Icy paused. "Are you happy with him?"

"I was once the daughter of a minor lord," she said, shaking her head. "When bandits killed my family, Silestin saved me. I owe him everything." She sighed. "But there are times when I wish it was not all speeches and appearances, that I was more than just an example of his beneficence."

Icy let out a long breath. "Perhaps," he said, "if you truly wish a life of freedom, I may offer my assistance...."

She was so pleased after that that she fell into his arms, and then into his robes, and then Icy and Naria discovered that if one has the proper balance, an awning is a wonderful place to entertain company.

Cevirt's training room was seeing more action than it had seen in years.

On one end, Hessler was summoning illusions and then examining them in the mirror with a critical eye. Off in a corner, Ululenia was making grass grow out of the training mats, while in the well-padded sparring ring, Loch was working out her tension by teaching Dairy how to fight.

The boy hit the ground and shook his head. "What did I do wrong that time?" he asked.

Loch helped him up. "You lifted your shoulder before you punched. Like I said, don't wind up like you're trying to knock over a house. At least, not unless you're distracting your opponent with your other hand."

"But…" Dairy put a hand to his jaw, a gesture he'd likely learned from Hessler. "That's how to get the most strength from your punch, isn't it?"

"Sure," said Loch, "but that's not always the goal." When the kid had his arm up like that, it made his sleeve fall down and show off the birthmark on his arm. It looked a little like a big bird and a little like a sword and a lot like a big silvery birthmark with no shape whatsoever.

Dairy lunged in with a battle cry, and Loch parried, stepped behind him, kicked his ankle out from under him, and gently laid him on the ground. "You fight like a knight, kid."

Dairy flushed, evidently pleased, as Loch helped him to his feet. "The farmer who raised me said that my father might have been a knight. There was a sword and a dragon stitched into the blanket they found me in."

"Listen. Fighting like a knight is good if you've got a good sword and a good shield and a good horse," Loch said as Dairy came at her again, "but in *this* world, the bad guys are better armed and better armored." As he wound back for a punch, Loch lunged in and stopped her speared fingers an inch shy of the kid's throat. "And if we fight fair, they win. Which is why we use every trick we know to stay alive."

Dairy sheepishly dropped his fist. "I suppose, Captain Loch. But…" He frowned, and then spoke with simple determination. "But it shouldn't be that way."

"No argument here, kid." Loch turned to see Icy and Kail returning. "Afternoon, gentlemen. How goes it?"

"Quite well." Icy was whistling and smiling vaguely. "I am feeling well prepared and relaxed."

"Everybody but me, I guess," Kail muttered. "Captain, can I have a word?"

"Certainly. Icy, work with Dairy, will you?" Loch gave the kid an encouraging nod. "We're teaching him some combat moves."

Icy continued to smile vaguely. "I am forbidden by my oaths from causing him injury, but I can evade. And perhaps throw him, very gently."

"Wonderful. Dairy, remember what I taught you. Kail, with me." Loch nodded to Ululenia and Hessler and left the training hall. "Meeting room?" she asked him after a moment.

Kail grimaced. "The free bar is ruining my appreciation for bad beer."

Loch grinned. "How about a kahva?"

"Cevirt's kahva tastes like dogs have been rolling around in it."

"I know a place in town."

They left Cevirt's palace and walked for a while in silence. Kail seemed troubled, but the range of things that troubled Kail was such that Loch wasn't overly concerned.

"Looks like Icy's getting some," she said. It was early afternoon, and Tern was right—the stones of the street didn't sound quite right.

"Who isn't?" Kail gave her a look. "I mean, besides me."

"You? I figured you were all worn out from passing time with everyone's mothers."

They reached the kahva-house. Loch got a kahva with cream, and Kail, as he always did, got some idiotic iced thing with too much sugar and spice and syrup. Still, after drinking rainwater collected from an old leather tarp behind enemy lines, one was entitled to a few creature comforts.

She sipped her kahva. It was a strong, fresh Urujar blend. "So, what's the trouble?"

"Why don't you tell me, Captain?"

She raised an eyebrow. "Tell you what?"

"Why we're still on this damn job." Kail leaned forward. "You said we'd back out if it didn't look do-able. I need you to tell me that this is looking do-able."

"We've got the invite," said Loch, sipping her kahva. "We've got a plan for both of the auras, and Tern thinks—"

"Tern's too busy trying to one-up the *death priestess* you signed on with us to be logical," Kail shot back, lowering his voice to a harsh whisper. "And the *plan* involves smuggling a damn zombie into Silestin's vault!"

"We can—"

"Is this about your sister?"

"Naria?" Loch sat back, laughing despite herself. "You think I'd come all the way up here to, what? Rescue her?"

"Does she need rescuing?" Kail asked evenly.

"She's playing politics," Loch said. Her fingers cupped the kahva mug. "That's her call. I've got no reason to interfere with that."

"Then why are we *doing* this, Captain?" Kail asked angrily. "Why don't you have Cevirt pull some strings, if you want your damn inheritance so much? Or," he added, "if you want to rob somebody, let's rob somebody who doesn't have the Republic's finest security at his disposal!"

"You know who I saw on the airship, Kail? Jeridan." At Kail's blank stare, she gestured angrily. "Jeridan, from the Cleaners. He was one of that snarling crew of madmen."

Kail snorted. "Jeridan couldn't fight."

"He could after whatever Silestin did to him," Loch said evenly.

"Are you saying—"

"I don't *know* what I'm saying, Kail. He attacked me, and he asked me to kill him while he did it."

"Did you?" Kail sipped his kahva.

"It didn't come up." Loch cupped her kahva mug again, holding in the warmth. "Whatever Silestin is doing, whatever power he wields, we need to stop him."

Kail put down his drink. "Last time I checked, you weren't wearing a justicar's stripes."

"He robbed *me*, Kail." Loch's fingers hurt. She pulled them away from the mug, saw color bleed back into the knuckles. "While you and I were fighting our way back out of the Empire, he was taking my home, my *sister*, and using it for his politics. I *need* this, Kail. I don't need him dead. I just need to beat him."

He laughed, and Loch felt a tension she hadn't been aware of loosen up in her shoulders. "You're a lousy liar, Captain. But I'll ride through Byn-kodar's hell for you anyway."

Loch smiled, took his hand across the table. "Thanks. Anything else you need to get off your chest?"

He grinned sourly. "Yes. Close the deal with whomever you're seducing. The tension is making you cranky."

"I don't see that being a problem," Loch assured him with a grin. "If I'm lucky, I'll have that wrapped up before Silestin's Victory Ball."

They finished their kahva and left in silence, but it was the silence of old friends.

At a table in the corner, out of sight but not earshot from the table where Loch and Kail had been sitting, Justicar Pyvic sat for a long moment in silence. Then he let out a breath through gritted teeth, paid for his kahva, and went to make his report.

Fifteen

PYVIC STRODE PAST THE PROTESTING ELKINSAIR AND INTO THE sitting room to find Silestin drinking a cup of kahva and looking at a book. "Archvoyant."

"Justicar." Silestin put down the book. "I don't recall us having an appointment."

"You'll want to hear this, sir." Pyvic took a breath. "I have a strong lead on the whereabouts of Prisoner Loch. My evidence suggests that she may be planning some action against you personally."

"You don't say." The Archvoyant smiled faintly.

"I also have reason to suspect that she may be operating with a member of the Voyancy to gain entry into your palace. If you'll allow me to make inquiries—"

"You vote Skilled, Justicar?" Silestin sipped his kahva.

"I don't believe that that's relevant at this stage of—"

"They were the ones who pushed for you," Silestin drawled.

Pyvic slammed a fist down on Silestin's desk, sending kahva dancing over the edge of the Archvoyant's cup. "I've overcome your political wrangling to solve this case, but even I know the chaos that would erupt if I walked in and arrested a Voyant. I'm bringing this to you first out of *respect*."

Silestin cocked his head. "Are you, now? After all the chaos you've caused, you look at the political ramifications *now?* That's awfully considerate of Voyant Cevirt."

Pyvic felt the blood drain from his face. "You knew?"

"What will it look like," Silestin asked softly, "when *my* people bring in the Skilled Voyant plotting against me, while the Skilled-appointed justicar does nothing?"

Pyvic looked at Elkinsair, then back at the smiling Archvoyant, and dashed from the room.

Silestin glared at the corner of the room. "I thought he knew nothing."

A man-sized silhouette of utter blackness shimmered from the shadows. "He did."

"Then it'll be close." Silestin gestured. "Go. Take Elkinsair and the hunter with you."

"Pardon my interruption," said Ambassador Bi'ul from the doorway, "but I wish to help." He gestured, and a massive figure in shadow-black armor clanked into the room. "And I have support."

"Ambassador Bi'ul," said Silestin with a lazy smile, "you are a treasure."

"Voyant *Cevirt?*" Melich repeated.

"How many justicars have we got?" Pyvic asked. "Right here, within shouting distance?"

"Twenty," Melich said, still distracted, "more or less. Cevirt?"

"I need them, Captain." Pyvic leaned forward and lowered his voice, so that the entire station-house full of justicars who'd watched Pyvic dash in couldn't hear him. "Silestin wants to do it himself."

"Byn-kodar's hell." Melich stood. "You've got them." He walked past Pyvic. "All justicars with me, *now*. Grab swords and move!"

They hit the street, Pyvic and Melich and about twenty men and women, some strapping on their swords or tugging on boots.

"Seven to five, Pyvic," Melich said quietly, one hand on his own sheathed blade, which was plated and gilded and generally impressive as hell because of his captain's status. His other hand clutched the walking stick, and he limped only a little as they marched. "Seven Learned and five Skilled means that the Learned can't pass major legislation unless they compromise to get two-thirds."

"I'm familiar with the math, sir." He'd have to tell Melich about Loch at some point. It could well cost him his job.

"If Cevirt is arrested, the Archvoyant picks an interim replacement."

"Yes, it goes to eight-to-four, and then the Learned can push anything through," Pyvic muttered through gritted teeth. "Well aware of the politics, sir. That's why I went to the Archvoyant first."

"Kind of stupid in retrospect, huh?" Melich asked without looking over.

"Might have been I was concentrating on the case and not the politics, sir."

"Bully for you, Pyvic. That's a comfort."

"Perhaps you can chew my ass out after we get this settled, Captain?"

Melich's walking stick clacked with a faster cadence on the cobblestones. "Deal."

Those who weren't out on the town were having celebratory drinks in the sitting room.

"I still don't see why the boy has to go with Loch," Hessler said to Tern as he mixed his drink. Loch and Kail were off somewhere, and Ululenia was trying to get Dairy to drink something.

"Because you're with me, Hessler," Tern said, toasting him gaily with her enormous cocktail glass. "We're the ones dealing with the crystals, and Dairy will be backup for Loch."

"And I'll be there, too!" Desidora chimed in. Tern glared and began flicking her expensive mechanical lighter. Desidora's wineglass briefly grew a skull, then shifted back to normal.

"Why can't he stay here in Cevirt's palace?" Hessler asked plaintively. "There's no logical *reason* for him to come to the party!"

"First, we might need a distraction," Tern said.

"Second, he provides a cunning camouflage for Loch as a simple attendant," Ululenia added, holding the drink up to the blushing boy's lips.

"And third, Loch insisted," Desidora finished, smiling winsomely, "and it's her job. Relax, Magister. The boy will be fine."

It wasn't as though Hessler cared about that kid. He was barely old enough to shave, and had far too much youthful idealism. If he screwed up, they could *all* get caught. It was really just enlightened self-preservation.

"I think we'd *all* be safer if he stayed behind," Hessler tried. "The kid always seems to press the wrong button or say the wrong thing...."

As if on cue, Dairy gagged on Ululenia's drink and spat it out in a great spray that crossed the tiny flame playing on Tern's lighter. The liquid ignited in a flaring arc of blue fire, missing Hessler by inches and setting fire to the drapes, the sofa, and Hessler's drink, which promptly exploded in a *second* gout of blue fire and set fire to the carpet.

"Case in point!" Hessler added acidly while Tern screamed and started stomping on the flaming carpet. Ululenia gestured, horn flaring, and fluffy white clouds near the ceiling began to shower the room with a gentle spring rain.

In a few short moments, everything was extinguished but wet and smoky. Cevirt himself arrived and offered some caustic commentary. Dairy, still coughing, apologized profusely, and Hessler observed that nothing would have happened had Tern not been playing with her lighter, which then made Tern glare at Hessler in the manner previously reserved for Desidora, who was laughing lightly and apparently unconcerned by the effect that a sudden spring rain had on her thin robes.

Ululenia shifted into her unicorn form and nuzzled Dairy aboard, and the two headed off to get something to make Dairy feel better. Desidora went with them at Tern's insistence, given that the unicorn had tried to get the poor kid drunk once already, and also given that Desidora's robes were *very* wet. Cevirt left to search for more towels.

"Well, *that* was a disaster," Hessler muttered, upending a wineglass to dump out the rainwater.

"Oh, I don't know," said Tern, the only other person in the room. She gave Hessler a sunny smile. "You and I finally have a chance to talk!"

Hessler squinted. "About what?"

Tern rolled her eyes and tugged at her sodden brown dress, which now clung to her tightly and outlined all the illegal things she had in her pockets. "Hey, Hessler, maybe you could help me out of these wet cl—"

She was interrupted by the great crash of the grand door of the palace bursting open.

Melich had used his captain's authorization to open the palace gates, but otherwise, it was Pyvic's show.

While Cevirt's palace was a pale shadow of the opulent masterpiece that was Silestin's, it still shouted wealth and taste and old magic. The walls were bedecked with fluted elven vases and priceless dwarven statues and rare fairy paintings that shimmered and glowed in little dances of color. The stairway to the second floor was lit by sparkling crystals set into the railing, and a magical chandelier cast a golden radiance across the hall.

Smoke poured from the sitting room off to the left, and as Pyvic headed that way, Voyant Cevirt, sopping wet, came around the corner. "What the hell is going on here? Who are you?" he asked with angry surprise.

"Justicar Pyvic of the Heaven's Spire Department of Justice," Pyvic said loudly as the others gathered behind him. "Your pardon, Voyant Cevirt, but we need to search the premises."

"My palace is of course open for you to search," Cevirt said smoothly. "But may I ask if you have a warrant, and what you hope to find?

Pyvic saw his chance, took it. "We have information suggesting that a group of criminals has been hiding in your palace, Voyant."

Cevirt gritted his teeth for just a moment, a barely perceptible tightening across the jaw. "I have not *knowingly* sheltered any criminals," he said in a cautious tone, as Pyvic gave him a tiny nod, "and in fact, I have no guests at the moment. Should you discover anyone, they—"

"Are your accomplices," finished Elkinsair, Silestin's oily little secretary, as he glided through the open main doors, his fussy robes barely moving at his feet. He was flanked by two hulking armored figures. One wore shining golden ringmail, a vibrant green cloak, and a long golden helmet that tapered to a point behind him like a teardrop. The other, even taller, wore an absurd suit of spiked black armor with a daemon-themed helmet, complete with glowing red eyes. Behind them, Ambassador Bi'ul sauntered in, smiling faintly.

"I protest these groundless accusations," Cevirt said without changing expression. "I am cooperating fully with an ongoing investigation-—"

"Byn-kodar take this little *uru*," rasped the figure in the spiky black armor, his metallic voice somehow familiar, and then he stepped past Pyvic and backhanded Cevirt across the room. "We know they're here! *Loch, you can't run forever! I'm coming for you!*"

And then Captain Melich was there, his walking stick clattering to the ground as he put himself in front of the armored figure. "As Captain of the justicars for Heaven's Spire, I am *ordering* you to—"

A knife rippled into view as it sank neatly between the captain's ribs, and he stumbled back from the shadowy figure that was already fading out of sight again. Without hesitation, the black-armored man slammed Melich to the ground with a punch that sent blood spraying.

"No!" Pyvic shouted, his own voice lost in the din of justicars yelling and drawing their weapons.

Cevirt, still on the ground with blood oozing from his shoulder, pulled a crystal wand from the pocket of his robes. "Not in my house, you bastard," he muttered, and activated the wand.

And any chance for a peaceful resolution went to hell as gem-studded security golems burst into the entry hall with crystal swords raised.

Loch was looking at earrings at a small outdoor stall when Kail came running over. "Trouble?"

Kail nodded and gave the merchant, a leathery old white woman, a look. She returned it, and Kail sighed and gestured for Loch to come with him.

"What have you got?" Loch asked quietly when they had a little room. Kail was breathing hard. He'd been looking at swords at a shop down the block when they'd split up.

"Two old guys sitting outside one of the shops." Kail gestured, and Loch squinted and saw them.

"I think we can take them, Kail."

"They saw Justicar Pyvic and twenty of his men heading through town."

Loch swore. "How long ago?"

"Quarter of an hour. It gets worse. A few minutes later, they saw some very large gentlemen in armor, along with Ambassador Bi'ul, heading in the same direction."

"Come on." Loch turned, one hand on her sword hilt from years of training.

"And do what? Loch…" Kail leaned in and lowered his voice. "If we go, all we can do now is—"

"Help. Come on." She took off at a run.

Kail swore, spat into the dirt, and took off after her.

"Hold," the little man said casually, holding up a glowing crystal wand of his own. The security golems froze in mid-step, and their eyes went dark.

"You son of a bitch!" Pyvic shouted, ripping his sword free from its sheath. The justicars were already moving to surround the others.

"Okay," said Hessler, peeking around the sitting room corner at the chaos, "the important thing is not to do anything hasty."

"Hasty in what sense?" Tern asked, and cocked her crossbow.

"If they fight each other," said Hessler, "we may be able to sneak out undetec…" Tern stepped around the corner, leveled her crossbow, and fired a bolt that exploded out into several coils of what Hessler suspected was *yvkefer*-lined chain. It snared the black-armored man as justicars lunged in at him. "…ted. Like that! *Hasty like that!*"

"Well, you could have been less ambiguous," Tern muttered as the justicars' swords glanced harmlessly off the spiked armor. With a roar, the black-armored man snapped the *yvkefer* bonds. "I was really banking on that slowing him down."

Meanwhile, as the justicars swarmed around the golden-armored man, he readied an enormous spear. He deftly parried a justicar's thrust, took another sword in a glancing blow across a shoulder plate, floored one man with the butt of his spear, and ran another through. With nobody between him and the doorway, he took a running leap, vaulted twenty feet up into the air to come down on the balcony overlooking the main entry hall, and disappeared into the palace.

Tern paled as the black-armored man reached out, grabbed a justicar, and snapped his neck. A second justicar fell a moment later, blood fountaining from a slash across the throat, and the black-armored man turned toward Tern. "Loch! I'll kill everyone in here if that's what it takes!"

"I'll bear that in mind."

Tern and Hessler turned to see Loch standing in the ground floor doorway. Her blade was drawn.

"*Aitha!*" Cevirt called from the floor. "Get out of here! In Gedesar's name, *run!*"

The black-armored man roared and clanked toward her, his spiked fists flinging blood in all directions, and Loch turned and ran the other way.

"Your warriors are gone, Elkinsair," Pyvic grated. He had the little man at swordpoint, while a ring of justicars surrounded the Glimmering Man. "You'll want to surrender *right now* before—"

"Defend," Elkinsair said with a smile, holding up the glowing crystal again, and the security golems returned to life. Pyvic dove back as a glowing crystal sword sheared through the floor where he'd been standing.

"Unless you'd like to attract more attention," Hessler muttered, "perhaps this would be an appropriate time to *leave*."

"You learn that at the universi... *crap*." Tern turned to the doorway where Loch and the black-armored man had gone.

A pair of justicars were pulling themselves to their feet between Tern and Hessler and the door. "I suggest simply running," Hessler said. "Given the violence that brute subjected them to, I doubt…."

The justicars turned to face them. One of them clearly had a broken neck, and the other had a massive throat wound that no longer pumped blood. Their eyes glowed green as they raised their weapons.

"I just wish Desidora were here." Tern cranked her crossbow again. "I'd have a hell of a zinger for her."

"Loch, you can't run forever! I'm coming for you!"

The armored man was behind her, and there were twenty or so justicars between Tern and Hessler and the real threats. Everyone knew the fallback point.

Loch had done everything she could to help.

"When I'm done with you," snarled the armored man behind her, "you'll be nothing but a dirty *uru* smear on the floor!"

Loch turned a corner and saw Ululenia and the kid down the hall.

Or perhaps she could play decoy for a bit longer. "Get out of here, *now!*" she shouted down the hall, then turned and ran back toward the armored man.

She was tired from running, but she was still faster than a man in full armor, and she reached the doorway she'd passed before and ducked inside with the armored man close behind her. It was a display room full of statues on pedestals, and the far wall opened to a courtyard that overlooked the rim itself.

"Die!" the armored man shouted, lunging at her without hesitation. He didn't even have a sword. Loch sidestepped his overhand blow and lunged in to stab him just under the arm, where he was protected by mail and not plates.

The sword hit cleanly... and stopped.

His backhanded swipe sent Loch crashing into the wall.

Ululenia danced briefly through Loch's mind, saw the distraction Loch was providing, and ran with her virgin clinging to her back.

She galloped for perhaps twenty heartbeats before the hunter, his armor shining gold and his cloak green, stepped out into the hallway ahead of her. His mind was closed, but he raised his spear as he saw her and called, "Run if you will, creature of magic! I am Hunter Mirrkir, and I sense your foul scent, wherever you flee," and his voice was metal and stone, and she knew that he was no mortal man.

She ran, as the deer ran when the wolf howled, and her virgin clung desperately to her mane. The hunter pursued, relentless, as Ululenia darted down hallways, her hooves clicking on the marble floors or making muffled clumps on the carpet.

She should have lost him, if not by the speed of her sparkling white hooves than by the number of times she had left the hunter's sight, but still he came.

"You cannot escape me!" he called, and the voice was calm. "I have slain hundreds of your kind!" Hunter Mirrkir raised his spear; angry blue magic crackled along its length.

She knew then that she must flee, for her virgin as well as herself. *We must part, my lovely one,* she told him. *Around the next corner, I shall leave you. Remember what Loch told us, and find me again in the garden.*

"But—" her virgin said, and then they were around a corner and a doorway presented itself, and she lunged inside and shifted, and then she was a bird, and her virgin fell behind her.

For twenty blessed heartbeats, she flew, horn flaring. And then an angry hiss split the air, and she sensed the spear. She darted to one side, then felt pain sear her soul as jagged tendrils of crackling blue light leapt from the spear as it missed her.

They coiled around her, cold and hateful, and she fell, four-legged and wingless, her horn fading as the jagged blue light tightened.

The dead justicars came forward, and with a quick backward glance, Hessler saw Bi'ul, the Glimmering Man, staring at them with a bemused smile. His hands were raised, and they glowed with the same crackling green light in the dead men's eyes.

"You summon zombies?" Hessler cried. "Contend with a daemon of Byn-kodar's own hell!" And then he threw out the tendril-monster illusion that had gotten him the second highest grade on last semester's midterm.

"That isn't a daemon," Bi'ul called casually. He raised one hand, clenched the fingers into a fist, and twisted sharply. "*Now* it's a daemon."

Hessler turned and saw his creation looming over him, and then the tendril blasted him across the room.

As the daemon turned to the justicars who *weren't* dead, the dead men continued toward Tern, who had just gotten the abjuration bolt into her crossbow when Kail tackled the two men from behind. "We got made!" he called, punching one of them in the kidney.

"You think?" Tern shot back. A lot of the justicars were down, but Pyvic was doing something to the body of his dead commander as a golem advanced upon him. He drew a crystal from the man's pocket, and a moment later the security golems froze in place. "By the way, those guys are dead."

"Oh." Kail grabbed a sword from one of them, punched the dead men a few more times, and then ran the blade through both of them, pinning them together. "Good to know. Uh…"

Tern looked. The daemon was turning their way.

"Protect Hessler! I've got an idea!" She ran into the sitting room, her brown dress sloshing with every step, as Kail swore mightily.

She came out a moment later to see Kail diving under a massive cloud of black tentacles whose claws cracked the marble of the entry chamber floor. She ignored that as best she could, hefting her lighter in one hand and an incredibly expensive bottle of dwarven whiskey in the other.

"Hey, Glimmering Man!" she shouted at Bi'ul, and threw the whiskey. "This should make you glimmer a bit brighter!"

The bottle shattered at Bi'ul's feet, sending whiskey everywhere, and Tern flicked her lighter and prepared to throw it.

Nothing happened.

"Son of a bitch." Tern looked at her dead lighter while the Glimmering Man turned her way.

"Besyn larveth'is!"

It turned out that even a *magical* crystal chandelier couldn't withstand a thrown warhammer.

It *also* turned out that whatever magic the chandelier used actually had a little fire in it.

As the whooshing flames engulfed the Glimmering Man, Tern spared Desidora, arm still extended in throwing position on the second-floor balcony, a quick wave. And then she helped Kail get Hessler to his feet, and *then* she ran like hell with her wet dress sloshing everywhere, because the Glimmering Man wasn't keeling over or flailing about in pain as the flames engulfed him.

He was laughing.

The hateful chains loosened, and Ululenia came back to her senses to see her virgin standing over her. She shifted to her human shape, and the chains loosened further still.

"But how…" she asked weakly, for her virgin was tearing the chains free with his bare hands, and they came apart like wet paper and fluttered into nothingness.

"It tingles," he said, "but it doesn't really hurt."

"It's evil," Ululenia protested. It was difficult to think, still.

"Evil is just an illusion," her virgin said with adorable sincerity.

"But I am not," came the horrible grating voice from behind him, and Ululenia looked up to see Hunter Mirrkir sauntering toward them, his golden armor shining. His spear had returned to his hand. Even at this close range, Ululenia could sense nothing behind the golden mask that shielded his face. "You are mine, creature of magic."

"I have apparently missed events of note," said Indomitable Courteous Fist as he stepped out from a doorway. "But I believe that you are inappropriately optimistic." He put himself between Ululenia and Mirrkir.

"Stand aside or die, mortal." His emerald cloak billowing around him, the hunter readied his spear. Ululenia struggled to her feet.

"I believe," Icy said calmly, "that a third option may present itself shortly."

Ululenia's beautiful virgin chose that moment to say, "But Mister Icy, you aren't allowed to hurt anyone!"

"My disciplines preclude violence against living creatures," Icy agreed, bringing his arms up with his thumbs and fingertips barely touching. "They do *not*, however, preclude demonstrations on nonliving material."

And then he struck the wall.

"Gosh!" said the virgin as the hallway caved in, putting several hundred pounds of rock between Ululenia and Hunter Mirrkir.

Icy rose slowly to his feet and snapped his palms in the air, sending little clouds of dust puffing out. "This concludes my demonstration of applied balance and momentum. It should also, coincidentally, buy us the necessary time to retreat," he said with a little nod, "though I suggest haste nevertheless."

Ululenia shook the last cobwebs free from her mind and shifted to her true form. *Astride me, quickly, both of you. Today, Indomitable Courteous, you are an honorary virgin.*

At some point, Loch had lost the sword. She'd stabbed the bastard in the armpit, the knee, even the damn *visor*. She'd taken hard hits for doing so, and for all that trouble, she hadn't so much as slowed him down.

"Getting tired, girl?" he gloated as she got back to her feet, wiping blood from her mouth.

"Tired of you, jackass." She grunted as he came in again, ducking under a swipe that tore the head off a statue and stomping on the back of his knee. It dropped him to a crouch, but he spun and hammered her back with an open palm, and she hit the ground a few yards away and pushed herself to her feet again, bleeding at the shoulder.

"What's the matter, Loch?" he roared. "Not ready to fight a real man?"

"Guess we'll know when I meet one." She probably should have run. Stupid to stand and fight. She could have ducked him for a few minutes, but she'd been so proud, so certain. The bastard was between her and the doorway now, and she was breathing hard and limping.

He came at her again, and Loch dodged, and then dodged again, and then came up with a statue to her back at a critical moment and couldn't quite get out of the way, and a spiked fist clipped her shoulder. She hit the ground hard, and the world went gray as she felt the armored gauntlets lifting her into the air.

The crushing impact slammed her back to wakefulness, and she cried out as she bounced back to the ground. The air over the balcony railing shimmered with pink radiance where he had thrown her.

"Oh, that's right," he declared heartily. "Bi'ul mentioned the safety barrier. Crystals that power it oughta be right about..." As she dragged her aching body to her knees, the armored man punched through the marble stones, sending shards of rock flying. "Here!" He stood, holding red crystals in his gauntlets, and then shattered them in his grip. The air hissed as the barrier blinked away, and Loch struggled to her feet, but not fast enough, as a mailed hand closed around her throat.

He dangled her over the railing, the magical armor granting him the strength to hold her at arm's length with a single hand. She grabbed at her throat with one hand, hammered her fist in vain against the back of his elbow with the other.

"You escaped with a long fall last time," said the man in the black armor. "Let's see if you can escape again the same way."

Both hands went to her throat, now, and with superhuman effort she loosened his grip enough to breathe. "At least," she gasped, "it was you that got me, not that slug Orris."

The armored man lifted his free hand to his visor, and the helmet opened to reveal the sneering face of Warden Orris himself. "That's what you think!" he cackled. "It *is* me in this—"

Loch's hands scissored, one hand slamming into the gauntlet that gripped her throat and the other hammering the *inside* of Orris's elbow. It buckled, and as his collapsing arm brought her in close, she drove her fist into the bastard's face.

He yelled, dropped her, and stepped away, and she hit the ground and stayed on her feet through sheer force of will. He reached up to close the visor, but she lunged in and broke his nose. Orris stumbled backward, flailing wildly, and she grabbed hold of the upturned edge of his visor and used the leverage to wrench him into the railing.

"I..." She hit him in that sneering face, again and again, still holding him up by the edge of his visor. "...knew...it... was...you!" The final punch struck him with such force that he spun and hit the railing, and he teetered over the edge.

Loch grabbed him by the feet and heaved, and Warden Orris left Heaven's Spire once and for all.

Loch would have given a lot to lean there on the railing, hurting from a hundred injuries and bleeding in at least four places, and watch Orris hit the ground. But if they'd found her then, she'd always have wondered if Orris had slowed her down enough to let her get caught.

Elkinsair and Bi'ul had taken Voyant Cevirt, leaving Pyvic and his justicars behind.

The daemon had vanished when the chandelier fell, and most of the justicars were still alive. When the golems had attacked, they'd reacted well. Melich would be proud.

Would have been proud, Pyvic corrected with a knifing grief, crawling toward his captain and ignoring the long and jagged pain where one of the golems had been too fast.

Melich's eyes fastened on him as he crawled over.

"Not your fault," Pyvic's captain rasped. Blood flecked his lips.

"It is." Tears burning his eyes, Pyvic finally collapsed. "I went to Silestin. I didn't get here fast enough. Damn the gods, I fell for her."

"Pyvic." The word bubbled in Melich's mouth. "Not your fault." He gestured with the hand that wasn't holding the wound at his ribs. "They're yours, now. Protect them."

"I will." Pyvic forced himself to his elbows. "We'll get you to a healer, Captain. We'll—"

"Protect them all, Pyvic." Melich lay back, shut his eyes with a final rattling sigh, and died.

Sixteen

"**T**HE ARREST OF VOYANT CEVIRT, A PROMINENT MEMBER OF the Skilled Party and the first Urujar in the Voyancy, comes as a shock to the Republic," the dragon proclaimed solemnly to the hushed crowd. "It also raises many political issues on Heaven's Spire."

"Well," said the manticore, rearing up, "I don't think you can have this conversation without asking whether this was a Skilled cover-up from the beginning."

"We don't even know why Cevirt was arrested!" the griffon protested. It tried to rear up as well, but the dragon tripped it with its tail to the laughter of the crowd.

"Voyant Cevirt was arrested for harboring the prisoners who had escaped from Heaven's Spire," the manticore said seriously, lashing out with its scorpion stinger. "The Skilled justicar who was assigned to the case did a completely unacceptable job, and it was Archvoyant Silestin's personal investigators who actually made the arrest."

"But witnesses saw the justicar going in first!" the griffon shouted. The manticore pounced on it, and the griffon ran away, trying to fling the manticore off.

"And now," the manticore shouted, "we've learned that the prisoner who masterminded all of this was in fact Isafesira de Lochenville, Voyant Cevirt's god-daughter, who was *presumed* lost behind enemy lines during the war!"

"The arrests would have been made peacefully without the interference of the Archvoyant's—" The griffon broke off as the dragon swatted it.

"Please, please!" it roared, belching flames as the griffon and the manticore cringed away and the crowd laughed. "Please try to keep this civil. This is *not* a forum for personal attacks!"

"The Skilled have been soft on Imperials for years, "the manticore declared, "and now a possible Imperial agent comes to the Spire and a Skilled Voyant helps her?"

"We have *no proof* that Isafesira de Lochenville is an agent of the Empire!" the griffon protested weakly.

The manticore wasn't even listening. "I think that decades from now, children in their schools are going to ask, 'How did they respond to this threat?' Now is not the time to question Archvoyant Silestin. Now is the time to let the Archvoyant do his job."

"Strong words in dangerous times!" the dragon declared, turning to the crowd and throwing out candy. "Remember, everyone, *it's your republic!*"

"Stay informed!"

"Explain to me," Pyvic said to Archvoyant Silestin, "why I shouldn't have you arrested."

"Because my assistants would break your arms," Silestin said, smiling faintly. "And then you'd be out of a job."

"Six justicars died because of your *assistants.*" Pyvic took an angry step toward Silestin, narrowing his eyes when the golden-armored man raised a spear.

"Six justicars died because Isafesira de Lochenville, sister of my adopted daughter Naria, refused to come along peacefully," Silestin answered without heat.

"That's garbage, Archvoyant." Pyvic considered the golden-armored man. He'd killed two of Pyvic's friends. "Maybe I'm arresting the wrong person."

"Hunter Mirrkir would be harder to arrest than you think." Silestin was still smiling. "And it doesn't matter what happened in that room. Would you like to know why?"

"Politics," Pyvic said in disgust.

"Politics," Silestin agreed, and then lost his smile. "So listen carefully, boy. You lost six, and that's sad. Those were good men and women serving the Republic. They're heroes." Silestin's voice was as commanding as when he'd led in the field. "Lochenville was lost behind enemy lines. The investigation determined that she'd likely deserted or turned for the Empire. Cevirt had that report changed, ostensibly to protect my daughter Naria. When Lochenville returns, she's arrested trying to break into the Spire. She escapes, then comes back up to the Spire *again,* and you yourself admit that she's planning something aimed at *me.* And when we find her, she's living with Cevirt, who's been blocking the vote on trade sanctions against the Empire for the past few months."

"You think she's an Imperial agent?" Pyvic asked skeptically.

"I don't know *what* in Byn-kodar's hell to think!" Silestin thundered. "But it's my job to *protect* the Republic! If she looks like an Imperial agent, I'm going to do whatever it takes to stop her! If it looks like the Skilled are being bought by the Empire to keep us weak and rudderless, I'm going to push legislation through however I can!" His voice lowered ominously. "And if a justicar tries to stop me, I will *cut off* the justicars like a diseased limb. Do you hear me, Pyvic? You lost six. How many more are in the temples with the Republic paying for their treatments? How many widows are feeding their children on a justicar's pension?" He stepped forward and stood eye-to-eye with Pyvic. "I've got no problem with them, Justicar, but if you force me to choose between protecting the Republic and protecting your people, I will. And you won't like the choice."

They're yours now. Protect them.

"I understand, sir." Pyvic stepped back, lowered his gaze respectfully.

Silestin nodded slowly. "I'm glad we do, Justicar." He smiled. "I mean, Captain. It's interim, I know, but I don't see any reason why it won't be approved."

Pyvic forced the words through the ashes that clogged his throat. "Thank you, sir."

"Dismissed, Captain. Oh, and please feel free to come to the Victory Ball." Silestin gave him a grandfatherly smile. "It'll be a good chance for you to meet people."

They'd all gotten to the garden where they'd first landed. On the way, they'd sneaked past a puppet show and heard the news.

"So," she said to them quietly, "the question is, do we continue?"

Tern gave Loch a stare that, magnified by her spectacles, took up close to half her face. "I thought the question was, *how do we get down?* Or maybe *how long can we hide up here?* Or possibly even *what the hell was I thinking to get involved in this in the first place?*"

"You were thinking of money," Hessler said shortly, "or pride, or the challenge of cracking the world's most difficult safe. Don't blame Loch. You got into this yourself, and it's intellectually disingenuous to suggest oth—*ow!*" He began hopping, holding one shin.

"Are we, in fact, Imperial agents?" Icy asked curiously. "If so, I will adopt the necessary patriotism."

"That's a big if, Icy." Kail looked at Loch, and she must not have kept the hurt and surprise from her face. "Captain, if there's any chance, I'm with you, but if we continue, we're doing it without Cevirt's invitation, without any more research on Cevirt's console, and without any special equipment. We've got a palace full of guards, not to mention Silestin's Blades and everyone who attacked us back at Cevirt's place."

Ululenia looked haggard, and her horn was dim, gray rather than incandescent white. Hessler had one arm bandaged. Loch herself probably looked the worst of all of them.

"You remember how Kail and I got stuck behind Imperial lines?" she asked. "And when we came back, my father's barony was gone?"

Kail grimaced. "Loch, this isn't the time."

"What I failed to mention," Loch went on, "was that the mission that sent me behind the lines was given to me personally by Colonel Silestin. He said it was a secret mission, and that we would meet with his army deep in Imperial territory and use the information I'd gained to plan an even deeper assault."

"Tactically sound," Icy noted.

Loch nodded. "And when we got to the rendezvous point, Silestin's army wasn't there." She grimaced. "We spent a long, ugly time behind enemy lines, then got home and found that we'd been written off as dead or deserted. I talked with a few old friends from other units. There *was no assault plan. Ever.*"

"He sent you off to die," said Tern in a small voice.

Hessler sniffed. "You expect us to believe that Silestin hated you enough to make up some phony mission?"

"Shut up, Magister," Loch said without looking at him. "While I was *deserting,* my father's well-defended and strongly fortified castle was overrun by *bandits,* and only the incredibly convenient arrival of *Silestin's* forces saved my sister, who was promptly adopted by Silestin so that he, as caretaker for my family's land, could use Lochenville's resources to fund his run for the Voyancy." She finally turned to Hessler. "Connect the damn dots."

Tern shifted, her boots squeaking on the wet grass. "He sounds like a monster. No argument. But I didn't sign on for assassination."

"Neither did I," Loch said firmly. "He killed my parents. He took my barony. I could kill him with a clean conscience. But I'd rather rob him." She looked around at the others. "The elven manuscript is worth more than Silestin could ever understand. If I sell it back to the elves and split it with you all, I can buy enough support to make Silestin pay for his crimes in public. That's all I care about. And in my opinion, Kail, *we can still do it.*" She let out a breath. "We had what we needed. The only thing that's changed is that we need a new way into the palace, but with the crowd swarming in for the Victory Ball, I think we can manage something."

"What of our foes?" Ululenia said, her voice shaky. "Their spearman's foul magic overcame me."

Hessler nodded. "And the Glimmering Man stole my illusion and gave it solid form, which... well, either one would be difficult from both an energetic standpoint and a conceptual metamagical perspective...." He coughed, seeing the stares. "He's powerful."

"Agreed." Loch nodded. "If we go forward, we need a way to avoid, distract, or negate them both."

"You can't just agree with me!" Hessler sputtered. "You agree and then act like that's something we tackle later. If we can't tackle it *now*, there *is* no later!"

"But we have to, Mister Hessler!" Dairy exclaimed. "We have to stop these men! Stealing this book won't defeat them, but it will hurt them, right, Miss Loch?" Loch nodded. "Then we have to do it," he finished. "We have to. I'm with you, Miss Loch, whatever anyone else says."

"Where my virgin goes," Ululenia said with a wan smile, "so go I." Loch nodded to her. That made three, or four if Kail stayed.

"You can't... Dairy, you don't have to...." Hessler waved angrily. "This isn't the proper way to.... Fine, I will remain, *pending* a plan for dealing with the spearman and the Glimmering Man and that fellow who was wearing the armor of shadows, which, as I recall, lent its wearer invulnerability and superhuman strength."

"But not flight," Loch said dryly. "He's out of the picture."

"I humbly wish to continue," Icy said without further explanation.

"I'm in," said Desidora.

"*Besyn larveth'is!*" Ghylspwr added.

"Oh, of course she is!" Tern said bitterly. "It's a chance for her to raise a zombie for a good cause! Maybe she can steal a few souls while she's at—"

"Want to know the truth about Byn-kodar, Tern?" Desidora asked conversationally. "Want to know why I left Tasheveth the love goddess?" Tern's apple cheeks paled at the death priestess's stare. "The truth is, I *do* make zombies, and I *can* steal souls if I need to." She crossed her arms, and her auburn hair slid to a glossy black. "Want to know something else? Byn-kodar is actually a degradation of the ancient language, as are the names of most gods. Ael-meseth, god of judges, has for a name a corruption of the phrase 'many oaths of trust,' for example.

"But the *full* name of Byn-kodar," Desidora continued as twisted thorny tendrils grew from the grass around the hem of her black robes, "is *Byn-kodar'isti kuru'ur.*"

"With sadness, we steal your life," Hessler translated. "But why 'we'? Or did I conjugate it improperly?"

"The 'we'," Desidora said with a smile that did not warm her alabaster cheeks, "alludes to the fact that *there is no death god*. The power over souls, the power over the dead, is held jointly among all the gods, kept in reserve until they agree that some great danger justifies bringing that power into the world. Then one luckless priest or priestess *loses* her connection to the deity she once served, and becomes what I am, instead."

Tern made a small noise.

"At least they're honest," Desidora continued, and now her eyes were pits of black, and the grass shriveled and died from the palpable aura around her. "*With sadness, we steal your life*. Do you know what I did as a love priestess, Tern?

I arranged marriages. I counseled bickering couples. I helped young lovers find each other. *Now,* I raise zombies."

She shut her eyes for a long moment, biting her lower lip as some great struggle took place inside her.

Then, slowly, the color returned to her hair and cheeks. And when she opened her eyes and spoke, it was her again, and not the thing she had been for a moment. "I'm not here for the money! I'm here because the gods told me that the fate of the world depends upon me!" Her voice broke. "I'm here because if I succeed, I *might* get to be a love priestess again."

"*Kun-kabynalti osu fuir'is,*" Ghylspwr said gently.

"Shut up, Ghyl." Desidora wiped at her eyes and turned to Loch. "I'm in. We're in." Icy held out an arm, but she waved him off.

Loch nodded. "I can't guarantee that the Glimmering Man will cross our path, but I'm grateful for your help for as long as you're with us."

"When do we start?" Tern asked in a small voice. She was sort of hunched over, and the hair that swept down over her face accentuated the mousy look.

Loch shut her eyes and allowed herself one quiet moment of victory. "Same time as before," she said. "We'll scout the palace until the ball to figure out how to get in."

She looked around at all of them, some angry, some injured, all exhausted. "Thank you."

"Don't *thank* us," Kail said in a shocked, horrified voice. "We're in this for the *money,* Captain."

Kail hadn't been the best of her scouts, but he'd been the one who could always make her laugh. "My mistake," she said primly. "Let's find a place to hide for the next few nights."

Orris drifted in a gray landscape, a place without pain or pleasure. He had forgotten how long he had been here. He could look around the landscape, but he could not move his feet. They were pinned to the shadow that lay on the ground behind him. The shadow had spikes on it. That had meant something to him, something important, when he first arrived. He thought.

A shining man approached, a man who walked as though the sun were behind him, shining in all the colors of the rainbow.

Orris remembered.

"No," he said.

"I am sorry," said the shining man, but his voice sounded like laughter. "A deal is a deal, and you did not get Loch's soul to save your own."

"Loch," said Orris. The name made him feel... something. "I... hate her, I think."

"Probably," said the shining man equably. "That's impressive, so hold onto it. You might even have haunted her, had you not had other commitments." He reached down to the shadow on the ground and, without ceremony, plucked Orris's feet free from it. Then he began to wind Orris's body up as though he were rolling a sheet of paper into a tube.

"No," Orris said again.

"You mortals often say that you wish to see interesting things," said the shining man. "It is *much* more interesting where you are going. At least, it is more colorful."

Orris was a little rolled-up ball, and the shining man held him, and because the shining man was just a silhouette with all the colors of the rainbow behind him, Orris was quite close before he realized that the shining man had opened his mouth.

It turned out that the gray landscape was not *entirely* devoid of pain.

Loch was in the kahva-house, looking for new insights in *The Uncovering of Bounty in Inhospitable Climates*, when Pyvic walked in.

She looked up at him for a long moment. He did the same with her. People seemed unsure of exactly what was going on, but there was a lot of staring.

When he became aware of it, he sat across from her. The crowd looked away. She raised an eyebrow.

"You shouldn't have come here," he said. He looked tired. She knew she was.

"It's the best kahva in town," she said. She'd stashed the sword, but had a knife up one sleeve. "I can't stay away just because things got complicated."

"Complicated?" He chuckled. It didn't reach his eyes. "I could arrest you right here... *Isafesira*. Six of my men are dead."

"And *none* of my men killed them. The Archvoyant's men took care of that." She raised an eyebrow. "Why did *you* come back here?"

"To see how stupid you were."

"Very, apparently. Are you angry because I'm robbing Silestin, or because you fell for me?"

"Fell for you?" Pyvic's lip curled in disgust. "How many mixed-race Urujar women do you think were both in Ros-Oanki and up here on the Spire? You didn't *fool* me, Prisoner Loch."

Her eyes narrowed. "So why the show?"

"They pulled me off of *real* cases to hunt you down," Pyvic said, quietly seething. "And I thought that maybe, *maybe* there was more to the story. More to why Silestin was so desperate to find you, why you were so desperate to take him down." He sat back. "But as it turns out, you're just a deserter and a thief."

"If you say so, Justicar. I'm sure you've done the necessary research to back up that claim."

"I could arrest you right here," he said again. "I could blow a whistle and have twenty guards here in a minute."

"You could do that." She sipped her kahva. "You could bring in your guards to attack an Urujar woman in an Urujar kahva-house shortly after the arrest of the first and only Urujar Voyant. I'm sure the people here would be just fine with that." She smiled. She didn't try for the seductive look this time. "And then you'd have to explain why you were sitting here sipping kahva with me. I'm sure someone saw us leave together that night. How would that look on your report?"

"You think I'd let you go because I might look bad?" he asked. "You don't know me as well as you think."

"Then why haven't you blown your whistle?" She was suddenly tired. Damn the kahva, damn Pyvic, and damn her for coming here in the first place.

"Because there *is* more to the story." He leaned forward, his voice low and urgent. "*Tell me* why you're doing this."

"*Find out yourself.*" She snorted. "You wouldn't believe anything a thief tells you."

"Are you working with the Empire, Isafesira?"

She shook her head. "You know who I am. Start hunting. I'm going to walk out that door now." She tried not to make it a challenge. "It was nice seeing you again. I'm not sorry about that night."

She walked out. He didn't stop her, didn't blow his whistle. She got out of sight fast.

About ten heartbeats later, she watched from the alley as he came out, half-hidden in the doorway, trying to trace her steps. He might have been waiting long enough for her to feel confident and make a mistake. He might have been trying to let her get away.

If he were less honorable, she wouldn't have been interested in him—he'd have been just another crooked justicar to play as the job demanded. If he'd been more honorable, he'd have been easier to dupe, and she wouldn't have been interested then, either. More honorable or less, either would have been fine.

Instead, he was... somewhere in between.

She shouldn't have told him her real name.

She left quickly, checking often to make sure that he hadn't found her trail.

Seventeen

THE DAY OF THE VICTORY BALL ARRIVED.

In a ring around Heaven's Spire, the palaces of the Voyants were decked with bunting and ribbons. Illusory heroes fought in the sky, and patriotic music played from behind palace gates. Two palaces remained conspicuously unadorned. The palace of Voyant Cevirt was quiet because of his scandalous arrest, its gates shut and its windows dark. The palace of Archvoyant Silestin was undecorated because he was hosting the Victory Ball, and, as he jokingly declared, he did not have the budget to decorate the outside as well as the inside.

Silestin's Victory Ball was the event of the season, and everyone on the Spire with political or financial pull had received an invitation. If the sheer grandeur of the ball were not enough incentive, there were always the whispers that Silestin was testing the waters with his beautiful young Urujar ward, Naria de Lochenville, who had announced that her older sister's criminal activities would not shame her into postponing her social debut.

The guests started arriving around sundown.

Loch, Kail, and Dairy had been standing in the guest line for some time, ignoring looks from nobles and businessmen.

Dairy was dressed in a page's gray doublet and breeches, which Loch had chosen because they went with the gray suede gloves Ululenia had bought him. With the gloves and the doublet, the silly birthmark on the kid's arm wasn't even visible.

Kail was dressed in the outlandish garb of a desert warrior, complete with the veil, the headdress, the flowing many-layered robes, and the brace of knives. He was serving as Loch's bodyguard.

Loch herself was wearing a shimmering copper dress with cream-colored lace along the neckline and sleeves, along with a matching headpiece covered with cream-colored flowers. Going by the stares, she looked like an orange-flavored dessert, both conspicuous and ridiculous.

Right according to plan, then.

"Invitation, please," said one of the guards at the gate.

"Don't just stand there like an idiot, boy!" Loch said helpfully after a moment of silence. "Present my invitation!"

"You... er... said that you wished to carry it yourself, my lady," Dairy stammered. Gods, but he was a lousy liar. They'd had to work on a reason for the discomfort.

"I said no such thing!" Loch exclaimed indignantly. "However can you say such a thing, you horrible little boy? Tell the guards you're sorry for losing my invitation!"

"I'm sorry," Dairy mumbled. The guards shifted restlessly, as did the people behind Loch's party.

"Good boy. Now, let us go—"

"My lady," said the guard, "we need that invitation to let you in."

She fixed him with an arrogant stare. "I do not *have* my invitation, as should be clear to you! It was lost by this... this little slug of an attendant. Now, you will let me in this instant, or when Silestin himself hears that I was delayed by this, this, this *harassment,* you will find yourself in a *great* deal of trouble!"

"My lady," said one of the other guards, "there are many people trying to attend the party who did not receive invitations—"

"Are you implying that my mistress is lying?" Kail asked in a deadly voice from behind his veil.

"Er," the guard stammered.

"Because I swore an oath to my ancestors that I would uphold the honor of my mistress, however many men I must kill to do so."

"Er."

"I can hear my ancestors' dread voices echoing in my mind even now, asking if I must slay you." Kail leaned forward. "Let me level with you: my ancestors are really pushing hard for me to strike you dead right this moment. Anything you can do to help me out would be fantastic."

"I'm sure this is a misunderstanding," the first guard said quickly. "Why don't you just go right inside? In fact, you can wear these red ribbons, which will mark you as special guests with full access." He shoved ribbons in their direction.

"I am certain that I would have been on such a list," Loch said airily. "Come, boy." She strode in with Kail and Dairy hustling to catch up.

"So that's it?" Dairy asked quietly once they were inside.

"So far," Loch said, glancing in both directions. The path led through a sumptuously ornamented front garden to the main palace itself.

"Red ribbons?" Kail muttered behind his veil. "Doesn't really go with my outfit."

Loch smiled. "I don't imagine we'll be wearing them long."

The aqueducts of Heaven's Spire were beneath the surface of the city. For large buildings, great chambers stored water in reserve and then filtered the new water in late in the evening to avoid shortages during the day.

The great chambers were also covered, and anyone who got inside would face a fifty-foot drop into the water below, since the ancient builders of the Spire had assumed that anyone doing maintenance on the water systems would be floating in mid-air through the power of magic.

Icy made barely a splash as he hit the water in a graceful dive.

Ululenia fluttered in on snowy white wings a moment later, changed into a great silver salmon in mid-air, and splashed into the water just as gracefully.

I shall determine the correct tunnel, she told him as he broke the surface and shook the water from his face. He nodded, and her scales shimmered beneath the surface, and then she was gone.

It was dark in the reservoir, and the water was not heated. Someone without the ability to channel his body's energy into a harmonious relationship with very cold water might have been uncomfortable.

The tunnel off to the right will lead us inside, Ululenia said moments later, *and I sense no magical wards, just as Tern predicted. However, the tunnel is long, and the water passes through a metal grate too narrow for you to fit through.*

"I am capable of slowing my breathing rate as long as necessary." Icy smiled. "And unless the metal is magical, it should bend easily enough. Shall we?"

With a brief mental nod of kinship, the Imperial and the unicorn made their way into the palace.

"You're sure you can make the shot?" Hessler asked.

Tern, Desidora, and Hessler stood on the roof of a bank across the street from the west wall of Silestin's palace. From their vantage point, they could see over the palace walls and into the gardens near the palace itself, and specifically near the palace mausoleum.

"I am *sure,*" Tern said, "that I can make the shot."

"Okay," Hessler said.

Tern lined up her crossbow. She had it set on a collapsible tripod and aimed at a ten-foot-tall bronze statue of Ael-meseth, whose arm was conveniently extended in a judgment-giving pose. She took off her spectacles, squinted into the scope (adjusted for her lousy eyesight already), and began to make tiny targeting adjustments.

"It's just that it's going to look conspicuous if you miss," Hessler added.

Tern turned around and glared at him. Her eyes looked tiny without the spectacles. "I am *not* going to miss, Magister."

"We believe in you, Tern," Desidora said firmly. Tern gave her a narrow look.

"Of course we do," Hessler said hastily. "We just want to make sure that, you know, you don't miss."

The bolt loaded into the crossbow was attached to a cable, which was in turn already attached to the wall behind them.

"Wait a minute," Tern said. "This isn't about me, is it, Hessler? You're afraid of sliding into the palace on the cable!"

"That is the most—I have summoned daemons who could rend my soul asunder if I misspoke a single word!" Hessler declared irately. "The very *idea* that I'd be afraid of sliding down a *rope* is ludicrous, provided that the rope is securely fastened and that you make the shot properly and it doesn't fall out when I'm halfway across the street."

Tern turned back to her crossbow. "Magister, I do this *all the time*. Hell, Icy usually walks down the cable instead of sliding. Of course, he's just a damn showoff." She licked her finger and held it up. "Half a tick...."

"Oh, *that's* hygienic."

"Hush, Magister. I'm dealing with daemons that could rend your soul asunder if you don't shut up and let me work." Tern moved the crossbow a tiny bit to the left. "Or at least dump you in the middle of the street," she added absently. "Now, the tightrope-bolts always drag a bit more in the wind, so maybe up *just* a hair... no, no, add a touch more velocity instead, don't want it to get caught up high in the wind. Aaaaaaand...." She pulled the trigger.

With a great snap, the bolt sprang free, sailed across the street and over the palace walls, and slammed solidly into the bronze arm of Ael-meseth. The bolt shattered, and a pair of coiling claw-hook lines sprang free from the central casing, tangled around the god's arm, and held firm. A thin cable now ran from the top of the bank across the street and into the mausoleum garden.

"Hah!" Tern stood up and popped her spectacles back on. "First try!"

"Wait, what do you mean, *first try?*" Hessler asked.

"Oh, you know how these things go." Tern snapped the crossbow free from the tripod and collapsed the tripod down to a series of small metal rods that easily fit into her pockets.

"No, really, I don't."

"I thought it was *wonderful*, Tern," Desidora said.

"Besyn larveth'is!"

"Well, thank you, both." Tern hooked the crossbow onto a pocket, then removed three small devices that looked like metal handgrips with half-circles at one end. "So, take your bar, attach it like so...." She gave one of the devices to Desidora and another to Hessler. Then she held the device up beside the now-taut cable so that the cable fit inside the half-circle of metal and pressed a button. The grip split into two halves, one in her hand, and the other snapping out a full hundred and eighty degrees and locking into place, so that now, instead of one handgrip, there were two handgrips, and the cable went through the hole in the middle. "And there you go. All you have to do is run and jump and hang on tight."

"Wait. That's it?" Hessler coughed. "Could we maybe try it a few times as you watch, or maybe you could hook ours on, or—"

"You're awfully cute, Hessler, but you need to lighten up," Tern said. "I'll see you both on the other side. Desidora, you've got the wards?"

"Of course," Desidora said with a smile. "Good luck."

Tern nodded, took a breath, gripped the handgrip, and leapt off the rooftop.

"By all the magic of Jairytnef!" Hessler said in a strangled voice as Tern sailed across the street, cleared the palace walls, and then dropped down behind a hedge and out of view.

"No kidding," Desidora said absently. "Calling you cute had to take you by surprise." She snapped her handgrip into place, locking it around the cable, then checked to make sure that Ghylspwr was secure on her belt.

"I *meant* that—" Hessler broke off in agitation. "Aren't you the least bit nervous about this procedure?"

Desidora laughed. "I was a love priestess, Magister. Helping young lovers break into each other's bedrooms required worse than this."

"I'm sure we'll... she called me cute?" Hessler blinked. "Oh, you know how Tern is."

"I do indeed. I might not be a love priestess anymore, but I can still read auras." Desidora smiled. "See you inside, Magister." She tugged once on the handgrip, then leapt.

Hessler watched her go, staring nervously into the twilight. Desidora dropped safely behind the hedges.

"She called me cute," he murmured. "Huh."

Loch, Kail, and Dairy were ambling through the gardens, listening to the chatter as the twilight set in and the magical lights filled the air, when suddenly there were guards all around them.

"I don't believe you were given an invitation, *my lady*," one of the guards said with a sardonic grin.

"Make a scene, and you'll regret it," another guard added. "Come quietly, and you'll be his guest after all... in a sense."

Loch looked around in alarm, saw the guards positioned casually at all possible escape routes.

"Damn," she said. "Red ribbons?"

"Red ribbons," the first guard confirmed.

Loch dropped her arms to her sides. "Can't blame a girl for trying."

Eighteen

A PAIR OF GUARDS IN ANCIENT CEREMONIAL ARMOR STOOD OUTSIDE the mausoleum. Tern, Desidora, and Hessler (who had landed safely, after all his worrying) got close by sneaking through the hedges, but then there was a wide open space, and the guards, and a large bronze alarm gong.

"So what's the deal?" Tern whispered. "They're a bit out of my range for darts. Diz, can you maybe do that throwing thing you do with Ghylspwr?"

"There's a ward around the mausoleum." Desidora shook her head, frowning absently. "I'm not certain, but it looks like it would stop anything we threw or shot from reaching the guards."

"Where's the ward?" Hessler asked. Tern guessed that he was trying to look with his wizardly senses, but it looked a lot like squinting. He was cute when he squinted, though.

"Protected under the overhang. I couldn't hit it from here even with Ghylspwr helping me."

"Besyn larveth'is!"

"Don't worry about it, big guy," said Tern. "We'll figure something out. Hey, Hessler, can you lure them outside the ward with an illusion?"

"I'll see what I can do." Hessler concentrated, and a moment later a pretty woman appeared behind a nearby hedge and called to the guards, "Excuse me, can either of you help me back to the party?"

She disappeared shortly after a flurry of crossbow bolts ripped through her. Hessler turned back to Tern. "No." Then he gestured, and Tern, peeking around the hedge, saw one of the guards strike the gong and make no noise whatsoever. "I can keep them from raising the alarm, though," he said with an effort, sweat beading on his brow.

They waited a moment.

"And that's it?" Tern asked, blinking. "They shoot at an intruder, ring the alarm, and then do nothing? Even when the alarm doesn't go off? What's wrong with these guys?"

"They're…" Desidora raised a hand, and her pink nail polish slid to black for a moment. "Ah." She nodded. "Mindless skeletal warriors. They only react as their enchantments dictate." She grimaced, and her color slowly returned. "I could crumble them into dust if they weren't behind the ward."

Tern began taking things out of her pockets. And to think, she'd been worried about being useful. "But their arrows fired out, right?" A pair of metal rods, some connecting joints, a pair of gear-driven wheel-legs. "So the ward might not protect against something that wasn't an attack?" The all-important wind-up assembly, of course, was in its velvet pouch.

"What are you doing, Tern?" Hessler asked as she snapped pieces together.

She smiled brightly as a spring clicked into place. "I'm going to throw Ghylspwr."

"Kun-kabynalti osu fuir'is?"
"Oh, relax, you big baby."

There were two guards in the water filtration chamber. By rights, it should have been a prime spot for the lucky and the lazy. But when the hatch covering the pipe abruptly tore free from its casing and clattered to the floor, the two guards had their swords free in an instant and lunged forward, snarls of hatred twisting their faces.

"Arrogant apple, babbling brook, creep... erk," said one of the guards, and then fell over.

"Dawdling duckling, excellent eggshells," said the second guard, fumbling with a whistle around his throat. He got it to his lips and blew a shrill screech of noise before finally mumbling, "Fondling fern, gullible goat," and keeling over.

Ululenia heard pounding footsteps and drawn swords in the hall outside, which was, unfortunately, located quite near one of the guard barracks.

Their minds are polluted, Ululenia thought sadly, looking down at them. *Their very essence corrupted. Be careful. They are as the crew on the airship. They will kill without hesitation.*

Then she transformed into a snowy-white wolf, howled at the group of guards who had just come around the corner, and darted down the hall in the opposite direction.

When she and the guards were gone, Icy pulled himself out and crept quickly to the guard barracks, leaving a little trail of watery footprints behind him.

"So," said Hessler as Tern stuck pieces of metal together, "why have the gods demanded that you stop the Glimmering Man?"

"That'd be ninety-seven feet..." Tern peeked around a hedge through a pair of telescoping lenses.

"I don't know." Desidora shrugged. "I only know that he must be stopped."

"Ninety-degree right turn, assume we go another foot forward while making the turn...."

"Have you a theory as to how he manipulated your illusion?" Desidora asked a moment later.

"Twenty feet after the turn, taking into account the change in surface...." Tern clipped a small spring and gear to the metal rod.

"The Glimmering Folk are said to be from a world that only brushes our own," Hessler said uncomfortably. "The only *reasonable* hypothesis is that the magical substance of illusion is drawn from the matter of their world. If this Bi'ul is a wizard in his own world, then manipulating the matter of his own world would be easier for him than it would be for me."

"Probably need an upward angle of maybe sixty degrees, force of... Ghyl?"

"Besyn larveth'is!"

"Yeah, see, that doesn't really help me."

"I think," said Desidora, "that the Glimmering Man made a reference to shadows. He said that you toyed with shadows, and then he made the shadows real."

"Well, yes, but—" said Hessler.

"Ghyl, if you were gonna be flung into the air, would it better to fling you straight up or end over end?"

"Kutesosh gajair'is!"

"End over end," Desidora translated, and then to Hessler said, *"Shadow-master, spirit-caster, drain the life and leave the husk."*

"Oh, *hell* no," said Hessler.

"Light shall mark the spirit stark that brings the Champion of Dusk." She cocked her head. "Would you say that the radiant aura of the Glimmering Man was a light that marked him?"

Tern held out her hand for Ghylspwr. Desidora handed him to her without looking, and Tern put Ghylspwr into what looked like a very tiny toy wagon made of metal spokes and wires. "Okay, here we go! Bessin-whateveritisyousay!" She placed the wagon by the hedge and pulled a tiny switch.

"Why do priests bring up prophecies every time something the least bit strange happens?" Hessler demanded as the little wagon rolled through the grass, ticking softly.

"Well, when the gods strip me of my priestly duties and demand that I go kill some powerful wizard from another world, I start to consider the possibility," Desidora said, raising an eyebrow. "Legends of the Champion of Dawn and the Champion of Dusk existed even in the time of the ancients. There's evidence that those legends are *why* the ancients left the land in the first place."

The little wagon ticked slowly toward the skeletal warriors, who watched it without evident interest.

"Oh, please," said Hessler. "It's your standard false duality designed to draw gullible believers into a world of monochromatic enemies and strip away any moral ambiguity—*usually* utilized by the ruling government to bolster whatever policies it wishes to implement." As it drew level with the mausoleum's entry gateway, the little wagon paused, then made a slow right turn and ticked its way between the skeletal warriors and into the mausoleum entryway.

"So, even though there's no way that your arcane studies can possibly account for it—"

"They *can* account for it, it's a dimensional warping crossover, and Ambassador Bi'ul, as a wizard powerful enough to breach the boundaries of his world to reach ours, is obviously quite talented—"

"—you see *no possible way* that Bi'ul could be the Champion of Dusk?"

"No, Desidora, as a matter of fact, I *don't,* because it's a stupid prophecy with no basis in fact!"

The little wagon finally finished its journey, ticking to a stop just past inside the arch. Something on the wagon went *snap,* and Ghylspwr whirled into the air.

"Kutesosh gajair'is!"

Something inside the archway exploded, and the air around the mausoleum flashed blue for an instant.

"So this Glimmering Man is a wizard who breached the worlds and came here?" Desidora reached around the hedge and made a hooking motion with two fingers. The skeletal warriors crumpled limply to the ground. "Would that be anything like *casting* his *spirit?"* Desidora stalked angrily across the grass with Tern and Hessler in tow.

"The prophecy is vague enough that it could mean *anything!"* Hessler insisted. Ghylspwr flashed back into Desidora's hand.

"Hey, guys, really, it was nothing," Tern muttered.

"But the gods don't create death-priests for *everything,* Magister!"

"Besyn larveth'is," Ghylspwr rumbled to Tern.

"Thanks, big guy."

Ululenia dashed through the hallways with guards behind her, their minds hateful and strange, warped by the same magic as the poor souls from the airship. She could have changed into a bird to escape them easily, but it was important that Indomitable Courteous have time to get to freedom. Her horn shone in the dim torchlight of the back hallway as she fled.

Hunter Mirrkir stepped out into the hallway ahead of her, his golden armor shining and his spear crackling with hateful blue light. "Again we meet, little unicorn. Another filthy creature of magic falls today."

With a panicked yelp, Ululenia staggered to a halt, turned, flashed into a bird, and darted for the nearest corner as though hell itself pursued her.

Behind her, Hunter Mirrkir ran as quickly as she flew.

Tern turned the mausoleum door's handle and then dropped to her knees. As the door opened, a spear flashed out from a nearby statue and imbedded itself in the doorframe a few inches over her head. "S'open," she called back.

"Thank you, Tern," Desidora said calmly, and stepped into the chamber, where a great stone sarcophagus had been carved in the likeness of a stern-looking man with a sword. She held out a hand and spoke in some old religious language.

"So, what's the deal with the prophecy thing?" Tern asked Hessler, who was frowning.

"Oh, it's nothing, it's…" He glared at Desidora with a cute little frustrated look. "There's a very old story that says that in the eyes of the gods, the world sits with the sun half-behind the mountains, and has been that way for eons. Er, not that it's actually like that all the time. It's more of—"

"Hessler, if you try to explain what a metaphor is, I'm going to kick you in the shins."

Desidora kept chanting. Her skin was pale, and her hair and robes were dark. The ancient statues of the gods had started to twist into gargoyles and skeletal monsters.

"Right," said Hessler. "Anyway, the gods don't know whether the sun is halfway risen or halfway set, and they said that one day Dawn and Dusk would each send a champion to do battle, and that would determine whether the world were entering into a bright and glorious day, or the cold darkness of eternal night."

"Your basic good and evil thing." Tern nodded.

Hessler cocked his head, looking at Desidora, who was surrounded by a field of coiling black in which countless humanoid shadows writhed. Her voice was cold and imperious, and her eyes were portals to a world of eternal darkness. Her skin was flawless as an ancient statue seen by moonlight. Apple-cheeked Tern would have *killed* for skin like that.

"Desidora," Hessler said derisively, "believes Ambassador Bi'ul might be the Champion of Dusk."

"He does seem pretty evil," Tern suggested. "And your spells didn't hurt him. Neither did that chandelier Desidora dropped on him."

With a faint glow of green-gold light, the lid of the sarcophagus drew back, and an ancient figure pulled itself upright with stiff, jerky movements.

"But if Bi'ul is the Champion of Dusk," Hessler said absently, "we'd need the Champion of Dawn to fight him. I haven't seen anyone untouchable by shadow or marked by the phoenix blade."

"Who dares summon me from the slumber of the dead?" rasped the figure in the sarcophagus.

"In the name of Byn-kodar'isti kuru'ur, I bind you to the will of the gods!" Lightning flashed from Desidora's hand and wreathed the zombie in green-gold fire.

"Right," said the zombie, dusting himself off. "What do you need?"

For a minute, Desidora was silent. The shadows writhed, clutching at her, and the gargoyle statues turned their tusked heads to hear her demands.

Then, slowly, her color returned.

"Tern, Hessler, I've altered his aura slightly to match that of his great-grandson," Desidora said in her own voice, breathing hard. "I've got to get to the console chamber. Tern, see you there. Hessler, remember what I said."

"Which part?" Hessler demanded irately, but Desidora was already walking out. "You're *leaving* us here?"

"We're behind schedule!"

"With *him?*" Hessler glared after her.

"Hey, look on the bright side," Tern said, elbowing him. "You've got me. Until I get you in through the side door, that is. Then you're on your own with Silestin's grandfather, here."

"I suppose it could be worse," Hessler said, grimacing, and then looked at Tern and tried to smile, which honestly didn't work as well as his frown, but it was nice of him to try.

The zombie looked at them both with a stern, if somewhat decayed, visage. "Are you going to give me an order? I *assume* I was wrenched back to the living realm for something other than the observation of your adolescent sexual tension."

Hessler and Tern stepped apart as though a sword had come down between them. "Get your dead ass out of the sarcophagus and follow along," Tern muttered. "And no yelling for guards, and no continuing forward when we stop and then stomping all over us and crushing our spines and skulls under your undead feet because we didn't explicitly tell you not to do that."

"The thought," said the zombie, "had not even *begun* to cross my worm-feasted mind."

Nineteen

WHEN THE HALLWAYS WERE WIDE, ULULENIA FLEW. WHEN THEY were narrow, she ran.

And still Hunter Mirrkir pursued.

She had lost her way, and now she thought as the deer, panting as it tore through the forest. Eventually the trail would end, and there would be only closed doors and guarded gates before her. Eventually there would only be her and the hunter.

He was tireless, his pace a sprinter's dash, though any mortal man should have grown weary by now.

Ahead of her, a small dining hall far removed from the main palace ballrooms. How many doors would lead away? The Hunter had not lost her trail yet.

Her heart quailed. She cried out in her mind to any soul that might help.

And still Hunter Mirrkir drew closer.

They had been taken not through the party-filled courtyard but through a small side passage, frequented only by guards and servants, to a cell large enough for the chained forms of Loch, Kail, Dairy, and the unchained Guard Captain Straithe.

"Thought you could sneak in during the Victory Ball?" he asked with a hearty smile. "Thought that old Captain Straithe would be a bit lax on the day of the party?"

"Yeah, pretty much," Kail muttered.

"Thought we'd get a little scratch," Loch said bitterly, "but all we got was pinched."

She was laying it on a bit, but you had to lay it on a bit for folks like Straithe.

"Well, you're at the party now," Straithe said with an avuncular smile, "with all the important folks! You'll have some wonderful stories to tell at the Cleaners."

Kail made unhappy noises without saying anything that would get Straithe angry. The key was not for Straithe to be angry. The key was for Straithe to be *gone*.

"You can't leave us in here!" Loch tried. "We've got rights!"

"Right now you've got the *right* to sit nice and pretty, young lady," the captain said, chuckling, "and I promise to be *right* back, once I've processed the papers."

Loch ducked her head. He was going to leave, any minute now.

"And you, young sir," he added, turning to Dairy, "should pray to Ael-meseth that the judge doesn't throw you into the Cleaners with these two!" He shook his finger in Dairy's face, and Dairy jumped back, flinching.

Something fell from his grasp and tinkled on the floor.

It was the lockpick Kail had passed the kid beforehand.

Hunter Mirrkir knew that the unicorn was his when her path took her back to the dark and unused ballroom.

Several times she had left his view, but each time her unclean aura, the aura that Mirrkir existed to cleanse from the world, led him onward.

His spear would pierce her unclean hide, and her stain would be washed clean. He had slain unicorns before. They were more difficult than satyrs, who foolishly tried to fight, but less difficult than fairies, who could play clever tricks.

She seemed to realize that it was over, for she stumbled in the ballroom, catching her foot on the carpet. She had assumed human form, a flash of bright white cloak ahead of him. It angered Mirrkir when they took human guise. Still, she did not beg. She had the grace to accept her fate.

He halted behind her, raised his spear to plunge it into her white-cloaked back. "Your time is ended, unicorn. What was mislaid shall be recovered."

And the unicorn said a peculiar thing, in a very peculiar voice, as she turned.

"Kutesosh gajair'is!"

Loch shut her eyes and sighed.

"Seems my men missed something while searching you." Guard Captain Straithe snatched up the lockpick. "Maybe you weren't just petty crooks." He stared at them grimly. "Maybe you *wanted* to get caught," he said slyly, "then break out of this cell and make a little trouble from the inside!"

"Dammit, I *knew* bringing the kid was a bad idea!" Kail growled.

"Shut up, Kail."

"No, Captain, I will *not* shut up!" Kail yanked on his chains. "He dropped Iofecyl on the *floor!*"

"You named your lockpick?" Straithe asked.

"I'm sorry!" Dairy blurted.

"Kid, you're a lousy thief." Kail glared at Dairy, then at Loch. "I don't know why the captain insisted you come along. This whole mission, you've stuck out like a sore thumb."

"Hear that, boy?" Straithe asked, leaning in toward Dairy. "You got yourselves involved with some nice customers, haven't you? Oh, they talked nice, but now they turn right against you."

"That's not true," Dairy said hotly. "Don't say that about Captain Loch!"

"Son, I hate to speak evil about the Urujar, gods know some of 'em are decent folk, but a certain type, you can just tell that they're no good." He chuckled.

"Don't *say* that about Captain Loch!" Dairy shouted, heaving at his shackles that chained him to the wall, and Straithe wagged a finger.

"You've got a temper like an Urujar, boy. That's why the Urujar don't make good criminals. Too lazy to work, too hotheaded to steal, 'bout all they're good for is fight—"

"Don't say that about my friends!" shouted Dairy, and he swung.

Three very distinct noises sounded in quick succession.

The first was the crunching sound that Guard Captain Straithe made when he hit the far wall.

The second was the sound of Iofecyl, Kail's lucky lockpick, ringing like a tuning fork as it flew end over end from Straithe's grasp. The noise ended abruptly when it landed in Kail's outstretched hand.

The third noise was a slow, metallic squeak, repeating slowly. It was the chain that had secured Dairy's right fist to the wall, now swinging back and forth while hanging from his still-outstretched arm.

"Huh," said Kail when Dairy's dangling chain stopped squeaking.

"I'm sorry," Dairy said softly.

"Don't worry about it, Dairy." Loch looked at Guard Captain Straithe. "You're doing *fine*."

Kail got to work on his shackles. "You didn't think I *meant* all that, did you? I was trying to create a distraction. Anytime I start yelling, assume I'm just making noise, okay?"

Loch gave him a wry look. "In fact, any time Kail opens his mouth, just assume that."

"But it *was* my fault," Dairy insisted, tugging at the chain that still secured his left arm to the wall. "If I hadn't dropped your pick, the captain would have left."

The cell door opened. Kail palmed Iofecyl. Dairy, showing amazingly quick thinking, raised his right arm so that casual observation would still show him as being chained to the wall. By the grace of the gods, Captain Straithe had landed directly behind where the door opened, so that when the guard stepped inside, he didn't immediately see the man.

"Captain, I'm..." He broke off in confusion. "That's odd. Captain Straithe said he'd be here." Any minute now, Loch thought, he was going to look behind him.

"He had to take care of something," Loch breathed throatily. "But while you're here, could I just *beg* for some assistance?" She lifted her arms higher than was absolutely necessary.

The guard licked his lips. He stared deep into her eyes, and then he stared a bit lower than that. Kail began quietly working on his shackles again. "W-what do you need?" the guard asked.

"Well, this cell is so *hot*," Loch breathed, "and Captain Straithe wouldn't let me take *anything* off, and I've started to sweat. There's this one drop of sweat that started at the side of my throat…" She arched her neck. "…and it's *slowwwly* trickling down to my collarbone…" She rolled her shoulders a little. "…and just making its way down between my… well…" She smiled. "It's just *intolerable,* and if you could just dab me dry, well…" She gave him a sultry, half-lidded gaze. "…you'd be my *hero.*"

"Uhm," said the guard, and fumbled in his pocket for a cloth. "I've got, um, a rag, um."

"Oh, I'm not picky." Loch smiled. "You can use *anything you like* to get it off."

"Uhh," said the guard.

"Man," said Kail, "that look you've got right now? That must be how I looked with your mother last night." He cold-cocked the hapless guard, who would, upon waking up, spend the rest of his life pondering those few seconds, sometimes paying great sums of money to recreate the experience in local pleasure-houses.

"That's lovely, Kail." Loch held out her hands meaning-fully. "Today?"

"Working, working. Nice distraction, Captain. Kid, close your mouth." Kail went through Straithe's pockets and came up with a set of keys. In short order, Loch and Dairy were both free. "If we can get the plan back on track, I believe I'm due for some shouting and running. Captain?"

"Go to it, Kail." Loch dragged Straithe and the guard out of sight from the door, then gestured. "I'll be ably defended by my attendant here if anything else goes wrong."

Kail grinned. Then he stepped out into the hallway, shouted, "You'll never take me alive, you bastards," and started running.

Loch and Dairy waited for a moment while a number of booted feet thundered past.

"I'm sorry," Dairy said again.

"Kid," Loch said, "no plan goes perfectly. If you hadn't dropped that pick, the other guard would've shown up before we were ready. The whole plan would have been blown at that point."

Dairy frowned. "So... what does that mean?"

"It means that the plan is going well. And if you need to punch your way free of any shackles, go ahead."

He blushed. "It was just loose, I think, Captain Loch. Nobody could pull a chain out of the wall."

"Then just keep getting loose chains, kid." Loch smiled. "You're my lucky charm."

The brigand in the inner palace had led the guards on a lively chase, picking corridors and servants' hallways almost as if he had studied the palace layout. Finally, when half the normal guards and a few of those sullen, silent guards who patrolled the high-security areas were after him, the brigand found himself surrounded outside a sitting room in the eastern wing. A pair of the vicious guards, the ones who didn't talk to anyone but each other, had been stationed outside the room, and they drew their weapons as soon as he arrived.

"Now, then," one of the normal guards said calmly, "let's be reasonable, shall we?"

"You'll never take me alive!" the brigand, a wiry Urujar with a mad expression, shouted in a crazed voice. "I'll kill you all!"

"You don't even have a sword," said the guard, who'd reached middle age by being the type of guard who talks a man into coming along peacefully instead of valiantly rushing in. He looked at the high-security guards with unease. Their teeth were bared, and their fingers were curled into claws. "Look, just settle down and come along—"

He might have talked him into surrendering had not another guard—not one of the strange ones, amazingly, but some town guard brought in for the Victory Ball—lunged in to bash the brigand with the pommel of his sword. The brigand caught the descending arm, wrenched the sword free, ran the man through, and then hurled the bloody body at the other guards, tangling several of them and clearing himself a path.

Then he ran from the room with guards shouting behind him—including the ones stationed at the sitting room. The old guard who'd tried to talk the brigand down paused for a moment to check the dead guard's pulse, but with a wound like that, there wasn't much guesswork.

When they were all gone and the room was quiet, Tern stepped out from behind a tapestry. "Wow. I really thought Kail got you that time."

"I am pleased that he followed my suggestion to strike realistically," the dead man said, sitting up slowly as his heart began beating again. "How fare Hessler and Desidora?"

Tern shrugged. "I don't think they're dating."

"I was, in fact, referring to our current mission."

"Oh. I don't know. They were arguing about prophecies and stuff."

Ululenia thanked Desidora in the silence of her mind. She flew through the hallways as a snowy white dove, taking her time and avoiding the servants, who shuffled along with minds bent to annoyance or excitement at the Victory Ball.

It took her some time to trace her path anew, but finally she found herself near the guests' changing rooms, where recent arrivals could add the final touches of artificial beauty before presenting themselves at the ball. Nesting in the rafters, she looked around carefully to make sure that the hallway was clear. Then she fluttered to the ground, shimmered, and took her human form.

She silenced the glow of her horn, and then altered the hem and neckline of her pale white gown so that its simple grace was slightly more fashionable. She would be remembered—a pale woman with ash-white hair in a snow-white gown could scarcely go unnoticed—but no more so than any other exotic guest.

She started as the hinge squeaked on a nearby door. When she turned, though, there was nothing, and she squinted, extending her senses as she scanned the room.

She felt the wave of anger and hatred before her, and turned to face it, only to see the knife sliding from the shadows.

There was no time to dodge.

"Captain Pyvic of the Justicars." He offered his invitation, and the guards looked at it, then nodded.

Protect them. That was what Melich had said. If that meant nodding politely at a Victory Ball so that funding didn't get cut, Pyvic would do so.

"Any guests, sir?" one of them asked.

Prisoner Loch, Isafesira de Lochenville, was no longer his problem. Silestin had made that clear.

"I figure you've got enough in here already," Pyvic said with a smile.

Protect them all.

"Both invited and uninvited," he added, still smiling.

The guards chuckled. "Figure a justicar would know about that sort of thing," one said.

"Some are clever," another added, "but there was one Urujar who thought she could yell her way inside! Don't know what she was thinking."

Pyvic laughed along with the guards.

"And she'd be taken to a holding cell inside, then?" he asked.

Hunter Mirrkir rose to his feet, using his spear as a crutch, and pulled his golden ringmail straight. When he was fully upright, he twisted his neck sharply, producing a cracking sound, and then raised the spear, showing no sign of pain from a strike that could have shattered solid steel.

"You can stand against the might of Ghylspwr." Desidora raised her hammer.

"Not lightly and not often," Hunter Mirrkir said with no trace of pride, "but as I must, yes. You falsified the trail of the unicorn."

"Death priestess." Desidora smiled slightly.

"Chosen by the gods in their hour of need." Mirrkir cocked his head. "Why ally yourself with an unholy beast?"

"You know the truth?" Desidora's cheeks paled, and her voice turned cold. "If *you* serve the gods faithfully, get out of my way."

"My orders come from the ancients, not the gods." Mirrkir stood straight and proud. "The magical creatures that spawned from the leakage of ancient magic are parasites. They will endanger the world unless removed. My orders are clear."

"Then say hello to Ghylspwr, last king of the ancients, who forged his soul into this hammer to defeat a great evil." Desidora raised Ghylspwr again.

"Can he supersede my directives through direct orders?" Mirrkir asked.

"Besyn larveth'is!" Ghylspwr said enthusiastically.

"Not as *such*," Desidora allowed.

"Pity." In the metallic rasp of Mirrkir's voice, there hung a trace of regret. "If you stand between me and the unicorn, I must strike you down."

"Let's see how that works out for you," Desidora said, and Ghylspwr threw in a *"Kutesosh gajair'is!"* for emphasis.

Mirrkir moved, and Desidora moved, and hammer met spear in the middle of the ballroom.

It was a fight that would have vexed armsmasters, had any been present to witness it. Ghylspwr moved with speed no normal hammer could match, but Mirrkir's spear was stronger than any normal weapon. The crackling spear swung in wide arcs of blue, and Ghylspwr blazed, a blur of silver.

The priestess blocked Mirrkir's high thrust, which had actually been a feint, then parried the low thrust, which had *also* been a feint, then arced Ghylspwr up to knock aside the *actual* attack, a slash at her face. She spun into a full-body swing that Mirrkir set his spear to block, but this time *she* had feinted, and instead she came in with a short overhand strike past Mirrkir's guard, and Mirrkir rolled away.

"You fight with spirit." Mirrkir leapt over a low sweep and stabbed down at her shoulder. Ghylspwr knocked the stab aside, then darted up the length of the spear to strike at Mirrkir's hands.

"Concerned?" Desidora panted as Mirrkir slid away. She lunged in with a sweeping strike that twisted at the last moment into a blow to Mirrkir's unguarded back.

Mirrkir turned, accepted the blow to the ribs, and trapped Ghylspwr with one arm. "No," he said simply.

And before Desidora could pull Ghylspwr free, Mirrkir drove his spear into her.

It sank into her breast, and she sat down stupidly, staring at it, as crackling blue energy swept through her and around her and *into* her, and then she screamed once, blue light shining from her mouth and eyes.

And then she was gone, and Ghylspwr dropped to the ground with a clatter.

"*Kun-kabynalti osu fuir'is,*" the hammer whispered.

Hunter Mirrkir leaned on his spear for a moment. The blow to the ribs had been necessary, but it had been a powerful strike nonetheless. His spear crackled with blue energy as the woman's soul became a part of Mirrkir's power, and then it lay dormant, ready to rid the world of the unclean magic.

"I wish you no evil," Mirrkir said to Ghylspwr, and stalked from the room. He could not sense the unicorn, but strange magic hummed elsewhere in the palace. He headed in that direction.

He would find her soon enough. He had all the time in the world.

Twenty

THE THING ABOUT ESCORTING A ZOMBIE THROUGH THE PALACE WAS that zombies were *slow.*

Tern had run off, hurrying to meet Icy Fist, which was fair, because she had to get the primary enchantment relay disabled in order for Desidora and Ululenia to reroute the aural detection grid, and all of that had to happen before Hessler and Silestin's great-grandfather reached the vault.

Judging by the zombie's speed, though, Tern could have walked and still gotten there in time. Some guards came by, and Hessler waved himself and the zombie into invisibility until they were gone.

"So what's with you and the girl?" the zombie asked when the guards were gone. Silestin Senior had not aged well since his death. There was still flesh on the bone, but it had dried and turned waxen, his muscles bare tendrils that pulled the shriveled flesh along. Hessler didn't know how the dead old bastard had the strength to waggle his eyebrows at him.

"We're simply colleagues." Hessler strode forward crisply, making it to the doorway before remembering that striding crisply was just going to leave the zombie behind.

"Fine," said Silestin Senior, "so don't tell me."

Hessler waited in silence, letting the zombie shuffle past.

"What's the job, anyway?"

"Job?" Getting interrogated like a slow-witted nephew hadn't been on Hessler's list of concerns about escorting the zombie.

"I'm dead, not dense, wizard." The zombie inhaled carefully in order to let out a snort, which left a little of the zombie's nose on the ground. "You needed the soul of an Archvoyant to get something in the palace."

No sense lying to him. "Actually, we needed your specific aura. Your great-grandson is Archvoyant now, and we're going to convince the security wards—"

"Sure, sure. So, the kid's the Archvoyant?" The zombie snorted again. No nose came off this time. "He was a nasty little bastard at six. Becoming an Archvoyant didn't make him any nicer, I bet."

Hessler blinked. "I thought you'd be proud to see your lineage continue."

"Hah!" Silestin Senior paused to pick up a tooth and stick it back into place. "I became an Archvoyant because I killed enough Old Kingdom Royals to keep the country safe. Don't get me wrong; power's lovely. But I'd hoped my line might do more than cling to what I won."

Hessler shook his head. It wasn't every day that he was surprised by a zombie.

"Are they gone?" Loch asked.

Dairy nodded. They were making their way toward the grand ballroom where the important people were, except that more guards had run by, and Loch had pulled Dairy into a storage closet.

Back when he'd lived on the farm, an exciting day was one when the cows had a calf. Well, that and the time when the blood-gargoyles had come in the night and picked mean old Burstin up by the throat and asked him where the orphan boy with the birthmark was while Dairy lay hidden in the hayloft.

"Good," Loch said. "We're close enough to the party. Keep the door shut."

"W-what are you doing, Miss Loch?" Dairy asked. He was having trouble forgetting about Loch in the chains talking in a much different voice from the one she usually used. She had talked about her neck. It had been a life-changing conversation for a boy Dairy's age.

"Giving you today's lesson," Loch said, and then did nothing to dispel Dairy's daydreams when she started ripping her clothes off. "Today's lesson, Dairy, is about the difference between *is* and *should*."

"Um," said Dairy desperately.

A sleeve decorated with fluffy lace fell to the floor. "When I was your age, I was all caught up in *should*. I *should* get to dress however I liked." The other sleeve joined it. "I *should* get to be a general in the army if I had the skill." A bunch of frilly lace along the hem fell away in a spray of ribbon. "I *should* get to do anything I've got the ability to do."

Dairy slowly realized that it wasn't the whole dress coming apart, just parts of it. Specifically, the frilly poofy parts.

"When I left home to join the army, I found out about what *is*. A general *is* someone all the troops can love and respect, and if all the troops can't love and respect an Urujar woman, then the general *is* a white man." Loch reached up to her neckline and peeled away the frills, as well as a lot of neckline. "A colonel *is* in charge, even if you worked your way up and he walked in as an earl and got his bars the same afternoon." She pulled on the side of her dress, and a thin slit appeared, working its way up from her ankle-length hem to well past the knee. "And a baroness *is* a woman in a killer dress, even if she'd rather be wearing riding leathers."

She tossed the big hat away and let her dark hair pool around her shoulders.

"You're... you're a baroness!" Dairy blurted.

The dress she *had* worn had made Miss Loch look silly. Now it was a form-fitting copper gown that showed off muscled shoulders and well-toned legs. With the red-gold of the dress against her rich dark skin, she looked like a hunting cat.

"As it happens," she said with a slow smile, "I *am*. But what I *really am* is more comfortable with good boots than silly ornamental slippers and a dress with a ridiculous neckline. This is a disguise, kid. It's just playing make-believe. Now come on. Escort me to the party."

She held out her hand, and her make-believe attendant took it in trembling fingers.

Icy and Tern found the secret panel quickly enough, and a bookshelf along the back wall slid aside to reveal a passage that led them to the most perplexing room either of them had ever seen.

"This would indeed appear to be the crystal lattice to which we were directed," Icy said slowly.

"I don't know, Icy. There might be another room made of giant crystal pillars somewhere else."

The walls of the enormous chamber were unfurnished, and the floor was bare, probably because it was made entirely of intricately paned crystal that flared with dazzling light in all the colors of the rainbow. The ceiling appeared to consist of a massive series of chandeliers, until Icy looked closely and realized that they were actually overlapping growths of magical crystal sprouting from the ceiling in patterns too complex for the mind to understand.

"And we are to disable this device?" Icy asked.

"This seemed *so* much more reasonable when it was a small little box drawn on a cocktail napkin." Tern kept looking at the shimmering patterns on the floor. "Desidora said there'd be a control panel. Do you see a control panel?"

Icy pointed absently at a small hub of glowing crystal studs set into a dais. It was on a raised platform at the far side of the room, a good forty feet away.

"I suspect," he said, "that simply walking across the room would raise an alarm."

Tern drew a pinch of powder from a small pouch and tossed it onto the crystal. It sizzled when it touched the floor, exploding into tiny multicolored puffs of smoke. "You know, it looks like something they don't *have* to alarm."

Icy digested this. Icy looked back up at the ceiling, approximately fifteen feet overhead, but with crystals poking down at various angles. "It is possible," he said slowly, "that I could leap up and catch hold of a crystal spur overhead, then leap from one spur to another and make my way across the ceiling." He frowned thoughtfully. "That particular section halfway across will likely be tricky. I may have to hurl myself at the wall and then leap back onto that *other* spur, as that particular handhold only appears to be accessible from—"

"I could just fire a grappling line across the room," Tern suggested.

Icy let out a breath. "I believe that would be simpler."

Tern grinned and dug out a grappling bolt. "But you weren't nervous." She loaded her crossbow, braced the base of the grappling line against the doorframe, took careful aim at the wall beyond the control panel, and fired.

The bolt exploded into sizzling flame midway through the room.

"Son of a bitch! Those are reusable!"

"Some sort of alarm system or latent magical energy?" Icy asked.

"No, Icy, I really cranked the hell out of it to build up speed, and the air resistance superheated the grapple."

Icy frowned.

"Yes," Tern muttered, "it's an alarm or the magic in the room. Hold on." She reached into a pocket, took out an iron bar, and pitched it into the room. It flew without trouble past the control console, bounced off the wall, slid back onto the crystal floor, and exploded into vivid green flame before disintegrating. "Velocity based. You should be fine to do those incredible acrobatics you weren't nervous about."

"While I am certainly capable of such maneuvers," Icy pointed out, "can we be confident that the crystal spurs on the ceiling will not react in the same manner as the floor?"

Tern tossed up the base of her now-disintegrated grappling line. It caught on a crystal spur and hung without evident distress. "All you, Icy."

"I shall perform a few stretching exercises first," Icy said. "This should not delay us significantly."

"Kail's been trying hard to teach you to lie, huh?"

The knife took Ululenia in the shoulder, and she stumbled back, gasping in pain. The being's thoughts had barely given Ululenia enough warning to avoid the killing blow, and she focused desperately on the mind nearby.

Sensed me before I struck. The shadowy figure cocked its head. *Doesn't move like a warrior, but perhaps she arrogant apple, babbling brook, creep—*

Then the mind snapped shut to Ululenia's senses as the figure rippled, like a reflection in a pond when a stone strikes the surface, and vanished into nothing.

One hand pressed to her bleeding shoulder, Ululenia looked around, then ran.

Ahead of her, the door slammed shut.

"Not so fast," came a voice, and Ululenia stumbled to a halt. "We aren't finished, you and I."

"You should seek gentler prey," Ululenia hissed. The mind was gone to her now, and unless the figure talked, she had nothing.

"You're no warrior," the figure taunted from Ululenia's left, and she spun. "With that wound, you'll be unconscious in minutes."

"Doubtful." Ululenia turned to run in the other direction, and another door slammed shut. No mortal man could have moved so quickly. "I sense not the aura of the fey from you, but you are no mortal."

"You're catching on," came the voice, very close now, and as Ululenia darted back, the figure added, "and you shouldn't run. You'll make that wound bleed out faster."

"What wound?" Ululenia held up her arm. The gown shimmered faintly, but no trace of blood remained.

"Shapeshifter," the voice hissed. "I'll make sure the next strike is lethal."

Ululenia backed up slowly until her back bumped into a support beam. She shut her eyes and said, with a confidence she didn't feel, "You assume I shall allow you to strike again."

"You can't fight me," the voice murmured as the figure came closer. "You can't see me. I can move faster than you can fly, and you'll be dead, dead, dead, just like all the others. You don't even have a weapon."

"I have no weapon save nature." Ululenia felt the hatred as the figure slid into substance.

Her horn flared with radiant light. She dove to the ground, and the knife struck the support beam.

The *wooden* support beam.

From which branches sprouted, twining around the shadowy figure's arm in a twisting embrace. With a wordless snarl, the figure rippled out of view again, but the twisting branches stayed tight around it.

"Nature will suffice." Ululenia shimmered and flew as a bird, then became a woman again when she reached the door. Not daring to look back, she yanked it open, dashed through, and slammed it shut behind her.

"Are you well, young lady?"

Ululenia looked up to see a matronly woman in a rich red dress staring at her in concern. Behind her, the ballroom shone in glorious glittering gaudiness.

"I am afraid," Ululenia said with complete honesty. "This is my first Victory Ball."

And with a chuckle, the matronly woman took Ululenia by the arm and led her out into the safety of the crowd.

"...and then he spits out whatever the unicorn gave him all over Tern's lighter, and it sets the whole damn room on fire!" Hessler finished grandly.

"Hah!" Silestin Senior had learned to cover his mouth to avoid spitting out teeth when he laughed.

"The unicorn conjures up a rainstorm, so we're safe, but sopping wet. Everyone has to run off and gather towels, and... well, that was when the justicar showed up. Not that *that* was the kid's fault."

The zombie shook his head. "At fifteen summers, I tripped over my own damn feet every five minutes unless I was in the field with some bastard trying to kill me."

"He has no place here," Hessler said, frustrated. "I can't send him away—he'd be hopeless on his own. And I promised Loch I'd finish this job."

"Man's got to stick to his word," said the zombie. A pair of servants came around the corner, and Hessler turned himself and Silestin Senior invisible. When the servants were gone, Silestin Senior said, "So how'd an academic end up walking a zombie through a palace on a heist job?"

"Whatever do you mean?" Hessler asked sharply. "It is a paying function. Wizards need money like anyone else."

"Fine," said the zombie, "don't tell me."

They walked for a moment in silence.

"I was in jail," Hessler finally said. "I'd been expelled from school, went to see an old advisor to petition for my reinstatement, and I ran afoul of some caravan guards I'd cheated at cards."

"Only cheat men you're sure you'll never see again," said the zombie. "Learned that one the hard way myself. Why'd they throw you out? You're good academic material." At Hessler's raised eyebrow, the zombie smiled. It wasn't pretty, but Hessler appreciated the attempt. "I was a general, Magister. I know a good soldier when I see one, good thief, good tactician…. You can't put a use to a man in ten heartbeats, you've got no business commanding men in battle. You're a book man, through and through."

Hessler let out a long breath. "It was my father."

The zombie waited, shuffling amiably while Hessler thought.

"My father died ten years ago and was buried in a pretty park outside the city," Hessler said, "near a great oak tree where he'd first seen my mother. That was his dying wish."

"Can't fault a man for that."

"When my mother died *this* year, she wished to be buried with him." Hessler grimaced. "However, since the time of my father's death, the park had become listed as a historical site, and it was forbidden to alter it without an official permit. The processing fee was more than I could save in a year." He sighed. "So I sold a few unlicensed magical artifacts on the side. One of the damn professors caught me and threw me out about a month after my mother was safely in the ground."

There was another long silence from the dead man beside him.

"Know what the worst part about coming back is?" Silestin Senior finally asked.

"What's that, sir?"

"Finding out that the men who held the power fifty years ago—ambitious, yes, but you've got to be ambitious to make any mark on the world—have been replaced by pampered toads who make laws to stay busy."

"Hard for me to say, sir," Hessler said a bit bitterly. "It's all pampered toads since I've been around."

"Wasn't always," said Silestin Senior, and as guards came around the corner and Hessler cloaked them both, he added in a tired voice, "Wasn't a damn golden age, but it wasn't like this."

"I'm so glad that Archvoyant Silestin isn't prejudging after that nasty incident a few days ago," an old woman in an ugly dress told Loch with a fond smile.

"As am I," Loch said, taking a drink from a passing waiter without looking his way and giving the old woman a wide-eyed smile. "It's such a *scandal!*" Off behind the old woman, Ululenia made her way through the crowd. She looked pale, but then, she always did.

"We'd heard rumors that Silestin would rescind the invitations of—" The old woman sputtered to a halt, evidently worried that "Urujar" might be an insult, and settled for "I think little Naria must have talked him out of it." Ululenia caught Loch's eye, gave a quick nod, and headed off toward the control room.

"She must have," Loch agreed, tossing back the drink in a single gulp. "She wouldn't see us shut out! Why, we're like *sisters*, all of us."

The old woman smiled and went off to hunt down an *h'ors d'oeuvres* tray, and Loch rolled her eyes and kept going. She had forgotten just how damn *easy* it all was.

"Were you at Voyant Kyndrik's party last spring?" a middle-aged rich man asked with a sleazy smile.

"I go to so many parties," Loch said with a sultry smile, "that it's hard to keep track."

"I'd have sworn I remember that lovely dress." His eyes were indeed looking at particular parts of the dress, even while he continued to talk. "Would you by any chance be interested in a cup of kahva?" He finally met her stare and grinned. "I like my kahva the way I like my women... hot and black."

"I like my kahva the way I like my men," she replied, her eyes half-lidded. "Ground up into tiny pieces and stored in a bag." As the man sputtered, Loch laughed in delight and moved on, tossing a friendly goodbye over her shoulder. Dairy followed, wide-eyed.

She'd hated these things as a child. Little Isafesira had wanted to swing wooden swords at the straw dummies in the courtyards. Little Isafesira had wanted to *do* things.

She was doing things tonight. Her father would have been proud of her. Scandalized by the dress, though.

And there was Naria, just now entering to a round of applause and joining Archvoyant Silestin in the middle of the room.

She hadn't grown as much as Loch would have thought. She was still slender. The smoked band of crystal she wore over her eyes had been magically transformed to a ruby red that matched her long, elegant dress and elbow-length gloves.

She hugged Silestin the way she'd hugged her father, and she smiled and waved at everyone.

Loch turned away. "Come on, kid."

"Loch, is that—"

"It doesn't matter."

As she turned to leave the room, the crowd ahead of her parted, and Ambassador Bi'ul of the Glimmering Folk appeared. His head was cocked, and he squinted as he looked her way.

"Miss Loch, I feel that tingle again, and…" Dairy took a step toward the Glimmering Man and bumped into Loch. "I think…" His skin was hot to the touch. "I think I'm…"

In the safety of her mind, Loch damned herself for a fool.

Then, without pause, she grabbed Dairy and hauled him into a crowd, ignoring the searing heat of his skin. "Boy!" she said loudly, and slapped him on the cheek. "What has gotten into you?"

Dairy shook his head and seemed to come back to himself. "I, er—"

"You've obviously become overexcited," Loch went on as the onlookers smiled and shook their heads and provided her with lots of cover. "I *knew* you were not ready for such an event."

The kid finally figured it out. "I'm sorry, my lady," he said contritely.

"You're no use to me this evening. Run back to my wizard and tell him you've need of a poultice." She looked at Dairy hard. "You *do* know where he is, boy?"

Dairy thought. "Yes, my lady."

"Good. Go now." She patted him fondly on the cheek. "Take care of yourself, boy."

Dairy nodded, smiled, and left in a hurry. Some of the nobles muttered about an Urujar woman having a white servant. Loch looked down at her hand. No blisters, but it had been like thrusting her hand into a fire.

A few heartbeats later, Ambassador Bi'ul walked by, looking quizzical. Loch took up a conversation with an elderly earl who complimented her dress and said that she was a good example for her people, and the Glimmering Man eventually straightened and walked away.

She mingled for a bit longer, to satisfy appearances, and then, with a confident smile, she headed for Archvoyant Silestin's personal rooms.

Ululenia quickly found the control chamber, which Kail had already unlocked for her. The room was a dark, unadorned cavern with a massive, glowing, control crystal-hub in its center. Across the floor, rune-traced crystals were laid out at regular intervals. Beyond the crystal hub, the ground fell away—the far half of the room was a great chasm.

"I don't know," Kail answered her unspoken question. He was sitting at the crystal-hub, twirling his lockpick between two fingers. "I have no idea why you'd have a giant magical cliff in the middle of a *floating* city. That makes less sense than *most* magical things. No offense."

Ululenia smiled. "None is taken. It may simply be as the blowhole for the great leviathan that is the control-hub, a means of venting that which is no longer needed."

"You're kind of reaching on the nature references," Kail said without rancor. "Got in without trouble?"

"The hunter found me." Ululenia shivered. "But Desidora was able to assist. And you?"

"Took off the helmet and guard's tabard and became a servant, and they never looked twice." He frowned. "Where's Desidora? I figured you'd both be here by the time Iofecyl and I got the lock opened."

"You named your lockpick?" Ululenia asked.

Kail opened his mouth to respond indignantly, and the door opened again.

It wasn't Desidora.

"I sensed an unusual flow of magical energies," said Hunter Mirrkir as he stepped inside. "I had hoped to find you here."

Icy took a deep focusing breath, and then did a one-handed pull-up, spun to face the other way, and swung back and forth before launching himself through the air and catching hold of another spur of crystal.

"That would be so much more impressive if you weren't, you know, going backwards," Tern called helpfully.

"A minor setback," Icy said. "I believe that if I swing several times to build momentum on *this* grip, then swing to the other handhold and immediately continue with a leaping swing, I should be able to reach the *next* useable grip."

"I didn't really understand that, but sure," Tern called. "Your arms aren't getting tired or anything, are they?"

"I have trained for much more arduous exercises, Tern."

"Because it would be bad if your arms got tired and you lost your grip or didn't jump far enough and fell onto the horrible magical floor," Tern said by way of encouragement.

"I shall endeavor to remember that, Tern."

Icy spun back around, pumped his legs to build momentum, then leaped. He grabbed, felt the spur of crystal crack under his weight as he pulled himself into the next leap, reached out as he swung, and caught the next crystal spur with his fingertips. As he swung back and forth, strengthening his grip, the crystal that had cracked finally fell behind him, exploding in a messy shower of heat and sparks as it hit the floor.

"Not a problem," Icy called calmly. "Now, if you fire another grapple, I can catch it, and you can swing across to the platform."

"Okay," Tern said doubtfully, "if you're sure I can swing across. I mean, you know I'm not *you*, right?"

"That thought is emblazoned upon my mind every waking moment, Tern."

"...need to be sarcastic..." Icy did not catch everything Tern said as she cocked her crossbow, but he understood the gist of it. "Okay, it's only half-cranked, so hopefully the speed won't trigger the disintegration ward. Are you ready?"

"I am ready."

"Icy, you're not even looking."

Icy patiently turned around and extended his free arm. "Fire at will, Tern."

Tern fired. Icy snagged the bolt in mid-air, then looped the trailing line around a spur of crystal.

"It is ready," Icy said, frowning as he looked down at the floor. "Are you certain that you have measured the rope distance properly?"

"It'll be fine," Tern said.

"Because it would be bad if you misjudged the timing or the length of the rope and fell onto the horrible magical floor," Icy said by way of encouragement.

Tern glowered. "The fact that I totally deserved that in no way excuses you. You ready?" Icy nodded. "Okay, *go!*"

Tern jumped, holding onto her end of the grappling line. Because of the length of the line, this would have resulted in her sliding along the floor, which would have been bad.

Which is why Icy, holding the other end of the line, which was looped once around the crystal spur, let go just as she jumped. He fell most of the way to the floor, pulling the grappling line with him and shortening its length so that Tern sailed across the room without touching the floor. As she whisked past Icy, her momentum pulled hard on the line, pulling Icy back up and taking Tern far enough to reach the platform, where she landed with a great deal of clanking... and let go of the grappling line.

Tern winced as lines of energy sizzled up from her trailing end and disintegrated the entirety of the grappling line. "Sorry!" she called to Icy, who now hung by one ankle from one of the crystal handgrips.

"The dismount is always the trickiest part," Icy said calmly.

"I'll bear that in mind." Tern looked down at the crystal dais. "I'll *also* see what I can do about deactivating this thing."

"A simple energy conduit," came a voice from the entryway, behind Icy. "Powerful, but hardly elegant." He twisted around and arched his neck to see.

Ambassador Bi'ul looked at him curiously. "That is extremely impressive, however you got there. You must be one of the thieves plaguing the Archvoyant."

"I do not believe that you can conclusively prove that based on the evidence at hand," Icy said cautiously.

"Don't be silly." Bi'ul waved an arm that trailed radiant light behind it. "Is there any chance you'd like to sell me your soul in exchange for me getting you down from there?"

Icy considered this. "I believe I can manage unassisted."

"Worth a shot." Bi'ul shrugged. "I suppose I'll just kill you, then."

An *yvkefer*-tipped bolt zipped through the Glimmering Man, who shimmered like a rainbow over a waterfall for a moment, then returned to his normal glowing form.

"Okay," called Tern, "that was significantly less effective than I'd been hoping."

"So you can sense her aura and stuff, right?" Kail asked as he got to his feet. "So anything I say about her *not* being a unicorn—"

"You are irrelevant," Hunter Mirrkir declared. His golden armor reflected the blue glow of his spear, and his green cloak rippled as a he strode forward. "I have already slain the death priestess. I have no need to kill the living." Under his feet, the runes on the floor-crystals began to glow.

Ululenia's mouth opened in a little "oh".

"You killed Desidora." Kail drew his sword and put himself between Ululenia and the hunter.

"She left me no choice." Mirrkir raised his spear. "Her death was a necessity."

He parried Kail's thrust, then went sprawling as Kail body-checked him. Kail got the sword up, only to have it swatted away by the slashing spear, and the butt of the spear slammed Kail hard to the ground.

Hunter Mirrkir rose to his feet, unperturbed. The runes on the floor where he had fallen continued to glow in the shape of his fallen body. "You have no magic. You cannot stand against me." He caught Kail's punch, grabbed his shoulder, and flung Kail to the floor. "Stand aside."

He got two more steps, then fell flat as Kail took him at knee-level from behind. A golden gauntlet batted Kail away, and he slid several paces along the smooth crystal of the floor.

A snowy white dove streaked past Mirrkir and Kail to the doorway, then fell back and collapsed into her unicorn form as tendrils of crackling blue energy wreathed around her.

"I took the precaution of warding the door," Hunter Mirrkir explained. "You have proven most resilient, and—" He broke off as Kail's punch glanced ineffectually off the golden helmet, then grunted as Kail's sword, recovered during Mirrkir's moment of distraction, punched through his shimmering golden ringmail.

Mirrkir's backhand slammed Kail to the ground again, and with a slight effort, he pulled the sword from his body. "Why do you continue to put yourself in my way?" he demanded, tossing the sword out over the cliff on the far side of the room. "You have no magic. You are not my enemy." The sword finally clattered at the bottom of the cliff. "You *cannot stop me* from killing the unicorn."

Kail pushed himself back to his feet. "It isn't about the unicorn!"

Hunter Mirrkir tossed out a negligent backhand, and Kail ducked, then lunged up and lifted Mirrkir by the waist. "She didn't ask to be a death priestess!" Kail yelled, staggering toward the cliff with Mirrkir over his shoulder. "She just wanted to be loved!"

He was almost to the cliff when the butt of Mirrkir's spear punched the base of Kail's spine. Kail went down hard, and Mirrkir regained his footing, then spun the spear to level it at Kail's neck.

"She deserved more," Kail muttered, grabbing the spear just below the head in a futile effort to stop it.

"You loved her."

Kail coughed. "She had nice eyes."

"Then I apologize," Hunter Mirrkir said without pause, "but she stood between me and my goal. As do you."

He does not, Ululenia thought. The blue shackles had faded, and she had gotten back to her feet in her true form. Her horn was dim and flickering, and she came forward shakily, shining hooves clicking on the crystal. *Take me, and let him live.*

Mirrkir stepped away from Kail and raised his spear. "Perhaps you are not entirely bereft of the spark of soul," he allowed. "Your death will save this one's life."

Agreed. And she knelt before him.

"Ululenia!" Kail got back to his knees. "Don't give arrogant apple, babbling brook...." He slumped back down.

Hunter Mirrkir raised his spear over Ululenia. "With your death, the magic of the ancients is reclaimed."

He struck.

He missed.

Badly.

Hunter Mirrkir stared down at his spear, which had, against all logic, bent double in the air to stab into his own stomach. "What..." he rasped, as blue crackling energy raced along the spear from where he gripped its base to where it had torn through his golden ringmail. "How..." The blue tendrils of energy flared brighter and faster, until the spear was a half-circle of brilliant blue light before him. "No!"

The blue radiance cast harsh shadows on every surface of the room, flared once, and then flickered and died.

And Desidora, priestess of Byn-kodar, stood before Hunter Mirrkir with one arm held high in his grasp and one fist sunk into his gut. Her skin shone like alabaster, and her hair and robes drew in the light from all around and returned only shadows.

"Did you *think*," she said coldly, "that you could *kill* a *death priestess?*" She pulled her fist from Mirrkir, then raised her open hand to the sky.

There was a flash of light, this one familiar, and a flare of silver in her hand.

"Besyn larveth'is!"

Hunter Mirrkir flew in a graceful arc, shattered golden armor spraying out in all directions from where the blow had struck, and hit the far wall before falling back into the blackness of the chasm.

You're alive! Ululenia shimmered back into human form, pale but smiling.

"I thought..." Kail was shaking his head. "I thought you were... Hey, you didn't hear anything we said while you were—"

"It doesn't matter." Ululenia stepped forward, arms outstretched. "All that matters now is that she's—"

"Finished." Desidora raised her free hand, and coils of absolute black snaked from her fingers to twine around Kail, who collapsed again, clutching at his throat. She turned to Ululenia, and her eyes were pitch black. "My quest cannot be allowed to fail," she said in a voice like razors. "The world needs me. I need power."

The crystals under Desidora's feet faded to a smoky black, and the runes traced into them slid into spiderlike patterns as Desidora the death priestess smiled, a slash of crimson across her chalk-white face. "I will take what I need."

Archvoyant Silestin's personal quarters and private vault were located in the western section of the palace. Loch ducked around a corner, slipped past a guard, and crept into the personal rooms.

The first was a sitting room. It had some chairs and a sofa and tables and a lot of knickknacks. Some of them were tacky, but the determining factor in displaying them seemed to be how much each had cost.

The second room was a small study. The desk, black marble with gold scrollwork, had some papers and a few gilded and bejeweled desk accessories.

The third room was a small kitchen. It had fewer exotic decorations, but it did have a nice pantry, a wide range of drinks and finger foods, and two lithe and scantily clad Imperial women sitting at a table.

The Imperial women slid to their feet as Loch came inside, their silk trimmings rustling exotically.

"Personal assassin guards?" Loch asked. "Or pleasure-girls? Or both?"

"Personal assassins," said the one on the right.

"Well, I'm both," said the one on the left, "but mostly personal assassins."

They assumed exotic combat stances that showed a lot of leg.

"Not a lot of muscle on you girls," Loch observed. She didn't have a sword. At least her dress had the slit up one leg, so she could move in it. She slid out of her high-heeled sandals.

"The Archvoyant's Blades do not need raw muscle," said the one on the right with a little sneer.

"Your own bulk will slow you down," added the one on the left.

Loch stepped forward. "That should be something to see."

The one on the left sprang into the air to execute a flashy kick, and Loch punched her in the face. The one on the right tried some acrobatic rolling maneuver, and Loch stepped into it, and as the woman stumbled back, Loch punched her in the face, too. Neither of them got up from where they'd landed.

She left her high-heeled slippers in the kitchen.

The next room was technically a library, although half of the bookshelves were taken up with vases and statuettes. One large display table held a gaudy golden plate that might have been dwarven, going by the runes.

"Gurdarik dynasty," said the Imperial assassin woman standing on the other side of the room. She was older than the girls, though still lithe and not wearing clothing you'd go outside in. "Extremely rare."

"Nice," said Loch. "What do the runes say?"

"Not a clue." The assassin shrugged. "I don't think Silestin bought it to read it."

"No," Loch agreed. "He's not the reading type."

She got the plate up just in time to deflect the assassin's throwing knife. Then she flung the plate at the assassin, who rolled smoothly out of the way. The golden plate shattered an ancient elven vase and clattered to the floor.

"So I'm guessing you're in charge," Loch said, slowly circling the room.

"Second Blade." The assassin mirrored her movements. "More than enough for you."

Loch batted aside a claw-hand strike, tried to catch the wrist but missed, then set her weight hard to stop the assassin's ankle sweep and drove forward with a punch. The assassin ducked it, then answered with a kick that Loch took on the arms. Loch moved in for an ankle sweep of her own but had to sidestep instead as the assassin kicked out with her other leg and leaped into a backflip. She came down perfectly and rolled out of range.

"You've trained."

"Here and there." Loch rolled out her shoulders. She'd have given a month's combat pay to be wearing a good pair of boots for this fight.

"A few years in the monasteries, and you could have been a master." The assassin leaped, and this time she was a glittering golden ribbon of death. One kick snapped into the back of Loch's knee just as the other kick slammed into Loch's jaw, spinning her away and dropping her to one knee with its force.

And as the assassin landed, necessarily off-balance for one critical moment, Loch lunged backward and threw an elbow into the assassin's gut. "Fancy trick might've worked…" Followed by a right cross to the temple. "…if I were a one-kick-to-the-head kind of girl…" Followed by a left uppercut to the chin. "…which I'm not." She stepped in, palmed the assassin's face, and slammed her head to the ground.

"You've trained too, lady," Loch said, panting. "A few years in the field learning to take as good as you give, and you could have been a real fighter." The assassin woman didn't get up. Not dead, but she wouldn't be serving as a pleasure-girl for a few weeks, either. "I'll be honest, though. I'd hoped for something a bit more challenging."

Behind her, a sword slid free of its sheath.

"I'll try not to disappoint," said Justicar Pyvic.

Twenty-One

"**D**ESIDORA," ULULENIA SAID CAREFULLY, "YOU DO NOT WISH to do this."

"You have *no idea* what I wish, puny beast." The death priestess glanced at her imperiously. Coils of energy continued to choke the life out of Kail. "The wishes of the woman are cast aside at the needs of the gods. I am that need."

Kail's eyes bulged as he clutched at his throat. "You are not a murderer," Ululenia insisted.

"I am what I must be." Beneath the death priestess's feet, the runes formed terrifying shapes that Ululenia could almost understand. "I am the last hope of the gods." The words cut into Ululenia's mind as she opened herself to the priestess. "I am the blade that tears away the rotted arm to save the patient. I am the thing that violates the souls of hundreds and kills thousands so that millions may live." She raised Ghylspwr. "I wield the last king of the ancients, who bound his soul to a weapon to forever fight the darkness. I am *justice*, beast, justice without hesitation, mercy, or regret."

"*Kun-kabynalti osu fuir'is,*" Ghylspwr said softly.

Ululenia stepped forward. "You are a priestess of Tasheveth. You *will* *not* kill this man. I am—"

"You are *what?*" the priestess asked with a sneer. "You think I do not know your kind, formed from the stray energies of the artifacts of the ancients? You are a *parasite*, a *tapeworm* in the belly of creation. If I could feed upon what laughably passes for your soul, I would drain you dry as well. You are *nothing* but stolen magic and a few mental tricks."

Such as this one, Ululenia said, and hit the priestess with everything that Kail, in his deepest and most secret places, held for Desidora.

The priestess staggered, shaking her head frantically as the darkness slid across her eyes. The dark coils wavered, grew frail and tenuous around Kail. She raised Ghylspwr, her arm trembling, and pointed the hammer at Ululenia.

Ghylspwr did not strike.

"Kill her!" the priestess screamed.

"Kutesosh gajair'is!" Ghylspwr shouted back, and did not strike.

"She *is* evil! She is making me *feel! I must not*—"

"Kun-kabynalti osu fuir'is," Ghylspwr said flatly. And did not strike.

The priestess turned a baleful stare upon Ululenia. "There will come a day," she hissed, and then collapsed, and a wave of cold washed across the room.

Kail gasped, bucked, and began to breathe.

Thank you. Ululenia nodded to Ghylspwr.

"Besyn larveth'is."

"I'm sorry," Desidora said softly, in her own voice. She was pale, but it was a natural pale, the pallor of exhaustion. "I'm sorry. I couldn't come back. I tried. I..."

"You…" Kail coughed and got back to his knees. "You got turned into a *spear*, Diz. I'm inclined to cut you a break." His eyes were watering, but he looked otherwise unharmed.

"I couldn't see anything but her." Desidora frowned, shook her head. "How did you drive her away? I sensed you sending something at her."

Ululenia glanced at Kail. "The arrogant apple trick," she finally said with a shrug. "Works every time."

"Glad to hear it," Desidora whispered as Kail shot Ululenia a grateful look. "But we must hurry. They'll be getting to the vault any moment."

"Kail, attend Desidora. I will handle the console myself," Ululenia said confidently, and strode to the podium. The crystals hummed under her fingers while Kail got Desidora propped up and breathing easily again.

The priestess, for all her vitriol, had been right. While Tern and Desidora understood the mechanics, Ululenia *was* a creature of magic, and as she opened herself to the energies, she could intuitively sense the steps necessary to force the Voyancy ward to stop drawing energy from several different matrices throughout the palace, and instead draw power only from one matrix… which Icy and Tern had hopefully disabled. It was as simple as the circle of life.

And had there not been a failsafe alarm to prevent exactly what Ululenia was doing, things would have gone perfectly.

Instead, a curtain of iridescent light, like a rainbow caught in the spray of a waterfall, rose up from the chasm, and from behind that shimmering curtain flowed the glowing forms of two spectral figures in ancient armor that shone like moonlight on water.

"*Ciel'urti ufa gaveth'isti,*" they proclaimed in hollow voices. "*Ynu gedesar'urti? Osu gedesar'urti, osku byn-kodar'isti.*"

"That could be a problem," Desidora said weakly.

After a moment of silence, the spectral knights looked at each other. *"Byn-kodar'isti,"* they agreed, and drew swords that crackled with blue flame as they drifted toward Ululenia.

"Keep working!" Kail shouted. He stepped over the still-fallen form of Desidora and called to the knights, *"Ynku isti ku-kutosh'urti!"*

The knights paused and turned from Ululenia to Kail. *"Ynu ur ku-kutoshi'is?"* one of them asked in spectral suspicion.

Kail grinned. *"Yeshki-aitha'al'ur, al-*ajetosh*'is!"* he proclaimed with a gesture that transcended the centuries.

"Gods, he knows it in *every* language," Desidora murmured as the two spectral knights roared wordlessly and floated his way.

Ululenia kept working on the crystals, bending them to her will. Off to one side, Kail dodged a strike and then dove back from another. "Be careful!" Desidora shouted. "They're backing you toward the cliff!"

"Hey, thanks, Diz!" Kail shouted. "I hadn't noticed the giant drop right there behind me until—" He paused and rolled away from another strike. "—you pointed that out to me!"

"Besyn larveth'is!" Ghylspwr shouted.

The knights paused.

"Ynu besyn larveth'ur?" one of them asked, still skeptical.

"Besyn larveth'is," Ghylspwr said again, more confidently this time.

"Ynu ufa osu gedesar fuir'ur?" the other knight asked.

"Kutesosh gajair'is," Ghylspwr said firmly.

The first knight gestured at Ululenia, then Desidora. *"Ynu alti veth'ur? Ynu alti iofelarur?"*

"Kun-kabynalti osu fuir'is," Ghylspwr declared.

The knights thought for a moment.

"*Hyur'urti,*" they finally said, and bowed once to Ghylspwr. Then they rose into the air back out into the chasm, where the rainbow veil shimmered into existence again.

One of them paused and turned to Kail. "*Ynku kumet'ur yeshki-aitha'al'is,*" he said flatly.

"I was totally mistaken," Kail said quickly. "Your mother was a saint."

The knights stepped into the veil and disappeared.

"Damn, Ghyl," Kail said after a moment, "if somebody had said that *you* were going to be the one talking us out of tight spots, I'd... well, I'd have bet heavily against it."

"I am finished," Ululenia said, sighing in relief. "The Voyancy ward is disabled, provided that Tern and Icy disable the energy conduit."

"They can't be having any more trouble than we had," Kail said sourly. "Let's get out of here. Every time we stop to catch our breath in this damn room, something goes wrong."

With Kail and Ululenia helping Desidora, they left to meet Loch and the others at the vault.

Bi'ul gestured at Icy imperiously. Nothing happened.

"Too much ambient energy," the Glimmering Man muttered. "Wasteful design by the ancient fools."

"So you can't use all the horrible magic?" Tern called from across the room. "Hah! What are you going to do now? Jump up there yourself?"

Bi'ul brightened, ducked into a crouch, and leaped fifteen feet into the air to catch one of the crystal spurs.

"I would appreciate it—"

"Sorry!" Tern started reloading her crossbow.

"—if you would refrain from giving the Glimmering Man helpful suggestions." Icy pulled himself up, switched to a handgrip, swung quickly to the next grip, and then swung off *that* with a big leap that ended with him landing feet-first on a large faceted plane and then kicking off to catch hold of *another* crystal spur some ways away.

Bi'ul flicked his wrist and swung a good twenty feet through the air to easily catch another handgrip. "Impressive," he called with no trace of sarcasm. "I admire the degree to which you have maximized the performance of your limited mortal shell. Are you *certain* that I cannot convince you to sell me your soul?"

"Losing my spiritual essence violates my personal code of conduct." Icy leaped off his spur and actually ran *on* the wall for a few steps before grabbing the next spur. He was coming closer.

But Bi'ul was practically flying. "Pity," he murmured, swinging without effort to another handgrip.

"Hang on, Icy!" Tern fired off another shot—this one silver-plated and soaked in the ichor of daemons. It went through the Glimmering Man without doing anything more than making him shimmer for a moment. "Okay, maybe the control panel, then. I'm sure there's a big..." Bi'ul was within a few yards of Icy. "...ancient-horror-from-beyond-stopping button. He's made of energy or... something, so... maybe...." She tapped the panel in desperation, looking for functions that might help. "Cold-reset of core functions? Sure, that might bleed off some magic. That could help. In fact, I'm sure...." She rapped on the crystal.

Long crystal rods shot out from the ceiling and walls, sprouted wickedly sharp multicolored crystal blades, and began to spin.

"Son of a bitch! Sorry, Icy!"

"I appreciate the attempts at assistance," said Icy, who had made a massive leap backward to avoid one set of spinning blades and was now suspended upside-down, balanced on the arch of his foot and bent nearly double to avoid the blades just a few inches beneath him.

"I know, I know! I'll turn them off!"

Icy flexed the arch of his foot and leaped up to grab hold of a long horizontal crystal rod. With a quick effort, he pulled himself up onto it, balanced like a tightrope walker. "Do not trouble yourself. I believe that from here, I can—"

Bi'ul swung through the air and caught a handhold between Icy and Tern.

"I shall have to kill you in such a fashion as to make the most of your athletic aptitude," Bi'ul said. "I've always wanted to see whether a human could survive without his skin." And he leapt from his handhold to the long crystal rod upon which Icy stood.

A bolt of dragon ivory sprinkled with fairy dust shot through Bi'ul's foot just as he touched down.

Like the shots before it, it passed through Bi'ul, doing no more than making him shimmer into insubstantiality for a moment.

And in that moment, Bi'ul reached the long crystal rod, and passed *through it*.

"And *I've* always wanted to see," Tern said as Bi'ul missed the rod and fell, yelling in outrage, "what happens to big bad horrors from beyond when they hit that floor."

Icy was running even before Bi'ul fell, and he leaped as the explosion blossomed beneath him, and then he was tucked tightly into a somersault, flipping in the air as energy roared. He hit the ground in a roll near the console and came to his feet smoothly beside Tern.

"Are you okay?" Tern asked, staring at the orange-and-red raging hail of fire that occupied most of the room.

Icy opened his mouth, then stopped.

"Yes," said Ambassador Bi'ul as he walked out of the flames, smiling. "In fact, I rather enjoyed that."

He was completely unharmed, though energy crackled around his legs.

On the other hand, he *was* still in the middle of the room.

Tern turned back to the console. "Then you're going to *love* this," she said, and input the command to overload the conduit.

Curling lightning roared in every color of the rainbow between the crystal ceiling and the crystal floor, a solid wall of twisting energy that rattled Tern's teeth in their sockets. She clung to the console, Icy beside her, as hot air battered her and purple-white tendrils seared her vision even through tightly shut eyes.

And then, as suddenly as it had come, it was gone, and the room plunged into complete darkness, silent as death and empty of everything save the smell of ozone.

Tern blinked and waited for her pupils to dilate. "Is he gone?"

"Yes," said Icy.

"Are we alive?"

"Yes," said Icy.

"I'm really sorry about the spinning blades."

"Don't worry about it," said Icy.

"Do you think the floor is cool enough for us to walk back out?"

"Let us give it a minute," said Icy.

"Okay," said Tern, and sat back to wait.

The walls of the chasm were too slick to climb, so Mirrkir had to drag himself through an access shaft, then crawl through the vents until he reached a vertical tunnel, whereupon he could drag himself back up.

He had not been back to his ancient home for millennia. The hum of the crystals around him was soothing, familiar. He could almost imagine the ancients themselves just around the corner, giving him his sacred duties.

If he carried them out properly, those last instructions delivered so quickly so long ago, they would return. Hunter Mirrkir knew it as he knew nothing else. When he reached the surface, he let his keen senses guide him to open air, then found the crystal-studded console that opened the secret door.

He closed it behind him conscientiously. The secrets of the ancients were not for the men of today. They had not proved their worthiness.

He walked slowly through the hallway. One of his legs dragged with each step. It would be dealt with later.

He could not sense the unicorn's trail—there was too much magic in the air. Someone had overloaded a major conduit, sending out such intense waves that Mirrkir could barely see the ground before him.

He turned a corner and found a new magic, even through the blistering haze. Death magic, and powerful. The priestess, again. He forced himself into a faster walk.

And soon he found them. A wizard, not the death priestess—the play of energies around him was different. He was walking alongside an undead creature, the source of the death magic.

The zombie sensed him first and turned, calling the wizard's attention. The wizard pulled at stuff of shadows, weaving an illusion of a fierce warrior between himself and Mirrkir. Mirrkir identified it, recognized it as shadow-substance, and walked through it.

At that moment, a young human appeared around the corner and ran to the wizard. He saw Mirrkir and stopped, and when the wizard saw him, he shouted in fear and summoned shadows to weave around the boy as a simple invisibility-cloak. Mirrkir had been instructed not to harm young mortals unless absolutely necessary. He approved of the wizard's willingness to sacrifice himself in order that the boy might escape.

But the shadow unraveled and drew back. The wizard gestured again, and again the shadow coalesced around the boy, then fell apart.

The shadow could not touch the boy. It was the same boy who had ignored the energy from Mirrkir's spear as he had hunted the unicorn before. Mirrkir had thought the boy a familiar empowered by enchantments.

He had been wrong.

Mirrkir turned away from the wizard. "My orders have been superseded," he said aloud, as sparks flashed from the wound in his torso. "*Nef-gajair* protocol engaged."

His ancient masters would be proud.

Falling-Petal was conscious but hurting badly. She kept her eyes closed and listened.

"Isafesira de Lochenville," Justicar Pyvic said, "Enlisted as Loch, captain of independent scouting unit nine, seventh wing of the Republic National Forces."

"Did some research?" said the woman.

"Convicted *in absentia* of desertion during a time of war, a determination subsequently classified by Voyant Cevirt. At least I know how you recruited Private Kail.

"And I also know...." He broke off, took a long breath. "I also know that as the daughter of a noble, you'd know about the value of Archvoyant Silestin's art collection."

Falling-Petal kept listening.

"He's got an old elven manuscript that will let me repurchase my title," the woman said. "Why don't you come along, Pyvic? Get out, live a little." She smiled—Falling-Petal didn't need to open her eyes to know when a woman was smiling. "I could keep you in luxury for the rest of your life."

"Would we have a mirror on the ceiling in the bedroom?" Pyvic asked, and Falling-Petal drew some conclusions about the relationship between the two.

"Oh, definitely," the woman purred.

"That's a shame," said Pyvic. "If I took the offer of a deserter and a thief, I'd never be able to look at myself again. I suppose I'll have to pass."

She drew in a sharp breath. "Your loss, Justicar."

Pyvic moved. Loch moved. Someone hit the ground.

"Your loss indeed," Loch said again, and Falling-Petal heard her walk away.

After a moment, Falling-Petal groaned, opened her eyes, and set about finding something to write all that down.

"Anything I can do?" Silestin Senior asked.

"Can you fight?" Hessler asked. He moved to stand between Hunter Mirrkir and Dairy. "Dairy, run!"

"I could paw at him a little," Silestin Senior said, "but I suspect he'd just tear me apart."

"I'm not leaving you, Mister Hessler!"

Hunter Mirrkir shuffled forward. Flares of magic sizzled from the cracked crystals in his torso. "I do this not out of hatred, wizard," he said, "but necessity. It is my protocol. It is what I was designed to do."

"Dairy, *run!*"

"No!" The *stupid* kid ran up and grabbed him by the shoulder. "I'm *not* leaving you. You stay away from Mister Hessler!"

"He can't stay away, kid." They could try running. The thing's leg looked injured. Maybe it would work for a while. Of course, he'd lose the zombie, but.... He tried to hit Dairy again with the invisibility cloak, and again it failed. "He's not a man. He's something the ancients made." Hessler started backing up, pulling the kid along with him. "Dairy, *run now.* I told you that I could protect you if I had to, right? I can protect you now, but... but I need you to get out of here so that I can do it!" They backed around a corner, Hessler trying to pull the kid into a run, and—

"Is there some difficulty with which I can provide assistance?"

Hessler turned. Icy and Tern stood behind him.

"We successfully overloaded the conduit," Icy said, "and we heard a commotion as we made our way to the vault." He nodded politely to Silestin Senior.

"You're working with an Imperial?" Silestin Senior asked in distaste.

Then Hunter Mirrkir shuffled around the corner as well. "Holy crap! He's a golem!" Tern shouted helpfully. "Why in Byn-kodar's hell did I use my *yvkefer* bolt already?"

"The rest of you are of no concern." Mirrkir had not stopped, and as Hessler and Dairy kept backing up, the hunter had increased his shuffling pace. "I seek the boy now."

"Which is why the boy needs to *run away now!*" Hessler shouted.

"Pardon me," Icy said politely, "but what has happened to Mirrkir's torso?"

"I was damaged," Mirrkir grated. "It will not stop me from my goal."

"He's a golem," Hessler said shortly.

"One of the magical creations of the ancients," Tern added helpfully.

"A nonliving object?" Icy asked. "Like a brick or a board?"

"He's significantly more complex," Hessler said acidly, "given his effective state of sentience and his impressive hunting abilities."

Icy sighed. "But he is a *nonliving* object?" he said again.

Hessler frowned. "I suppose that depends upon how exactly one classifies life. It cannot likely reproduce, but it may learn from—"

"Oh," said Tern, and then, "Oh! Yes. *Hell* yes! Completely nonliving. Powered by sophisticated enchantments. No soul."

"Like a brick or a board," Icy said in satisfaction, and stepped past Hessler and Dairy toward Mirrkir.

Mirrkir lashed out to swat him aside. Icy ducked it, leaped into the air, and kicked Mirrkir three times before he landed. Mirrkir lunged in with a punch, and Icy leaped over it, kicked Mirrkir in the head, then somehow managed to scissor his legs around Mirrkir's punching arm in midair with force that produced an audible crack. As Mirrkir grabbed at Icy with his other arm, Icy leaped from Mirrkir's arm into the air, caught the grabbing arm, and did some kind of somersaulting joint-throw that sent Mirrkir crashing to the ground yards away.

"I have often wished to try those techniques on a moving target," Icy said in satisfaction. "Magister, would it be safe to assume that the golem is composed primarily of crystalline substances?"

Hessler thought a moment. "That would be fair, yes."

"Excellent." As Mirrkir rose back to his feet, Icy raised his hands overhead, the fingertips just touching. Hessler thought they looked blurry, as though they were vibrating very quickly.

"My protocols will not be denied," Mirrkir growled, and leaped at Icy.

Icy leaped forward as well, his whole body pivoting in one movement of perfect efficiency.

The golem exploded.

"Although I am chagrined to admit it," Icy noted, "there is a great deal of potential enjoyment in the practice of hitting enemies."

"I've always thought so," Tern noted.

"You're working with an Imperial?" Silestin Senior asked again.

"Times change," Hessler said absently, walking past the zombie and through the debris. He stopped before the golem's head, the largest part of him still in one piece. Crystals sparked at the base of the neck, and the metal faceplate had shattered to reveal a crystal lattice inside.

"He... must... die..." the head said. "He must... or he will fight... and the choice shall be maa-a-a-a...." The crystals flared once more, then faded to darkness.

Hessler turned back to the others.

"We should get to Loch and the others," he said. "We're behind schedule."

"I will leave by a different means," Icy said, dusting off his palms. "There is something else I must attend to."

Tern raised an eyebrow. "You sure?"

"I will be fine." Icy smiled faintly, and then, as Tern looked at him, blushed.

"Oh. Well, aren't *you* just full of surprises." Tern grinned. "See you at the meeting point."

Icy headed off toward the main ballroom, and Tern, Hessler, and the kid headed for the vault, with the kid slipping back to talk with Silestin Senior about what it was like to be a zombie.

"What did it say?" Tern asked quietly once the kid was out of earshot.

Hessler glanced back. Dairy was smiling nervously, and when he gestured, the birthmark on his arm was visible.

"Nothing important," Hessler said, and turned away.

When Loch reached the sumptuous room with the hidden door that led to the vault, Ululenia, Desidora, and Kail were already there. Kail looked shaky, and Desidora looked like hell. "Trouble?"

"Nothing we couldn't handle," Kail said.

"I died," Desidora said. Loch looked at her, and Desidora shrugged weakly. "I got better."

"There is someone in the palace," Ululenia said. "An assassin who moves unseen. We must be wary of the shadows."

"Everyone is *full* of good news," Loch said acidly.

"Sorry we're late!" called Tern as she, Hessler, and Dairy stepped inside and shut the door behind them. "We got held up by the guy with the spear."

"Mister Icy blew him up!" Dairy said enthusiastically.

Loch looked at Tern with one eyebrow raised.

"Golem."

"Ah."

Hessler's face was drawn and bleak. "Loch, I need to speak with you." Then he turned and waved a hand, and a zombie shimmered into view. "What, no trouble dealing with Urujar?"

The zombie shrugged. "Some of the best damn soldiers I've known have been Urujar. Anybody who survives what they've survived has to be tough. Silestin, ma'am."

Loch gave him a quick soldier's nod. "What's the problem, Hessler? Desidora, can you and Silestin do the honors?" She stepped over to the corner of the room, and Hessler followed. Behind them, Desidora grew pale while the zombie pressed his hand to a crystal plate hidden behind a painting. Kail looked nervous, staring at Desidora as though he expected something bad to happen.

"I've been thinking," Hessler said, "about why a trained thief would allow an untrained kid to come along on a mission."

"Everyone's gotta start somewhere, Hessler."

Hessler shook his head. "Something twisted the world around us. It pulled me into that cell with Dairy, and it pulled you to that cell to find us, so that I'd come with you, and he'd come with me, and... Loch, are you familiar with the Champions of Dusk and Dawn?"

A hidden panel slid back next to Desidora. No alarms went off. Loch grinned. "I've heard of it."

"I think… I think that Dairy is the Champion of Dawn."

"Took you 'til now, huh?" Loch nodded at the doorway and raised her voice. "Let's go. Tern, you're on the vault. Where's Icy?"

"He's fine." Tern grinned. "We think there might be a woman."

"You… you *knew?*" Hessler asked in a furious whisper.

They all moved into the hidden room, which looked like Cevirt's vault room, only larger. Tern took out the duplicated crystal, a tuning fork, and some other tools, and began to tinker with the vault door. "Give me some room," she said. "This is… well, I have no *idea* what this is, but I think having room will help."

"You heard the woman," Loch said. "Stand back in case she botches it and there's a massive explosion." As everyone hurriedly stepped away from the glowering Tern, Loch turned to Hessler and lowered her voice. "Saw the birthmark that first night, remembered a bit in the old poem about going to a city in the sky, and figured that I was supposed to help him out with his destiny," she said with a little smile.

"You're dragging him into *danger!* He's supposed to fight the Champion of Dusk to determine the *fate of the world!*"

"Right. That's written into the prophecy. And, if that's really destined to happen," Loch added, "it stands to reason that he *has* to survive to get *to* that fight." To Hessler's open-mouthed stare, she said, "Look, we were going to arrive at the port, where it turned out that guards were waiting. Luckily for us, the kid screwed up, and the ship crash-landed instead. You and the others were in that sitting room right before Pyvic and everyone else came to arrest you. Then the kid screwed up, and most of you went elsewhere in the palace just in time.

If he's going to get to that fight, he *will* survive. And as long as we stay near him..."

"By all the gods..." Hessler put a hand to his face. "He's your *insurance policy.*"

"Lucky charm," Loch corrected, and then looked around to see everyone except Silestin Senior and Dairy himself looking at them, wide-eyed. Dairy was listening to Silestin Senior tell stories about the old days. "Tern, the safe? Today?" Loch lowered her voice again. "Look, Magister, if the kid's going to fight for the sake of the world, nothing can change that. But if he's picked up a few pointers from tagging along with us, that can only help."

Tern was still tinkering with the vault door. It glowed with a pearly radiance, and Tern pulled more things out of her pockets every few seconds. "Tern?" Loch called. "We have a problem?"

"I'm sure we're fine!" Tern called back. "But if anyone can make a broken additive-magic algorithm stop from overloading and blowing us all halfway to the Empire, that would be great."

I will attempt to assist you. Ululenia closed her eyes, and her horn blazed in the dim light of the room.

"As will I." Desidora grew pale again, and Kail nervously took a step away.

The zombie finished whatever story he was telling Dairy with a laugh that made a bit of his nose fall off, and Dairy lurched back in surprise, lost his balance, and fell into Tern, who banged one of her crystals heavily against the vault. With a short musical chime, the pearly radiance faded.

Everyone looked at Dairy. Everyone looked at Loch.

"To be fair, that could have been one of us," Desidora said.

"Sorry!" Dairy cried. "Tern, did I mess anything up?"

"You're doing fine, Dairy." Tern's eyes were wide as she looked at him, and she turned back to the safe. "I'll just… yeah. You're fine."

"Lucky charm," Loch murmured to Hessler.

"Your amoral plan has a tiny problem, *Captain.*" Hessler leaned in close. "Bi'ul appears to be the Champion of Dusk. You've just put a sixteen-year-old boy in the same palace as the thing that's going to fight him to determine the fate of the world!"

The vault opened.

"Hah! Take that, stupid ancients!"

"Besyn larveth'is!"

"Er, no offense."

"I was really hoping that tingly feeling was just youthful vigor," Loch muttered. She stepped into the vault chamber, a featureless room of black stone lit only by pale crystals overhead.

In the middle of the room, a single book lay alone on a square of velvet. Loch picked it up, folded in the corners to turn the velvet square into a velvet bag, and ushered everyone else in.

"You knew that *too?*" Hessler's face reddened with what looked like the academic version of a killing rage.

"Found out at the party," Loch said quietly, "which is why I sent him out to you. Relax, Magister. If the world falls into eternal night, that's going to hurt my plans to sell this book and get very rich." She smiled. "Now come on. The hardest part's over. Everybody ready?" She looked around. "Tern, activate the failsafe and transport us out of here."

Tern traced a pattern into a crystal panel on the wall. "Everyone get ready. This might feel a bit—"

With a great crash, the vault door slammed shut and the lights went out.

"Hessler, light. Tern?" Loch asked, pinching the bridge of her nose.

Tern's voice was carefully steady. "I'm sure it's just a—"

A great metallic screech cut off the rest of what she was saying.

It was, Loch saw as Hessler's magic illuminated the room, the sound of the ceiling closing down on them.

Twenty-Two

AMBASSADOR BI'UL REFORMED IN HIS GUEST ROOM SOME TIME later. Very little could hurt him in this world, since the foolish mortals were interacting with a shadow-formed simulacrum made manifest across the worlds.

Nevertheless, the sheer energy of the conduit had been too much for him. He had been forced to give it up as lost and go through the tiresome process of re-forming a shadow in which to place his consciousness again.

He made himself a little taller this time.

When he finished, fully solid and glowing radiantly, he returned to the room where the mortals had gathered to engage in their social charades.

He found Silestin, who was speaking with the Urujar girl and a young man wearing a noble's vestments.

"Now, Naria, this man is from a wonderful house, and—"

"Your palace is being robbed," Bi'ul greeted Silestin. "Some mortals were vandalizing an energy conduit, likely to disable a security ward."

What Bi'ul liked about Silestin, inasmuch as he liked anything in this pitiful world, was that Silestin could dismiss the casual charades of this world almost as well as Bi'ul himself. "Take a walk, Naria," said the Archvoyant, and dismissed the young man as well. He pressed a small crystal on one of his rings, and a moment later Elkinsair arrived. "The ambassador here indicates that we are being robbed. Any thoughts?"

The little security chief paled. "I was examining the entry wards, but detected no changes within the... of course, if they are already inside... I will see to it directly, sir."

"Good man. Inform the others. Bi'ul, I am in your debt." Silestin nodded to him, then walked off, the matter evidently concluded.

What Bi'ul *respected* about Silestin was that phrases like "I am in your debt" were constructed to avoid mentioning exactly *how* that debt would be paid.

"Thank you for bringing this matter to my attention," said Elkinsair. "I take such things quite seriously—"

"I was discorporated while dealing with the thieves," Bi'ul said. "If I am inconvenienced again in any way, I will ensure that you remain alive while I violate you with the fused verte-brae of your own spinal column."

Elkinsair swallowed. "That seems fair, Ambassador."

Then he trotted off, and Ambassador Bi'ul decided to mingle.

Icy had changed out of his guard uniform and into his traditional golden silk robes, which Ululenia had thought-fully dried for him after leading the other guards away.

He strode into the palace ballroom with an expression of benign serenity, the picture of the exotic and untouchable Imperial.

"And on this most important day of victory," Archvoyant Silestin was saying to a quiet room, "we must not forget that no victory is without cost—that even now, we must be prepared to defend the freedom we won from our oppressors."

Technically, the Republic had started the war, but Icy was confident that it was not taught that way on this side of the border. Some of the guests gave him dark looks.

"The Republic will defend itself and its legacy of justice wherever they are threatened, be it in the homeland of those who fear our liberty, or here in my own home," Silestin continued. "The Republic demands strength, and I intend to represent our proud heritage without flinching. These recent Imperial assaults upon our financial sovereignty...."

The Empire was evidently calling in its loans. More people glared at Icy. His disguise as an Imperial ambassador was causing more problems than he had hoped.

A hand closed over his arm, and he turned and looked into Naria's dark and beautiful face. "You shouldn't be here." Behind the smoked lenses that hid her eyes, he saw the anguish.

"I agree." Icy nodded. "Neither should you."

"Indomitable, I cannot—"

"Are you happy, Naria?" Icy looked at the crowd. "Your adoptive father is scapegoating my homeland for his own purposes. You legitimize his claim by providing the veneer of racial harmony. Does this please you?"

"What would you have me do?" she demanded. "Become a thief like my sister? I did not ask to represent all Urujar as a noble, but if I must, I must do so with honor."

"Is this honor?" Icy gestured toward Silestin angrily. "And I have not asked you to join us, Naria. I have only asked you to come with me." As tears slid down Naria's cheeks, Icy stepped in closer. "Meet the sister you believed dead and choose a course for yourself. That is all that I ask."

A guard, one of the ordinary men who had not been corrupted, was approaching them, and bystanders were murmuring. Icy stepped away and offered Naria a polite bow. "I apologize for upsetting you," he said, and left.

He was in the outside gardens when her hand slid around his arm, and she leaned in close, her warm skin smelling of exotic spices.

"Take me to my sister," she whispered. "Take me away from here."

Loch looked at the descending ceiling. "I'm open to suggestions."

"The energies of the vault have shifted," Ululenia said, "as new buds shooting forth in the spring."

"I'm open to *relevant* suggestions."

"Hey, what could be more fun than cracking the vault from the *inside?*" Tern muttered, kneeling in front of the door with a small crystal rod between her teeth and a pair of tiny copper tweezers in her hands. "With, you know, a running hourglass."

"It's shielded," Hessler said. "Ululenia, can you put what you sense into my... thank you. It's... it's incredibly complex, Loch. Someone has tampered with the artifacts of the ancients to an absurd degree. When we tried to activate the teleportation failsafe—"

"I'm less concerned with cause than effect, Magister." Loch raised her hands experimentally, braced herself, and utterly failed to halt the ceiling's descent. "Okay, that's not going to work. How's it coming, Tern?"

"Oh, are we under time pressure? I hadn't noticed."

"If you can't do it…" Loch dropped to her knees as the ceiling bumped her head gently. "Priestess?"

"The vault's shielding the magical auras," Desidora said. In the pale light Hessler had created, her skin was already chalk-white. "Even if the unicorn puts the images into my mind, it would take too much power to manipulate them from here."

"Too much?" Loch asked as everyone slowly dropped to their knees. "How much is too much?"

Desidora's hair began to writhe. "I *might* have the necessary power if I drained the souls of every living person in this vault," she said coldly. "I assume that you do not consider that a viable option."

"Not for the moment. Ululenia, how big can you get? Could you do a bear or something?"

"*Besyn larveth'is?*" Ghylspwr asked, jerking in Desidora's hand toward the ceiling.

"I'm *almost* sure that would be a bad idea," Kail said. "Uh, Tern, do you need help? What does Icy do?"

"The safe isn't usually *closing* on him, and he's usually not off trying to redeem Loch's sister."

"My sister? He's off with Naria?" Loch had to duck her head, even down on her knees.

"He's got a soft spot for damsels in distress."

Loch opened her mouth to respond, and at that moment, the vault door opened.

"Trouble?" Silestin Senior asked, and then shuffled aside as everyone scrambled out.

"Your grandson did something to the transport rune," Loch muttered. Behind her, the vault ceiling clanked into the ground. "The gods only know what."

"Actually," Hessler began, "while trying to map the magical patterns, I believe that I have calculated—"

"Am I going to like it?"

Hessler squinted, opened his mouth, and then closed it. "No."

"Any reason you can't tell me later?"

Hessler sighed. "No."

"Then off we go." Loch turned to the group. "Nothing fancy. Ululenia, you and Hessler are with the kid. Priestess, take Kail and Tern. I don't care how, and I don't care how much noise you make. Just get yourselves out safely. We meet in the alley by Cevirt's palace."

"What about you?" Kail asked.

"I'll be along," Loch said grimly, and shoved the velvet into Dairy's hands. "Just keep running when the alarms go off. Silestin, thank you for the assistance."

The zombie grinned. "Pleasure to watch you work, Captain."

She nodded, gave them all one last look, and then rolled out her shoulders and started running.

It was evening in the Republic. Heaven's Spire had left Ros-Oanki and was making its way through the night sky toward the next city.

This turned out to be fortunate.

An hour before midnight, Warden Tawyer, who was hosting a small Victory Ball of his own, received an emergency message from a runner reporting unusual activity from the *lapiscaela.*

The warden was almost to the Cleaners before the wave of energy ripped through the city and knocked him clean off his feet.

Nobody at the Cleaners saw what happened firsthand. The prisoners were in their cells for the evening, and of the guards who patrolled the grid during the evening, no trace was ever found.

But everyone who could make it to the Rim could look over the edge and see the great crater burned into the ground below.

Archvoyant Silestin was on his feet moments after the shockwave knocked everyone to the ground. Unlike most of the people in the room, he had absolutely no doubt what had just happened. "We hit a mountain or something?" he called to the chief lapitect with a laugh. The lapitect, pale and already fiddling with his damned crystals, gave a weak chuckle, and Silestin turned to the nobles he'd been talking to. "Excuse me, gentlemen. I expect I've got a few meetings to get to."

Elkinsair was by his side moments later. "Sir, it appears—"

"Noted. How are we coming on that break-in I was just warned about, Security Chief?" Silestin put a little acid on Elkinsair's title.

"I'll have a status report for you in one hour," Elkinsair said without hesitation. "But based on my current information, it must be your personal vault."

Silestin nodded, thinking hard. The most pressing question was how much truth to mix in with the story. "The ball is over. Security precautions in light of the night's events. Get people out, then release the hounds. Full aggression."

"It will take time for everyone to get outside," Elkinsair pointed out.

"Then the criminals who just attacked may claim a few more victims," Silestin said calmly. "Get me Bi'ul and then get to work." Elkinsair left without another word.

Silestin straightened his formal jacket and adjusted his sword. The public story would be a maintenance error. The chief lapitect could come up with someone to throw on the pyre. Behind closed doors, the solemn declaration could be more pointed, but he'd have to be careful....

Captain Pyvic of the justicars was beside him suddenly. The man had a bruise coming up nicely along his jaw. "Archvoyant," he said grimly, "I believe you're being robbed."

"I'm aware of that, Captain," Silestin said without heat. Still, it did him good to see the young man adjusting to his new role. "What can you tell me, other than that you got yourself knocked cold by one of them?"

"It's Isafesira de Lochenville," Pyvic said. "I found her in your quarters and tried to stop her."

"Looks like it worked out well for you, Pyvic." Silestin smiled sourly. "Now, if you'll excuse me, this party just ended. The malfunction with the *lapiscaela* requires my attention."

Pyvic snorted. "That was no malfunction, Archvoyant. And if I'm the captain of the justicars—"

"Then you'll tell the story I want you to tell," Silestin said sharply. "If we go around saying that an Imperial saboteur tried to destroy the Spire and blew a three-acre hole in the ground below instead, we'll have panic in the streets." Pyvic paled as Silestin went on. "You served in the military, Pyvic. You don't order your army to charge until everybody's standing up with their boots laced and a weapon in hand. Your job is to keep the peace. My job is to make that peace possible. Now, if you'll excuse me…"

Not as refined as he'd have preferred, but it would do.

Captain Pyvic bowed and stepped aside. Silestin exchanged grim nods with a few Voyants as he left the ballroom, and met Ambassador Bi'ul at the entrance to his personal quarters.

"Someone activated your weapon prematurely," the Glimmering Man said without preamble as he fell into step beside Silestin.

"Looks that way," Silestin agreed pleasantly. "Elkinsair thinks they used the vault."

"I did note that a misfire was likely for anyone attempting to utilize the escape rune."

"If you would accompany me, I'd like to make certain that they're gone."

"Not at all, Archvoyant." Bi'ul smiled, a glittering rainbow across his lips. "I never tire of making myself useful to you."

They walked through Silestin's personal quarters. A few of Silestin's personal attendants lay unmoving, but he ignored them for now.

Finally, they reached the vault. The door was open, and as Bi'ul had told him would be the case, the ceiling had collapsed in order to merge the crystal matrixes required to power the weapon. Standing by the vault was a long-dead figure that Silestin recognized after a moment as a relative.

"Used you to beat the security systems, did they?" Silestin asked dryly.

The zombie grinned gruesomely. "My grandson doesn't miss a trick."

"What were they in here for?"

"The Urujar woman has a code of honor." The zombie snorted. "All she wanted was something you stole from her father."

Archvoyant Silestin threw back his head and laughed long and loud.

When he was done, he gestured at the zombie with one signet-ringed fist. "Goodbye, grandfather." A blast of lightning slammed into the zombie, driving it to the ground sizzling. Silestin let the electricity play over his ancestor until only a charred husk remained, and then he turned to Bi'ul.

"The elven manuscript?" Bi'ul asked politely.

Silestin's smile was wolfish. "At last."

Twenty-Three

"So what do we do now, Ululenia?" Dairy asked as they tromped through the hallways. Ululenia was in her human form, but she was letting her horn show and making guards and servants fall asleep.

"Now, my virgin," she said with a sly smile, and Dairy felt the tingly feeling again, more like he'd felt while Loch had torn her dress apart than the way he'd felt when the Glimmering Man had looked at him, "we shall leave this palace and then spend the night sharing a room in the most expensive inn in the city."

"Ululenia," Mister Hessler said firmly, "you are *not* corrupting the boy."

"Is the room expensive enough to have *two* beds?" Dairy asked, and Ululenia laughed and stroked his cheek, and then she stopped, and her eyes went cold, and she and Mister Hessler spun around.

A thin little man in a long robe was standing before them. "*Well*," he tittered, "not only am I to guard the safety of my master's palace, but now I must guard the honor of this helpless young man."

"Elkinsair." Ululenia narrowed her eyes and stepped between Dairy and the little man.

"Ululenia," said the little man, and his smile was small and cruel.

"You know each other?" Mister Hessler asked.

"Passing acquaintance," Elkinsair said, and then rolled his eyes. "Oh, dear. Ample assets, buxom barmaid, comely courtesan, am I getting it right? If it's alliteration that excites you, how about *unoriginal, unctuous, undefended unicorn?*" And he pursed his lips and squinted.

Beside him, Ululenia gasped and began to tremble, one hand going to her forehead. Dairy reached out to steady her, and she pushed him away. "Back, *back!*"

"Oh, that's right," said the little man. "Lust would hit you rather hard with one of your virgins nearby, wouldn't it?"

Ululenia was sweating, and her horn flared with ugly red light. "Get out... of my.. mind!" White light flashed around her as she changed into a great white bear, her claws as long as Dairy's fingers.

"Isn't that *just like* a unicorn?" Elkinsair rolled up his sleeves. "Bringing a bear to a *magic* duel." He flung open his robes.

And then Dairy understood, for he had a magical shining horn, just like Ululenia's. Only not on his head.

Also, he had goat's legs.

"Come on, boy!" Mister Hessler shouted, and grabbed Dairy by the hand. "We need to get you out of here!"

"I won't leave Ululenia!" Dairy shouted.

"No release for you since Woodsedge?" asked Elkinsair the satyr as his horn, which Dairy was trying very hard not to look at, flared with light, and Ululenia dropped into a crouch with a growl of pain. "And this supple young virgin is right here, tantalizing your frustrated desires. I can feel you slipping away even now. Deep down you want to give in and lose yourself, don't you?"

Ululenia shifted back into human form, her horn now mostly red. "*Run,* my virgin," she hissed, turning away from him. Her skin was flushed.

Everyone kept telling Dairy to run.

"No, Ululenia," he said clearly. "I'm not going to run. I... I believe in you."

Elkinsair spared Dairy a glance. "Well, isn't that just adorable apple, babbling brook, creeping cat, *son of a bitch!*" He stumbled backward, and Ululenia's horn flared again, and Elkinsair flew across the room and hit the wall.

Hessler grabbed Dairy by the arm. "Now, while he's distracted!" he cried. "Ululenia can catch up!" He ran down the hallway with Dairy in tow, then turned and flung out his hand, filling the hallway behind them with a wall of pure darkness. When it was in place, he pulled Dairy through a side door. "That should make it harder to find us," Mister Hessler gasped.

"What about Ululenia?" Dairy asked, easily keeping pace with Mister Hessler.

"I don't think she could lose your mind if she tried." Mister Hessler smiled.

"I'm worried about her," Dairy admitted.

Mister Hessler pulled him into a hallway. "That's very noble of you, Dairy, but... well, trust me, she's better off without you there."

"Oh."

"We need to get you out of here, Dairy," Hessler said quietly. "Nothing else matters. Not the book, not Loch, not Ululenia. All that matters is keeping you..."

They came around a corner into a large room. There were a lot of guards in the room, and just like the guards up on the airship, their faces were twisted into snarls of hatred, and their eyes were wrong.

"...safe."

Loch came out of Silestin's personal quarters to find the dining hall emptied of guests, except for a couple of people who had already been killed by the dozen or so soul-drained guards who now occupied the room.

The guards turned to her, their eyes cold and empty and their bestial snarls in place. Two of them stopped stabbing the already-dead guests who hadn't left quickly enough and raised their blades along with the rest.

"I know that Silestin did something to you," Loch said slowly, walking into the hall. "I know he's got you under his control."

The blades followed her movement, and the guards slowly began to circle. Some of them were panting.

"If there's any of you left in there," Loch said, "fight it."

She was in the middle of the dining hall now. They almost had her surrounded. She forced herself not to tense up.

"I will find some way to bring you back. I swear it. But I need your help. Show me that you're in there."

The guards moved in.

Loch lunged, caught a descending arm, smashed her elbow into the attacker's face, wrenched the sword free with an off-hand slash that eviscerated another guard, ducked under a slice that mistakenly killed the guard she'd just disarmed, and brought her blade up in a great two-handed arc that killed another even as she kicked another one in the chest to knock him down.

She parried an overhand strike, ran the man through, and then used *his* sword to gut another one while her free hand collapsed the windpipe of a third.

After that, things got a little messy.

When it was done, she dropped the two bloody blades she'd ended up with and looked at the fallen men.

"Sorry," she said.

Then she turned and started running again.

None of it would have happened if they hadn't found out about him selling the magical artifacts on the side, Hessler mused.

He'd been careful, but not careful enough, unless it was part of the prophecy that had caused him to get caught, and kicked out, and thrown into that cell so that Loch would find Dairy and bring him up to Heaven's Spire.

Hessler didn't know. A few weeks ago, he wouldn't have shared a drink with anyone foolish enough to believe in prophecies, which were obviously propaganda promulgated by religious figures in order to reinforce the predominant morality of the time at the expense of the undereducated working class.

Now he stared at the guards, and then at Dairy, and then at his own slender hands.

"Dairy," he said quietly as the guards drew their weapons, "I need you to trust me."

"I'll do anything you ask, Mister Hessler." The kid stepped between him and the guards, who growled wordlessly and raised their weapons.

"I need you to run back to Ululenia," Hessler said, and his voice caught a little. "I'm going to leave an illusion of myself here for them to fight, but I'll be with you, invisible and silent. Do you trust me?" Dairy nodded, and Hessler shut his eyes for one selfish moment. "Then go. I'll be right beside you. I'll always be with you, Dairy. Remember that."

The kid ran, and as the soulless guards moved to chase him, Hessler threw up an illusionary wall of fire that blocked the doorway behind him. "He's gone," Hessler said with quiet pride. "All you get is me."

He didn't go easily. As they moved in on him, Hessler plunged all of them into darkness, then tried to creep to a corner, ducking below their blind slashes. One of them bowled him over by blind luck, though, and the distraction killed his illusions.

A frantic blast of light blinded the guard who'd knocked him over, and he formed a shadow-Hessler across the room that drew the attention of a few of them, but two more were coming his way, and even after he made himself invisible and rolled to the side, they were following, kicking at the area where he had lain.

A boot caught him in the ribs, and his cloak fell away as the stabbing, crushing pain made it impossible to breathe. He blinded the other two with another flash of light and pulled himself back to his feet, but every breath was pain lancing through his lungs, and he couldn't concentrate.

He is safe, Magister, came Ululenia's voice in his mind, and her grief made it clear that she understood. *You will not be forgotten.* And Hessler knew that it would not be painless, and he feared that it would not be swift, but in that moment, it was enough.

He made it three more steps before a blow drove him to his knees, and then he was being held up by two of them, their swords ready, and as Hessler looked up through the thudding pain, he saw Justicar Pyvic walk into the room, sword raised and face contorted with grim fury.

It wasn't the same mindless snarl that the guards had, and Hessler's heart hammered with desperate hope.

"You don't understand," Hessler gasped. "Bi'ul is...."

Pyvic struck without hesitation, and the crushing blackness that shattered Hessler's vision was the last thing he felt.

The gardens were dark, lit only by the moon. Behind Icy, the palace windows gleamed with a crisp blue-white glow.

The western gardens were overgrown, the hedges untrimmed and the wildflowers watered but unchecked, creating a lush and verdant forest that mixed several different climates for a singularly beautiful effect.

Icy picked his way along a gentle path, looking up at the dim silhouette of the trees above.

"I'm always frightened to come out here at night," Naria admitted, her voice a whisper. "Will we be here long?"

"My friends should arrive shortly," Icy assured her. "We shall be gone soon enough."

The path led into a small clearing lit gray by the moon. The wind rustled the leaves, sending little crackles through the foliage.

"And then will we..." Naria paused. "Will we have to stay outside? I... I *can*, I'm not afraid to, but—"

"No," Icy said, chuckling. "There is a kahva-house with a small inn upstairs. I imagine we will stay there. For the moment, however, we are simply heading to an alley near Voyant Cevirt's palace."

She smiled, then stiffened in sudden alarm. "Indomitable!"

He turned, putting himself between her and the danger, peering into the darkness of the trees.

Something leaped at them from the other side.

Icy spun as Naria hit the ground with a cry, saw the figure standing over her, and moved forward, hands raised in combat positions he had practiced for years but hoped never to have to use against a living being. But for Naria—

"If you want to court my sister, Icy, there are three things you have to know," said Loch, standing over Naria's fallen form. "The first is that she'd *never* date a peasant Imperial unless she had an ulterior motive."

Icy opened his mouth to respond indignantly, and then stopped when he saw the dagger in Naria's hand.

"Too late, Isa. He already told me where your little gang is meeting." Naria swept Loch's legs out from under her with a smooth kick and rolled to her feet in the same motion. Then she lunged, the blade moving in a smooth arc toward Loch's throat.

Loch caught Naria's wrist, lunged back to her feet, and body-checked Naria into a tree.

"The second," Loch said, "is that with all the money and power she has at her command, she'd never settle for crystal lenses to cover her ruined eyes... unless they're magical lenses. My money'd be on mental illusions to compensate for the blindness."

"They do more than that," Naria hissed, and vanished from view.

"She is not simply invisible," Icy said quietly. "Her movements are not disturbing the grass or creating any noise."

"And the third," Loch said, "is that she was too delicate to handle a real fight. The only time she ever beat me in anything is when she cheated. Which makes her..." She broke off, spun, and threw a hard, nasty punch directly behind her.

As Naria shimmered into visibility directly behind Loch, her knife raised to slit her sister's throat, the punch caught her square in the face. She went down bonelessly and didn't move.

"...easy to predict."

Icy dropped to his knees, the breath sucked out of his stomach. "She was..."

"The Archvoyant's First Blade. Last one anyone would ever suspect. Add in whatever shadow-magic Silestin picked up for her, and she's a damn fine assassin." Loch's face relaxed. "And she was always good at twisting men around her finger." She shook her head, then picked up Naria's slim knife.

"I told her where we were meeting." Icy hated himself for saying the words, but would have hated himself more for not saying them.

"I know." Loch reached down with the knife, and Icy shut his eyes.

He heard fiber snap and opened his eyes to see Loch pulling the lenses away from Naria's face. The cord that bound them to Naria's head was neatly cut, and Naria's knife lay discarded in the grass.

"We'll be long gone by the time she wakes up," Loch said. "And I don't think she'll be pulling any more assassin-y surprises." She rose to her feet, dropped the crystal lenses to the ground, and stomped hard. Icy winced as magical crystal crunched in the darkness. "Come on."

Icy followed Loch out of the clearing, though he did turn once to look back.

Ambassador Bi'ul followed Archvoyant Silestin into a small sitting room. The Archvoyant gestured, and Bi'ul sat.

"The problem, Ambassador, is that I know what you want," Silestin said without preamble.

Bi'ul nodded, unoffended. "The ward set by the ancients was quite specific."

"You need souls." Silestin smiled. "And much as I appreciate your assistance, I have no intention of offering mine."

"So we find ourselves at this impasse." Bi'ul smiled, toying with a goblet of wine.

"Pretend for a minute, though, that there was no impasse." Silestin sat down and filled his pipe. "Pretend I've got some souls—not voluntarily given, but mine nonetheless. Convince me that allowing your kind into the world doesn't lead to the destruction of everything I hold dear."

Bi'ul blinked. "You value nothing save your own power." Silestin waved at him irritably. "Ah. You fear that if the Glimmering Folk return, you would lose power. Charming." Bi'ul smiled. "What *you* fail to consider is that as mortals find fragments of the ancients' power, someone, somewhere, *will* allow us into the world. It is only a question of when and where."

"Not good enough." Silestin puffed on his pipe.

"The world as you know it will end, one way or the other," Bi'ul noted. "Would you prefer to be the capital of the new and glorious empire of the Glimmering Folk, with the world bowing to what was once your Republic and you living in luxury as a regional governor? Or would you prefer that your Republic be one of the conquered nations ground into dust, your last thoughts before your soul is forcibly extracted that you *could* have had the power, but were too worried about the risks?" He smiled, rainbows shimmering across his face. "But this is merely an academic question, as you have no souls to offer me."

Silestin withdrew a slim emerald crystal wand from his vest. "The prisoners who work on the underside of the Spire? They clean the floating stones and keep everything running."

"Wasteful." Bi'ul shrugged. "Before the ancients fled this world, maintenance was performed by golems."

"The prisoners say that it's unlucky to talk near the stones." Silestin spun the crystal wand between his fingers. "They say that your voice gets caught in the stone, that the stones can steal your soul."

"An entertaining story, Archvoyant."

Silestin grinned. "I believe you about the golems. I'm certain that the ancients never intended for anyone living to be near the stones for long. They would *certainly* never have intended the voices of the workers to imprint in the crystals in such a way as to allow soul-binding." He touched his ring to the crystal wand, and its emerald glow flushed to a dull and angry red. "Luckily for you, Bi'ul, the old men weren't infallible."

Bi'ul stared at the crystal for a long moment, his mind tracing the energy pattern.

He smiled. "Luckily for me indeed, Archvoyant."

"Kutesosh gajair'is!"

"That the last of them?" Kail asked, panting, as Desidora's swing sent one of the snarling guards crashing into the far wall of the small dining room where they'd been ambushed.

"No more on my end," the death priestess said coolly.

"I'm good," Tern chimed in. She'd gotten a couple of the guards with an alchemical bolt that splashed a quick-drying glue everywhere. "So, Diz, what *are* these guys?"

"I don't know." Desidora looked at them without expression. "Their auras are polluted somehow. I don't know what Silestin did to them, but it isn't natural."

"And that's *you* saying that," Tern noted, and then coughed when Desidora stared at her. "Well, it is. Is it reversible? Maybe rather than fighting our way out, we could cure them."

"Unlikely," Desidora said, dismissing it with a wave, "and dangerous. It would require too much investiture of power to even be possible." She looped Ghylspwr back into her belt and started walking.

"Wait," said Tern, leaning against a table that Kail had knocked over before leaping up onto the chandelier and bringing it down on a bunch of the guards. "That's it? It's too *hard* for you, so we just leave these people?"

"Tern," Kail said quietly, "let it go."

"Why? It's cold, Kail. The whole reason Loch put this job together was to hurt Silestin. If he's got people enslaved, freeing them has got to hurt him as much as stealing a *book*."

Kail was still looking at Desidora as she peered around the corner for more guards. "She shouldn't use that death priestess power unless she really needs to. It's not...." He grimaced. "She just shouldn't have to, is all."

"She doesn't *need* to? It's too much *investiture?*" Tern raised an eyebrow. "How is it that as somebody who took a while to get on the zombie-loving bandwagon, *I'm* the one pushing for her to try something? Either she's with us, or she's not."

"Tern...."

"No! If I could pick a lock to get us outside right now, I wouldn't be complaining that it was *too hard.*"

"It's dangerous. When we were in the—"

"I'll try," Desidora said from the doorway. "You're right, Tern. It's worth making an effort." She moved to stand over an unconscious guard. "You should both stand back and avoid making any sudden movements. With the complexity of the aural tampering, I will have to...." She looked at Kail, then at Tern.

"You're going to get really pale, and any nearby artwork is going to get spiky?" Tern guessed.

Desidora smiled. "Most likely."

Kail stepped forward. "You were right before. This isn't the time to try. We've got more pressing—"

"Too late," Desidora hissed, and her smile was a scarlet scratch across her alabaster face. "Did you *think* I would not see?" She flung out a hand, and shadowy coils sprang from her fingers and wrapped around Kail's throat. "No unicorn to hold me back this time."

Kail fell to his knees, eyes bulging in their sockets. Desidora's eyes were jet black, and her hair twisted and writhed in a wind that touched no one else in the room.

Then Tern's sleep-dart caught her in the shoulder, and she had time to shout, "Pitiful *fool!*" in a truly baleful voice before keeling over.

"See, we tried, and it didn't work," Tern said briskly, hoping Kail was going to get up on his own and not make her go over and help him up, because that was about the only thing that would make her feel worse. "The important thing is that we tried, and now we can move on with a clear conscience."

"*Kutesosh gajair'is!*" Ghylspwr called from Desidora's waist.

"I know. We're going to help her, Ghyl."

Kail got to his feet shakily. His back was to Tern—he was still looking at Desidora—but she could see him sucking in great lungfuls of air, and she gave him a moment.

Finally, he said, "No, we aren't."

Tern sighed. "Look, I'm sorry. You were right, okay? Both of you. I don't know what happened, but—"

"*Kutesosh gajair'is!*"

"I *know!*" Tern snapped, striding past Kail to kneel beside Desidora's fallen form. "We'll help her. There's no need to use the… phrase you use… for evil…."

She spun, but the crossbow was knocked from her hands before she could bring it to bear.

"Change in plans," Kail said, smiling, but his eyes were dead like those of the guards as he caught her arm and stepped in. "The three of you will be staying."

Tern didn't have time to scream.

Twenty-Four

IT HAD ALL SEEMED WONDERFUL, STEALING BACK WHAT THE EVIL Archvoyant had stolen. It had seemed like justice, except more exciting.

But now, as Dairy stood in the shadows of Voyant Cevirt's palace, it didn't feel that way.

Miss Loch looked angry and sad. Icy stared at the ground, and Ululenia kept wiping at her eyes, although she smiled and told Dairy that she was fine.

"But Mister Hessler said he would be with us!" Dairy insisted. "He said!"

"Magister Hessler was very brave," Loch said quietly.

"Courageous as the mother bird luring the hunter from her children," Ululenia added, and wiped at her eyes again. Her horn lit her pale face in the darkness.

"He said he was going to escape," Dairy said. "I wouldn't have left, but he said he could escape."

"Maybe he did." Loch looked over at the walls.

"Loch," Ululenia said quietly, "I was in his mind."

"Maybe he escaped," Loch said firmly, looking at her squarely, and Ululenia nodded, looked at Dairy, and tried to smile again.

"What about Kail and Miss Tern and Sister Desidora?" Dairy asked.

"It's Mister Kail," said a voice from the shadows, and everyone jumped as Kail stepped out. "And I'm alone. Captain, they got Tern and Diz."

"No!" The cry escaped from Icy with a force that surprised them all. "Loch, we cannot—"

"Patience, Indomitable." Loch turned to Kail. "Captured?"

Kail nodded. Now that he was with them, the energy that had gotten him here seemed to drain away, and he sagged where he stood. His hands were shaking as he explained what had happened, and Loch seemed more worried by that than by what Kail was saying, the way she looked at his shaking hands and twitching fingers.

The guards had come upon them. Tern had been knocked out, and Desidora had drawn the guards to her. "The security guy used something to knock her out," he finished, "and I ran. No way to save them."

"Of course there is. You did just what you were supposed to do, Kail." She leaned in and took his trembling hands. "You did just right."

"What happens now, Miss Loch?" Dairy asked. "Mister Hessler, and Miss Tern, and... what happens now?"

"You remember I told you about the difference between *should* and *is?*" she asked, and Dairy nodded. "We *should* get a whole heaping lot of money for what we did tonight. But we *are* going to trade this book..." She held it up. "...for a tiny little bit of money and the freedom of our friends. The elf you contacted, Ululenia. He can get them out?"

Ululenia nodded. "Of course, Little One. If anyone can do it, the elves can. The wards of the ancients are like their own hearts' blood, and for one of their manuscripts—"

"Good." She turned to Kail. "Ululenia already contacted the elf. The deal is set for tomorrow before dawn, in the same park we arrived in. Go spend the night as you will, everyone. Have a few drinks at any tavern that's still open, or just get some sleep." She stared hard at Ululenia. "*Just* sleep."

Ululenia turned away. "I have no heart for celebration this night, Little One."

"We will soon enough." Loch waved grandly. "Go. I'll see you all at the park an hour before dawn." She touched Kail on the shoulder. "We'll save them all."

And with that, she walked off into the night.

Archvoyant Silestin looked at the two women strapped to Security Chief Elkinsair's devices.

"That's them." The Archvoyant grinned. "Funny how things change, *Priestess.*"

They were both strapped to moveable tables shaped like Xs, their arms and legs bound wide apart. Thick leather straps made movement impossible, and bands across their throats made even breathing difficult.

"You are trafficking with a creature the gods have sent me *personally* to destroy, Silestin." Desidora met his gaze squarely. "If you care about the fate of all creation, much less your mortal soul—"

"You said she felt like one of Ael-meseth's," Silestin said to Elkinsair.

"A death priestess," Elkinsair explained. "Formerly a love priestess. Her latent ability to affect auras has been greatly enhanced." He frowned. "That's likely how they breached the vault."

"Makes sense." Silestin smiled up at Tern, who was stripped to her shift. "Do whatever you want to the tinker."

"Son of a bitch!"

"Make certain the priestess lives at least until I return. I might need another playing card." He clapped Elkinsair on the shoulder and left.

Elkinsair waited until Silestin was gone, and then he did a little capering dance, shrugging out of his robe so that his horn shone. Tern's knowledge of satyrs was heavily influenced by *jokes* about satyrs, and a quick application of what she knew to be the fact that his horn was located, as Icy would have said, about five chakras down from Ululenia's, gave her a couple of guesses.

"Ah, *finally*," Elkinsair murmured as he removed a crude silver amulet. His horn blazed even brighter. "Had to wear this old thing to mask my aura from that dreadful Mirrkir. He has some dreadfully backward ideas about my people. But since you've killed him, I'm free to…" He looked over at Tern and raised an eyebrow. "…be myself."

Tern began to struggle.

"Don't bother, little mouse." Elkinsair fixed her with a ruddy grin. "As deaths go, heart failure from sheer pleasure is enviable. You'd thank me before it was over. *But…*" He turned to Desidora. "…the mouse will live… at least, as far as I am concerned."

Tern tried to relax. "See, that *sounds* reassuring, until that clause on the end."

"I must be honest, Priestess," Elkinsair said with a self-deprecating laugh. "This is something of a dream come true for me."

"You have some messed-up dreams," Desidora said without inflection.

"I've heard of death priestesses, but to actually *meet* one...." Elkinsair smiled. "Don't be coy, Priestess. Try your full power on me. Wrench my soul from my body."

"I traveled with a unicorn," Desidora said coldly. "We both know that my magic won't affect you."

"So why do I taunt you?" Elkinsair asked with a tittering laugh. "It's quite simple, Priestess... and it's to your advantage." He slid his gaze to Tern. "Though not hers."

"See, again, reassuring *right up until the end.*"

"If you know what I am," Desidora said evenly, "then you know that it goes against the will of the gods to stand against me."

Elkinsair laughed again. This time, the delicate little titter grew into a wrenching, inhuman cackle that had Elkinsair's eyes watering while he pounded on the walls.

"Satyrs don't care about the will of the gods?" Desidora asked as his cackles finally died down.

Elkinsair fixed her with a glassy-eyed stare. "Oh, my poor dear, I care deeply for the will of the gods. Even if I didn't, I'd be a fool to stand in their way." He shook his head wistfully. "No, precious priestess, my amusement comes from you... that you think the gods have destined you to succeed."

"They granted me these powers." Desidora kept her gaze level. "They came to me in my dreams and told me their will."

"And when you were a *love priestess* and you wished to bring two young lovers together, I'm *certain* that you told your charges the truth about what they should do." He let out a fond sigh as Desidora flushed. "My dear, you are a bolt fired from a divine crossbow. You might *think* you were aimed at the enemy's heart, but it's far more likely that you were fired as a diversion so that their *real* blow can strike true." He sneered. "A *love priestess?* Against one of the *Glimmering Folk?* Really."

"She's cut through every security ward *you* put in place," Tern fired back.

Elkinsair nodded. "Yes. This death magic of hers... it's fascinating. Which is why I'm willing to go against Silestin himself... to let you walk free, Priestess."

Desidora's eyes narrowed. "I'm listening."

"The lock binding your right arm is magical, warded by layers of abjuration." Elkinsair leaned in. "If you use your clever aura-magic on it, it will render you unconscious and alert me to your attempts." He smiled, running one finger along her bonds. "But there's a weakness. The lock is set to automatically release five minutes after the prisoner dies, to simplify removal of the body."

"You've out-thought yourself." Desidora shut her eyes. "My magic won't let me transcend death. Not in that way, at least."

"Don't worry." Elkinsair tugged the strap across Desidora's chest a little tighter, then leaned in to whisper. "It's keyed to the tinker's table." He glanced at Tern, then broke into a broad grin as her face went pale. "Ah, she understands. Clever tinker."

"I'll kill you," Desidora said, heaving up, her face going red with exertion. "I'll get loose, and I will *end* you, satyr!"

"It is a question," Elkinsair said quietly, "of faith. If you believe so firmly in your cause, then sacrificing a friend should be worth it. You can walk out of this room, free to continue your quest, and I will have a clear recording of your magic to use in *my* studies. If you do not...." He shrugged.

"Fail to escape, and I shall gain my data about your death-magic through *significantly* less pleasant means."

"Don't waste your time," Tern said confidently. "I'm seventy or eighty percent sure that she wouldn't even *consider* falling for such an obvious ploy!"

"I'll leave you two ladies alone." Elkinsair smiled absently. "I must go attend to Prisoner Ghylspwr, now. I have some *very* exciting experiments in mind for him as well."

He walked out, and the clanging of the interrogation-room door was the only sound he heard behind him.

Everyone who'd made it was there in the gray pre-dawn light.

Loch had ditched the sleek evening gown and come up with tan leathers that were suitable for riding, hiking, fighting, or running as the case demanded. Kail looked tired and forewent his usual quips. Ululenia and Dairy both looked nervous. Icy appeared calm as always, and his robe was clean and pressed.

The steel-gray sky was cold and clear as Loch led them back through the side streets to the little park one last time. The soft clump of her boots on the false cobblestones that lined the city no longer sounded strange in her ears.

She sent Kail out ahead when they reached the last few streets, and he came back a few minutes later to report that the elven ship had arrived. Loch nodded, waved briefly, said a quiet prayer for the captured and the dead, and motioned them forward.

The sound of clopping hooves surprised her, and she turned to see that Ululenia had assumed her natural form, and Dairy was astride her. *It may prove to the elf that our intentions are pure,* she said.

Once through the line of trees, there was nothing beyond but the lawn and then the rim itself, and the city was just a skyline behind them, dark shapes fading into the cold morning mist. The wet grass squelched as Loch and the others tromped through the garden.

At the edge of the rim, a new tree had grown overnight.

As Loch drew closer, the great leaves resolved into dozens of rich green sails that shone even in the wan light, and the trunk became a great twisted mast, and the massive bunching roots became the body of the living ship itself, which had pierced the wards of Heaven's Spire and now rested a great root over the garden's safety rail as an organic gangplank.

At the foot of the gangplank, standing in the mist in a posture of perfect serenity, a tall cloaked figure waited. The others fell in behind Loch as they drew close, so that she was the point of the wedge approaching the elf. His cloak shimmered, blue and green and gray flickering across its surface like a waterfall on a cloudless day. His arms were crossed, the hands tucked into the opposite sleeve like a monk's posture in walking prayer.

"Isti ciel'ur, ufa eurufuir'isti," Loch said with a polite bow. The elf nodded, his features still a mystery beneath the cloak. Loch had heard stories, but even her father had never met one of the sylvan folk in person.

Since she didn't speak any more of the ancient language, she switched to Darish. "By the sun and stars, this book was given freely to the blood of my blood. I offer freely to return it to its creators." She'd gone over this with Ululenia back at Cevirt's, combining the unicorn's knowledge with what Loch remembered her father telling her.

The elf was still a long moment. Then one hand swung free of the other and waved her forward. Loch stepped forward slowly, withdrew the book from the leather bag she carried it in, and handed it to the elf. He held it up to his cloaked face with slow reverence.

Then he said, "Never could read this gibberish," and struck Loch with a savage backhand.

An uppercut slammed into her gut before she got her balance back, and then a right cross slammed her to the ground. There were shouts behind her, and the sound of drawn steel.

"I have to tell you," said Archvoyant Silestin, shrugging out of the shimmering cloak and tossing it and the book to the ground, "that I am awfully impressed, young lady." He was dressed in his formal military uniform, his jacket set with medals and his dress sword at his waist.

"Screw you," Loch muttered, coughing. Guards had appeared from the trees and stood in a loose semicircle around her team, crossbows raised. They were cloaked as well, but there was no mistaking the identical postures of the soulless creatures.

Dairy was holding very still, tears of frustration filling his eyes. Ululenia had a light scratch across her throat and a blade still pressed there to discourage tricks.

The man Loch had trained, the man she'd trusted with her life dozens of times, was holding the knife.

"Kail?" Loch coughed again, then saw the look in his eyes, the soulless snarl. She turned back to Silestin. "You bastard."

Silestin chuckled. "You remember all those stories about the *lapiscaela*, what they do to the prisoners? Turns out there's a grain of truth in there." He smiled at Kail. "And a man with time and resources can make use of that truth."

"You've got to be running low," Loch said, forcing herself back to her feet. "The ones you lost on the airship, the ones we cut down during the job...."

Silestin glanced at the men with the crossbows, then shrugged. "I can always get more. A transfer here, a disappearance there... nobody ever misses a prisoner."

"You're tampering with their *souls*," Loch said slowly. "What if the Voyancy found out about this?"

Silestin laughed. "The Voyancy? I *own* the Voyancy, thanks to you. You came along at *just* the right time. A little scare with the Imperials," he said in a singsong voice, gesturing at Icy, who returned his stare evenly, "a tragic betrayal that *proves* that Urujar like your Voyant Cevirt just can't be trusted, and suddenly I've got an eight-to-four majority and can pass any legislation I want. None of the seven other Learned would *dare* oppose me, and the Skilled don't have the nerve to spar with live steel." He snorted.

"I wonder if they'll feel that way when they see *this*," Loch said, and held up the ring she'd stripped from his hand when she handed him the book. It was gold, set with one large ruby. "Kiss your soul-stealing magic goodbye," she said, and wrenched the ruby from the socket.

There was a moment of silence through the clearing. The ruby fell to the ground, twinkling wanly in the pre-dawn light.

"Kail," Silestin said pleasantly, "take her down."

The blow caught her between the shoulder blades before she could turn.

In the control room where Kail, Ululenia, and Desidora had not long ago disabled the personal-aura ward, Ghylspwr hung suspended in a curtain of shimmering light. Elkinsair watched him closely, pressing glowing crystals on the console and frowning from time to time.

"*Kutesosh gajair'is!*"

"May I tell you a story?" The satyr pressed another crystal, and the light around Ghylspwr changed color subtly. "If you are indeed one of the ancient kings, you may even know it yourself."

"*Kutesosh gajair'is!*" Ghylspwr declared again, shivering in the magical field.

"Once upon a time," Elkinsair said, "the ancients were fighting the Glimmering Folk. The ancients were losing, and they realized that as long as they existed in the world, their enemies could enter the world as well. But if the ancients left, they could place a barrier between this world and the world of the Glimmering Folk. The ancients would be gone, but this world, and all the worlds it touches, would be safe."

Ghylspwr stopped shivering. "*Besyn larveth'is,*" he said, in a far different voice.

"I am certain you do," Elkinsair agreed. "As the story goes, a few heroes held the line while the rest of the ancients erected the barrier. And as the story goes, the greatest of these heroes was the prince of the ancients." Elkinsair smiled wistfully. "He wielded a magical hammer that carried the soul of his dead father, who had been the wisest king the ancients had ever known."

Ghylspwr was silent.

"They fought for a very long time against the Glimmering Folk and their minions," Elkinsair continued. "There were only a dozen ancient warriors left, and then there were only six, and then there was only the prince, fighting with his great hammer. *As the story goes*, the hammer was called *Galarros'pir*, which meant 'speaks like a great fire,' in honor of the eloquence of the great king."

"*Besyn larveth'is*," Ghylspwr said quietly.

"Then the prince suffered a grievous blow," Elkinsair said, "and a *curious* thing happened. A light flashed from the hammer, and the prince's wound was healed. And then it happened again, and the light flashed again, and *again* the prince was healed. As the ancients erecting the barrier listened, they noticed something." Elkinsair smiled. "Each time the prince's wounds healed, the hammer became... how to put this delicately? *Less.*"

"*Kun-kabynalti osu fuir'is.*"

Elkinsair chuckled. "How very true. The great and eloquent speech began to falter, the words growing simpler each time the prince was healed, until finally the ancients erected their barrier, and—*as the story goes*—the prince, struck with one last mortal wound, flung the hammer away, crying 'Father, it is enough. Let me go.' And he died just as the barrier sprang to life and drove the Glimmering Folk away, banning them from touching the ground of this world until they possessed a true soul."

"*Besyn larveth'is.*"

"When one of the few mortals to witness this great battle and survive picked up the great hammer, its eloquence was gone, and it could only say a few phrases. The great king had bled away his very essence to save his son... who then died anyway." Elkinsair shook his head. "Such a tragedy."

"*Kutesosh gajair'is.*" It was a bare whisper.

"Such simple phrases. *I destroy the enemy. I protect life.* And my personal favorite—"

"*Kun-kabynalti osu fuir'is.*"

"*None shall die while I watch over them. The irony is *so* beautiful.*" Elkinsair wiped at his eyes. "But do you know what fascinates me?" He leaned forward. "The notion that magic of the soul may be drained to grant power to another."

Ghylspwr went suddenly still.

"Oh," Elkinsair said in surprise, "did you think I had just come to tell a story? Oh, no, dear weapon." He pressed another crystal, and the light changed. "If your pathetic faculties can sense me, you know that I am born of the stray magic your people left behind. I enjoy my life, and I enjoy the power your lost magic gives me. I think it only natural that I wonder how much *more* powerful I might become if I could *steal* a bit more for myself."

Ghylspwr thrashed in the shimmering curtain of light. "*Kutesosh—*"

"*Gajair'is,* yes, I know." Elkinsair pressed a few more crystals. "Hence my voluntary servitude of that fool Silestin, which lets me work around all this lovely magic. Sadly, the power here on the Spire is too pure for me— poison in my veins if I try to siphon it away. *You,* however, already gave your magic away once. It stands to reason that you can do it again." He pressed one last button, and the shimmering curtain began to flicker into random patterns. "With the proper encouragement." He stood, letting his robe fall open, and his horn flared a blinding white as he smiled in naked lust at Ghylspwr, who continued to struggle uselessly.

"Do you always talk to your toys?" came a voice from behind Elkinsair. He turned in irritation, then paled.

Ambassador Bi'ul raised an eyebrow, a dark slash over his shining eyes.

Elkinsair pulled his robe shut. "The Archvoyant has asked—"

"I thought you too intelligent to lie to me," Bi'ul said, ignoring Elkinsair and looking at Ghylspwr. "Leave us. I would speak with the trinket alone. We have..." Bi'ul paused, then smiled. "...unfinished business."

"You... you know—"

"Leave us," Bi'ul said, sparing Elkinsair a glance, "now. Any threat I make is infinitesimal compared to what I would actually *do* should you disobey my wishes."

Elkinsair nodded quickly and darted out of the room, looking back longingly at Ghylspwr before he shut the door.

Bi'ul smiled slowly. "At last."

"You stupid girl," Silestin sneered above her. "Did you *think* you could play me?"

Kail knelt on her back. One hand clutched a fistful of her hair and yanked her head back so that the other hand could hold the knife to her throat. Her sword was in the grass a few yards away.

"You were a *captain*," Silestin went on, "when I was a *colonel*. Did you think I didn't *know* about scout-sign? Did you think that when I closed my fist around your man's soul, I'd tell him not to betray you by *saying* or *writing* anything and forget about your little hand signals?" He spat on the ground near her head.

"It was a risk," Loch gasped. "He told me it was the ring. I could free him, bring the Voyancy on you...."

"You got greedy," Silestin said, leaning down enough so that she could see his smile. "That's why I beat you, Isafesira.

If you hadn't thought you could take me down with some elaborate double-cross, you'd be free right now. All you had to do was run." He glanced up, then made a gesture Loch couldn't see before turning his smile back her way. "I'm so glad you decided not to."

The soulless men approached, and at a gesture from Silestin, Kail dragged Loch back to her knees, though the knife remained pressed against her throat. "Here," Silestin said, "take a look."

Most of the soulless men moved into protective positions around Silestin or close guard positions around Ululenia and Dairy, while a pair marched up into the elven ship and came back with the real elf. He was a thin creature with pale green skin, and he wore green and brown clothing that looked to be woven from plants. Crystals of lavender and light blue were set into his face like tattoos, glowing softly. He was bound with iron shackles, and his face was tight with pain.

"You did all this to get the *buyer?*" Loch asked in disbelief, her voice still tight as the knife threatened to draw blood.

Silestin sniffed. "Greedy *and* shortsighted." He gestured, and the soulless men dragged the elf closer. "Do you know what's going to happen today?" He pointed at the ruby lying on the ground. "Every Voyant just got an emergency summons indicating a threat to the Republic. When they get to the Hall of the Voyancy, they're going to learn that the Empire is preparing to launch a devastating attack, and that they've already tortured one of the elves to death in order to gain ancient magic to use against us." He grinned. "I didn't anticipate you activating the weapon I've had Elkinsair and Bi'ul working on, but that plays well as Imperial sabotage that *luckily* revealed a failsafe weapon left by the ancients."

"You bastard." Loch shut her eyes for a long moment. "You're going to start a war."

"Actually," Silestin chuckled, "*you* are. The elves only deal with those they trust. In order to lure one of them out of hiding, I needed someone to steal that book and then try to sell it in good faith. You think I couldn't have locked down my palace to stop you from escaping once I learned about the breach?"

"We escaped." Loch's voice broke.

"You were *allowed* to escape. That ring you just broke? It sends the emergency message only if the user believes in the rightness of his cause with the utmost conviction, and Elkinsair never managed to crack that for me. But *you* believed that what you were doing was for the best, didn't you? When the elves find one of their own killed and mutilated with Imperial soldiers dead nearby as well, they'll unleash the power of the forests on the Empire. When the Voyancy gets this message, they'll believe anything I tell them." He shook his head, frowning as he thought it over. "A loyal soldier who deserted during the war, then spent all these years planning an act of sabotage as the first strike in the Empire's attack upon the Republic. So sad. I doubt the history books will be kind."

He broke into a smile again, a boyish grin. "You know what the best part is? You didn't even steal the real manuscript." He picked up the book again. "I had a forgery placed in my vault, just to be safe. The real elven manuscript is in my library." He tossed the book aside. "After all, young lady, that's where books *go.*"

"There was no cure," Loch said softly. "There was no way to save Kail."

Silestin snorted. "Not that he could tell you about." Stepping back carefully, he removed a red crystal wand from a jacket pocket. "*This* is what you should have been after. Sadly, it's a little too late—"

"Finally," Loch snapped. "Pyvic?"

"With pleasure," said the cloaked man next to Silestin, and knocked the crystal from Silestin's grasp with a sharp blow.

Twenty-Five

"**J**UST GET IT OVER WITH," TERN SAID QUIETLY. THE INTERROGAtion room was built to muffle the screams of its victims, and the walls seemed to soak up the words.

"It's not going to happen." Desidora lay still, trying to stay relaxed.

"Of course it is." Tern struggled for a moment, then lay back in defeat. "The gods slapped their big death priestess thing on you. The only reason you signed on with us was to get a shot at Bi'ul. The freaky little satyr is right. If you believe in what you're doing...."

"It's not *about* whether I believe it," Desidora said, keeping her voice steady. "It's about not playing the satyr's game. Death magic is too dangerous to be toyed with by someone like him."

Tern sighed. "That's a really great justification, and if I hadn't heard Loch's little talk with Hessler by the vault, I'd be coming up with a whole *collection* of reasons for you not to kill me. But it's important, Diz. It really *is* fate-of-the-world stuff you're dealing with. It's worth killing me for."

"That's not what I was taught." Desidora grit her teeth. She could feel cold blossoming deep in the pit of her soul.

"Damn it, Diz!" Tern's voice broke. "Let it be me deciding, okay? Just do it." She was crying. "That way I'm a hero, and not just some… thief you killed because she stood between you and the quest. Let me have that much."

"If I do it…" Desidora felt her skin inching toward white, her hair darkening. "I don't know if I'll come back."

"Well, as the person who'd be *dead*, that breaks my heart," Tern said acidly, sniffling.

"I nearly killed Kail," Desidora said softly. "Back in the control room, and then again with you. I just reached out and started tearing at his soul. I don't want to be that person. The auras, the zombies… that's just a trick. It's an ugly trick, but… I was one of *Tasheveth's*, Tern. I was *love.*"

"And I was a moderately wealthy girl who was more interested in science than arranged marriages." Tern rolled her eyes. "And yet, here we are."

"I don't *want* to be what the gods are trying to make me, Tern." The leather of Desidora's restraints was black, and the bindings were silver. Her own voice was cold, and the reasons for her words hard to remember. "Do you know how that feels?"

"Like I said: arranged marriage."

The unyielding light of logic cut through everything else. "The gods were either wrong or right, Tern. If they were wrong, then letting it take me over again could release an insane death-priest."

Tern coughed. "I thought, uh, priests weren't supposed to go around saying things like 'if the gods were wrong.'"

"And if they were right," Desidora continued coldly, "then I'm no good as a *tool* unless I serve in the capacity for which

I was designed. In which case, I must trust my own intuition, flawed as it is. And my flawed intuition says...."

It came at her, tore through her self, wrenched at her very being. It could not be stopped, could not be reasoned with. It was need, the survival instinct of the gods themselves, the sheer ferocity of absolute imperative action.

And there in the darkness, the one-time priestess of Tasheveth clung to a fragment, tattered and shunted aside, of the feelings that Ululenia had given to her.

A long moment passed.

"...no." And when Desidora, shivering and sweating, weakly opened her eyes, her skin had a healthy flush.

"Disappointing," came Elkinsair's voice from the doorway. "Your faith lasts only as long as you are not asked to do something unpleasant. Fine." He shut the door, shrugged out of his robes, and stood before them, his vile horn glowing. "I see that the death-magic *wants* to come through. You're using... ah, you used *love* to hold it back." He sneered. "Charming. I wonder if I could help you out with that?"

He stepped up to the table and placed his hands on Desidora's legs.

"Get the hell away from her!" Tern shouted.

"Be at peace," Elkinsair crooned. "You'll have your chance. At least, you will if the priestess here doesn't give in and kill you. Being a *love priestess*, she should be ideally suited to enjoy what's about to happen to her." He turned back to Desidora. "I can do things to you that you've never even imagined. I can make you beg for it. I can make you *die* from it." His smile was hard and ugly. "And it's been too long since I've passed time with an unsuspecting maiden in the woods."

Desidora shut her eyes, tried to relax. He would only enjoy it more if she struggled.

It was coiling inside her again, and she tried to keep it locked down, but the fear was there, human and mortal, and now the fear wanted it to come help. His hands pulled at her robes.

There was a flash of silver at her hand, and then her hand tore free of its bonds with inhuman strength, guided by another.

"Kutesosh gajair'is!"

Constrained as he was by Desidora's imprisoned state, Ghylspwr could only swing in a limited area, down and about at the height of the table. Nevertheless, he had at least *one* good target.

When all you are is a hammer, every problem starts to look like a nail.

Desidora heard the impact, which sounded like a flare of powerful magic followed by someone hitting the wall. A moment later, Ghylspwr twisted in her grasp and began smashing things nearby. A moment later, the restraints fell away, and she sat up to see most of the table smashed.

"Ghyl!" Tern shouted. "I am *so glad* I didn't talk Desidora into killing me!"

"Besyn larveth'is,"

"You too! Hey, any chance you could destroy this damn table I'm strapped to?"

"I think I can just undo the straps," Desidora suggested, and went to work. In a few short moments, Tern was free, rubbing at her chafed wrists and flexing her legs.

What was left of Elkinsair was crumpled in the corner. His glowing horn had vanished, and his skin had already turned a dull gray.

"You okay?" Tern asked, and put a hand on Desidora's shoulder.

"I will be," Desidora said, and gave Tern a ragged smile. "Come on. Let's find our clothes and get out of here. When we get back to Loch and the others, I'll tell you how to get Hessler into bed."

"What?"

Ambassador Bi'ul was standing in the doorway.

It coiled inside her again, and this time there was no reason to hold it back, for the final fight was upon her, and—

"Get me into bed?"

"*Besyn larveth'is!*" Ghylspwr said happily.

"I was coming to help, although it looks you had the situation under control."

Desidora checked Bi'ul's aura. "Hessler, could you please avoid impersonating my nemesis without telling me about it first?"

"Ah. Sorry." In a flash, the rainbow faded around him, and the wizard's features shifted back to normal, although he had a nasty black eye. "I was attempting to infiltrate the palace. Appearing as the ambassador provided me with enough leeway to free Ghylspwr." He blinked. "What were you two talking about when I arrived?"

"What happened to your face?" Tern asked very quickly.

"Oh." He touched it and winced. "I was fighting men like the guards on the airship. They're under some sort of—"

"We know," Desidora said.

"Ah. In any event, they had me captured, and Justicar Pyvic arrived just in time to help me. He knocked me unconscious so that they wouldn't see me as a threat."

Tern pursed her lips. "Can't argue with that. So, Diz, ready to go?"

Desidora hefted Ghylspwr. "Let's see what we can find."

The wand tumbled end over end, its angry red light searing in the gray pre-dawn sky.

It landed next to Ululenia, who raised a hoof and brought it down hard.

Kail dropped his knife and fell down behind Loch, retching.

"What in Byn-kodar's—"

Loch's uppercut caught Silestin square in the jaw and knocked him flat on his ass.

"Did you *think*," she said dryly, "that I wouldn't recognize one of my men betraying me? I spent years behind enemy lines with Kail. I spent leave-time dragging him out of taverns. He can lie to a lot of people, but not me."

Around the garden, the soulless men crumpled slowly to the ground. Some of them were crying. Some of them were still.

Three cloaked figures stayed on their feet and drew back their hoods.

"Isafesira," Pyvic said with a brisk nod, "this is Voyant Bertram, Learned Party Leader, and this is Voyant DeVieux, Skilled Party Leader." He gestured to two middle-aged white men who held their crossbows with undisguised distaste. Bertram was a big man who'd gone fat and bald later in life, while DeVieux looked like a former dock worker in an expensive outfit. "Gentlemen, I believe that the admissions we all just heard constitute reasonable cause for a recall hearing."

"The Learned do *not* condone this behavior." Voyant Bertram nodded grimly. "We had no idea that the Archvoyant had such designs, and we fully support any investigation."

"After passing every bit of legislation he put in front of you," Voyant DeVieux said dryly, "you're willing to turn on him now?"

"We're not going to let this turn into a political nightmare." Pyvic glared at DeVieux, then turned to Silestin. "Archvoyant, *Sir,* I'm arresting you under suspicion of treason, murder, corruption, and about a dozen other charges. We'll let the judges figure out the specifics."

Silestin rubbed his jaw. "When did she turn you, Captain?"

"Last night." Pyvic smiled. "I did indeed encounter her, but... statements I had received from both you and Prisoner Loch led me to conduct my own investigation. What I discovered raised some questions."

"I talked with one of my girls." Silestin turned to Loch. "You took her down, but she heard your conversation."

"Justicar Pyvic led a scouting unit during the war." Loch raised a hand. "Your *girl* doesn't fake unconsciousness very well, and Pyvic and I both kept in practice on those scout-signs you were so proud of knowing about earlier."

"You set me up." Silestin was almost saying it to himself. "You were out to take me down from the beginning." He looked up at her suddenly, and his gaze was almost desperate. "Did you even *care* about the manuscript?"

Loch grinned. "As a matter of fact, yes." She reached into the leather satchel and withdrew another book. "It belonged to my father. And I thought you might try something clever with a decoy, so I made certain I checked the library. After all, that's where books *go.*"

"That's a nice bit of maneuvering." Silestin chuckled and shook his head.

Then raised his head to the sky and shouted, "Bi'ul, *we have a deal!*"

"Excellent," came a voice from the trees, and the Glimmering Man stepped out and let his radiance burn through the pre-dawn mist.

A dozen man-sized figures, their black claws and horns wreathed in flame and their scaly red hides oozing smoke, flared into existence. "Consider this an advance payment in good faith." Bi'ul smiled, and his eyes were like prisms set before a bonfire. "Fetch my price, and the rest shall be yours."

"Blood-gargoyles!" cried Dairy, who had been watching the last few minutes with varying degrees of anxiety and bewilderment. Ululenia danced back toward the railing and the elven ship, her horn flaring. The Voyants were doing the same thing.

"Damn it, Loch!" She turned at Pyvic's cry to see Silestin leap into the air and soar out over the garden railing, faint green light sparkling around him as he flew.

"Farewell, young lady," Silestin called with a cold smile. "For what it's worth, you played it well." Then he dipped down below the rim of the Spire.

"Souls," Pyvic said. "He's getting the souls of everyone in the Cleaners to pay Bi'ul."

Loch swore, dove for her sword, and came up between the Voyants and the creatures. "Kail! You ready to make amends?"

Behind her, there was another cough, and then, weakly, "Do they have mothers?"

She smiled despite herself. "Get the elf out of his shackles." The Glimmering Man and the blood-gargoyles were moving slowly, confidently.

Then a cylinder of shimmering amber light sizzled into the air around them, and Loch turned to see Voyant Bertram holding a slender crystal wand. Loch looked at the elf. "I have

friends at the Archvoyant's palace. A tinker, a death priestess, and a wizard who specializes in illusion. In exchange
for the manuscript, I need them here *now*, I need a delay on
those things coming toward us, and I need a sum of money to
be negotiated later. Deal?"

With a weak grin, Kail unlatched the elf's shackles, and
the elf pulled away, massaging the burns on his wrists. The
crystals on his face blossomed with sudden light. "Multiple
parameter considerations, estimating negotiative assertion
probability... equitable."

The elf ran for his ship, the roots slithering back from the
railing even as he approached. He vaulted over with the grace
of a leaping gazelle, and the ship's sails crackled with green
light and went taut.

As the ship roared away, Loch turned. "Pyvic?"

He was by her side, sword raised. The blood-gargoyles
had destroyed the light-barrier, but vines had grown from the
ground and were now coiling around the creatures. Bi'ul himself simply waited. "One justicar-grade flight charm, ready
and waiting," Pyvic said. "But do you trust the elf?"

"Go." Kail was on his feet, pausing only to pick up a pair
of fallen swords. He raised his eyes to Loch. "I'll hold them.
Stop the bastard. Don't let him... don't let him do that to anyone else."

Loch turned to Ululenia and Dairy. "Stay alive. I'll be
back as soon as I can."

We will not fail you, Little One, Ululenia promised.

"Come on, kid!" Kail shouted, and tossed Dairy a sword.
"Time to earn your share."

The vines coiling around the blood-gargoyles were
smoldering from the heat the creatures gave off. Loch gave it
another minute, tops.

"You heard the man." She sheathed her sword, put both arms around Pyvic, and held on tight. "Let's go."

Then the wind swirled around them, sparkling green as the magic lifted them into the air.

Kail's whole body ached. Desidora probably would have said it was the pain of his soul returning to his body, but all Kail knew was that he had the worst hangover of his life, combined with a gut-wrenching sadness that made him want to crawl into a bottle and stay there.

"What do we do, Mister Kail?" the kid called as the blood-gargoyles burned free of the vines that the elf had summoned.

Beside Kail, one of the Voyants used a wand and blasted Bi'ul with a crimson beam of pure light. As far as Kail could tell, it did absolutely nothing.

"We stay alive, kid." Kail turned to the blood-gargoyles, who were loping forward with easy grace. "Only a dozen of you?" he shouted. "I was worried for a moment!" And brandishing his sword, he charged.

They moved like hunting cats, lithe and deadly, baring obsidian fangs as he drew near. Pound for pound, hunting cats were the deadliest creatures a man in the wilderness could encounter, far more dangerous than wolves.

But wolves worked together. Hunting cats didn't. And all the legends Kail could remember about the blood-gargoyles had them working alone.

He dove into the middle of the pack, spinning and swinging wildly, and caught one of them on the arm. Flames flared from the wound, and Kail dove to the side and drove another one back with a desperate slash. Fast and deadly, the gargoyles leapt at him—and into each other as he ducked away. One of them went down under a whirlwind of flaming black claws, finally dissolving into sooty embers as its ally sank its fangs into its throat.

"That all you've got?" Kail slashed, ducked, stabbed, and leaped away, and the gargoyles banged into each other, hissing in fury. "Your mother leaves bigger scratch marks on my back when I— ah!" He dropped to a knee as one of them caught him on the leg.

For a moment three of them loomed over him, claws raised, and then a golden flash of color slammed into Kail, and he was rolling hard and coming up to a pained crouch a few yards away.

Icy Fist stood between Kail and the blood-gargoyles, his fists raised. "I do not believe your attacks will succeed," he said as they leaped at him, "due largely to your ineffective tactics…" He ducked, and two of them slammed into each other, snarling. "…and your moral inadequacy." Another one slashed at Icy, who redirected the attack, and the attacker's slash opened up a flaming wound on one of its allies. He sneaked a glance at Kail and, with a gentle smile, called, "Disharmonizing influence!"

"You're my hero, Indomitable Courteous."

Over near the rim, Dairy and Ululenia were surrounded by half a dozen of the creatures. The kid, now fighting on foot, killed one with a massive two-handed swing that left him completely unguarded, but as another blood-gargoyle lunged at his unprotected back, Ululenia's hooves caught the beast squarely in the chest. "Keep moving!" Kail shouted.

One of the Voyants was down, smoke rising from his chest. The other was surrounded by a nimbus of golden light, but green tendrils of energy were slowly constricting around it.

"Not my problem," Kail muttered, and charged into the group around the unicorn and the kid as one of the blood-gargoyles got onto Ululenia's back.

He slashed one down the back to get its attention, then kicked another one into a third. "Come on, you fiery bastards! Picking on a kid and a horse? Where's the fun in that?"

He'd betrayed Loch. Not by choice, which should have helped, but didn't. He'd been a tool.

The second Voyant hit the ground, green tendrils of energy crackling around him.

Kail slugged a blood-gargoyle in the jaw as it lunged in to bite, then got himself between the creatures and the kid while the kid whacked the one on Ululenia's back. In the other pack, a flash of white light flared for a moment, and when it faded, Icy lay unmoving in the grass, the creatures around him all unharmed.

"Dodge that," Bi'ul said with a hint of satisfaction.

It was suicide to even consider it.

But it was a choice. It was *his* choice.

Kail's sword cleaved through the one standing over Icy, and he body-checked another one to the turf, crying out as a third raked claws along his side. He spun and swung, but the blade caught on the bone spur just behind it below, and when it twisted, Kail's cheap blade snapped.

He shoved the broken blade into its face, snarling in triumph as it dissolved into sooty flame that scorched his arm, and then fangs sank into his shoulder. He got his fingers into the damn thing's eyes as claws raked a line of fire across his chest, and then he was on his knees, and a brilliant pain tore into his gut as one of them kicked him with taloned feet, and he dropped to one knee, levered to ready a lunge, and then saw the great slash coming at his ribs a moment too late.

"Besyn larveth'is!"

As his vision blurred and went dark, Kail saw the blood-gargoyle standing over him explode into flames tinged with silver, and with the last of his fading strength, he turned to look at Bi'ul, who stood several yards away with an expression of surprised displeasure.

"I win," Kail said, and the darkness took him.

"You'll forgive me if this isn't quite how I'd hoped to hold you again," Pyvic muttered as he and Loch swooped down below the rim and under Heaven's Spire. Overhead, the *lapiscaela* were dull and quiet, resting in their cradles and waiting for the morning light. Below, the world was lost in a sea of mist just starting to lighten as the sun eased over the mountains.

"Hoping to hold me?" Loch asked, trying not to look down again and holding onto Pyvic a bit tighter. "I thought I was an unprincipled thief and possible Imperial agent."

"An unprincipled thief with great legs." Pyvic smiled, then squinted. "I don't see him. He must have landed above."

"Bring us in, then. If his deal with Bi'ul is what I think it is, he'll be stealing souls from the stones." Seeing a familiar landmark, Loch grinned. "I see they got the Tooth back in."

"I don't remember Orris being happy with how you returned it, though." Pyvic brought them up slowly to the lower grid, watching for ambushers, then lifted them to the safety of the upper grid and set Loch down.

"How's Hessler?"

"Awake and fine. He was trying to free the priestess and the safecracker when I left."

Loch nodded, testing her balance on the pipes. After a moment's thought, she kicked off her riding boots and socks.

"You really wanted to fight the Archvoyant *barefoot?*" Pyvic asked, hovering at her side and watching as Loch's footwear fell away and finally vanished in the mist.

"I want to reach him. The boots don't have enough grip." She drew her sword. "Ready?"

He drew his own blade. "Where do you think he is?"

"Start from the middle." She ran at an easy jog, her bare feet making almost no noise on the iron piping. Beside her, Pyvic floated, watching for an attack. "And Justicar?"

"Yes, Captain?"

"I'm really glad you're here."

The familiar run came to her almost immediately—narrow steps along the pipes, punctuated by sudden shifts at the corners, with her free arm pulling her from handgrip to handgrip. The Cleaners was empty this early in the morning, and the only movement was Pyvic floating gently at her side and Loch's own breath puffing in the cold morning air.

And then, through the twisting pipes that made up the grid, the white flash of a military jacket caught her eye. "There!" She changed direction, cut the corner of a wide stone with a short leap, and charged.

Silestin was leaning down over one of the *lapiscaela*, another crystal wand extended toward the stone, but he caught Loch from the corner of his eye and came upright as she approached. "Come to watch me make history?" he asked with a lazy smile.

She slowed to a walk, keeping her breathing even and her sword up. "You're done, Silestin."

"The Glimmering Folk say otherwise," Silestin said with a chuckle. "When they return, the Republic will be the heart of their land. The Empire, the old kingdoms over the sea... they'll be ground down to dust, while we live in luxury. I'll be a hero. A legend."

"*Mister* Silestin," Pyvic said formally, landing gently beside Loch, his own sword out and leveled, "as I said before, you are under arrest. You can surrender and get a fair trial, or we can cut you down here and now." He smiled grimly. "I'm really fine either way."

Silestin raised an eyebrow. "Pyvic, son, that's a powerful argument with one tiny flaw. You see, I'm the only one hovering... and these pipes are solid iron." He brought up his ring.

Loch dove on instinct before the lightning started crackling. The sizzle of burning air and the crackle of lightning along the pipes hit her ears as she came down hard on one of the *lapiscaela*. She took it on the side, rolled while keeping her sword-arm outstretched to avoid skewering herself, and looked up.

Pyvic had jumped out of Silestin's aim, too, but not far enough. He clung to the pipes, arched back in a rictus posture of tortured pain as the lightning played across the pipes—and him. Then it faded, and Pyvic fell. Loch's breath caught in her throat, but after a few heartbeats, Pyvic's flight charm kicked in, and he drifted lazily and safely downward.

Then she looked up at Silestin, who grinned and held up his ring-hand.

"You have any idea what using your lightning ring could do to the stones?" she asked, and sheathed her sword.

Silestin frowned. "You're right. It could be dangerous. I suppose—" And then he fired, and fortunately Loch had read it coming and already taken a desperate leap that brought her high enough to catch the piping of the upper grid as lightning crackled across the surface of the *lapiscaelum* behind her. The stone gave off an angry high-pitched whine behind her.

She kept the momentum of her swing and flung herself at the next stone, knowing what any soldier with a ranged weapon would do with a target like the one she was presenting. Lightning flared along the pipes behind her, and a moment of tingling numbness thrilled through her body. She hit the stone hard, slid, and missed the catch on the far side. As her body went over, she had one aching moment of time, balanced on the edge, to see Silestin raising the ring again, and she gritted her teeth and kicked off hard.

The jolt as she hit the lower grid nearly wrenched her arms from their sockets, but she held on, swung desperately for a moment, and then pulled herself up to get the pipe under her armpits. The stone flared a bright red and began to whine like the one before it as the electricity crackled.

She was out of options. She edged over to the next pipe and pulled herself up slowly, agonizingly slowly, to a crouch. Her ribs ached—bruised, not broken—and her shoulder twinged with the sharp pain of a torn tendon.

She climbed to the upper grid, waiting for the shot. It didn't come.

Silestin was making his way to her as she pulled herself up, and his sword was out. She raised an eyebrow. "No more ring?"

"If you think I need a magic ring to finish off one arrogant Urujar thief," Silestin drawled, "that speaks to your own stupidity."

"No more ring." Loch grinned cruelly. "How much money did you just spend trying to kill me?"

"I can always buy another one." Silestin pursed his lips. "So... what's the trick?" At Loch's questioning look he sniffed. "You planning to run off under an illusion? Maybe your unicorn will fly you away? You've had an angle this whole time. I respect that. So… what's it going to be this time, young lady?"

"The trick," Loch said, drawing her blade, "is that this time, the young lady kicks your ass."

The first rays of dawn shimmered off their blades as steel met steel.

They had just reached the palace gardens when the elf arrived in his marvelous living ship. The flight to the garden had taken mere heartbeats. As Desidora leaped off the gangplank and into the garden, Ghylspwr held high, she saw Kail fall to a group of *pyrkafir*. It seemed that fortune had decreed she arrive at just the right time.

Or perhaps fortune had nothing to do with it.

"Besyn larveth'is!" Ghylspwr shouted as she threw him. He tore through one of the *pyrkafir*, blasting it to ashes, and as the smoke cleared, she saw Ambassador Bi'ul staring at her with an expression of displeased surprise.

"Who are you?" he called in irritation.

It coiled inside her, and this time she stretched out her soul and welcomed it.

"Death," she said, and held out one pearly white hand.

"Insipid," Bi'ul sniffed. "If you wish to bluster—"

"Kutesosh gajair'is," Ghylspwr said in a voice as cold as the death priestess's own as he flared into that open hand.

Behind her, the tinker and the wizard were trying to help the unicorn and the boy. They were irrelevant. She stepped forward as the *pyrkafir* charged. "I am the averted death of the gods." She swatted one aside. "I am the sacrificial death of all who must fall to serve their will." Ghylspwr swung up to blast one into the sky. "And I am your death, Glimmering Man." A blinding slash of silver destroyed two more. "Your time in this world or any other has passed."

There were no more *pyrkafir* between the death priestess and the Glimmering Man. Behind her, three mortals and a fey who had once been her friends fought for their lives with magic and steel, bolts and bravery.

"Pitiful," Bi'ul said absently, and hurled a searing flare of prismatic light.

She called upon her power and raised her weapon. Though the light drove her to her knees, she remained when it faded. In a ten-foot circle around her, the grass was withered and dead, sacrificed for her.

"Impressive," Bi'ul murmured, "but how much grass are you willing to kill?"

She stood. "As much as is necessary."

"Forget us, Mister Hessler!" came the cry behind her. "You've got to help Desidora!"

She could feel their auras moving toward her, the two who had been with her on the ship. She said nothing. They could prove useful.

She swung, a testing blow, and Ghylspwr struck multicolored sparks off the rainbow shield that sprang up on Bi'ul's arm. His right hand had become a ball of living light; he lashed out, forcing Ghylspwr to parry, and the shock of power drove the death priestess back on her heels. The shield knocked Ghylspwr aside, and the blast of light caught her with a glancing blow. Desidora hit the ground, and the trees at the edge of the garden shivered and shed their leaves in a sudden collapse of brown and red and black.

Bi'ul stood over her, shining fist raised, and then stumbled back, his radiance dimming as a field of gray washed over him. A bolt ripped through his glowing shield, and he cried out in shock and pain.

"I had a little time to study," the wizard said, "and it struck me that if you are a creature of illusion..." He raised his hand, and another gray field washed over the Glimmering Man. "...then magic that *abjures* illusions might cause you some discomfort."

"And I borrowed a little dirt from Silestin's garden." The tinker cocked her crossbow. "Since that prophecy says you're not allowed to touch the earth, I figured I'd let the earth touch *you*."

The Glimmering Man snarled. "You think you can hurt *me?*" He flung out his hands, and waves of force slammed the two to the ground, where they lay unmoving. "Your best efforts are at best an *irritation!* This pitiful death priestess—"

"Is back on her feet," she said coolly, raising Ghylspwr again in her pale hands. The sacrifice of the others had given her the time she needed. "Will you talk all day, or shall we end this?"

He opened his mouth to answer, but a scream silenced him.

It tore through the mind, not the air, and both the priestess and the Glimmering Man turned.

The *pyrkafir* had obviously been leaping for the boy's unprotected back, and the unicorn, with one creature already clinging to her mane and another clawing at her haunches, had placed herself in the way.

The slash had ripped cleanly across her throat.

As she fell, the boy destroyed the one he was fighting, then turned and, with a cry, killed the three who slashed and snapped at her helpless body.

She was a priestess of death. She could see the pitiful thing that the magical beast had for a soul already tearing loose from its mortal shell.

The boy fell to his knees, shouting words the death priestess did not hear. She saw his face, uncomprehending, the grief intruding at the edges. She saw the unicorn, kicking weakly.

She saw the last *pyrkafir* closing in on the boy.

He was pathetic, weak-willed, unwilling to utilize the sacrifice granted to him. He was nothing. Nothing more than mortal.

Her hair fell into her face, whipped by the morning wind.

And in the light of the first rays of dawn, those unkempt strands were auburn.

"*Kun-kabynalti osu fuir'is,*" her friend said quietly.

"I know."

She threw, and the *pyrkafir* died, and a moment later the wave of power slammed her to the ground, and the world swam around her, sick and dizzy. The Glimmering Man was a blinding radiance standing over her.

"Touching," he said, and raised his shining fist. "The gods will be so disappointed."

And then he paused and looked up, and his prismatic eyes widened.

"Step away from my friends, Mister Bi'ul, and surrender," called Rybindaris, the Champion of Dawn, "or else I'll have to hurt you." In his hands, Ghylspwr shone with silvery radiance.

On the horizon far to the east, the sun stopped rising.

Loch was younger and faster. Silestin had stayed in practice and paid good money for every health and youth charm on the market. It worked out to be pretty close.

She parried a thrust, riposted, then swore as he turned her blade to catch on the piping. "We didn't have to be enemies," Silestin said, his slash leaving a thin trail of blood on her arm as she gave ground. "You're a resourceful girl. Why go after me?"

"Why the hell do you think?" She danced back from his following stab, leaped to cut the corner on another *lapiscaelum*, then kicked back off immediately and lunged in, catching him by surprise. "*You killed my family.*" As he parried, she locked blades and came over the top with a left cross that sent him stumbling back.

"I *saved* your sister," he corrected, sidestepping Loch's slash and flicking his blade at her eye. She parried, then caught a fist in the ribs she'd banged on the stone earlier. She stumbled back, pain lancing across her vision. "That's what always annoyed me about the Urujar." She caught Silestin's slash just above the guard, and his blade circled and sliced down across her arm.

As her vision cleared, Loch saw her sword fall silently, catching the morning light as it disappeared forever. Then she looked up the length of Silestin's sword into his sneering face. "Always blaming others for your problems."

She feinted left, went right, accepted the cut on the heel of her hand as she knocked his blade aside, and caught him with a right cross to the jaw. "You son of a bitch!" As he rocked back, she hammered on his sword arm, and his own blade fell free and joined hers on the long trip to the ground. "You kill my family, you *own* it!" She stepped in hard with an uppercut.

He took it on the shoulder, lunged in, and caught her with a shot just below the breastbone. "Somebody has to think about the Republic!" She stumbled back as he followed with a flurry of jabs. "Somebody has to make the hard decisions! Somebody has to get the job done!" Her bare foot slipped on the piping as she gave ground, and she fell back, catching herself on a vertical pipe. "Who's it going to be? You? All you care about is blame!" He raised a boot, brought it down hard. "All you care about—"

She dove to the side, holding herself over the mist far below with one straining arm, and trapped his kicking leg. "I care about the Republic. That's why I went after you." Then she hauled herself back in and slammed her free fist into his crotch. "Because there are lines you don't cross." With a grunt, she kicked him off the grid.

He fell into the air, face purple with pain, and floated over one of the *lapiscaela*. "Or what?" he gasped, hovering out of her reach as he regained his composure.

"Or me." Loch pulled herself back to her feet. "You don't serve the Republic." She pointed off to where the two stones he'd hit with the lightning were vibrating hard enough to rattle the pipes. "Look at yourself. You're going to bring down Heaven's Spire, the most powerful weapon the Republic *has*."

"You *forced* me to do that!" Silestin shouted. "And Bi'ul can fix it! He can make it right! All I need to do is—"

"Sell him some souls?" Loch shook her head in disgust.

"What does it *matter?*" Silestin yelled, balling his fists as he raged. "If it gives us a golden age and destroys our enemies, *what difference do a few souls make?*"

"To a *real* leader," Loch said, "everything," and jumped.

She caught him squarely, and her weight drove him down to the stone. They both hit hard, and she scrabbled to catch his arm. Then a fist slammed into her side, a knife of pain through her lungs, and as she gasped, Silestin kicked away from her and got back to his feet.

She couldn't breathe. It was agony, lancing through her, and she got to her knees before his boot caught her *other* side, and then she was on her back, coughing, curled up to protect herself, and Silestin stood over her, his carefully styled hair matted and undone, his jacket torn, his face red.

"Thought I forgot the ribs?" he sneered. She took another kick on the arms, another jolt of agony that stole her breath. "Silly girl. *That's* why you never made it past scouting captain." Another kick. "Too headstrong, too idealistic. A shame, too." He rolled out his shoulders and shook his head regretfully. "You're a hell of a fighter."

Loch spat blood and grinned fiercely. "I'm a better thief." And in one tightly clenched fist, she held up the flight charm she'd lifted when she'd tackled him.

Her kick swept his legs cleanly, and he bounced hard on the stone, scrabbling frantically, and slid over the edge.

This time, he didn't float.

The sun had gone a peculiar pale color, and the sky was midway between the pale blue of a sunrise and the warm orange-purple of sunset.

"The Champion of Dawn." Ambassador Bi'ul laughed. "The living vessel that holds the wards of the ancients in place. Your soul must have died and been reborn hundreds of times while we found a way back to this world."

"I don't know anything about that, sir." Dairy's voice was steady, but his birthmark burned hot and angry on his arm as he looked at the Glimmering Man. "But you hurt my friends, and I'm going to have to stop you."

"*Kutesosh gajair'is,*" Ghylspwr added, thrumming in Dairy's hand.

"You, beardless boy?" The Glimmering Man rolled out his shoulders, his glow growing stronger with each heartbeat.

"Me." Dairy swallowed. "You're a bad man, and you hurt people. If the ancients sent you away, then you should stay away." He straightened his shoulders and stared at the Glimmering Man straight-on. "Or I'll send you away, sir." He lifted Ghylspwr, and shining silver light blazed through the garden.

"*Besyn larveth'is!*" Ghylspwr shouted.

"Do your best, child." Bi'ul held out his arms, laughing in delight. "Don't hold back. Show me what you and the tattered soul of a dead old man can do."

With that, Dairy leapt forward, Ghylspwr swinging back in one arm and then coming down at Bi'ul with a blow that could shatter mountains, so great was the force behind it.

Bi'ul sidestepped it, sneering. "Pitif—"

And then the fingers of Dairy's *other* hand raked across Bi'ul's face, and the Glimmering Man flinched, and Dairy stepped in and drove the point of his elbow into Bi'ul's gut, and then he kicked Bi'ul between the legs, and *then* he drove Ghylspwr's pommel into Bi'ul's nose, and the Glimmering Man stumbled back with rainbow ichor on his face.

"It's called a feint, sir," said Dairy. "Captain Loch taught it to me."

"I cannot be denied!" Bi'ul shouted, his face a mask of blazing fury.

Dairy hefted Ghylspwr. "That's what your mother said last night, sir. At least, that's what it sounded like. Her knees were pressed against my ears at the time."

And as Bi'ul leaped at him, a shimmering prism of rage, Dairy swung.

The world went black for one long moment, and there was only the sound of a glass breaking, a glass containing all the oceans in the world, and those oceans held back the fires of a thousand suns, and it all burst forth in one massive wave of power that spread across creation in an instant.

Then the light returned, and Bi'ul was gone, but a rainbow began where the Glimmering Man had stood, and its arc carried it over the rim, far into the sky, and finally down to the ground.

"Well done, lad," said Ghylspwr in a rich, deep brogue.

Dairy blinked, and looked at the hammer. Where before it had glowed silver, it now shone with the golden light of the sun, and the runes along the handle glowed in all the colors of the rainbow. "Thank you, Mister Ghylspwr. You can talk?"

"With the stolen magic of the Glimmering Man freed, I am..." Ghylspwr paused. "...more of what I was." The hammer twitched in Dairy's hand. "You defeated a force that I myself could not, lad. Though few will ever know what you did, the world rejoices."

"I..." Dairy looked at Hessler and Tern and Icy and Kail, all unconscious on the ground. At Desidora, still on her knees, tears flowing freely down her cheeks. At Ululenia. "It isn't my honor."

"The gods themselves will welcome her into paradise." Ghylspwr's runes shone blazing white. "Though her soul is a construct of stolen magic, she proved herself as true as any child of man. She dies a hero, lad."

Dairy walked toward her. Her horn was gone. Her snowy white flank was turning gray. "She shouldn't," he said, eyes stinging as he knelt beside her.

"Lad...."

Dairy laid a hand gently on her flank. "Captain Loch showed me the difference between *is* and *should*. She shouldn't be gone, but she is...." She was still trembling. Tiny whickers of breath barely made puffs of steam in the cold morning air. "But she shouldn't be. Someone needs to start *should*."

The morning clouds parted, and the sun rose above the mountains as a bright new day dawned.

"You're right."

Behind Dairy, Desidora gasped.

"A wise old man from a long time ago said, 'None shall die while I watch over them,'" Ghylspwr said gently. "I'd almost forgotten that man. Thank you for reminding me."

"Ghyl," said Desidora softly, "no."

"I protect life, Desidora." The hammer flashed, and the rainbow energy flared and poured into the runes. *"Besyn larveth'is."*

Ghylspwr moved in Dairy's grasp, and the head touched Ululenia's torn flank gently. The runes flared one last time, and then went dark.

Ululenia's horn blazed radiant white, and then her whole body did, and then she was a woman again, her white gown torn but her pale skin unscarred. "Thank you," she whispered, dark eyes shining.

"Kun-kabynalti osu fuir'is," Ghylspwr said fondly, and pulled Dairy's arm around Ululenia's waist.

The stone beneath Loch's bare feet shivered, and the upper and lower grids rattled around her like a horse's tack. Even stones that *hadn't* been hit by the damn lightning ring were starting to glow red.

With one hand clutched to her battered ribs, Loch limped to the edge of the stone and looked down.

He wasn't dead.

"You were right," Archvoyant Silestin called up, hanging by his fingertips from the pipes of the lower grid. As he shifted his grip, the vibrating pipe snapped a strut under his weight and began to bend with a slow squeal of protest. "You were right, Isafesira. I killed your family."

She raised an eyebrow. "You picked a hell of a time to tell me."

"Do you..." He grunted and shifted his grip again, but another strut snapped, and the pipe started to rock, squeaking with the movement. "Do you want to know why?"

"You already told me, Silestin. Power." The stone was growing hot beneath her bare feet. She jumped to the pipes of the upper grid and held on carefully, the iron trembling beneath her fingers.

"For the *Republic*." Silestin shifted his grip, nearly slipped, and kicked his legs wildly for a moment to right himself. "The things I'd seen in the war, heard in the halls of power... Isafesira, the war with the Empire is coming. The Republic barely held on last time. I needed the power to keep us safe."

She stared down at him. The whine of magic from the stones slowly grew louder.

"I'm not going to apologize. It wasn't because your family was Urujar. I... it's important that you know that. I just needed someone in the right place, at the right time. But..." Another strut snapped. There was only one left to connect the pipe Silestin hung from to the rest of the grid. "But we need the Spire, Isafesira. We need Heaven's Spire."

"You should have thought of that before you shot the rocks with your *ring*, then."

"I didn't know! I swear by the gods, I wouldn't endanger the Republic's greatest strength for my own gain." He looked up at her, his eyes wide. "Would you?"

"Go to hell, Silestin." The iron was getting hard to hold. She needed to start climbing, get up and out of here before things started breaking.

"I can fix it!" he cried. "I can get Bi'ul to do it. Or Elkinsair. Hell, maybe even the elf. I know more about this island than—" The iron shook one of his hands free, and he swung wildly. "Let me make it right! Let me—"

The last strut gave way.

One brown hand, battle-scarred but strong, caught Silestin's fingertips.

She looked down at him, at the abject relief, an old man's fear. And then she heaved, her ribs screaming, her shoulder on fire, her legs trembling, and swung Silestin over to a stable pipe, high enough that he could pull himself up with shaking arms.

"That's the difference between us," she said softly through clenched teeth. "I'm—"

His fist slammed into her injured ribs, and she fell with a wordless gasp as the pain knocked the breath from her. One hand grabbed at the pipe, caught it, but her vision was black-tinged with the screaming pain that stole the wind from her lungs.

"You're a fool," Silestin said easily, pulling himself up to stand over her. "That's the difference between us." He lifted one of his fine expensive boots. "A fool who lacks the conviction to follow her beliefs to—"

A knife blossomed in his throat.

He looked up in surprise, and the hand he'd been holding on with came free, grasping the knife gently, and then he fell back like a man falling into a feather bed after a long journey.

Loch watched him fall out of sight for a long moment, and when her body would bear it, she brought her other hand up to strengthen her grip. Then she looked up.

"I didn't know," Naria said, looking down at Loch. The lens she wore over one eye was cracked, sparkling with stray magic. The other eye was milk-white and scarred. "I swear, I didn't know."

Then she turned and vanished, the shadows closing around her.

Loch held on for a long moment, the pipe vibrating in her grasp and the whine growing steadily louder in her ears.

Then she pulled herself up with two strong hands, ignoring the pain that flashed across her ribs, and started climbing.

Epilogue

"**A**ll i'm saying," the manticore huffed, arching its wings and raising its stinger, "is that you have to look pretty hard at Voyant Cevirt after everything is said and done."

"But," declared the griffon, leaping forward with claws bared, "Archvoyant Bertram himself ordered the charges dropped! *Your own Archvoyant* ordered it!"

The manticore lowered its wings and swished its tail. "He's everybody's Archvoyant now, and I'll hope you remember that," it groused. "This is a period of mourning, not a time for partisan attacks."

"Indeed," rumbled the dragon, belching flame and throwing candies to the crowd. "Please, let's all remember that an Archvoyant is dead. Let's try to be respectful."

"But out of respect," the griffon pressed, stalking forward, "shouldn't we learn from what happened? After funding for the prison reforms committee was slashed, Voyant Cevirt had to send a friend and former soldier undercover to investigate safety hazards among the *lapiscaela*."

"I fail to see what this informal audit—" the manticore began, rising back up.

"If we'd had the funds to properly perform an official study," the griffon declared, "we might have uncovered the dangerous malfunction in the stones before it became so dangerous. Archvoyant Silestin might still be with us today!"

"I can't believe you're dragging politics into this!" the manticore snarled, backing up slowly. "It was Silestin's own last-minute negotiation with the elves that *saved* Heaven's Spire."

The griffon spread its wings, and its lion tail swished angrily. "Nobody is denying Silestin's heroic sacrifice, but with proper maintenance of the Spire's prison facilities, these malfunctions would *never happen*. That's what's important here."

The manticore cowered in the corner. "I just think it's disrespectful to use a man's heroic actions as fodder for politics," it muttered. "That's disrespectful, and that's all I'm saying."

"I think we can all agree that Archvoyant Silestin died as he lived," rumbled the dragon with a puff of flame, "fighting for the Republic." It tossed out more candy to the crowd. "Remember, everyone, *it's your republic!*"

"Stay informed!"

"What do you mean," Tern said, scratching at her bandaged shoulder, *"we aren't getting paid?"*

Voyant Cevirt's sitting room had been quickly restored, as had Voyant Cevirt. Hessler sat in the overstuffed chair, his splinted leg up on the ottoman next to Tern and his drink diluted only by three olives and a tiny onion.

Desidora, who had bar duty, wore Ghylspwr, the robes of Tasheveth the lover, and an expression of mild amusement as Dairy tried to help a heavily bandaged and recumbent Kail drink his beer.

Icy sat cross-legged on the floor with his tea, and Ululenia, human for once, sat at the edge of the sofa and blew what she called a gentle and rejuvenating wind into Kail's face. Cevirt himself stood next to Loch in the doorway.

Loch would have laughed, but it would have made her ribs hurt again. Instead, she sipped her red wine, then turned back to Tern. "The thing is, the whole Spire was going to fall out of the sky."

"Right," said Kail, "because of Silestin."

"*Totally* not our fault," added Tern, sipping her fruity drink. She was pleasantly flushed, and her eyes looked a bit unfocused behind the big spectacles.

"But the elf had to fix it before the *lapiscaela* all exploded," Loch went on, "and since he had to do so after being captured and mistreated by Silestin...."

"Tell me," said Hessler, "that you didn't just *give* him the book."

"He fixed the stones," Cevirt said, ticking it off on his fingers, "he delayed the gargoyles—"

"*Pyrkafir,*" Hessler said irritably.

"—for a brief but critical time," Cevirt went on evenly, "and he got you all to the garden in time to stop Bi'ul."

"They just *gave* him the book," Tern translated in a loud whisper.

"*Damn* it."

"There is a deal, however," Cevirt went on with a faint smile. "All charges have been dropped against you, and any of you with criminal records have just been granted a clean slate. Republic airships will drop you off wherever you wish to go."

"So... we're not getting paid," Kail said.

"Pretty much," Loch agreed cheerfully, and finished her wine. "*Except* for Dairy."

Dairy slowly turned pink. "Why me, ma'am?"

Cevirt pursed his lips. "Ambassador Bi'ul was evidently charged with several crimes, and as you were the one who... *apprehended*... him, there is a reward coming from the justicars."

"The justicars are paying the youngest thief on the team?" Kail asked.

"Dairy's too virtuous to be a good thief, anyway," Tern said, leaning back to sip her drink and slowly falling off of the ottoman.

"I don't know about *virtuous*." Desidora smiled. "After those wicked things he said to Bi'ul...."

Dairy blushed. "I don't even know what... what I said... means. It's just something Kail told a sailor in a tavern one night."

"Hey, *thanks* for bringing me into it, kid."

"What did you say?" Ululenia asked curiously, and gave Dairy a gentle stare. "Oh," she said after a moment, and her pale cheeks went as pink as Tern's. "Well. I'll show you what that means later."

Loch stood back from them all, watched them laugh and flirt and rest their wounded bodies and souls. She finished her wine, thought about having another glass, but decided to hold off.

They broke up soon after, with plans to meet at the kahva-house that evening before the airships took them back to ground the next morning. Dairy gave Hessler a goodbye hug before being led off by a most determined Ululenia, and then Tern invited Hessler to visit the museum of magic, choosing her words carefully and making discreet eye contact with Desidora, who was nodding and mouthing the same words.

Kail wasn't well enough to leave the couch, but Desidora offered to stay with him while the others left. Icy, incredibly, left to go meditate in the garden where the great battle had been fought.

Loch left her wineglass in the sitting room, gave Cevirt a hug and a promise to see him again before she left, and started walking.

The kahva-house was quiet that afternoon, and she found an empty table easily enough. She ordered a kahva, opened the book Cevirt had given her, and lost herself for a while.

When the coin landed on the table, she looked up with a smile.

"How did they take it?" Pyvic asked as he sat down. His uniform was clean and pressed and extremely formal. He'd been in Voyancy meetings for the past week.

"Could have been worse," Loch said with a shrug. "The kid insisted on splitting your reward money among everyone."

"One born every minute." Pyvic smiled, reached out, and took her hand. His fingers were warm.

"It's enough for all of them to live well for a while," Loch said with a small smile, "even split nine ways. Thanks."

"I heard the paperwork finally went through on Lochenville." Pyvic squeezed her hand gently. "I'm sorry."

"Naria will make a fine baroness." Loch closed her book. "She's got the training, the connections, and the public persona for it. The barony will be well taken care of."

Pyvic let out a long breath. "It should be you."

"*Should* and *is*, Justicar. Clean record or not, if it were me, there'd always be questions. It wouldn't look right."

"So out of all this, you get nothing." Pyvic signaled for a kahva to match Loch's.

Loch stirred her kahva. "Not quite nothing," she said after a moment. "Freedom for me. A clean record. The man who killed my family gone for good. A couple of prophecies fulfilled." She took a sip, swished it. "Could be worse."

"Do they know how close the Voyancy came to tossing them all into the Cleaners and throwing away the key?" Pyvic's kahva arrived. He closed his eyes and tasted it. He still looked good, even dressed in his silly uniform in the middle of an Urujar kahva-house. Damn.

"It didn't come up," Loch said with a smile.

"What do you do now?" Pyvic asked. "Any other nemeses who wronged your family I should know about?"

She laughed. It hurt her ribs a little, but it was worth it. "I could always try being a bookseller. I'd need some books, but I could probably lift a few from Cevirt without him minding."

"You'd make a hell of a justicar," Pyvic said suddenly, and as Loch nearly spat out her kahva, he added, "After seeing what you can do, the Voyancy was quite amenable to the idea of you being a blade in their sheath and not their back."

Loch raised an eyebrow and gave him a half-smile. "A justicar?"

"Think about it," Pyvic said, giving her hand another squeeze. "Free travel around the Republic, the joy of righting wrongs, mental challenges as tricky as the old scouting missions but with better sleeping arrangements...." He let the word hang just a bit, and his index finger traced tiny circles on her wrist.

She looked at him again, really looked at him. A justicar, of all things. She'd faced down an Archvoyant last week, and one justicar with dark eyes and really good fingers had her sweating. "You do know," she said, voice low, "that they're meeting me *here* later this evening?"

"How *much* later?" he asked, and his eyes twinkled as he said it, and there was still enough left of the scout captain for her.

There were rooms available in the inn over the kahva-house, and Pyvic left to go get one very, very quickly.

Freedom for her friends, she thought absently, watching him go and then come back, flushed but smiling. The man who'd killed her family gone for good, and a couple of prophecies fulfilled. And some free time with Justicar Pyvic.

She decided not to mention the trinkets from Silestin's palace that she'd pocketed while moving through his personal chambers. Even split evenly with the team, Loch figured she'd have enough to make a generous donation to the Republic Urujar University Fund.

Pyvic caught her look, stopped, and raised an eyebrow. "What?"

Loch gave him her sultry smile. "Not quite nothing," she said again, and led him upstairs.

The smile worked.

Made in the USA
Middletown, DE
13 April 2024

52931317R00262

About the Author

 Patrick Weekes was born in the San Francisco Bay Area and attended Stanford University, where he received a B.A. and an M.A. in English Literature.

In 2005, Patrick joined BioWare's writing team in Alberta, Canada. Since then, he's worked on all three games in the Mass Effect trilogy, where he helped write characters like Mordin, Tali, and Samantha Traynor. He is now working with the Dragon Age team on the third game in the critically acclaimed series, and he has written tie-in fiction for both series, including Tali's issue in the Dark Horse "Mass Effect: Homeworlds" series and *Dragon Age: Masked Empire*, an upcoming novel to be released in July 2014.

Patrick lives in Edmonton with his wife Karin, his two Lego-and-video-game-obsessed sons, and (currently) nine rescued animals. In his spare time, he takes on unrealistic Lego-building projects, practices Kenpo Karate, and embarrasses himself in video games.